They thought their time together,
which began with such
love and joy, had ended long ago.

But for Ellie and Tucker,
the journey has just begun....

continued . . .

Always in My Heart

Always in My Heart

*

Catherine Anderson

A SIGNET BOOK

SIGNET
Published by New American Library, a division of
Penguin Putnam Inc., 375 Hudson Street,
New York, New York 10014, U.S.A.
Penguin Books Ltd, 80 Strand,
London WC2R 0RL, England
Penguin Books Australia Ltd, Ringwood,
Victoria, Australia
Penguin Books Canada Ltd, 10 Alcorn Avenue,
Toronto, Ontario, Canada M4V 3B2
Penguin Books (N.Z.) Ltd, 182–190 Wairau Road,
Auckland 10, New Zealand

Penguin Books Ltd, Registered Offices:
Harmondsworth, Middlesex, England

First published by Signet, an imprint of New American Library,
a division of Penguin Putnam Inc.

First Printing, August 2002
10 9 8 7 6 5 4 3 2 1

To our son John, the game biologist and woodsman extraordinaire, who sees the face of God in the turn of a leaf and hears the whisper of His voice riding on the wind.

Chapter One

Ellie Grant tugged her son Kody's basketball jersey from between the cream-colored sofa cushions. The white knit was streaked with mud and covered with black dog hair, and the team name, TROJANS, in green lettering across the front was smeared with what appeared to be mustard. Scrunching the nylon in her fist, she almost lifted it to her nose—and then caught herself. What on earth was she doing? Granted, she missed her boys, but they'd be gone only until tomorrow night. She could survive another weekend without them, no shirt sniffing allowed.

Turning, she stared at the television, which was usually on and blaring when the kids were home. Light from the adjoining dining room reflected off the dusty screen, highlighting the words, WASH ME. Ellie grinned in spite of herself. The brats. In the time it had taken one of them to scrawl that message, he could have polished the glass.

Her smile slowly faded. The quiet inside the house seemed to echo against her eardrums. Most mothers would probably take advantage of the reprieve to read a good book or take a luxurious bubble bath, but Ellie just felt lost. For two weeks straight, she hadn't had a second to call her own. Now she suddenly had twenty-four hours of emptiness stretching before her.

It was always this way when Tucker had the boys. She never knew quite what to do with the time. She stared at the dog hair on the mauve carpet and considered hauling out her old Kirby, but like a recovered alcoholic tempted by drink, she shoved the thought away. Instead, she stepped to the entertainment center and punched on the stereo. Zach, her fourteen-year-old, kept the CD player filled with his favorite country and western disks. Garth Brooks would chase away the silence and lift her spirits in short order.

She cranked up the volume, grabbed the portable phone from the end table, and headed toward the kitchen. As she passed through the dining room, the first strains of "Every Breath You Take" by The Police thrummed in the air. She stopped dead in her tracks. In July of her sixteenth year, that song had been blaring on the radio of Tucker's rattletrap Chevy when she lost her virginity. She hadn't listened to it since the divorce, and she knew Zach hadn't, either. He disdainfully called all songs from his parents' era "oldie moldies."

Ellie almost swung around to change the selection. But, no, she assured herself, it wasn't a problem. Two years ago, she might have fallen apart if she'd listened to that song, but she could handle it now. A stroll down memory lane might even be good for her, proof at long last that she was completely and forever over Tucker Grant.

Continuing toward the kitchen, she let the music carry her back to that summer night nineteen years ago. The details came so clear in her mind that it might have happened yesterday. She could almost smell the breeze rolling in off the river, redolent with the perfume of wildflowers and the scent of pine. She and Tucker had climbed into the back, where they could stretch out on the seat without the steering wheel and gearshift getting in their way. Heads bent, hands shaking with nerves, they'd shyly undressed, neither of them completely sure how to proceed once they got naked. Finally, Tucker had simply taken her in his arms. *Don't be scared, Ellie girl,* he'd whispered. *I'll love you forever—until the rivers stop flowing and the ocean goes dry.*

Snapped back to the present by the coldness of the worn kitchen linoleum under her bare feet, Ellie sighed and shook her head. Talk about a sappy line. She was surprised she hadn't giggled. Back then, of course, it had seemed terribly romantic, just the sort of thing a young girl yearned to hear.

She shifted her gaze to the stack of bills on the breakfast bar, a fair third of which were due. Then she stared at the broken faucet, which she couldn't afford to replace until well after Christmas. Since there was no sign of Tucker Grant in this charming picture, the rivers must have stopped flowing and the oceans gone dry. Or maybe Tucker was just lousy at keeping promises.

Ah, well—who needed him? Judging by things the boys had told her, he hadn't changed a bit. After ten years with the state, he was still a field biologist, turning down promotions because he didn't want a desk job. At the top of the pay scale for that position, he received occasional cost-of-living raises, but that was it. She, on the other hand, was the big kahuna at the House of Interior Design, and she'd gotten two salary increases in the eleven months since she'd been hired. In short, she was on her way up, and he was dead in the water.

Though she'd never been inside his new house, the boys had given her a sketchy description. Instead of investing his half of their marital-home equity into a solidly built older place that could have been renovated, he'd bought on the cheap in a modest housing development with cookie-cutter floor plans and lots the size of postage stamps. No big surprise. The only time in Tucker's life that he'd ever shown good taste was when he married her.

Determined not to think about him for a second longer, Ellie advanced across the floor. Halloween was only a month away. She would put this time to good use, making sugar cookies for her sons—great big round ones decorated to look like jack-o'-lanterns. In the morning, she'd go up to the attic and dig out the Halloween decorations. By tomorrow night, the house would be cheery and bright with pumpkins and witches hanging at the windows, and she'd welcome the boys at the door with a big smile and a plate of treats. They'd love that.

As she drew the old green mixing bowl from a cupboard, Ellie thought of her mother, who'd once mixed cookies in this bowl before it had been passed down to her only child. As a little girl, Ellie had stood on a stool, watching the mixing process in fascination and snitching morsels of dough whenever her mom turned her head. Years later, Ellie's sons, Sammy, Zach, and Kody, had followed the same tradition, forcing her to make double batches every time she baked so she'd have something left to put in the oven.

Images flashed through her mind of those holiday baking sprees when her boys had been much younger, their faces smeared with icing, their pudgy fingers gooey and coated with multicolored sprinkles. The kitchen had fared no better than their faces, and afterward she always felt compelled to scrub the floor on her hands and knees.

Looking back on it now, Ellie wished with all her heart that she'd let the floor go and just enjoyed having milk and cookies with her sons. But, no, before Sammy's death and the ensuing divorce, her priorities had been seriously skewed. She'd been caught up in the supermom syndrome back then, convinced she had to be a perfect wife, mother, and homemaker, all while she pursued a career. She'd had no time to sit around on a winter afternoon, eating cookies with her precious boys.

It had taken a tragedy to make her realize that nothing was more important than her kids. *Nothing.* These days, if it came to a choice between devoting time to her sons or scrubbing the floor, the floor lost every time. When the boys were grown, they wouldn't remember how clean her kitchen had been, but they'd have fond memories of this holiday season and the goodies she'd baked for them.

Ellie stopped the sink and squeezed in dish soap. While the water ran, she lighted the candle on the windowsill that Kody had given her for Mother's

Day, a misshapen lump of yellow wax he'd poured for her at school. He'd used one of Bucky's empty dog food cans as a mold, and the rings in the aluminum had left telltale lines. Every time she looked at it, she smiled.

Beyond the windowpane, the drizzly gray of afternoon had given way to the deeper shades of early evening. Still leafy from summer, hydrangea, lilac, and camellia bushes crowded the weathered board fence, creating a dense jungle of rain-drenched foliage that needed to be pruned. Lending some bright relief from all the green, splashes of autumn-orange decorated the drooping maple trees. Soon the grass would be hidden beneath a carpet of fallen leaves that would crunch underfoot.

The wavering candlelight washed the glass with patterns of gold. As the flame licked its way down the wick, the sweet smell of vanilla wafted to Ellie's nostrils, reminding her of the task at hand. She turned off the faucet and spun from the sink. Studiously ignoring the range top, which got washed only when one of the boys decided to give it a few swipes, she climbed on the stepstool to get salt and vanilla from the spice cupboard above it. As she hopped down, she kept her gaze averted from the stove's crusty burner plates. A vow was a vow. No matter how filthy they got, she would never scrub them, so why drive herself crazy noticing the buildup?

Singing along with Bonnie Tyler, she belted out the refrain of "Total Eclipse of the Heart" as she measured ingredients. She was about to soften some butter in the microwave when the portable phone on the counter rang. She jumped and then stared at it;

it was probably Marvin calling. *Great.* She had grown very fond of him over the last few months, and most of the time, she was glad of his company, but she didn't want to have him over when the boys weren't home. Whenever she was alone with him, he grew amorous, and it was becoming increasingly difficult to fend him off.

Ellie wasn't ready for intimacy. She couldn't say why, exactly. Marvin was more than ten years her senior, and at forty-six, he wasn't a bad-looking guy. A tad overweight, maybe, and starting to go bald, but things like that didn't matter to her anymore. She'd had a deliciously handsome man once, and just look where that had gotten her.

Marvin was decent and kind and dependable. That mattered far more to her than looks. Given their mutual careers in interior design, they also had a lot in common. All the makings were there for a fabulous relationship. It was just, well—she didn't know what the problem was, really. When he kissed her, no matter how hard she tried to get into it, she found herself thinking about stupid stuff, like what she needed to pick up at the market on her way home from work the next night. Not good.

After dating Marvin for nearly six months, off and on, Ellie knew he had every right to be feeling impatient with her. *Soon*, she kept telling him. She just needed a little more time. Taking the relationship to a more serious level was a big step for her.

What to do, what to do? The phone jangled again, urgent and demanding. She considered not answering. But what if it wasn't Marvin? It was always possible that one of the boys might call.

On the fourth ring, she groaned and wiped her hands, trying to fabricate a believable excuse not to invite him over even as she grabbed the phone and pressed the TALK button. Menstrual cramps, she decided with an evil grin. Not very original, but it was a surefire way to cool his jets.

"Hello," she said, doing her best to sound miserable.

"Ellie?"

She would have recognized that deep, silky tenor anywhere. *Tucker.* Her hand tightened over the phone as an image of him took shape in her mind. Tawny hair, hazel eyes sharp with intelligence, and sun-burnished features, every chiseled plane of which had once been engraved on her heart. Just thinking about him filled her with resentment.

She pictured him in a sunshine-yellow kitchen with fake butcher-block counters. He'd be leaning against a wall, she decided, his booted feet crossed at the ankles, his rangy, well-muscled body show-cased in a wash-worn flannel work shirt and faded denim jeans that hugged his long, powerful legs like a second skin.

"Hi," she said stiffly. He seldom called, so she had to grope for more to say. She opted for a note of humor. "If you're about to tell me the state has screwed up the child support again, I'll jump off a tall building. I just dropped a hundred and sixty bucks on football cleats and basketball shoes."

She hoped he would offer to kick in a little extra this month to cover the expense just so she could turn him down. He'd argued against her moving to Springfield, predicting that the cost of living would be much higher in the Eugene area and she would come to regret the decision. *In your face,* she wanted to say. *I'm doing just fine over here. I love my job. I just got a raise. I have a fabulous new boyfriend. I don't need your help, thanks very much.*

Instead of offering her money, he said, "No, it's nothing like that, Ellie."

His tone was taut and oddly neutral. After being married to him for thirteen years, she knew when he was upset. Alarm raised goose bumps on her skin. "What's wrong?"

"I don't know how to say this."

Oh, God! Memories sped through her mind, all splashed with crimson. Her vocal cords felt like overstretched rubber as she struggled to speak. "What happened?" She braced a hand on the counter, feeling as if her knees might buckle. "It's one of the boys, isn't it? Who's hurt? Tucker, answer me."

"No, no, it's nothing like that. As far as I know, they're both all right."

"As far as you know?" Her heart was pounding so hard that it pained her. She pressed a fist over the spot. "Something's wrong. I hear it in your voice."

"They've taken off."

For a moment, the words circled in her mind, making no sense. "What do you mean, they've taken off?"

"Exactly what I said. I just got home, and the little snots are gone."

She stared stupidly at the roses on the faded hunter-green wallpaper. "Gone? This is your weekend. You're supposed to be watching them."

"I worked today."

"So? I have a job, too. Have I ever called to tell you the kids were gone?"

"That isn't fair. Zach's fourteen, for Pete's sake, and Mrs. Robinson next door is always available in case of emergency. You leave them alone on Saturday all the time while you're working."

"I also call to check on them. If they don't answer the phone, I hightail it home to see what's wrong."

"I was way out past Wickiup Reservoir, overseeing a team of stream surveyors. I tried to call home on my cell phone and couldn't get out."

Ellie knew the cell phone reception wasn't as good in central Oregon as it was in the valley. There were fewer towers over there, and the mountainous terrain sometimes interfered with the signals. Knowing that and admitting it were two different things. She wasn't obligated to give Tucker Grant a fair shake. When the shoe had been on the other foot, had he been fair to her?

She pushed a shank of blond hair from her eyes. She was shaking so hard that the strands shivered back down over her forehead the instant she withdrew her hand. "Where do you think they went?"

His voice turned gravelly. "According to the note they left, they're somewhere in the Baxter Wilderness Area."

Ellie knew the place. While they were still married, they'd taken the boys camping there several times each summer. "*Somewhere* in the area? I'm not following. That's a long way from Bend. How did they get there?"

"I think they rode their bicycles." He paused as if the next words came hard. "Ellie, they've run away."

"They've *what?*"

She heard a rustle of paper come over the line. "The note is in Zach's handwriting, but Kody signed it, as well."

Iridescent hues of blue and pink shimmered in the froth of dishwater suds. The scent of vanilla from the candle suddenly made her nauseated.

"Ellie, are you still there?"

She nodded and then realized he couldn't see her. "Yes. I'm here. I'm, uh, just trying to assimilate this. Are you *sure* they've run away, Tucker? Maybe they just got bored while you were gone and—"

"No. I wish that were the case, but it isn't. They've definitely run away."

"Why? Did something happen to upset them?"

"Nothing that I'm aware of."

This was so unlike her sons, she knew there had to be an explanation. Suspicion slammed into her brain. "Have you been letting your friend Liz stay the night when they're there?"

Even over the phone, she felt him bristle at the question. "That is so typical. Why is it that you always have to assign blame?"

He was a fine one to talk. He'd held her responsible for Sammy's accident and walked out on her during the most difficult time of her life. "Just answer the question. Has she been spending the night there?"

"The particulars of my sex life are none of your damned business."

"They quickly become my business when you play fast and loose in front of my children."

"May I remind you that they're my children, too?

Fast and loose? You know better than that. Not around my kids."

Ellie closed her eyes. He was right; deep down, she did know better. "H-how long do you think they've been gone?"

"My guess is that they left shortly after I did this morning. All that's in the dishwasher are two cereal bowls. I don't think they had lunch here. It would also take them quite a while to reach Baxter on bicycles. At least five or six hours, depending on how often they stopped to rest. They had to leave here fairly early to get there before dark."

Panic clawed at the edges of her mind. She held it at bay by trying to concentrate on absolutes instead of possibilities. "Did they take camping gear?"

"Yes. All that's left in the garage is mine."

She pictured her boys pedaling along the shoulder of that busy road, and her self-control took another hard hit. She caught the inside of her cheek between her teeth.

"Ellie, don't," he said softly, as if he knew exactly what she was thinking. "They've done this expressly to scare the bejesus out of us."

"And they've succeeded. Highway 97 is the most dangerous road in Oregon."

"Ah, now, it's not that bad."

Ellie remembered another time when he'd poohpoohed her concerns, and she'd ended up standing over her child's grave. "I've warned them a *hundred* times not to ride their bikes in heavy traffic." Pain bunched in her temples. *Sammy.* She couldn't help remembering the day he died—how the pavement had turned black with his blood.

"I'm sure they're both fine. If anything happened, someone would contact me."

"They don't carry ID."

"No, but the bicycles are licensed. The cops could easily trace them back to me. They're fine, Ellie. We need to keep our heads."

That was true. Panic would accomplish nothing. She took a deep breath. "Right." Kody's face flashed through her mind, and she wished she'd never let him out of her sight. "We'd—um—better call someone. We need to find them as quickly as we can."

"I can find them, Ellie. You know that."

She made a small sound of agreement. Tucker's reputation as a tracker was well known in Deschutes County. Search-and-rescue teams frequently called upon him to help locate lost hikers.

"I'll gather my gear and head up there as soon as we get off the phone," he said. "By first light, I'll be on their trail. Riding bicycles, they weren't able to take the dog with them. Bucky can help sniff them out. They'll be fine for the night."

"In a wilderness area?"

"They have warm sleeping bags, and they ransacked my cupboards and fridge, so they shouldn't go hungry. Even if they run low on food, they both know how to catch fish with whatever they have on hand, and I've taught them damned near everything I know about the edible plant life in that area."

"There are cougars and bears out there, Tucker. They're just little boys."

"Not so little anymore. Zach's fourteen, and Kody's eleven. I know grown men with less wilderness savvy. No worries, Ellie, I promise."

"We still need to find them as fast as we can." She shoved rigid fingers into her hair. "No offense to your tracking skills, but the best way to do that is to call in help."

"I'd rather try to find them myself first."

"Yes, well . . . my vote carries half the weight."

He sighed. "Ellie, think. I know you're scared, but let's not go off half-cocked. The boys have run away. Do you know what may happen if the authorities get wind of it? Kids don't do things like this without a reason. If a bunch of do-gooders start digging for dirt, we could end up with a hell of a mess on our hands. Our sons could become temporary wards of the court until it all gets straightened out."

"That's absurd. They aren't going to make our kids wards of the court. We're perfectly good parents."

"Are we?" A humorless huff of laughter came over the line. "Excuse me, but I'm holding a note in my hand that says we've done a piss-poor job somewhere along the way. If you think children's services won't investigate us, you're dreaming."

Ellie gripped the phone with both hands. "Better that than one of them getting hurt."

"I'll find them, I said. Name me a better man for the job, damn it."

He had a point. And he was probably right about children's services, as well. When kids ran away, it raised a red flag, and the authorities might suspect the worst. "I can't believe they've done something so harebrained."

"Yeah, well, they have. As for finding them quickly, I'll have them home tomorrow night, guaranteed." He released another weary sigh. "You know, Ellie, getting them back isn't my primary worry. We have to figure out what the hell we're going to do once we get them home."

"Shaking them silly sounds highly appealing at the moment." She stared at the half-mixed cookie dough, remembering all her grand plans for a cheery welcome-home party. How many kids got home-made cookies, just because? She lived with ring around the toilet, dirty grout, and dust bunnies under her furniture, and this was the thanks she got? "I can't believe they've done this. What earthly reason do they have? It's not as if we abuse them or anything."

She heard the rustle of paper again. "They've made a couple of demands."

"What kind of demands?"

He hesitated before answering. "They refuse to come home until we agree to get back together and go to counseling."

"What?"

"You heard me. They want us back together again, no discussion, no bargains. It's that or nothing. They've made it very clear they won't settle for less."

In the background, Kim Carnes belted out the lyrics of "Bette Davis Eyes." Now Ellie understood why Zach had put that particular CD in the player. He knew she usually turned on the stereo while they were gone, and he'd been hoping to soften her up with old favorites from her and Tucker's dating days. How long had he and Kody been planning this, anyway?

Ellie's blood pressure went up several points. Candle wax was about to drip on the windowsill. She leaned over to blow out the flame with an angry expulsion of breath. "It isn't as if we arbitrarily decided to get a divorce."

"I understand that, and you understand that. But do our boys?" The question hung there, stark and razor sharp, between them. "They're miserable, Ellie. They have to be. Happy kids don't run away."

Her kids were *not* miserable. She devoted every spare moment to making them happy. She couldn't remember the last time she'd taken a bubble bath, and she hadn't shaved her legs in over two weeks. She'd even started cutting her own hair, using the money she would have spent at a salon to buy Nike running shoes and name-brand jeans. How could they possibly be miserable?

Dimly she realized that Tucker was still talking. "You know how far it is from Bend to Baxter, most of it uphill," he said. "They pedaled every inch of the way. Kids don't put themselves through an ordeal like that without good reason. Whether this makes sense to us or not—whether we understand it or not—this is very important to them."

Her throat felt raw, and her voice had gone raspy when she spoke again. "What are we going to do?"

"I have no idea. Maybe—" He broke off without finishing the thought.

"Maybe, what?" she pressed.

"I don't know. Coming home to find them gone and then reading this note, I've just been thinking that—" He broke off again and cursed under his breath. "Did we do the right thing? Maybe getting a divorce wasn't best for our kids."

The hair at her nape prickled. "What are you saying?"

"That maybe we screwed up."

We? It was all she could do not to scream the word at him. He'd left her, not the other way around. Just packed his stuff and walked out. She could still remember the deafening report of the door slamming shut behind him. She had almost run after him, would have gotten on her knees and begged him to stay if she'd thought it might change his mind. Now he wanted her to share the blame for their divorce?

"We obviously have two very disillusioned kids on our hands," he continued. The paper rustled again, and she envisioned him crumpling the note. "They've run away, for God's sake. Maybe we should stop thinking about ourselves and start thinking about them for a change."

Ellie's heart squeezed, and the word she'd tried to swallow back blurted from her lips. "*We?* Excuse me, but the way I remember it, *you* were the one who left, Tucker." She'd also gotten it straight from their elder son that he'd been the first to start dating other people after the divorce.

"Like there was anything to hold me?" he shot back. "You're damned right, I walked out."

There had been a time when hearing him say that would have broken her heart, but now she felt nothing but anger. What would he say, she wondered a little wildly, if she told him the whole truth? He would really despise her then.

"What's changed?" she fired back. "Have I missed something?"

"Nothing's changed, obviously." His voice vibrated with frustration. "Here we are, three years later, and it's still the same old bullshit."

"And it's still all my fault. Amazing."

"Well, it sure as hell wasn't mine."

"Nothing ever is."

He swore under his breath.

"No need to whisper. You're taking the Lord's name in vain, either way."

"Do you work at being impossible, or does it just come naturally?"

"I work at it, of course. It's so rewarding when I'm dealing with you."

Silence. Ellie couldn't remember what they'd been talking about. "Where were we?"

"I was trying to point out that how we feel about each other isn't the issue. Not when our kids lay something like this on us."

"Ah, yes. And I was pointing out that you're three years late in reaching that conclusion. Thanks, but no thanks. I think how we feel matters a lot. What are you suggesting, that we live in misery for the rest of our lives just to make our kids happy?"

"As I recall, I was the one who was miserable."

"It was no picnic for me, either." Ellie remembered how he'd turned his back on her, night after night. Nothing on earth could induce her to go through that again. "I love my boys, and I'd do anything for them. You know that. But I honestly don't see how we could ever live together again."

"Forget I offered."

That went without saying. He'd used up all his chances with her. They had nothing left between them now but memories, and even those brought more pain than joy.

"I'm sorry, Tucker," she said wearily. "If I thought for a moment we might make it work, I'd agree for the boys' sake, but I just don't—"

"Forget I suggested it, all right?" He bit out the words. "As we both very well know, sorry doesn't fix much, does it?"

She held tighter to the phone. That sentiment of his had destroyed their marriage. The irony of it was, he hadn't known the half of it, and he still hadn't been able to forgive her. Buried pain knifed to the surface. She swallowed hard, stared at the faucet, listened to the *plip-plop* of the drips. As far as she was concerned, he could go to hell on greased runners.

"Well . . ." He cleared his throat. "I guess there's no point in pissing up that rope. Right now, we've got more pressing concerns, namely two mixed-up kids. Once I find them, we'll have plenty of time to discuss what, if anything, we should do to prevent this from happening again."

Ellie thought of her boys, out there alone in the dark. Were they cold? Hungry? Afraid? They were all she had left.

Reaching a snap decision, she pushed away from the sink and turned toward the breakfast bar. "Where do you plan to camp tonight?" She grabbed a notepad and pencil. "I'll drive up and meet you."

"You don't need to be there, Ellie."

"Yes, Tucker, I do."

"Look, no offense, all right? But how long has it been since you went hiking in rough terrain?"

"A while."

"As in three years?"

Ellie bristled. "What's your point?"

"I think it goes without saying."

"Just tell me how to find the camp, Tucker. This isn't up for discussion."

"Come on." Irritation put an edge in his voice.

"You know you're out of shape. You wouldn't last an hour out on the trail. You'll only slow me down."

"If the shoe were on the other foot, would you sit at home?"

"For once in your life, be reasonable."

"I'm being perfectly reasonable. They're my children. I can't sit here, doing nothing, when I know they're out there, upset, alone, and possibly lost."

His tone turned cajoling. "I'll take my cell phone along. How's that? You'll know something the moment I do."

"Why are you so reluctant to have me tag along?" She arched an eyebrow. "Oh, I get it. Your little friend Liz is going, isn't she?"

"What's it to you?" he snapped back.

"Nothing except that I'll be damned. They're my kids, not hers. If anyone's going to help search for them, it's going to be me."

"Ellie, you get turned around the minute you leave the road."

"And she doesn't, is that it?"

"I didn't say that. Look, let's back up and—"

"No, you look. I'm going, end of discussion. Just give me directions to camp."

Chapter Two

Tucker ran a thumb up the bridge of his nose to rub the throbbing spot between his brows. He was getting a bitch of a headache. No small wonder. Just the thought of spending time with Ellie again had him grinding his teeth. For all the reasons he'd just cited to her on the phone and several more he preferred not to think about, he didn't want her to join him.

He blinked to clear his vision. Shopping bags still sat on the counter. After finding the note from his boys, he hadn't bothered to put the groceries away. He'd planned to make a vegetarian stew for supper with fresh fruit compotes topped with fat-free yogurt for dessert. Given his druthers, he would have preferred a giant meat-lover's pizza with extra cheese, but what kind of a father taught his kids to eat like that?

Now, despite all his efforts to be a good parent, his sons had run away on his watch. Why couldn't they have taken off while their mother had them? Ellie, bless her vindictive little heart, would never let him live this down.

Filled with a sense of urgency he couldn't shake, Tucker left the groceries sitting there and went out to the garage. As he grabbed his backpack off the shelf, his gaze landed on the small cassette player he'd once carried on wilderness hikes so his wife could listen to music at night. Next to the electronic device were some dusty plastic containers for fresh eggs and bread, two other luxuries she had been unwilling to do without even on camping trips.

His life was a lot simpler now, he thought fiercely. The only reason he'd offered to go back to her had been because of the kids. Like he wanted the old ball and chain around his neck again?

The single life agreed with him. When a buddy called and invited him to go fishing, he could be ready in thirty minutes—no fuss, no muss. He liked the spontaneity of that. He also enjoyed being able to spend his money any damned way he pleased. Granted, by the time he made his mortgage and child support payments, there wasn't much left over, but it was his. If he wanted to buy the boys something special, there was no one to say he shouldn't. The same went for a half rack of beer. Being a bachelor was great. The only drawback was doing his own laundry, and even that wasn't so bad. Pink socks were starting to grow on him.

Jerking his pack off the shelf, he checked the contents to be sure Zach and Kody hadn't removed anything important. He always kept his gear in perfect order just in case he got an emergency call. In central Oregon, it wasn't uncommon for hikers or cross-country skiers to lose their way, and he never knew when his services as a tracker might be needed.

Somehow, he just hadn't expected the next emergency to involve his own kids.

Even after rereading their note several times, he couldn't believe they had done something so stupid. As a general rule, Tucker didn't resort to corporal punishment, but he had a good mind to do so this time. As a field biologist for the Oregon Department of Fish and Wildlife, he knew better than most people how dangerous a wilderness area could be. His only consolation was that his boys were well trained, which greatly reduced their chances of getting lost or injured.

Tucker had just finished checking his pack when he heard the faint peal of the doorbell. Frowning, he stepped to the door that opened onto a covered breezeway at the front of his rambler. Because the porch was recessed, he couldn't see who was there.

"Yo!" he yelled. "I'm out here."

Liz Brighton, a new field biologist at ODF&W, peeked around the corner. Her long, curly red hair flared like a torch in the dim glow of the porch light. "I wondered why you didn't answer my knock."

They had been dating occasionally for a couple of months, but only in the most casual of ways, so he was surprised to see her on his doorstep. "Hey, Liz. What're you doing on this side of town?"

She shrugged as she moved along the walkway toward him. "I was just out driving around and gravitated this way."

Informally attired in snug blue jeans and a tight green sweater that enhanced far more than her emerald eyes, she looked good enough to eat—a tall, long-legged beauty with generous breasts and an incredibly small waist. A guy would have to be blind and half-dead not to find her appealing.

Tucker had excellent vision, and he was a long way from dead. Unfortunately, a little voice at the back of his mind kept warning him to be cautious. Liz said she planned to stay focused on her career for the next few years, that a serious relationship was out of the question for her right now. In the interim, she only wanted to have a good time with a man she liked and respected. No strings, she promised, and no hard feelings when it was over.

On the surface, that sounded like a mighty fine arrangement. Only there was something in Liz's eyes, an eager intensity that made Tucker edgy. He couldn't shake the feeling that she might be looking for far more in a relationship than he was willing to give. He didn't need any more complications in his life right now, especially not ones that involved a female subordinate from the department. With two kids to support, his job was a top priority, and nothing—absolutely nothing—could be allowed to jeopardize it.

As Liz drew up in front of him, she flashed a sexy smile that made him wonder if he needed his head examined. "I got lonesome to see you. I, um, thought I might watch a movie with you and the boys. Do you mind?"

Tucker thrust a hand through his hair. "I wish I could say yes, Liz, but my boys aren't here."

"I thought you had them for the weekend."

"I did. Rather, I do. They took off while I was at work."

"Where to?"

"The Baxter Wilderness Area." The next words came hard. "They've run away."

Her eyes widened. "They've *what*?"

"You heard me." Eager to be on his way, Tucker retreated into the garage. "I'm packing right now to go find them."

She pushed through the doorway after him. "Baxter? Oh, Tucker, they could get hurt up there."

He showed her his back as he bent to retrieve his pack. "Hopefully, I'll find them before anything happens."

"How long have they been gone?"

"I think they took off shortly after I left for work this morning."

"On foot?"

"No, they rode their bicycles. I'm heading up now so I can hit their trail at first light."

"Those crazy kids. What on earth possessed them?"

"That's the way of it with boys that age. Sometimes they have the collective IQ of a gnat." He slung the straps of his pack over one shoulder. Turning to meet her gaze, he said, "I'm sorry, Liz. I'll give you a call when I get back to town, all right?"

She rested her hands at her hips, her expression thoughtful. "What part of Baxter are you going to search first?"

"I'm assuming they entered at the north end where we usually camp. They're familiar with that area, and it's closest from here. I'm taking Bucky along to help sniff them out. With his nose to give me an edge, I'll have them home before the sun goes down tomorrow."

She narrowed a lovely green eye. "I'd be a much better search partner than that silly dog."

Tucker held up a staying hand. "I appreciate the offer, Liz. Really I do. But that's not a good idea."

"Why not?"

"My ex is driving up to meet me."

"Oh. I see." The expression in her eyes said she didn't see at all. "Well, then." She lifted her shoulders in a shrug. "Ha."

"It's nothing like that." He sighed, trying to think how he might best explain. "It's over between me and Ellie. Honestly. It's just that things could get sticky if—" He broke off, the thought suddenly occurring to him that Liz's offer might be a blessing in disguise. Being alone with Ellie out in the middle of nowhere wasn't high on his list. "What am I saying? Here you are, a wilderness expert, offering to help find my kids, and I'm turning you down?"

Her expression brightened. "I'd love to help."

"Are you sure? It really would be great if you could come along."

"Consider it done." She glanced at her watch. "Can you give me thirty minutes? It'll take me that long to run home and grab my gear."

Tucker needed to hurry, but he guessed a few minutes, one way or the other, wouldn't make that much difference. He couldn't pick up the boys' trail until daylight, anyway.

"Thirty minutes," he agreed. "Try not to be any longer, though, all right? I imagine Ellie is already driving over, and it's only a three-hour trip. If I don't have a fire going to guide her in, she'll drive past the spot and get lost."

"You're kidding, right?"

"Unfortunately, no."

"Surely she's not so inept at finding her way as all that."

Tucker frowned slightly. "Inept. Now there's a word."

By the time Ellie reached the Baxter Wilderness Area, she was heartily glad that Marvin had appeared unexpectedly on her doorstep before she left and had agreed to come with her. It was so horribly dark up there in the woods, with tall pines crowding the shoulders of the highway. The only moonlight that peeked through the trees was directly along the road, a thin stream of faint luminescence that limned the asphalt, making it look like an ever-narrowing, ethereal blue ribbon that curled into the yawning blackness ahead of them.

"I'm so glad you stopped by tonight, Marvin." Taking her gaze off the road for a moment, Ellie glanced across the car at him. "Thank you so much for coming with me."

He ran a finger under the knot of his tie, then rolled his shoulders and stretched his neck. "You've thanked me at least a dozen times." He grinned. "I'm just sorry about the Chinese food. If I'd known we would eat in the car, I'd have gotten something easier for you to manage while you were driving. Sweet and sour over rice doesn't make for great finger food."

"I wolfed down enough tempura to do me." Nerves had Ellie's stomach churning, and she hadn't really felt like eating. "And stop trying to change the subject. When someone drops everything like you did to go traipsing off into the wilderness with me, I can say thank you a dozen times if I like. You're a good friend, one of the best. I just can't tell you how much I appreciate your willingness to help me out."

"Hey, I haven't been camping in eons. I'm looking forward to it. Honestly."

Ellie worried the inside of her cheek. He'd had to borrow camping equipment from his brother-in-law, and she could only hope he'd brought along everything he would need. "It won't be your usual outdoor experience. No outing with Tucker ever is. Imagine one of those survival camps where they put people through hell, teaching them how to live off the land, and you'll pretty much have the right picture."

"I'll survive. Surely you don't think I'd let my best girl drive up here alone?"

His best girl? Ellie's hands tightened over the steering wheel. She liked Marvin. She really liked him a lot. But lately he'd been making noises that made her nervous. With two sons to complicate the situation, she needed to take this relationship business just a little more slowly than he seemed willing to go. She had tried to explain that to him, but apparently she hadn't put it in terms he could understand.

"I hope I didn't come off like a big chicken back at the house."

"Bluck, bluck, *bluck*." Tucking his fists in his armpits, he flapped his elbows, doing a comical rendition of a clucking hen.

Ellie rolled her eyes and sighed. "Okay, so I came off like a big chicken. I don't usually mind traveling by myself. Honestly. It's only in remote areas like this, with forestland stretching forever in all directions, that my confidence feels a little shaky. I don't know what I'd do if a tire went flat or the car broke down."

"You'd do exactly what I would, call Triple A."

"Oh, that's a comfort."

He winked at her. "Do I look like a mechanic?"

Dressed in a Ralph Lauren shirt and neatly creased dress slacks, with takeout cartons littering the floorboard at his feet, he looked to be exactly what he was: a slightly plump, middle-aged guy who'd been a salesman most of his life. Marvin hadn't gone back to college to study interior design until after his divorce. Before that, he'd worked for twenty years at Sears in the drapery and household section.

In that moment, it struck Ellie what a grand gesture this was for him to make. He wasn't the rough-and-rugged type, yet he had agreed to accompany her without any hesitation. That meant more to her than she could say.

"If we have to call road service," she said, "it'll be just my luck the cell phone won't work. In mountainous areas like this, the signal can get blocked."

"Bite your tongue. I've happily avoided the macho ritual of changing flat tires for almost fifty years."

"You mean you don't know how?"

"I've got a basic idea. Never had a flat but once, and that in town. I pulled over and walked to a garage one block over. Got it fixed in twenty minutes."

"That's one of the things I like best about you, Marvin—no baloney. Most guys would pretend they could change a tire with one hand tied behind their backs."

"The instant I lied, we'd get a flat, sure as it rains little green frogs."

Ellie smiled in spite of herself. "In a pinch, I think I can change a tire." Weary of the oppressive darkness, she leaned forward to adjust the dash lights. The heightened green glow bathed Marvin's round face, making his skin look chartreuse. "Years ago, Tucker showed me how. The lug nuts might be a problem. As I recall, even he strained to get them off sometimes."

Marvin made a show of flexing a bicep. "I can loosen a few lug nuts." He waggled his eyebrows. "I'm not totally useless."

"I never said you were." Ellie was so worried about her boys that she didn't feel much like smiling, but his teasing coaxed another grin from her. "Let's just keep our fingers crossed that nothing goes wrong." She fixed her attention on the road as she took a sharp turn. "Walking back down this mountain in the dark doesn't sound very appealing."

"Hoo-ooo-oo," he said softly, doing a fair rendition of a ghost.

"I'm not afraid of the dark," she hastened to explain. "Not very, anyway. I'm just cursed with an abysmally poor sense of direction. We've made several turns. I'm not sure I can find my way out of here."

"Never fear. I come equipped with testicles."

She shot him a bewildered look. "What?"

"Practically all men have a great sense of direction, and most women don't. I've always attributed it to anatomical differences."

"Ah. Is that why Moses wandered in the desert for forty years?"

He chuckled. "You've got me there." Drawing a fortune cookie from a sack, he added, "Considering you were married to Rambo for so long, I'd think you'd be perfectly at home up here. Didn't he teach you how to get your bearings?"

Ellie smirked at the disparaging nickname. *Rambo.* She had to remember that one. "He tried. I wasn't a very apt pupil. I can determine east and west by the position of the sun easily enough, but I tend to let my mind wander while I'm walking. If you aren't sure which direction you've been going, it's a little hard to double back."

"True," he agreed with an indulgent smile.

"I'll also remind you that in this day of satellites, it isn't easy to locate Polaris at night. I finally gave up and just followed Tucker everywhere. In short, all the Rambo stuff never rubbed off on me. I developed a halfhearted appreciation for the great outdoors, but that was about it."

"You didn't get into the stick-rubbing stuff, then?"

"Definitely not. Tucker carries a small square of magnesium. Supposedly, it'll burn even under water. You scrape off shavings over the kindling and light it with a flint."

"That should simplify building a fire."

"As simple as one, two, three."

"What's so impressive about that?"

"I never said it was impressive."

Loud crackling sounds filled the car as he chewed the fortune cookie. "Sometimes I get the feeling you're still pretty damned impressed."

"Not even."

"You're not still hung up on him?"

"On Tucker? Give me a break. We can't even talk

on the phone without taking shots at each other. That's the main reason I asked you to come, so I wouldn't have to be alone with him."

"I know. That's what worries me."

Ellie frowned. "I'm not following."

"You aren't exactly the fainthearted type who avoids confrontation at any cost. Why are you so reluctant to be alone with him?"

"Because I find the prospect nauseating?"

After peering at her through the gloom for an interminably long moment, he asked, "Deep down, are you afraid of what may happen?"

She rolled her eyes. "As in, afraid I may murder him, you mean?"

"Why all the anger?"

"Can we change the subject?" Ellie flipped on the turn signal, realized there was no need, and shoved it back to the off position. "I really don't want to talk about him."

"Fine. It's not a particularly pleasant subject for me, either. I care about you, Ellie. It doesn't make me happy to think you may still be carrying a torch for the bastard."

"Don't worry about it. I just don't want to be alone with him, that's all."

Just the *thought* set her teeth on edge. On the rare occasion that she had seen Tucker since the divorce (which, thankfully, hadn't happened for nearly a year), she'd felt—well—distinctly uncomfortable. He'd always had this way of looking at her—a quick glide of his gaze over her body that made her tongue stick to the roof of her mouth. No matter how determined she was not to let him rattle her, all it took was one heated glance to make her forget what she meant to say and stammer like an idiot.

She knew it would be a million times worse if she got stuck out in the woods alone with him, especially in these woods where they'd camped so often during their marriage. They'd had intimate encounters practically everywhere. She could just imagine stopping for lunch and thinking, *I remember that rock*, as she tried to swallow trail mix that suddenly tasted like road gravel.

Looking back on it, she could only wonder how she could have been so shameless, sometimes in broad daylight, no less. Even after the kids came along, Tucker had always managed to steal moments alone with her, and Tucker being Tucker, he'd known exactly how to make the most of them.

"What are you smiling about?"

Ellie gave a guilty start. "I wasn't smiling."

"Yes, you were. It's a refreshing change, actually. You're so worried about those kids, you've been pulling a long face most of the evening."

Her brows snapped together. Had she really been smiling? Surely not.

Just then she glimpsed a green-and-white road sign. Relieved to have a reason to change the subject, she cried, "There's the turnoff!"

Stepping hard on the brake, she jerked the wheel to execute the turn. With the sudden deceleration, the Honda's back tires lost traction on the asphalt. She let off the brake and began tapping the pedal. Marvin grabbed the dash and threw her a worried look.

"Black ice," she explained. "Thank goodness I spotted the sign. I almost went right past it."

"What's that you're doing with the brake?"

"The tapping? You do that on ice. It keeps the tires from locking up."

He rubbed his arms. "I can't believe there's ice at this time of year. It's not even October yet."

"It's common at high elevations even in summer and fall." Just then, the front tires of the Honda bumped onto the rutted side road, jarring her teeth and making her fight the wheel. She leaned forward to peer out the window. "Keep your eyes peeled for the four hundred road. I don't want to miss it in the dark."

He turned to stare out the glass. When a small brown sign came into view, he said, "There it is."

She stopped and flipped on the dome light to review Tucker's directions. "About a quarter mile in, we'll come to a fork. There, we go left."

He nodded. When the fork of the road popped up in the headlights, Ellie made the turn. After driving about a mile, she said, "Knowing Tucker, he'll be camped way back off the road, so watch close for his campfire."

"Back off the road. Of course. What self-respecting Rambo would do otherwise?"

Ellie peered out the windshield again, searching for a flicker of firelight in the vast expanses of blackness. Her eyes had started to burn by the time she spotted the campfire, a small splash of amber in the darkness. In the play of light, the massive, cinnamon trunks of Ponderosa pines were visible around the clearing.

As the car bumped over the ruts and carried them closer, she could make out Tucker's forest-green Land Cruiser parked under the shelter of a tree. Two pup tents had been erected side by side near the fire. Ellie's hands knotted on the wheel. Two tents meant that Tucker had invited his girlfriend.

She glanced over at Marvin, more relieved than ever that she'd asked him to come along. At least she wouldn't look like the pathetic ex-wife without a new man in her life.

She nosed the Honda off the dirt forestry road and across the field toward the fire. As the car lurched over uneven ground, Marvin straightened on his seat and grabbed the door armrest to steady himself.

At the sound of their approach, a woman emerged from the shadows into the firelight. She was tall and slender with a cloud of red hair that ignited to fiery gold in the flickering amber. *Liz.* The boys called her Frizzy Lizzy. The unflattering nickname had given Ellie the foolish hope that she might be homely. *Not.* She was infuriatingly gorgeous, and even though Ellie searched hard, she detected not one strand of frizz on her regal head. Her snug jeans showcased long, shapely legs that Ellie would have killed for, and the green sweater she wore accentuated large, firm breasts the size of late-summer melons.

If Tucker Grant had searched a hundred years, he couldn't have found anyone more Ellie's exact opposite.

Chapter Three

Tucker's mood had gone from bad to worse over the course of the evening. Driving in from the main highway, he'd hoped to spot his sons' bicycle tracks along the edge of the road, but he hadn't. That might mean nothing. The boys could have come in on another road to a different campsite in this same area. Unfortunately, it could also mean they were in another part of Baxter entirely. If the latter proved to be the case, establishing a search grid would be a real bitch.

After assuring Ellie that he would be on the boys' trail by first light, Tucker dreaded having to tell her that the kids' whereabouts might be more difficult to pinpoint than he had first thought.

Ah, well. Nothing he said or did made her happy these days, which was exactly why it had been almost eleven months since they'd had a face-to-face. When he picked up the boys for visitation, he stayed out in the driveway and honked the horn. It was easier that way. For the kids' sake, both he and Ellie tried to be civil when they saw each other, but somehow they never quite managed. Invariably, one of them ended up making a snide remark, the other fired back, and the fight was on. Tucker figured it was better for everyone involved if he just steered clear.

No such luck tonight. He thanked God that Liz had come along. This way, at least, he wouldn't have to be alone with Ellie up here, where both of them had so many memories of happier times.

He was chopping firewood behind the tents when he heard a car approaching. Just as he registered the sound, Liz called, "She's here, Tucker!"

Sighing, he dusted his hands on his jeans and stepped out into view. It was funny how drastically things changed over the course of a man's life. There'd been a time when his heart had lifted at the sight of Ellie. It seemed corny now, but back then he'd always felt as if a cloud had moved over the sun when he wasn't with her.

Headlight beams bounced across the clearing. Squinting against the glare, Tucker watched the silver gray Honda roll to a stop some ten feet behind his Land Cruiser. When the engine died, absolute silence blanketed the campsite for a moment. Then, as loud as a rifle shot, a coal in the fire popped, followed by the ping of the cooling metal on the car.

Auburn brows arched like wings over her green eyes, Liz angled him a questioning look over her shoulder. Tucker shoved his hands into his pockets and moseyed closer. Since the divorce, Ellie had lent a whole new definition to the word *difficult*. He wasn't looking forward to this.

The heavy boughs of a towering Ponderosa cast her in shadow as she emerged from the sedan. When she moved forward into the firelight, Tucker was so shocked by her appearance that all he could do was stare. During their marriage, she had always worn her hair in a cloud of blond curls to her shoulders. Now it was as short as a boy's and looked as if it had been cut with a pair of hedge trimmers. She wore no makeup, not even any liner to enhance her big blue eyes. Even on camping trips, Ellie had always looked like a fashion plate. The only time Tucker had known her to go barefaced in public had been the day of Sammy's funeral.

For just an instant, a feeling akin to panic coursed through him. Something was wrong, had to be. Was she sick? She'd had a great aunt who died of breast cancer. Maybe it ran in the family. *Shit.* Why hadn't the boys said something?

An awful, weak feeling attacked Tucker's legs as he studied her delicate features. Smudges of exhaustion underscored her eyes, and she was so pale it frightened him. Even her soft, full mouth looked bloodless. Given the fact that he'd once believed her to be the most beautiful woman he'd ever seen, Tucker hated to even think it, but she looked—well, *terrible* was the only word that came to mind.

All animosity aside, he didn't know what he'd do if something happened to her. In a perverse way, she was still a driving force in his life, even if the feelings she now inspired within him were mostly hostile. Because of her, he'd saved his half of the equity from the sale of their home and scraped together all the other cash he could to make a down payment on another house. No way had he been going to rent when Ellie planned to buy, absolutely no way. He'd even traded in his new Land Cruiser for an older model and sold all but one of his hunting rifles. Because of her, he vacuumed the corners with a crevice tool now, for Christ's sake, determined not to let her best him at anything, not even housekeeping.

God, if something was seriously wrong, what would his boys do without her? Tucker had enough trouble being a good single parent on weekends. He had no idea how he'd manage if it became a full-time job.

"Hi, there," she called, rubbing her palms over her thighs the way she always did when she felt nervous. "You haven't lost your knack for giving great directions. I drove straight to the spot without a hitch."

Her voice sounded fine. Tucker narrowed an eye and studied her more closely, trying to determine if she'd lost any weight. At five feet three inches, and only a little over a hundred pounds, there never had been a whole lot to her, but as near as he could tell, she wasn't emaciated. The oversize flannel shirt she wore was soft from countless washings, and in the slight breeze, the cloth molded itself to her torso. The small but temptingly plump breasts he remembered so well still thrust pertly against the flannel. The curve of waist and hip that had once felt so perfectly formed for the weight of his hand looked just as it always had.

The tails of the shirt reached to the juncture of her thighs, a shifting tease of plaid that drew his attention to the snug denim that skimmed her legs. Maybe she wasn't sick, after all, he decided, but only showing the strain of an exhausting evening. God knew his nerves had been strung as tight as piano wire all night.

He realized he was staring at her legs. He jerked

his gaze away. He'd only been looking out of concern for her health, he assured himself. Knowing Ellie, she had hacked her hair off and gone without makeup on purpose, just to scare the hell out of him.

"Tucker always gives good directions," Liz said in a chirrupy voice. "It comes from working with so many kids fresh out of college. Once off the road, they get turned around and can't find their way back to the rig. He guides them in on a two-way."

Bucky, who'd been out christening bushes, gave a glad bark at the sight of Ellie and ran up for a pat. The dog seemed accustomed to her appearance, which blew Tucker's theory about the awful hairdo and lack of makeup. Evidently she had been neglecting herself for quite some time. What really griped Tucker—what really, *really* griped him was that she still managed to look beautiful, even with her hair going every which way and her face so white.

She leaned down to scratch the dog's ears. In the firelight, her wispy cap of blond curls shimmered and gleamed like molten gold. Still bent forward at the waist, she looked up at Tucker. Her flannel shirt gaped at the front, giving him a bird's-eye view of cleavage and lace.

"Any sign of the kids yet?"

She had to know he could see down her shirt. Well, he thought testily, she didn't have much to show off. Definitely nothing that interested him, anyhow.

"No," he found the presence of mind to reply. "I can't get out there and look until daylight."

He didn't add that it might take hours or even as much as a day to find their trail, even with the dog to help sniff it out.

Ellie straightened, much to his relief. Scanning the dark woods around them, she hugged her slender waist and nibbled her bottom lip. "I just pray they're all right."

"They'll be fine for one night." Tucker mentally crossed his fingers that one night didn't stretch into two.

"Oh, I hope so," she said shakily.

The awful, frightened look in her eyes took Tucker back in time to that fateful afternoon when she'd been worried that Sammy might get hurt on the motorcycle he'd been about to buy for him. With the memories came pain that ran so deep it made his bones ache.

He had overridden Ellie's concerns that day, and less than a week later, Sammy had been dead. Ellie had never forgiven him for that. Not that he blamed her. Tucker would carry the guilt and regret with him to his grave.

A movement inside the Honda caught Tucker's eye. Straining to see past the glint of firelight on the windshield, he made out the vague shape of a man on the passenger side. He appeared to be eating something. After licking his fingers, he wrenched open the door and climbed from the car.

He was a short, stocky fellow and dressed like a department-store salesman. Tucker had nothing against neckties; he wore one himself occasionally. But a wilderness area was no place for one.

Introductions weren't necessary. The boys had told him all about good old Marvin, namely that the guy was a dweeb and they couldn't understand what their mother saw in him. Tucker had to admit he was mystified, as well. As Marvin stepped around the front of the car to stand beside Ellie, Tucker noted that he had the beginnings of an impressive potbelly and was going bald. In Tucker's opinion, Ellie could do a hell of a lot better for herself.

Looks weren't everything, of course. Maybe Marvin had a great personality and a fabulous sense of humor.

Or maybe he was just damned good in bed.

Tucker wanted to kick himself for allowing that thought to slip into his mind. The particulars of Ellie's sex life were none of his business. As long as she chose lovers who were nice to his kids, he didn't care who hung his britches on her bedpost at night.

Waving a hand toward her current sidekick, she said, "Marvin, I'd like you to meet my ex-husband, Tucker Grant. Tucker, this is my friend and co-worker, Marvin Baines."

Tucker didn't miss the fact that Ellie had honored Marvin by introducing Tucker *to him* rather than vice versa. It was a subtle social nuance, one that many people no longer observed, but Ellie, the highfalutin physician's daughter, had been raised in upper crust circles where such things were important. Now in her mid-thirties, she still hadn't lost all her social grace, though God knew how she'd managed to retain any of it after thirteen years of marriage to a rough-mannered logger's brat.

Instead of feeling angry at the slight, Tucker almost grinned. Seeing her in action brought back memories. She was the only woman he knew who could so politely say, "Up yours." In his circles, people were more direct, and polish was something they put on their dress shoes.

He stepped past Liz to shake Marvin's hand. The guy's grip was as soft and clammy as a soggy marshmallow. "Good to meet you."

"Yes, well," Marvin replied, "I only wish it were under happier circumstances. I hope you don't mind that I came along to help with the search."

Tucker angled Ellie a sharp glance. The last thing he needed was a tenderfoot on his hands. Before he could think what to say, Liz cleared her throat. Tucker met her sparking gaze, realized he hadn't introduced her yet, and hastened to rectify the oversight.

Ellie smiled and thrust out her right arm. "Hello, Liz. It's great to finally make your acquaintance. The boys have told me so much about you."

All of it bad, no doubt, Tucker thought sourly. The boys didn't like Liz and made no secret of the fact.

Liz hesitated before shaking Ellie's hand. Then she relented, only to wipe her palm on her jeans afterward as if the contact had been contaminating. Tucker frowned. Had he missed something? As far as he knew, Ellie had been politeness itself so far, her manner warm and cordial.

Ellie shot Tucker a questioning look. Pretending not to notice, he gestured toward the fire. "The coffee's on. Feel free to help yourselves if you need a pick-me-up after the long drive."

Marvin nodded. "That sounds great. Man, it's chilly as all get-out up here. I'd swear it was the middle of winter."

"At this elevation, it's always cold at night and early in the morning, especially in the fall and spring," Tucker explained.

Ellie touched Marvin's sleeve. "We should pitch our tents first. Then we'll have coffee."

Marvin shrugged. "It shouldn't take that long to put up two tents. Can't we do it later?"

"Just in case we have problems, I'd rather do it now. Daybreak will come early. I don't want to be up half the night, assembling our shelters and getting our gear ready to go."

With a smile for Liz, Ellie excused herself, grabbed Marvin by the arm, and started for her car. Tucker watched the pair rummage through the trunk of the Honda for a moment. Marvin rested a possessive hand on Ellie's shoulder as she searched through a box, his pudgy fingers tracing light circles over her flannel shirt. Tucker knew it was bad of him, but he couldn't help but wonder how she could stand having those soft, clammy hands on her body.

Memories assailed him of other camping trips when he and Ellie had still been together. If Marvin had dared to touch her in such a familiar way then, Tucker would have ripped his chubby arms from their sockets and bludgeoned him with the bloody ends.

But, hey, that was history. If she wanted to sleep with the Pillsbury Doughboy, it was no skin off his nose. He just plain didn't give a rat's ass.

Firelight created a small circle of illumination in the clearing, but beyond that, the woods were darker than dark. As Zach whittled pointy ends on sticks so he and Kody could roast fat-free hot dogs for supper, he kept feeling as if something was staring at him. Occasionally, he heard twigs snap, but no matter how many times he turned to look, he saw nothing. The thought of cougars and bears sent a chill crawling up his spine.

Maybe he shouldn't have gone along with this crazy plan of Kody's, he thought sourly. Back in town, getting their folks off alone together for a few days had seemed like a good idea. But now Zach was sort of scared. All he and Kody had for protection was a couple of pocketknives. What would they do if a huge animal came charging out of the trees at them?

Zach tried to distract himself by thinking about other stuff—like these hot dogs their father had bought, for instance. Cold, they tasted awful, and when Zach chewed on them, they made funny squeaky sounds against his teeth. What had gotten into Dad, anyway? He never let them have fast food anymore, and the only snack foods he kept on hand were lean cold cuts, fresh fruits and vegetables, rubber hot dogs, low-fat potato chips, and nasty carob-coated raisins. Even the hot dog buns were whole wheat. It was enough to make a guy barf.

Sometimes Zach wondered if his parents had switched bodies or something. A year ago, he would have laughed at the suggestion, convinced that such things happened only in movies. But now he wasn't so sure. When he and Kody still lived in Bend, their dad had been totally laid back, never making them study or go to bed on time, letting them eat whatever they wanted, and not really caring how the house looked. Then, right after they moved to Springfield, he'd suddenly become a health-food nut, a clean freak, and a fanatic about homework. Even weirder, he made little lists and taped them up everywhere to remind himself of dumb stuff, like what day of the week the toilets had to be scrubbed. If he forgot, he got all bent out of shape, like the health inspector might show up any minute or something. It gave Zach a headache just thinking about it.

As for Mom, she kept the cupboards stuffed with unhealthy snacks, hardly ever asked if they had schoolwork, and didn't bother to clean up the house anymore. She was way too busy reading *Football for Dummies*, taking him to the park to throw spirals, or playing basketball in the driveway with Kody. She was the only mother on the block who could recite football stats and dribble better than a guy. Sometimes she came by the junior high to watch Zach practice. Instead of sitting on the bleachers like a normal mom, she stood on the sidelines with all the fathers and yelled at the coach. Once she even stuck her pinkies in her mouth, let out a shrill whistle, and gave him the peace sign, her version of the finger. Zach had wanted to put his helmet on backward to hide his face and walk off the field. It was bad enough that she dressed like a bag lady and had a boy's cut. Did she have to make a spectacle of herself?

It was almost as if she was trying to take their dad's place, and he was trying to take hers. Zach guessed both of them were only trying to make up for getting a divorce, but instead they were making things worse. He missed having his mom walk around, picking lint off the carpet. He even missed having her nag at him to eat his vegetables and gripe at him to wash behind his ears. As for his dad, Zach wanted him back the way he used to be, all relaxed about stuff, with dishes in the sink and a pile of dirty socks by his recliner.

In short, he wanted his mom to act like a mom, and he wanted his dad to act like a dad. Hello? Why was that so hard for them to understand? It was, like, *normal*, okay?

Nothing in Zach's life had been normal since Sammy had creamed himself on that stupid motorcycle.

"Maybe they aren't coming," Kody said forlornly.

Wearing the holey T-shirt that made him look like a war refugee, Kody huddled at the opposite side of the fire, rubbing his hands together over the sputtering flames. Zach thought about telling him to get a jacket on, but then he thought better of it. Kody hated to be bossed around, and Zach didn't want to start a fight.

"It's almost midnight," Kody noted after glancing at his watch. "Maybe Dad's so mad at us for running away, he's just gonna leave us out here."

"You know Dad would never do that."

Kody's chin quivered. When he met Zach's gaze over the fire, his hazel eyes sparkled with tears. "They have to come. If they don't, it'll ruin our plan."

"I'm starting to think it was a bad plan, anyway," Zach muttered.

"Oh, yeah? Like your idea was so great? 'Let's make Mom and Dad jealous,' you said. Now just look at the mess things are in."

"Don't start."

"Well, it's true! Both of them are dating other people for real. First thing we know, one of them will do something really dumb, like get married to someone else, and you aren't doing anything to fix it!"

Zach had nothing to say in his own defense. Lying to make his folks jealous had been a really bad idea. "I am too trying to fix it. I'm here, aren't I?" He shot his brother a resentful look. "Get off my back, why don't you? I screwed up. I admit it. How could I know they'd get so bent out of shape? They'd been divorced for two whole years. It wasn't like either one of them would have been doing anything wrong if they really had been dating."

Tears shining on his cheeks, Kody shoved at a piece of wood in the fire. "Yeah, well, now they hate each other. At least they used to talk on the phone and stuff."

"You lied, too," Zach reminded him. "You told Dad that Mom was dating a guy who looked just like Tom Cruise. Remember? And you told her he was hot on some lady prettier than Jennifer Lopez."

"Only because you said!"

"I never, either! Like Dad would date Jennifer Lopez? Meg Ryan, maybe. She looks more like Mom. And why did you say Tom Cruise, for Pete's sake? He doesn't look like Dad at all."

"You never said to pick movie stars who look like them."

"I never said because it's so totally obvious, dumb butt. If you'd picked people who resemble them, they might not have gotten so pissed."

"Now you tell me. You're just trying to make it partly my fault. It was *your* stupid idea, not mine."

"Yeah, yeah, blame it all on me." Zach tossed

Kody's stick across the fire. "Cook yourself a hot dog and shut up."

Zach whittled angrily on his roasting stick for a moment. Then he heard Kody sniffle, and he started to feel bad. "They'll come, Kode," he said with far more confidence than he felt. For almost five hours, he and Kody had waited on the knoll above the clearing where they figured their dad would camp, and nobody had shown up. "They probably just got a late start or something."

Kody gazed out into the darkness. "Maybe we shouldn't have made Dad guess where we are. What if he went to the wrong place?"

Zach whittled more furiously. "He'll figure it out."

"Baxter's a really big place."

The same concern had occurred to Zach, but Kody was already so upset he wasn't about to admit it. "He'll figure it out, I said. We ran away to get our family back together. Right? Where did we last camp as a family?"

"Tabletop Mountain."

"Exactly. It's symbolic." Zach jabbed his chest with a thumb. "If I thought of that and you thought of that, it stands to reason Mom and Dad will think of that."

"Are you *sure*?"

Zach wondered what he was going to do if their dad and mom didn't show up. "Of course I'm sure. Do I look worried?"

Chapter Four

Ellie could scarcely believe her eyes when she saw all the gear and supplies Marvin had stuffed in the trunk and on the rear seat of her car. Back at the house, she'd been so upset she hadn't paid much attention to what he was bringing. He'd borrowed a folding table, a three-burner propane stove, and a nine-by-twelve tent from his brother-in-law. In addition to that, his pack was bulging, and he'd brought along enough groceries to feed an army.

"Marvin, how on earth do you plan to carry all this?"

He gave her a bewildered look. "Carry it where?"

His question confirmed Ellie's worst fears. He had absolutely no clue what this search would entail. "We won't be camping down here every night," she explained. "We'll stop wherever we happen to be when it gets dark, hopefully near a stream, and pitch our tents there." She inclined her head at the huge pile of canvas at her feet. "You need a pup tent." *Not*, she added to herself, *a canvas version of the Taj Mahal.*

"This was the only tent I could get on such short notice."

Ellie knew he'd had virtually no time to prepare. She crouched to test the tent's weight. "There's no way you can carry that thing in a backpack. We'll have to improvise."

Marvin peered through the gloom at the heap of canvas. "I guess you're right." He gave her a sheepish look. "I'm sorry, Ellie. I just naturally assumed we'd have a base camp and come back to it every night."

"Hey." She held up a hand. "No apologies necessary. Until I met Tucker, I wouldn't have known what to bring, either. As for returning each night to a base camp, there's no telling how far in the boys may go. Once we find their tracks, we'll have to stay on their trail until we catch up with them."

He shivered and rubbed his arms. "It's freezing up here."

"Did you bring a jacket?"

"Of course. Unfortunately, that doesn't solve the tent problem. You're right. This one's far too heavy to carry. If I poop out somewhere along the trail, Rambo will probably leave me behind. Maybe I should just forget it and head back home."

Ellie's heart caught at the suggestion. If Marvin left, she'd be a fifth wheel (okay, a third wheel) the whole miserable way. "We only brought one car," she pointed out.

"After you find the kids, I'm sure Tucker will give you a ride back to Springfield." He glanced toward the fire. "I didn't miss the expression on his face when he found out I was going. To say he wasn't pleased is an understatement."

"Yes, well, he can get over it." She touched his

hand imploringly. "Please don't leave, Marvin. I need you here for moral support."

He puffed air into his cheeks. "I don't want to go, but what'll I do for a tent?"

"I'll think of something." She glanced once more at all the food. There was a huge bottle of pancake syrup poking up from one bag. "First things first. Before we worry about shelter, let's get your backpack organized. Okay?"

As she spoke, Ellie reached into one of the sacks and withdrew a half-gallon jar of peanut butter. She stared at it for a long moment, then returned it to the bag. "That can't go."

"Peanut butter's a really good fast energy food and high in protein," he argued.

"Yes, and it weighs a ton. You can't take it."

He shrugged. "You know a whole lot more about this than I do. What kind of food *can* I take?"

It took Ellie twenty minutes to arrange Marvin's pack and sort through his groceries for edibles that would serve well as trail rations. She decided that the nylon rain shield on her pup tent would work as a lightweight shelter for him. He could drape it over a low limb and use sticks as pegs to anchor each corner.

After getting Marvin's things ready, she spent the next ten minutes erecting her tent and rolling out her sleeping bag for the night. When she was finally finished, she went in search of Tucker, hoping to talk with him about his plan of action for tomorrow.

She spotted him and Liz crouched at the edge of camp. Separated by a large rock, they were perusing a forestry map stretched out between them. Overhead, they had suspended a lantern from a tree limb.

As Ellie walked toward them, she couldn't help but think how good it felt to be in the woods again. There was something about central Oregon—a feeling in the air, for want of a better description—that always energized her. Beneath her feet, the earth was spongy with layer upon layer of pine needles that had fallen and turned to dust over the years. The musty, decayed scent mixed pleasantly with the sharp smell of pine and sage.

As she drew closer, Ellie took a moment to study Tucker. Though she hated to admit it, he looked sexier at thirty-six than he had at twenty. Hard work had kept him superbly fit, padding his shoulders with muscle and giving his chest an impressive breadth. Yet he'd still managed to retain an overall leanness—compliments, she felt sure, of the incredible distances he walked every day.

Crouched on one boot heel, he sat with his shoulders hunched forward, one arm resting loosely on his knee, a posture that stretched his red shirt taut over his powerfully sculpted back. Looking at him made Ellie's throat go oddly tight, a reaction she felt sure stemmed from resentment. Even though she no longer loved him, it wasn't easy, seeing him with another woman, especially one so beautiful. Could that bright red hair really be natural? Only Tucker and her hairdresser probably knew for sure.

Ellie might have felt more charitable if Tucker had had the good grace to deteriorate a little with age, but all maturity had done was lend his face a tough, pared-down look, accentuating his high cheekbones, the strong, angular cut of his jaw, and the stubborn thrust of his square chin. Tiny crow's-feet fanned out from the corners of his hazel eyes. The dimples that she'd once loved had become elongated creases that bracketed his firm mouth. At the moment, that mouth was set in a humorless line and tucked in at the corners, his upper lip drawn thin, the lower shimmering like moist silk in the lantern light.

"Hi," she called out to warn of her approach.

Tucker glanced up, his tawny hair catching the light, the sun-streaked strands gleaming like polished brass. Tendrils curled lazily over his high forehead to touch straight, gilded brows with no hint of an arch.

"Hi," he said in that soft, silky tenor that had once set her heart to skipping.

After he issued the greeting, his jaw muscle started to tic. Then he gave her one of those looks she'd been dreading—a slow, heated glide down her body. She nervously trailed her fingers up the line of buttons on her shirt and promptly forgot why she had walked over there.

Fortunately, her gaze fell on the map, which saved her from stammering like a fool. "I, um—noticed that you're studying the area. I thought I might sit in on the discussion."

He nodded. "Did you get all set up for the night?"

"Pretty much." Ellie rubbed her palms on her jeans, feeling absurdly ill at ease. As she drew up near the rock, she said, "Marvin's pitching his tent." She bent at the waist to look at the map. It was a confusing network of lines and squiggles, but with Liz watching her and looking so superior, she pretended to be making sense of it. "What area are we going to search first?"

"We?" Liz repeated. "Your time might be better spent helping your boyfriend with his tent. Tucker and I can coordinate the search."

There was no mistaking the dislike that burned in Liz's green eyes. Ellie couldn't think what the woman's problem was. She'd tried her best to be friendly. "I'm sure Marvin can handle his tent by himself. If you don't mind, I'd like to be in on this discussion."

"Do you know anything at all about the area?" Liz asked. "Or, for that matter, how to read a forestry map?"

What Ellie knew about this area struck sheer terror into her heart. The terrain was treacherous. Every year, at least one hapless hiker became a statistic. "I'll be the first to admit my ignorance about wilderness areas and forestry maps, Liz, but that isn't really relevant. My kids are out there."

The redhead nodded. "Yes, and the sooner Tucker and I can plan a search strategy without interruption, the sooner we'll find them."

"I won't interrupt," Ellie assured her.

"Excuse me, but you're interrupting right now."

Ellie hadn't driven all this way to spar with Tucker's girlfriend. All she wanted was to find her boys, take them home where they'd be safe, and pick up the threads of her life again. She straightened and planted her hands on her hips. It wasn't often that she encountered such unveiled animosity, and she wasn't quite sure how to handle it. She waited a beat, hoping Tucker might intervene. When he didn't, she met Liz's gaze straight on and said, "Let's get something understood from the get-go, shall we?"

Tucker had seen that glint in Ellie's eyes too many times to ignore it now. Liz was about to discover what he'd learned long ago: his ex-wife could go from zero to sixty in less than a second when someone stepped on her toes.

"Ladies." Tucker held up a hand, sent Ellie a warning look, and then settled his gaze on Liz. "Let's all work together on this. Okay?"

An angry flush pooled in Liz's cheeks. "Whatever." She smoothed her hand over the map, her mouth tightening into a thin line. "All I did was suggest that her time might be better spent helping Martin."

"Marvin," Ellie corrected as she crouched with them by the rock. After giving the map a quick study, she asked Tucker, "Do you have any idea where they may be heading?"

"If we knew that, we wouldn't need to lay out search grids," Liz inserted with a saccharine-sweet smile.

Ellie's already pale face blanched a shade whiter, a sure sign that she was about to lose her temper. "I'm sorry. I assumed that to plan a search, you must have a general area in mind. Baxter's a big place."

Tucker hated to take sides in this, but it seemed to him that Liz was out of line. Ellie had done nothing to deserve these not-so-subtle jabs. For reasons beyond him, Liz seemed to have taken an instant dislike to her.

Thinking quickly, he pushed to his feet and said,

"Liz, could I get you to help me for just a second?" With a glance at Ellie, he added, "We'll only be a minute. While we're gone, maybe you can familiarize yourself with the map."

Liz flashed him a bewildered look but nevertheless stood to follow him. Tucker led her around their tents to where he'd been chopping firewood earlier. When he turned to face her, he asked, "Did I miss something?"

Her gaze flicked up to meet his, then danced away. "What do you mean?"

Tucker tucked his thumbs over his belt. He didn't want to cause hard feelings, but at the same time, he didn't feel he could let this slide. "You're not being very friendly to Ellie."

"I didn't realize I needed to be." She lifted her eyebrows. "You haven't spoken of her very often, but the few times you did, I got the distinct impression there was no love lost between you."

Tucker scraped a hand over his jaw. "Ellie and I have our personal problems. I'll be the first to admit that, but in all fairness, it's probably as much my fault as hers. She's a nice person, Liz. If you'll give it half a chance, you'll probably like her a lot."

She stared past him into the trees. After a long moment, she shrugged and said, "I guess I was being a little bitchy. It's hard for me to be nice to her." Her gaze shifted back to his. "You never talk about it, but I know she hurt you. It's written all over you."

Tucker didn't care to discuss what had happened between him and Ellie. If the truth were told, he wasn't even sure he could. Looking back on the horrible weeks after Sammy's accident, he had trouble even putting the blur of events into chronological order. Their marriage had fallen apart; that was the bottom line. What more was there to say? He'd been responsible for their son's death, Ellie couldn't forgive him, and that was the end of their story.

"The hurt went both ways, Liz. It always does in a divorce."

As Tucker uttered those words, he knew truer ones had probably never been spoken. Ellie undoubtedly had her side of the story to tell, and in her version, he was probably the villain.

"I guess a divorce leaves everyone with wounds that take a long time to heal," Liz said, echoing his thoughts.

"Yeah," Tucker agreed, his voice suddenly husky. He kicked at a splinter of kindling. "It hasn't been easy on either one of us, or our kids, for that matter. This latest mess is proof of that." He scuffed at more wood chips. "Here's the thing, Liz. Tension is already running high. The last thing we need is more. You know what I'm saying? You don't have to like Ellie. But I am going to ask that you at least be polite to her."

Liz folded her arms. "I'm sorry, Tucker. Maybe I'm just out of sorts because I'm tired."

"It has been a long day." He glanced at his watch. "It's after midnight. You were up at—what?—five?"

"Four-thirty, actually." She flashed an apologetic smile. "My disposition sours after eleven and goes downhill from there." She gave him a questioning look. "Would you like me to tell Ellie I'm sorry?"

"Probably better to just let it go. You didn't say anything that bad, and tomorrow is another day."

"I'll be a model of good behavior from now on, I promise."

He chuckled and gave her a little push. "Why don't you call it a night? I can map the grids without you."

"Oh, I don't mind helping."

"Got it covered. Really. Go on to bed."

She hesitated, her gaze shifting toward the lantern light. "You sure? I don't think her talent for color coordination will come in very handy."

"No worries. She's a quick study. I'll put her to work duplicating the grids on a second map so you and I'll both have a copy for tomorrow."

She retreated a step. "Well, good night, then."

Tucker was about to reply in kind when she suddenly moved back to him. Before he could think what she meant to do, she pressed herself full-length against him and wrapped both arms around his neck. Settling her open mouth over his, she kissed him deeply and thoroughly, her tongue tangling with his. She tasted faintly of coffee and wintergreen Tic Tacs. Through her sweater, he felt her nipples go hard as they rubbed over his chest.

Tucker's first instinct was to step back. Ellie was sitting only a few feet away, and heaven only knew where Marvin was. He didn't want anyone to walk around the tents and catch them. But even as he settled his hands at Liz's waist to put distance between their bodies, his mind hazed over. It had been so long for him—*too* long. He couldn't feel a woman's softness smashed against him and not respond. When she pushed her hips forward, a certain part of him went rock hard.

Her breathing changed, going shallow and quick. She grasped his wrist and pushed his hand under her sweater. The next thing Tucker knew, he had a warm, naked breast cupped in his palm. She nipped his lower lip and trembled.

"Touch me," she whispered urgently. "Oh, please, Tucker, touch me."

He almost obliged. He was horny, and she felt damned good. After three years, almost any woman would. That was what sobered him, he supposed, the realization that she was nothing but a body to him. Maybe some men could take her on those terms, but he didn't want to be one of them, not when he sensed she might be wearing her heart on her sleeve.

He tried to pull his hand away. She held fast to his wrist. "You want to," she whispered. "I know you do."

Yeah, the part of him that had no conscience wanted to, all right. But he'd never allowed his actions to be ruled by physical needs, and he didn't mean to start now. He tensed his arm against her. "Not now," was all he could think to say. "Not now, Liz."

"Why not?" She rubbed her nipple over his palm, her breath hitching at the sensation. "Just for a minute. *Please?*" She kissed him again, thrusting her tongue past his lips to drag the tip over his teeth. "Feel how I want you?" She moved his hand over her. "How I need you?"

What *he* needed, he thought dizzily, was to focus on what *he* wanted. And for reasons he couldn't define at the moment, this wasn't it. With a hard jerk, he got his wrist free of her clinging fingers. Then he clamped his hands over her shoulders to hold her at arm's length. Ragged and shallow, his breath wheezed from his lungs. He trembled with the effort it took to lock his elbows against her.

With distance between their bodies came some clarity of thought. He looked into her big green eyes, and what he saw there made him feel like a lowdown skunk. She was dreaming big dreams, he realized, just as he had feared. She wanted far more from him than just sex and good times, namely a ring on her finger and the rest of his natural life, all wrapped up in a bow. He wasn't ready for that, not with her, not with anyone.

He'd lost a child and come through a bitter divorce. He needed time to just *be* for a while. He'd fallen in love with Ellie at sixteen, and from that point forward, his life had been inseparably entangled with hers, his identity so completely defined by the roles of lover, husband, father, and breadwinner that he wasn't even sure who he was anymore.

He didn't want to hurt Liz with a flat-out rejection. She was offering him her body, after all, and he could wound her in ways that might never heal if he didn't choose his words carefully. Rather than risk that, he grabbed at the first excuse that came to mind.

"I'm sorry," he whispered, his voice grating like a blade over sandpaper. "I'm sorry, Liz, but the timing's wrong. We're not alone out here."

For a moment, she stared at him with a befuddled, incredulous expression on her face. Then the tension drained out of her, and she smiled. "What's the matter? You afraid we might get caught?"

That was exactly his fear, only his concern was

mainly for himself, and not in the way she meant. Knowing in advance that she was starting to care for him, he couldn't make love to her and then walk away when the shine wore off. And it would wear off, guaranteed. He'd loved only one woman in his life, and it was going to be a good long while before he took the plunge again.

He realized that he was digging his fingers into her shoulders and forced himself to gentle his grip. "Yeah, I guess you could say I'm afraid of getting caught. Call me peculiar, but I prefer privacy for this sort of thing."

"The chance of getting caught only makes it more fun." She tried to press closer and frowned when his arms didn't give with her weight. "Come on, Tucker, don't be a stick-in-the-mud. I promise you won't regret it."

He already had regrets. He'd sensed all along that she was angling for more than he was prepared to give. When a man knew he couldn't step up to the plate, he had no business being in the game.

He kissed her forehead, gave her a half turn, and said, "Good night, Liz. It's a fantastic offer, but for now, I've got to pass."

She sent him a come-hither look over her shoulder. "If you come see me later, I promise to be quiet," she called softly. "Nobody will ever know."

He would know. Tucker couldn't think of a kind way to decline the invitation, so he settled for winking at her. She ran a hand over her hip, slowly and suggestively, then slid it up her side to touch her breast through her sweater. His gaze dropped like a stone to where her fingers toyed with her nipple, tweaking and rubbing it to a hard peak that was discernible even in the dim light. His mouth went as dry as dirt. With an impish grin, she disappeared around the side of her tent.

Standing there in the shadows, he hauled in a sharp breath and held it until his temples pounded. Then he rubbed a hand over his face—up, then down, making his nose ache from the drag. *Shit.* Where was a cold shower when he needed one?

"Good night," she called softly from inside the shelter. "You know where to find me."

Tucker gazed stupidly at the quivering wall of blue nylon. "Good night," he finally said.

He heard the zipper of her sleeping bag rasp. He swallowed hard, feeling proud of himself on the one hand, but also wondering if he'd lost his frigging mind. Three years without sex, and he turned down the first tempting offer he got? There was something not quite rational about that.

Okay, fine, so he was certifiably nuts. He could live with that. What he couldn't live with was the knowledge that he'd used someone without any regard for her feelings. He'd still be able to look himself in the eye when he shaved in the morning. That was something. Right? A man couldn't put a price on his self-respect.

Somehow that wasn't much of a comfort when he glanced down at himself and pushed uselessly at the bulge behind his fly. *Hell.* Now what? No way was he stepping back into the light until that went away. Ellie would be sure to notice and think the worst. Not that he cared what she thought. It was just—

well, as he'd told Liz, there was a time and place for everything, and this wasn't it.

He rubbed a hand over his face again and blinked. Then he walked a circle around the pile of firewood. It was one of life's ironies, he decided, how quickly this condition could come over a man, and how blasted long it took to go away.

"Sorry I was so long," he told Ellie a few minutes later when he rejoined her at the rock.

"That's fine. I've been trying to make sense of this map while you were gone." She looked up. "Where's Liz?"

"She's pretty tired and decided to turn in."

"Ah." Ellie glanced over her shoulder. "I get the impression she doesn't like me."

Tucker assumed what he hoped was a bewildered look as he crouched across from her. "Really? I think she's probably just worn out. We were both up before five this morning."

Her gaze sharpened on his.

"She at her house, I at mine. No, she didn't spend the night at my place."

Her shoulders relaxed. "The only reason I even care is because of the kids. I don't want them getting the idea that it's okay to—well, you know—engage in casual intimacy."

"I agree."

She shrugged and smiled, her eyes darkening with curiosity. "If this thing with Liz is serious, Tucker, and you'd like to have her over when the boys are around, maybe you should sit them down and explain that she's someone very, very special to you."

"Fishing, Ellie?"

For just an instant, she looked nonplussed. Then she gave him a brittle smile. "Dreaming, Tucker?"

Her quick retort made him chuckle.

She patted the map. "All I care about is finding our kids."

"Amen to that."

Bucky trotted up just then. Angling his nose under Tucker's arm, the Australian shepherd begged for some petting. Tucker obliged the dog with some scratches under the chin. Finally the canine had had enough and settled by the fire for a snooze.

"First, the good news," Tucker told Ellie, dreading the moment when he would have to share the bad. "I've brought the boys up here a lot. They know this part of Baxter very well, and I think it's safe to say they can't possibly get lost in here."

She nodded, but her gaze clung worriedly to his, telling him she knew much grimmer information was to follow. "That's good to know."

Tucker wished he could leave it at that. "Now for the bad news. Tonight when I drove in, Liz shone a flashlight out the passenger window, searching for bike tracks on her side of the road. I watched the other shoulder and the center with my headlights. We saw no tire tracks."

Her slender throat convulsed as she struggled to swallow. "What does that mean, that the boys aren't in this area?"

"No. It only means they didn't come to this particular place or use this road. We've frequented several campsites in this part of Baxter. Most recently, we've spent a lot of time here, so I naturally assumed this is where they would come."

She bunched her hands into fists and pressed them hard against her knees. In the lantern glow, her knuckles gleamed white. "So now what'll we do?"

Tucker tapped the map with a fingertip. "We'll have to drive the highway tomorrow and drop off onto all these forestry roads until we find their tracks. When we discover where they ditched the bikes, we'll know where they headed in. That's where we'll start the ground search."

She nodded and took a shaky breath. "Will that take much time?"

"We'll only be combing a small section, and we'll have two vehicles. It shouldn't take that long." He indicated the map. "I'll divide the search area into grids so we don't drive any of the same roads twice. Come daylight, we'll break camp and work in teams, with certain grids assigned to each. It'll take a little longer than I hoped, but I think we'll be starting in after them well before noon."

She looked relieved to hear that.

"Worst-case scenario, the boys may get a half day's jump on us," he added. "If that happens, we may not catch up with them before dark."

Tucker didn't think it was possible for her to grow any paler, but she did. "Are you saying they may be out here alone another night?" When he nodded, she pressed her lips together and closed her eyes for a moment. As her lashes fluttered back up, she said, "Maybe we should just call Search and Rescue, Tucker." Before he could protest, she held up a staying hand. "I know you're one of the best trackers in the county. I'm not saying you aren't. But isn't that what parents usually do when their kids get lost?"

He wouldn't out-and-out lie to her. "Yes. But our children aren't lost."

"You're splitting hairs. They're out there, and we don't know where they are. That's pretty damned lost. How do you even know for sure that they're in this area?"

After driving in tonight and not seeing bike tracks, Tucker didn't know that for sure, and he was worried. Evidently that showed on his face because Ellie suddenly stiffened.

She waited a beat and then held up a hand. "Hold it a minute." She laughed humorlessly and lifted her gaze to the lantern for a moment. When she looked back down at him, she asked, "Am I reading this right?"

Probably, he thought. "Ellie . . ."

She held her hand higher. "Don't Ellie me. Do I look that stupid to you?"

"No, of course you don't."

"Then don't play games with me," she said, her voice going shriller with every word. "They're my sons, too. I deserve to know exactly what we're up against. No bull feathers, no coloring of the facts. They may not be in this part of Baxter. Isn't that the truth of it?"

"It's possible that they aren't, yes."

"So why did you wait until now to inform me of that? I am their mother, and I've been here for well over an hour."

Tucker passed a hand over his eyes. "I wanted to break it to you gently, for fear you'd panic and call for help."

She started up from the rock. He grasped her arm.

"Ellie, please, at least hear me out. I should have filled you in. I'm sorry I waited. I just don't want a bunch of inexperienced volunteers out here."

"If the kids aren't in this section of Baxter, I'd rather have inexperienced volunteers helping to find them than none at all. This is a *huge* wilderness area to cover."

"Inexperienced volunteers may tromp through the woods and destroy the tracks, not to mention that they could get lost themselves. That would cost us valuable time."

"And you were afraid, if you leveled with me, that I might disregard your concerns?"

Releasing his hold on her, he said, "Yes."

"I had a right to know, and I had a right to hear it immediately. You've no business keeping stuff from me, no matter what your reasons." She flung her arm to encompass the woods around them. "My babies are out there, damn you! I've already buried one. Do you think I want to lose another?"

"You won't, honey."

"Don't call me honey!"

"Ellie, then," he quickly revised. *"Jesus!* Would you listen to yourself? We're not on opposite sides, here. I love those kids, too. They'll be fine for a night or two. I've trained them well. They'll be absolutely fine."

She cupped a hand behind her ear. "Do I hear an echo?" Her blue eyes, brilliant now with anger, looked like huge blue splotches in her white face. " 'He'll be fine,' you said. Remember that? Now you think I should take your word for it again?"

Tucker felt as if she'd slugged him. He was suddenly so angry, he wanted to grab the map and slap it in her face. "Pardon me, but you were the one at home when it happened." At the reminder, he saw her flinch. "I bought him the goddamned bike. For that, I'll take the blame. But he wouldn't have killed himself on the blasted thing if you'd been watching him like you should."

Silence. They stared at each other, their angry words hanging between them. For an awful moment, Tucker thought she might burst into tears. Given the fact that he hadn't seen her cry since the day their son died, that would have been his undoing. Instead she closed her eyes and bent her head. She was shaking—shaking horribly. He felt sick.

Why did it always come back to this? Sammy was dead. Nothing they said or did would ever reverse that. Why in God's name couldn't they comfort each other instead of trying to draw each other's blood?

Tucker guessed if either of them had been able to do that, they never would have gotten the divorce. The sad fact was that all the love they'd once felt for each other had been buried with their child. Now there was nothing left but bitterness and regrets and fatal mistakes that could never be rectified.

"I'm sorry," she whispered tremulously. "I started it. I'll finish it. Please accept my apology. I shouldn't have said that."

Tucker released a shuddering sigh. "I'm sorry, too. I shouldn't have said what I did, either."

Head still bent, she hugged her waist, took several deep breaths. Tucker stared hard at the map. He was so upset that his vision had gone blurry. "If you want to call in a search party, Ellie, if you believe in your heart that's the best thing to do, I'll go get my phone and make the call myself."

She finally raised her head. Her eyes had an awful, empty look now. "You made a good point. If they bring in a bunch of volunteers, they could destroy the boys' tracks." Her bloodless lips curved in a ghost of a smile. "The best tracker available is already on the job. It's not as if they'll send out anyone better."

Some of the tension eased from Tucker's shoulders. "Thank you for that."

"The truth is the truth. You're very good. Just understand that I'm not giving you carte blanche. If you haven't found their bike tracks by noon tomorrow, all deals are off. Then we'll be faced with searching all of Baxter. We'll need a lot of manpower to do that efficiently."

"That sounds fair enough to me," he agreed. "And, just for the record, if it comes to that, I'll call for help myself. I don't want my kids wandering around out there alone any more than you do."

She nodded and rubbed her arms. Tucker wondered if she might be cold. Even with the warmth from the nearby fire, the night was nippy, and she wasn't wearing a jacket.

Before he could offer to find her a coat, she said, "How much danger are they in? I promise not to fly off the handle and call anyone. Just level with me, all right?"

"It's no walk in the park out there," he admitted. "You know that. The bear and cougar populations have exploded. Rattlesnakes aren't thick in this country, but they're around, even this late in the year.

There's also the possibility that one of the boys could fall and get hurt. Any time you venture into a wilderness area, you're taking a few risks. On top of that, they're only kids. Having said that, I have to add that they aren't ordinary kids. They know more about getting around out there than most men. If I didn't believe with all my heart that they'll be okay for two nights, I already would have called for help."

She pushed her fingers through her hair. When she withdrew her hand, the uneven wisps slipped free in disarray that was oddly becoming, the tendrils curling over her forehead and in front of her ears to create a nimbus of gold around her face. Tucker still preferred her hair long, but the short cut was starting to grow on him. It was more practical, certainly, than the way she'd worn it before. He guessed maybe that was why she'd stopped wearing makeup as well, to free herself up for more important things, namely their sons. It couldn't be easy, working six days a week while she was raising two kids, one of them a teenager.

The sound of approaching footsteps snagged Tucker's attention. He glanced around to see Marvin walking toward them. The older man rubbed his plump hands together and trained interested brown eyes on the map. "Sorry it took me so long. That damned tent's a nightmare to erect." He crouched down beside Ellie. "Well, now, let's get down to business, shall we?"

"I was just telling Ellie that we'll have to drive the roads tomorrow." Tucker went on to explain about the absence of any bike tracks in the immediate area, and how he planned to divide the north end into search grids. "If we head out early, it shouldn't take us that long to cover the area."

Marvin nodded and leaned closer to study the map. "How do we go about setting up search grids?"

Tucker drew three pencils from his folder and began sectioning off the area into manageable chunks while Marvin and Ellie duplicated the markings on another map. When he finally felt satisfied, it was nearly two in the morning, and Ellie looked ready to drop. The blue smudges under her eyes were now edged with gray, and her skin was almost translucent.

"We'd all better grab some shut-eye," Marvin advised with a huge yawn. "What time does it break day?"

"In about four hours," Tucker replied.

"I'm gone." Marvin pushed to his feet, leaned down to kiss Ellie on the forehead, and raised a hand in farewell to Tucker.

Ellie gazed after him for a moment. Then she struggled to her feet. In the firelight and shadows, she could have passed for a teenager in the flannel shirt and jeans. Rubbing her arms against the chill, she bade Tucker good night. He watched her walk to her tent, which was set up at the opposite side of the fire, about five feet from Marvin's nine-by-twelve monstrosity and some ten feet from his own.

As she lifted the flap to duck inside, she glanced back over her shoulder. Their gazes traversed the distance, locking on and holding for what seemed an interminable time. Silent messages, memories—a wealth of both was transmitted between them.

The last time they'd been out in a wilderness area together, Sammy had still been alive.

Tucker was the one who finally broke eye contact. Or was it Ellie? He didn't suppose it mattered. All that really counted was that they both turned away, just as they had three years ago.

When it came right down to it, what else mattered?

Chapter Five

Ellie started awake the next morning to the feeling of a cold, wet nose in her ear. It was pitch dark, and, still groggy with sleep, she couldn't think clearly enough to identify the source. Jackknifing to a sitting position, she flung out her arm to ward off attack, only to find herself embracing a cheerfully affectionate Australian shepherd. Taking unmerciful advantage of her lowered defenses, Bucky licked her face and managed to nail her on the parted lips at least twice before she could turn away. His breath smelled of dog kibble and soured grass, a nauseating mix, especially before her eyes were completely open.

"Bucky, no!" Ellie sputtered, swatted halfheartedly at the nose pressed so lovingly to her cheek, and ducked her head. "Not in the *mouth*."

She heard a deep chuckle come from just outside the tent. Given the fact that Marvin would be hard-put to emit a sound that gravelly and masculine, Ellie had little difficulty identifying the culprit. *Tucker*. It seemed totally unfair that thoughts of him should bombard her before she'd even had a cup of coffee.

Grumping under her breath and keeping her chin

tucked against her chest to avoid any more dog slurps, she crawled out of her sleeping bag. A blast of frigid predawn air sliced through her clothing, making her grateful that she'd had the foresight to sleep fully clothed. She patted the damp floor of the tent in search of her boots, coating her palms with grit. Unless there was a stream nearby, water for washing would be at a premium. Oh, how she *adored* camping. On her list of favorite things, it ranked just below her annual mammogram. At least having her breasts squeezed flat by a cold, steel vise was over with quickly.

One down, she thought acidly as her hand closed over a cold lump of leather. She swung her arm in search of the other boot, connected with the encrusted heel—she did hope that hardened glob wasn't dog doo-doo—and grabbed hold of the stiff leather to drag it toward her.

"Go away, Bucky, *please*." Defeated, Ellie sank back down on her sleeping bag and spent a moment petting the silly mutt. He poked her all over with his wet nose, leaving dots of slobber on her face, neck, hands, and undoubtedly on her clothing, as well. She told herself it didn't matter. Out camping like this, personal hygiene standards plunged to an all-time low. "I love you, too. Yes, I do. And good morning right back at you."

When the love session had lasted long enough to satisfy the happy canine, Ellie set herself to the unpleasant and difficult task of stuffing her feet into age-hardened boots. The creases on the insteps just above her toes felt like ridges of cement digging into the tops of her feet, and there was a squeeze across one heel. Given the fact that the boots had once been top of the line—Tucker spared no coin to make sure everyone in his family had quality footwear—and had fitted her perfectly, Ellie hoped they would loosen up with wear.

As she was tying the second set of laces, she heard Marvin's whiny alto ring out through the darkness. "Why is it necessary to break camp if all we're going to do this morning is drive around on roads? Wouldn't it be simpler to leave everything here so we can come back later for lunch?"

Her eyes weren't even open yet, and Marvin was thinking about lunch?

"If we find where the boys dropped off the highway onto a dirt road, we'll follow their tire tracks to where they ditched their bikes," Tucker replied. A faint swishing sound punctuated the statement. "If that happens early today, we'll immediately start tracking them. If it's late in the afternoon, we'll make camp and head out after them in the morning."

Not, Ellie thought. She'd given Tucker until noon— no ifs, ands, or buts. If he hadn't found the boys' bikes by then, she was calling Search and Rescue.

"It seems like a big waste of time to me," Marvin complained. "Judging by what I saw of the map last night, the grids we're going to search cover only about ten square miles. It'd be a lot simpler to drive back here and be all set to cook the midday meal."

"We won't be doing much cooking," Tucker replied. "Only at night along the trail. Otherwise, it'll be a grab-what-you-can and eat-while-you-hike affair."

Ellie heard aluminum poles clank and knew by the

sound that Marvin was disassembling his canvas Taj Mahal. "It seems to me it's important for all of us to eat regular meals and keep up our strength."

When she stepped from the tent a moment later, firelight engulfed her. She gravitated toward the source, rubbing her arms and chafing her hands, so cold she felt like a human icicle. Blinking to clear the sleep from her eyes, she saw Tucker's three-cup camp pot simmering on the rocks, a speckled blue mug perched beside it. *Coffee.* Using the cuff of her shirtsleeve to protect her hand, she lifted the pot. Much to her dismay, it didn't feel as if there was much coffee left, a suspicion that was proved correct when barely a half mug dribbled from the spout.

Ellie was grateful for whatever she could get. She returned the pot to the rocks, her mouth all set for that first wonderful sip. *Coffee.* Oh, yes. As she cupped the mug in her hands and lifted it to her face, the steam wafted to her nostrils, so rich and deliciously aromatic she could almost taste it.

Just then a movement to her left caught her eye. Still half-asleep, she glanced around to see Tucker, naked from the waist up, standing over a stump. He was shaving, she realized, which explained the swishing noise she'd heard earlier. On the log before him rested a small enamel washbasin, and in one big hand, he held a twin-blade razor. His lower jaw sported a swath of shaving cream, the whiteness stark against his tanned skin. His hair, still damp from a recent dousing, gleamed dark bronze in the flickering firelight, and tendrils of steam rose from his bare shoulders.

Still groggy from sleep, Ellie tried to look away,

but instead, her gaze dropped to take in the play of strength in his back and arms each time he moved. In the amber light, every ripple and mound was accentuated by shadows, creating a mesmerizing exhibition of masculine beauty that sucked her mouth dry and made her feet go numb. Unable to stop herself, she looked even lower, following the cleavage of hard muscle and flesh that delineated his spine. Bad move. It was a downward path that led unerringly to the waistband of denim that rode tantalizingly low on his narrow hips. Just as she reached that mark, Tucker bent forward to rinse his razor, providing her with a stunning glimpse of his tan line and the two dimples just above his buttocks.

Ellie lost her grip on the cup. It dive-bombed and hit the rocks with a loud explosion of noise, and the coffee, which had seemed such a miserly amount a moment before, sprayed in all directions with impressive coverage, the giant's share splattering her jeans.

Pain. The liquid was scalding. Ellie shrieked and leaped back from the rocks, slapping at her pant legs and stomping her feet. "Ouch! Oh, *God!*"

Tucker was on her in less than a second. One side of his face still streaked with shaving cream, he seized her by the arms and ordered, "Be still!"

Before Ellie could think what he meant to do, he tugged open her jeans and dropped them with one hard jerk. The frigid air instantly eased the burning sensation on her thighs. Nevertheless, she found herself standing in the firelight with only French-cut lace panties and flapping flannel shirttails to conceal her private parts.

A hot wave of embarrassment washed over her. The sexy panties, which she'd kept at the bottom of her lingerie drawer since the divorce, had only recently been brought back into service because her sensible cotton briefs had worn out. Rather than buy new underwear no one would ever see, she'd opted to spend the money on her boys instead, while she wore the lacy strips of elasticized nothing that Tucker had given her their last Christmas together. He no doubt remembered this pair. After the kids were asleep that Christmas Eve, she'd modeled them for him in front of the tree, and the next morning, they'd both awakened with bits of tinsel in their hair.

"What are you *doing*?" she cried. Her coffee-doused britches lay in a puddle around her ankles, and she couldn't even run for cover.

Making no reply, Tucker wheeled back to the stump. Grabbing a green plastic water container beside it, he soaked a hand towel, then returned to slap the wet, freezing cloth over her thighs. The shock made Ellie gasp and leap back, a reaction that nearly sent her sprawling with the jeans shackling her feet.

As Ellie struggled for balance, Tucker curled his big hands over her legs to anchor the towel in place. "Would you hold still? That coffee was scalding. It'll blister the hell out of you."

If he hadn't been parading around half naked, she never would have spilled it in the first place, she thought angrily.

Drawn by the commotion, Marvin stepped into the ring of firelight. He reeled to a stop and stared at her lower body with a hungry look on his face. Ellie splayed her hands over the juncture of her thighs, feeling like a takeout carton of sweet-and-sour.

"Oh, for God's sake," Tucker said, his tone biting with impatience. "Like I've never seen it before?"

Ellie looked back at her ex-husband. Maybe it was the unwelcome reminder of the intimacy they'd once shared, or maybe it was the absolute disdain in his voice when he referred to that part of her anatomy as *it*, but she was suddenly, furiously angry.

"Maybe you *have* seen it before, Mr. Grant," she blurted, "but it's not yours to look at now."

"Thank God."

She wanted to hit him. The patch of shaving cream on one lean cheek presented her with a perfect target. Mightily tempted and barely resisting the urge, she knotted her hands into fists and jerked her gaze from the spot.

"What the hell are you staring at?" Tucker asked sharply.

For an instant, Ellie thought he was speaking to her. Then she realized Marvin still stood frozen in his tracks, his eyes trained on her rump.

At the question, he jumped as if he'd been jabbed with a pin. "N-nothing," he stammered. Even in the firelight, the guilty flush that pooled in his plump cheeks was obvious. "I just thought you might need some help, is all."

"If we needed help, we'd ask for it," Tucker bit out. When Marvin didn't immediately move, he added, "Beat it!"

Marvin wheeled away just as Liz stumbled from her tent, her long red hair in a stir. "What on earth's happening out here?"

"Ellie spilled hot coffee on her legs."

Liz rubbed her eyes and proceeded to give Ellie's backside a disdainful once-over. "Hmm," she said.

Not "Oh, my, are you hurt?" Just "Hmm." Ellie ground her teeth, thinking that Tucker's new girlfriend must have been in the back row when personalities were passed out. Not that he would care. What Liz lacked in that department, she more than made up for in physical attributes, none of which Ellie possessed. If that wasn't a slap in the face, she didn't know what was.

Tucker finally drew the towel from her legs. When he brushed his hard fingertips ever so lightly over her blotchy thighs, she jerked and almost toppled over backward again.

"I can't tell if it scalded you or not," he said.

Her legs felt fine. She just wanted her pants back on. As she leaned over to tug them up, Tucker pushed erect. Their heads smacked together like two pumpkins, the hollow-sounding *plunk* reverberating through her brain. Pain exploded across her forehead. He cursed viciously. She saw so many stars that an expletive was beyond her.

"Are you okay?" He clamped a hand over her elbow. "Ellie?"

Blinking away spots, she flattened a hand on his chest to steady herself. Warm, vibrant flesh and springy chest hair had her snatching her hand away before she could even see clearly again. "Fine," she managed to say. "I'm just perfect." She rubbed her throbbing eyebrow. "How about you?"

"I've taken harder licks." He still gripped her arm. "Sorry about that. I didn't know you were bending over."

After saying that, he treated her to the final indignity by jerking her britches up for her. Ellie fumbled with the metal button and zipper. One didn't necessarily have to drink coffee to wake up quickly, she decided. Taking a bath in the stuff worked just as efficiently. All her nerves were humming, anyway, certain ones more than others. Her thighs still tingled where Tucker had so lightly grazed her skin with his fingertips.

She sent him a fulminous glare as he walked back to the stump and quickly finished shaving his jaw. While slapping astringent on his cheeks, he stood with his booted feet braced apart, the bunched muscles in his thighs pulling his faded jeans taut to showcase his long legs. Ellie forced herself to look away.

He'd seen it all before, had he? Well, that went two ways. She wouldn't give Tucker Grant a second look if he were the last man on earth.

The tantalizing smell of his aftershave trailed after her as she marched to the trunk of her Honda. Fumble-fingered from the cold and frustrated by shadows, she filled her small aluminum coffeepot with water from the five-gallon jug she'd brought along, then assembled the basket and scooped in some grounds. She grabbed her parka while she was there, grateful for its protective warmth as she shoved her arms down the sleeves.

When she returned to the fire, Tucker had finished shaving and was, thank the saints, fully clothed. He wore a blue chambray shirt and a lined denim jacket that added breadth to his shoulders and gave him a rough, rugged, ready-for-anything look. Liz stood beside him, looking disgustingly gorgeous for a woman who'd slept in her clothes and hadn't brushed her hair yet. The green sweater skimmed her large breasts, the knit so tight over her nipples that Ellie could have sworn she saw aureole bumps. *Disgusting*. What was the woman, a D cup? She had "boob job" written all over her. The evil wish slipped into Ellie's mind that Tucker would hug her too hard and pop one of her sacs.

Entertaining herself with a picture of how Liz would look with one half of her glorious chest flattened, she put her coffee on to heat. Droplets of water slid onto the hot rocks and made hissing sounds that suited her mood perfectly. She didn't spare Tucker or his voluptuous sidekick so much as a glance while she stood, waiting for the coffee to perk, an endeavor that reminded her of the adage, "A watched pot never boils."

Seconds stretched into seemingly endless increments of time. She heard the rise and fall of Liz's feminine voice as she carried on a whispery exchange with Tucker. Occasionally she tittered, making Ellie wonder what was so damned funny. Were they laughing at her, by any chance? *Up yours*, she thought acidly. As if she cared? Tucker Grant meant nothing to her anymore.

Her pot had just perked for the requisite three minutes when Marvin returned to the fire. Grabbing Ellie's cup, which she'd set on the rocks, he helped himself to coffee. By the time she had fetched another mug from her mess kit, all she could squeeze from the pot was a measly half a cup again, and even that she had to gulp down.

"Everybody ready to hit the road?" Tucker asked.

"As ready as I'll ever be," Marvin said sourly.

Tucker turned to Liz. "I got the search grids mapped out last night. Since you and I know our way around out here, I think it's best if we each drive a vehicle. Marvin and Ellie can pair off with us. I'll give you a marked map before we head out."

Liz flashed Ellie a hard look. "You mean I'm going to be stuck with Twinkle Toes all morning?"

Tucker's jaw muscle started to tic, a sure sign that he was clenching his teeth. He waited a beat, and then he said in that soft, silky tone that boded ill, "I was going to suggest that, yes, but given your attitude, I've just changed my mind. Ellie can ride with me."

Marvin planted his hands on his hips. "Why can't Ellie and I go together in the Honda? It *is* her car."

Tucker looked Marvin dead in the eye. "Are you familiar with wilderness areas?"

"No, but we're not actually in a wilderness area yet. We'll just be driving around on the roads."

"If you wander off any of those roads in the right direction, you'll be in a wilderness area fast enough, and it's extremely easy to get turned around out there. I already have two kids to find. I don't want two adults added to the list."

Listening to this exchange, Ellie wanted very badly to side with Marvin. Being stuck in the Land Cruiser all morning with Tucker wasn't appealing. Unfortunately, she knew just how easy it was to get lost out here. In a mature stand of conifers, the canopy was sometimes so thick, you could see only patches of sky overhead, and the light was so diffused, it was difficult to pinpoint the position of the sun.

"We want to ride together," Marvin insisted.

"Ellie?" Tucker fixed her with a hard look. "It is your car. What's your vote?"

"I, um . . ." She flicked her gaze to the still-dark woods around them. Only the faintest trace of pink had yet to brighten the sky. She thought of her boys, out there all alone. This was no pleasure outing. Finding those kids had to be the number one priority, and if that meant enduring a few hours in Tucker's company, so be it. "I'll ride with Tucker, Marvin."

His eyes bugged. *"What?"*

"It'll only be for a couple of hours," Ellie rushed to add. "Tucker's the expert, and he is in charge. If he says that he and Liz should each drive a rig, that's the end of it, as far as I'm concerned."

Liz tossed the remainder of her coffee into the fire. The liquid spewed when it hit the hot embers. "Ellie and I can ride together. I don't mind."

"I think it'll be better if she goes with me." Tucker's tone brooked no argument.

He bent to collect his coffeepot, turned his back on an unhappy Liz, and went to collect the rest of his gear. Liz's green eyes cut into Ellie like lasers. In a huff, she spun away from the fire to break down her tent. Ellie took that as her cue to collapse her own tent and get her stuff packed up. If there was one thing she knew about Tucker Grant, it was that he hated having to wait for anyone.

For once in the last three years, they were in perfect accord on something. The sooner they began searching for the boys, the happier she would be.

Less than ten minutes later, which barely gave her enough time to splash water on her face, brush her teeth, and run a comb through her hair, Ellie was sitting in the passenger seat of his SUV. The morning sun had finally peeked up over the ridge, washing the horizon with streaks of rose and providing them with just enough light to see. Bucky, settled in back for a nap with his yellow front paws dangling over the edge of the seat, started filling the cab with soft snores before Tucker even started the engine.

He drove slowly from the bumpy clearing. As he pulled onto the rutted, dirt side road, he started to hand her the map, then seemed to think better of it and stowed it above his visor.

"Did you get a good sleep?" he asked pleasantly.

Ellie's mood wasn't the best, and she wasn't about to assume a cheery façade just for him. "Delightful. A rock poked me in the back all night, if 'all night' is the appropriate term to describe a measly four hours."

He chuckled. "Rule number one when you're putting up a tent, check the area for rocks first. A pebble can feel the size of a boulder when it's digging between your shoulder blades."

Ellie stared straight ahead, feeling so nervous she couldn't decide how to sit. If she hugged her middle, he might interpret it as a defensive posture. If she rested her hands on her thighs, she might look tense. She finally settled for leaning against her door with one arm propped on the rest, her other hand tucked between her knees. Let him read it any way he liked. At least she was comfortable.

The smell of his aftershave teased her nostrils. It was English Leather, her all-time favorite. During their marriage, she hadn't been able to keep her hands off him when he wore it. Knowing him, he'd deliberately splashed on extra to drive her crazy.

"Once I fell asleep, I rested fairly well," he informed her. "I spent the first thirty minutes tossing and turning, of course, but when I stopped obsessing about the boys, I slept like a baby."

"I did a little obsessing myself," she admitted.

"We wouldn't be parents if we didn't worry, I guess." As he gained the main forestry road, he said, "Keep your eyes peeled for bike tracks, just in case we missed them in the dark last night. I'll keep watch on my side."

Glad for something to distract her, Ellie straightened on her seat to peer out the passenger window. She saw nothing that remotely resembled the tracks of two bicycles. There were animal tracks—some paw prints that she thought might be bear, and a number of hoof marks left by deer—but no skinny tire lines anywhere. Nevertheless, she kept close watch, hoping to see something.

When they reached asphalt, Tucker stopped to glance at the map, then made a right turn. "We'll work our way west for two miles. There are a number of roads off this highway that lead to trailheads. We'll need to check all of them."

Ellie nodded, praying they saw bike tracks soon. It would be better all around if this remained strictly a family affair. She didn't want to notify the authorities any more than Tucker did.

A tense silence reigned for the next twenty minutes. In that time, they checked three dirt roads that turned up nothing. They'd just returned to the main highway when Tucker broke the quiet by saying, "I hope Liz and Marvin are finding more to talk about than we are."

For some reason, until that moment, Ellie hadn't

considered what Liz and Marvin might be talking about. Her stomach clenched with sudden anxiety. It would be just her luck that Liz would try to pick Marvin's brain for intimate details about her relationship with him. Given the fact that there were no intimate details, Ellie felt some cause for concern. Under no circumstances did she want Tucker to learn that she'd been without a lover for three whole years.

It was just a pride thing, she assured herself. He'd been dating other women for several months now, the first, according to Kody, a Jennifer Lopez look-alike with tongue studs. *Grrr.* Every time Ellie thought about it, her blood pressure rose. She couldn't help but wonder what had attracted Tucker the most, the woman's gorgeous body or the gewgaws in her mouth. A coworker had cheerfully informed Ellie that tongue studs were to fellatio what melted butter was to popcorn.

She flashed a strained smile. "Given their respective relationships with us, I imagine their conversation is a *lot* more interesting than ours." She rubbed her hands on her jeans. "Not that Marvin is the type to talk out of school." She hoped.

Tucker gave her a sidelong glance. "Liz isn't very happy with the driving arrangements. I have a feeling anything she says about me right now will be less than complimentary."

"Ah, well. What do we care what they're talking about?"

He shrugged. "Right."

Silence. Ellie tried to look straight ahead, but she discovered she had fantastic side vision. Whenever he worked the clutch or stepped on the brake, his thigh muscles bunched under his jeans. Each time he shifted gears, she noticed how his big hand completely engulfed the column knob. Pouring through the windshield, sunlight ignited the silky hair at his wrists, making it shimmer like threads of copper.

The visuals, coupled with the inescapable scent of his cologne, worked on Ellie's senses like a drug. She could vividly recall the feel of those big, hard hands on her body—the rasp of his fingertips over her skin, the heat of his palms, the way her nerve endings had thrilled at every caress.

The interior of the Land Cruiser suddenly seemed too small for the both of them, and her lungs felt oxygen deprived. She got a twitchy feeling, way low in her belly. She tried to tell herself it was merely road vibration, but that was so silly, she discarded the thought.

Wake-up call. Whether she wanted to be or not—whether it was pleasant to accept or not—she was still wildly attracted to Tucker Grant. It didn't seem to matter that he'd broken her heart and walked all over the shattered pieces on his way out the door. It didn't seem to matter that her good sense told her she was every kind of an idiot. Her mind and heart might be inviolate, but her body still hummed every time he got within three feet of her.

Ellie swallowed and stared fixedly at the dash. No biggie. Sexual attraction was a knee-jerk sort of thing. The chemistry had always been good between them. There was no point in denying that, and she'd be a fool to try. What she needed to concentrate on was the fact that she didn't *like* the man anymore. He had proved himself to be supremely arrogant, judgmental, and unforgiving. Even worse, he'd been arrogant, judgmental, and unforgiving when he hadn't known the half of it. Despite that, he'd still laid all the blame for Sammy's death at her feet and walked out, leaving her to weather the storm of grief alone.

Where had he been when she'd paced the floors every night, sobbing their son's name?

Where had he been when she'd staggered sleepily into Sammy's room to check on him, only to remember, after she was standing over his empty bed, that he was gone and she would never be able to touch his forehead or smooth his hair again?

Where had he been when she'd stood in front of the medicine cabinet, reading labels in a frantic search for something—anything—that might help her to sleep? And, damn it, where had he been the night her innocent search for a sleeping aid had become something far more sinister, prompting her to read labels for an ingredient that might prove fatal if she took a large enough dose?

Ellie didn't like to remember those dark days. Only the love she'd felt for her two surviving sons had pulled her back from the edge. She was better now. The road to recovery had been slow and painful, but she'd finally come out on the other side, stronger than before and much wiser, determined to enjoy every precious minute she could with the two sons she still had left.

She couldn't forget, would never forget, that she'd made that journey alone. Tucker Grant, the father of her children and the man who'd sworn to love her in sickness and in health, for better or for worse, had been nowhere around.

A sound like a bird twittering jerked Ellie from her

musings. Tucker reached for the cell phone in the ashtray. "Hello." He listened for a moment and then thrust the phone at Ellie. "Lover boy."

Ellie took the phone. "Hello?"

"Hi, just me," Marvin said. "Anything at your end, yet?"

"No." Ellie leaned over to look out her window as Tucker dropped off onto another dirt road. "No sign of them yet."

"Nothing over this way, either," Marvin reported. "So, um, what're you doing?"

Ellie frowned at the question. "We're driving around. What are you doing?"

"Driving around. I, um . . . well, you know. Just checking to make sure everything's going all right. You aren't having any problems, are you?"

His concern tugged at her heart and was, in her estimation, inarguable proof that he was a far better man than the one beside her. "No, none at all, Marvin, but thank you for calling to check."

"You sure? I know you don't want to be alone with him."

Still watching the road, Ellie smiled at the concern she heard in his voice. "It'll only be for a while. I can handle it."

"Okay. Just bear in mind, if things go south, I can drive these roads without a problem. I mean, really. Who's going to get lost out here?"

A lot of people, Ellie thought, but she saw no need to argue the point. "Ah, well, it's always better to be safe than sorry."

He sighed. "So, what time do you think we'll stop for lunch?"

Ellie hadn't even thought to grab something from

her pack for breakfast. "I don't know. When we all get hungry, I guess."

"I'm hungry now. Aren't you?"

Actually, her stomach was so upset from nerves she doubted she could swallow any food. "Not really, no. Right now, all I can think about are my boys."

"Right. I'm thinking about them, too, honey. They'll be okay. Don't worry."

"I'm trying."

A moment later, when Ellie finally broke the connection, Tucker returned the phone to the ashtray. She looked back out the window on her side. Nothing. "Are you positive this is the best area to search first?"

"This is where I've taken them hiking the last two years. There are countless trailheads in here, and this area is within easier biking distance from my place. It only makes sense that they'd head for the closest and most familiar terrain."

"I can't fault your reasoning, I don't suppose. It's just that we've seen no bike tracks, and Liz and Marvin aren't having any luck, either."

He conceded the point with a nod. "I still think this is the most logical place to start. If we find nothing, I'll have to put my thinking cap back on."

Kody sat on the knoll, elbows braced on his upraised knees, chin resting on his fists. He stared glumly at the vacant clearing below them, his dusty cheeks tracked with tears.

"They aren't coming."

Zach was starting to think his brother was right.

"I can't believe Dad and Mom won't come, Kody. Something's holding them up, is all."

"What makes you so sure?"

"We're their kids. Parents don't leave their kids in a wilderness area. They'll show up, I'm telling you."

Kody rubbed his cheeks, smearing the tears and dust to form watery mud. The corner of his mouth, which sported a glob of mustard from his hot dog last night, quivered as he struggled not to cry. "I hope you're right."

Zach looked out over the trees. For as far as he could see, there was only forestland. He'd been so sure that his folks would know exactly where to come. Tabletop Mountain was the very last place they'd all visited together as a family.

How could his parents fail to remember that?

Tucker was starting to get an uneasy feeling. What if the boys hadn't come to this section of Baxter, after all? Just the thought had him leaning over to rifle through the glove box for the bottle of ibuprofen he kept on hand. It didn't improve his mood when Ellie turned on the seat and pressed her knees against the door to avoid the brush of his arm.

Her big blue eyes widened as she watched him shake five tablets onto his palm while he drove with his elbows. Ignoring her, he reached in back for his ever-present water bottle.

"If you take the entire container at once, I've heard they give you a rebate to help out with final arrangements."

He smiled humorlessly at the sarcasm. "I checked with my doctor. I'm a big man. For the occasional headache, he said a dose of four or five won't hurt me."

After washing the pills down with some water, he returned his attention to the road, one thought dominating his mind. On his say-so alone, Ellie had refrained from calling in Search and Rescue last night. If the kids weren't in this area—if they got lost in unfamiliar terrain or one of them got hurt—it would be on his head.

Again.

Tucker's hands clamped over the steering wheel. His shoulders were as broad as the next guy's, but he honestly didn't think he could handle having the death of another child on his conscience. Not without losing his mind.

"Are you okay?" Ellie asked faintly.

"Hell, no, I'm not okay. My kids are out there somewhere. How can I possibly be okay?"

She averted her face. Tucker immediately felt ashamed. They were her kids, too. Where did he get off, jumping down her throat? He was about to apologize when the phone chirped again.

"Hello," he snarled.

"I've had it."

It was Liz, and she sounded grumpier than he felt. "You've had it with what, Liz?"

"With this *idiot* you've saddled me with. Twinkle Toes would be a giant step up."

Tucker winced. "I hope he can't hear you."

"No. He's off in the trees, taking a piss. The third time already, I might add. Little wonder. He's guzzled three cans of Pepsi since we took off. After every few gulps, he belches. Have you ever been locked in a Honda with a gassy fat man?"

"No, I can't say I've had that pleasure." In all fairness, Tucker thought it would be more accurate to say that Marvin was slightly overweight. "Is that why you called, to share the experience?"

"Very funny. I'm telling you, the man's gross. No wonder your kids call him Starvin' Marvin. He never stops eating."

"Is that right?"

"He just polished off a whole bag of potato chips, and he hadn't even licked his fingers clean when he started worrying about lunch."

Tucker sneaked a look at Ellie. "Hmm," was all he felt free to say.

"He's also a chronic bitcher," Liz continued. "He hates the dust. He thinks we're doing this all wrong. In the movies he's watched, searchers always have a base camp, and they communicate on two-way radios."

Tucker thought the cell phone communication was working quite well. As for a base camp, that might be a hell of a good idea. He could put Marvin in charge of operations, call him every once in a while to make him feel important, and leave his slightly overweight ass behind. "I'm sorry, Liz."

"He's also totally useless at reading the map," she harped. "Can you believe he actually got me turned around? Took me down a road, said there was an intersecting finger to the next one, and the first thing I knew, I had no idea where I was."

"You found your way out okay, I take it, no harm done."

"That's where you're wrong. He cost us valuable time. I think we should send them both back to town. Can you imagine what it'll be like out on the trail?"

"I understand what you're saying, Liz, but that simply isn't possible."

"Why? Because Twinkle Toes is the mother of your children?"

Tucker glanced over at his search partner and bit back a grin. *Twinkle Toes.* Liz might be in for a big surprise if she said that to Ellie's face a second time.

"Give me a break," Liz went on. "You don't owe her anything just because she bore your children." Silence. Then, "Where are you, anyway?"

He glanced out the windshield. "We're coming up on the Indian Horse trailhead."

"You haven't made very good time. What's been the holdup?" Brief, tension-laden pause. "Is she coming on to you?"

Tucker arched an eyebrow. There was an unmistakable ring of jealousy in her voice. "Our kids are lost, Liz. We're both very worried. What do you think the answer to that question is?"

She heaved a shrill sigh. Tucker could almost see her, pushing at her brilliant red hair. "I *know.* I'm sorry, Tucker. It's just—oh, man, here he comes. God, he forgot to zip his fly. Should I tell him, do you think?"

"It may be more entertaining if you don't."

She huffed in disgust. "*Hardly.*" In the background, Tucker heard a male tenor. "He wants to talk to Ellie," Liz said crisply.

"Here she is." Tucker handed over the phone.

Ellie pressed a cupped palm over her free ear. "Can you speak up, Marvin? There's static." Then, "Wind? Why are you standing outside the car?" Jaw set, she listened for a several seconds. "On a *what*?

You're kidding." She shot Tucker a burning look. *"Really?"* Her brows lifted. "No, it doesn't bother me. Why should it?" A pause. "Okay. Yeah, me, too. Bye." She depressed the button, gave Tucker another scorching look, and thrust the phone at him. "The flame-haired sex goddess says she'll call you back later."

The flame-haired sex goddess? Tucker wasn't *even* going to bite on that one.

Chapter Six

When the clock on the dash read twelve sharp, Tucker pulled over to the shoulder of the road, dialed a number on the cell phone, and handed it to Ellie. For a moment, she couldn't think what he was doing.

"It's noon," he said, his expression deadpan. "We haven't found any bike tracks yet. A deal is a deal."

Ellie cradled the phone on her palm and stared out the windshield. A part of her wanted very badly to depress the CALL button. Another part of her hesitated. Exactly what did she hope to accomplish by contacting Search and Rescue? As she'd told Tucker last night, they couldn't send a better tracker.

Tracing her thumb over the button, she met Tucker's gaze and asked, "If we call in reinforcements, what are the advantages?"

He stared out the windshield with a distant expression in his eyes. "More than likely, they'll send out a large group of searchers to do a sweep. With that much manpower, we'd probably find the boys' bicycles a lot more quickly."

"Probably?"

"It'll take a few hours for them to get out here. They have to call people in, and each of those people has to gather his gear and make personal arrangements before he can take off." He shrugged. "Some of them are working, others not. At best, it'll take them an hour or so to get a group together, plus driving time to get up here. By then, we may find the bikes ourselves."

He rubbed a hand over his jaw. "After that, a large group of men will be overkill. I feel certain the boys have a particular destination in mind, and most of the trails around here lead into mountainous areas. In places the paths widen out, but we'll have to walk single file much of the way up."

"So essentially what you're saying is that two or three men could execute the search just as efficiently as forty."

"Once the bikes are found, yes." He sat sideways on the seat, his left arm draped over the steering wheel. He watched her solemnly as she struggled to reach a decision. "In case of emergency rescue, it's nice to have trained, well-equipped people along to work as a team. I won't lie to you about that. But I honestly don't expect Zach and Kody to get in a jam. They're sharp kids, and they've had extensive training themselves. Unless they do something totally harebrained, they should be okay until we find them."

"If we make this call, we may be sending them a very negative message," she mused aloud.

"That's true," he agreed. "They've made several demands. If we call for help, we're ignoring their note completely. They may see it as a power play."

Ellie let her head fall back against the seat. She didn't want to make the wrong decision. "What do you think we should do?"

"I told you what I thought last night. Having said that, though, I'll understand and support you all the way if you want to get a full-scale search effort under way. This is a pretty scary situation, even to me, and I know firsthand how wilderness smart our kids are."

Ellie stared at the dome light. As though he sensed her distress, Bucky roused himself to poke his head around the seat and lick her cheek. Ellie was so emotionally drained that she couldn't even muster a sputter.

She handed Tucker the phone. In a voice gone thin with exhaustion, she said, "Let's give it a few more hours. What's to say we won't find bike tracks on the very next road?"

He returned the phone to the ashtray. "I can't promise to find them right away, Ellie. Last night when I phoned you, I felt sure I could. Now . . ." His voice trailed away. "It's possible they aren't even in this area."

Ellie had no answers. The only certainty in her mind was that if anyone could find them, it would be this man.

"I'm tired!" Kody complained. "Can you slow down? What's the big rush, anyway?"

Zach turned to walk backward up the trail. "I want to lay these tracks and get back to the knoll."

"What's the big hurry about getting back to the knoll? Nobody's there."

"They'll show up. The way I figure it, Dad thought we went somewhere else. Probably where he usually takes us hiking. When he doesn't find any sign of us over there, he'll think about it and come here."

"You *hope*. What if he doesn't? I think it was a big fat mistake, not telling him where we went. Now everything is all screwed up."

"Everything isn't screwed up. Look at the bright side. This gives us time to lay a fake trail. It'll lead Dad on a wild goose chase for at least part of a day. That'll buy us time. Remember the plan. The longer they're stuck out here alone together, the better the chance they'll fall back in love. If we head straight for Tabletop with Dad on our heels, they'll only be together for two days, max."

"That's true." Some of the worry slipped from Kody's expression. "Dad sure will be mad when he figures out we tricked him."

By late afternoon, Ellie's stomach burned with nerves. She'd been staring out her window for so long that her eyes burned, as well. Tucker had just pulled onto the shoulder of a dirt road to study the map again. They'd long since driven the grids that he'd designated last night, and now they were searching the general area at random, keeping in touch with Liz and Marvin by phone.

During the lull, questions circled in Ellie's mind. What if she had made the wrong decision by not calling for help? What if Tucker was mistaken, and the kids were less adept at getting around out there than he believed? If they got lost, they could wander aimlessly for days.

The thought terrified her. In many Oregon wilderness areas, the forest floor was left in its natural state, creating an obstacle course of deadfall. Even more worrisome, the woods were full of what Tucker called "widow makers," trees uprooted by high winds that had caught on other trees and never dropped to the ground. They shifted precariously in a breeze, and the least little disturbance could bring them crashing down. A hapless hiker who happened to be beneath one when it fell ended up badly injured or dead.

Why had the boys done this? If they were so miserably unhappy, why hadn't they simply said so?

Therein lay the problem, she supposed. They *had* said so. They'd come to her plenty of times, complaining about school and how much they missed their father. Committed as she'd been to a new job and a house payment, she'd seen no way to remedy the situation, so now they'd taken matters into their own hands.

In a way, Ellie supposed it was fitting that they'd run away to Baxter. The very last time they'd gone camping as a family before Sammy died, they'd come here.

At the thought, a chill of excitement washed over her skin. She gave Tucker an incredulous look. "I just figured it out."

He glanced up from the map. "You just figured what out?"

"Where they are." Ellie's throat went tight. Her gaze clung to his. "Think, Tucker. Where did we last go camping as a family before Sammy was killed?"

His mouth tightened and his eyes went dark with shadows. "Tabletop Mountain. That's clear on the west side, Ellie. On bikes, it would have taken them from early morning until nearly dark to get over there."

"That's where they've gone. I know it." She pressed a hand over her heart and closed her eyes. After a moment, when she could speak again, she continued. "This is all about our family. Don't you see? They want things back the way they used to be. You said yourself that they're making a statement, and you're absolutely right. That's a very special place in their memories. *Our* place." Unshed tears seared Ellie's eyes. "They're taking us back to Tabletop."

The map slipped from Tucker's hands. A stricken look came over his face. After a heavy silence, during which he stared at her with his heart breaking in his eyes, he whispered, "Oh, Ellie, you're right. Of *course* they're heading for Tabletop." He thumped his forehead with the heel of his hand. "Of *course*. It makes absolute sense. I don't know why that didn't occur to me."

He grabbed the cell phone to call Liz. After explaining as briefly as possible, he said, "Meet us at the Tabletop trailhead."

It took them forty minutes to drive around to the west side. When Tucker took the cutoff that led to the trailhead, Ellie saw bike tracks along the shoulder of the dirt road.

"*Yes!*" she cried, thrusting a fist triumphantly above her head. "They're here, Tucker. They're *here!*"

He flashed her a relieved grin, gave her a thumbs-up, and said, "Good job, Ellie."

They'd no sooner parked in the tree-encircled

clearing and exited the Land Cruiser than Liz and Marvin pulled in behind them, sending up a cloud of yellow-brown dust. Liz gave a glad whoop as she climbed from the Honda. "Way to go, Tucker. Talk about homing in on your prey." She inclined her head at a cluster of manzanita off to one side of the clearing. "There are the bikes!"

Ellie had missed the glint of a bike fender poking out from under the brush. She walked over to the spot, her heart twisting as she pushed aside the branches. In a way, it eased her mind, knowing she'd guessed right about the boys' destination. But it also saddened her. Before Sammy's death, this was where they'd always come as a family. She couldn't count the times she and Tucker had camped here with their three boys before starting up to Tabletop Mountain the following morning.

It seemed to her in that moment that the faint echo of her sons' laughter drifted on the breeze. Arms clasped over her chest, she looked off through the trees. *Sammy.* It still hurt when she thought of him, the grief so sharp and poignant that her stomach twisted. She would never forgive herself for what had happened to him. The guilt would be her cross to bear for the rest of her life. She caught the inside of her cheek between her teeth and bit down hard enough to sting.

"You okay?"

Ellie whirled to find Marvin standing behind her. He stared solemnly at the bikes. For a long moment, he said nothing. "It must be hell, coming back here," he murmured. "I know it makes you remember things you'd rather forget."

Ellie never wanted to forget Sammy. *Never*. But she knew Marvin meant well, so she only nodded. "Mostly I'm just worried about Zach and Kody." She gestured at the woods all around them. "They're out there alone somewhere, Marvin. It makes me feel so helpless and afraid for them."

He wiped a hand over his mouth. "Yeah, I imagine it does. Look on the bright side, though. When they ditched the bikes here, they were still safe and sound."

The thought eased some of the tension from her muscles. "Yes, and unless Tucker has failed miserably as a teacher, they still should be. He's devoted a lot of time teaching them how to take care of themselves out here."

Marvin's eyes darkened. "Too bad he didn't spend a little more time teaching them other things."

"Like what?"

"To have some consideration for their mother, for starters." He inclined his head at the larger bike. "Zach is old enough to know better than to pull a stunt like this. I know you don't want to hear that, honey, but the boy's out of control. If he'll do something like this at fourteen, what'll he be like at sixteen when the real attitude problems start?"

A prickle of irritation moved up Ellie's spine. "Zach isn't out of control, Marvin." She thought of all that had happened in her son's life over the last three years. "He's lost a brother, his parents have gotten a divorce, and to top it all off, I uprooted him eleven months ago, taking him away from his dad and all his friends. He's a sweet boy. He's just confused and unhappy right now. And who can blame him?" She pushed her shaggy bangs from her eyes. "I thought they'd get used to it in Springfield over time, that as difficult as it might be for a while, we'd all settle in and be better off in the long run. We were leaving all the sad memories behind. Being hired as manager was a big step up for me as well, and the salary was so much better. I really believed I was making the right decision when I accepted the job. Now I just don't know anymore."

"A lot of kids have to move, Ellie, and they don't do stuff like this."

She lifted her hands. "Can't you understand how he must be feeling?"

Marvin bent his head. When he looked back up at her, his expression was imploring. "I can, yes. Now I've got a question. Can you understand how *I'm* feeling? I've seen this coming for weeks, and my hands have been tied. That boy needs some stability in his life, namely a full-time father." His larynx bobbed as he swallowed. "I'd like to take on the job. I'd like that more than anything. But you keep making excuses and putting me off. We haven't even had sex yet, for God's sake. 'Soon,' you keep saying, but so far, I haven't made it to first base."

Not now, Ellie wanted to cry. "This isn't the time to discuss our personal relationship," she managed to squeeze out. "My sons are lost. That's all I can think about right now."

"It's the perfect time. Get your head out of the sand, Ellie. Those kids are on a downhill skid, Zach especially. He needs a firm hand." He swung his arm toward the vehicles. "Rambo sure as hell isn't doing anything to remedy the problem."

Ellie couldn't argue the point. Since she'd moved to Springfield, Tucker's time with the boys had been cut back to almost nothing. He phoned them frequently, trying to make up for the miles that now stretched between them, but a father could accomplish only so much with long-distance telephone calls.

She hugged her waist, feeling sick. What had she done? Her career be damned. Money and advancement were wonderful, but not at the expense of her kids. Because of her selfishness, the boys had been separated from their father. As deeply as she resented Tucker on many levels, she had to give him credit where it was due: he loved his sons, and he'd always been a wonderful parent.

Searching him out with her gaze, Ellie saw that he was standing with Liz at the back of his Land Cruiser, one big hand resting lightly on her shoulder. Tawny head bent, he seemed to be listening intently to something she said. Only a few inches separated their bodies. Watching them together, it wasn't difficult for Ellie to imagine him holding the redhead in his arms.

She had no claim on Tucker anymore, Ellie reminded herself. It shouldn't hurt to see him with another woman. But somehow, reason played no part in her feelings. *Damn him.* It was one thing to know he had girlfriends galore back in Bend, but did he have to carry on like this directly under her nose?

"Will you at least promise to consider it?" Marvin asked.

Ellie jerked. "What?"

He turned away. "Never mind. God knows why I even bothered to ask."

She caught his sleeve. "Don't go, Marvin. I'm sorry. What did you say?"

When he swung back to face her, his eyes burned with anger. "I just asked you to marry me, damn it. Not that you noticed!" He jabbed a finger at her face. "You're too damned busy watching the action over there to pay attention to me at all."

Ellie winced, wishing he'd lower his voice. She didn't want Tucker to overhear this exchange. "Marvin, please. You're yelling."

"You're damn right, I'm yelling. Just look at you, mooning over him like a lovesick teenager. Shit! Why don't you save us both a lot of trouble and just go back to the bastard? That's what you really want, deep down."

"That isn't true!"

"Prove it," he snarled. "I just asked you to be my wife, goddamn it. If you aren't still hung up on him, say yes, and let's set a date."

Ellie felt as if she were poised on the edge of a cliff and being urged to jump. "Marvin, I told you, now isn't the time for this."

"When will it be time?"

Ellie had grown very fond of this man, but in that moment, she realized she didn't and probably never would love him. That was why she hadn't gone to bed with him yet, she realized, why she continued to put him off. To share that kind of intimacy with a man, her heart had to be engaged, and she thought of Marvin as a friend, and nothing more.

"I don't mean to put you off," she tried. "I'm just very upset right now, and—"

"You're upset? What about me? It's not easy, knowing the woman I love still has the hots for her ex-husband!"

Ellie wished she had a sock to stuff in his mouth. "This is a discussion that might be better saved for Springfield, where we have some privacy."

He held her gaze for a long while, his expression stony. "Fine. When you're ready to talk, let me know. Just understand that I'm not going to play this game much longer."

As he walked away, Ellie gazed sadly after him. He was absolutely right; the games had to end. She had hoped to develop deeper feelings for him and had honestly believed she would over time. *Stupid, so stupid.* Love sprang from a hidden place within the heart. It wasn't an emotion that could be forced. It either happened—or it didn't.

With Marvin, it hadn't. It was as simple as that.

She passed a hand over her eyes, feeling sick and angry with herself. She'd never meant to hurt him, but there was no denying that she had. And as soon as the boys were found, she would have to hurt him even more. Under the circumstances, she couldn't possibly keep seeing him. It would be cruel to string him along, knowing that nothing could ever come of the relationship.

Stunned by the conversation he'd just overheard, Tucker gave himself a hard mental shake and tried to concentrate on what Liz was saying. He forced himself to look straight into her green eyes, his brain still swimming with shock and incredulity while her voice hummed in his ears like a swarm of bees. Ellie had been putting Marvin off about having sex? Even more disturbing, what on earth made Marvin think that she was still in love with him, Tucker?

Liz waved a hand in front of Tucker's face. "Hello? Have you gone comatose?"

He blinked. "Pardon?"

"You're not listening to a thing I'm saying."

"Of course I'm listening."

"What'd I just say, then?"

Tucker hated when people asked that question. "I'm sorry. I guess I'm tired and not tracking very well. What did you say?"

She pouted her lips and gazed up at him through her lowered lashes. "Nothing that important." She ran a slender hand over his chest. "Poor fellow. You probably didn't get much sleep last night, worrying about those darned kids. You should have come to my tent. I've got a sure cure for what ails you, Mr. Grant, better than any tranquilizer you'll ever find."

Tucker forced himself to smile. "I'll bet you do."

"There's always tonight. If you're worried I'll wake everyone up, I promise I won't." Her eyes gleamed with dark promises. She stepped closer and grazed his jeans with her pelvis, the tips of her breasts burning through his shirt like hot pokers. "My word of honor."

Tucker curled his hands over her shoulders and set her firmly away from him. Been there, done that. He wasn't going through the rub-and-grind routine again. Liz was a pretty woman, but he was quickly coming to realize that the beauty ran only skin deep. In short, he wasn't interested.

"Would it be possible for us to shelve the personal stuff for now, Liz? I have two kids to find, and right now, that's all I can think about."

She danced her fingers up the buttons of his shirt and smiled saucily. "I'm very fond of your sons, too, Tucker. I couldn't be more worried if they were my own."

Worried mothers didn't rub against a man like a cat in heat. He moved back another step. "I figure we have only about an hour of good light left, two before it's fully dark. I'm thinking we'll be better off camping down here tonight and heading up the mountain in the morning."

"Suits me." Her voice went husky. "Given the fact that we can't start looking for them until then, will you promise to come see me tonight?"

Tucker was tempted, mightily tempted, to just lay it on the line for her. But that wasn't his way. Even though he was quickly coming to realize he didn't really like Liz, he hated to hurt her feelings if he could avoid it.

"Not with other people in camp, Liz. Like I said last night, I'm a private man when it comes to that sort of thing."

She sighed and wrinkled her nose. "You're no fun at all."

"Sorry. A leopard can't change its spots." On that light note, he stepped quickly away. "I need to study my map of the area for a few minutes." He glanced over to see Marvin pulling a camp stove from the trunk of Ellie's Honda. "Would you mind passing the word that we'll be staying here tonight?"

"It appears to me he already knows."

"He's probably just hungry and plans to fix a quick meal."

Liz rolled her eyes. "He never stops stuffing his face."

"Be nice."

She tucked her thumbs in the hip pockets of her jeans as she started across the clearing. "I always am." She threw him a mischievous smile over her shoulder. "Remember me tonight when you're counting sheep."

By the time Ellie returned to the vehicles, Liz was gathering wood for a fire, and Marvin was assembling his brother-in-law's propane stove. On the ground nearby lay his tent. It appeared to Ellie that Tucker planned to spend the night here. Given the fact that it was still broad daylight, she wondered why.

Tucker stood at the front bumper of his rig, studying a map he'd spread over the dusty green hood. At Ellie's approach, he glanced up. With one sharp look into her eyes, he said, "We can't head up the mountain tonight, Ellie." He swung his head at the sky. "It's getting too late. There's a stream down here, and the ground is nice and flat for the tents. We'll stick tight, break camp before dawn, and head out at daybreak."

It bothered Ellie that he could read her thoughts and answer her questions before she even asked them. Did he really know her so well? After a moment's reflection, she supposed that was only fair. She knew him pretty well, too. She'd seen the hot flash of desire that crossed his dark face when he'd been cozying up to Liz a minute ago, and she recognized the resultant bulge behind the fly of his jeans for exactly what it was, as well.

Planting her hands on the fender, she angled her

body toward him, her gaze giving no quarter. "It won't get dark for at least two hours. I want to start up the mountain *now*."

He gave her a querulous look. "At the most, we'd get in an hour of tracking before we had to start looking for a place to camp. Better to stay put."

"An hour is an hour. I don't want to waste precious time."

He sighed and passed a hand over his eyes. "Come on, Ellie. Be reasonable. I'm as worried as you are."

"Like hell. Don't waste your breath trying to convince me of that."

"What the Sam Hill is *your* problem?"

She slapped her palm down on the map. He flinched at the sound of her flesh connecting with the metal. Ellie was so mad she barely felt the sting. "I'll tell you what my problem is. My kids are out there in those woods somewhere, facing God knows how many dangers, and their father is more interested in getting a piece of ass than he is in going after them."

"I beg your pardon?"

"You heard me. I'll be damned if we're going to make camp before dark. Tell Liz and Marvin you've changed your mind, that we're heading out."

He straightened away from the front of the vehicle, drawing the map with him as he went.

Ellie dropped her gaze to his belt and curled her lip. "There's no point in trying to hide it. I already saw."

His eyes heated with anger. He tossed the map back on the hood. "What the hell are you implying?"

"You know exactly, and I didn't imply anything. I said it straight out."

"Then get your mind out of the gutter. There's nothing like that going on."

"Right. I do have eyes in my head."

"And you only see what you want to see. Just for the record, whatever is or isn't going on between me and Liz has nothing to do with my decision to make camp here."

"*Your* decision?" She shook her head and thumbed her chest. "Half my kids, half my decision. We're leaving. *Now.*"

"Understand something. You're welcome to join in on this search. As the mother of my sons, you have that right. But I'll be calling the shots. That includes deciding when and where we'll make camp."

Ellie knew when Tucker had dug in his heels. "Fine, then," she said, flinging the words over her shoulder as she swung away. "I'll find their tracks and go after them myself."

Tucker watched Ellie rummage in the trunk of her Honda for her gear. Her movements were jerky, her cheeks flaming. After being married to her for over a decade, he knew when she was in high dudgeon. Damn her stubborn hide, he'd be wasting his breath if he tried to talk to her. She was determined to go after the boys right now, and knowing her, she'd go, come hell or high water.

He was tempted to let her. Like he needed this? Unfortunately, the woman could walk fifty feet into the trees and get lost. He didn't dare let her traipse off alone.

Tucker sighed and sauntered toward her. When he drew up at the rear fender, she flicked him a searing look, then went back to grabbing her stuff. She didn't look up again as she shoved her arms through the straps of her backpack.

"You take off alone, you'll get lost," he said.

"I'm not a complete idiot, Tucker." She dangled a piece of plastic before his nose. "I know how to use a compass."

"I came out here to look for my kids, Ellie, not chase after you. Get turned around out there, and you're on your own."

She shrugged. "Look on the bright side. Maybe Marvin will crash early, and you'll have a clear playing field with carrottop. The two of you can try out the hood of your Cruiser. Who knows? It may be almost as fun as the porch swing."

Tucker had no idea what she was talking about. He didn't own a porch swing, and he sure as hell hadn't been rocking his way to oblivion with Liz. He clenched his teeth. He didn't know why, but this slip of a woman could make him mad faster than anybody else on earth.

"Not that it's any of your business, but there's nothing like that going on."

"Uh-huh," she sneered.

"Quick biology lesson, all right? If, and I do stress *if*, you'd seen what you believe you saw, it wouldn't necessarily mean anything. A man has no control over certain bodily functions. That part of him reacts to stimulus. His mind doesn't have to be engaged. Neither do his emotions. If a woman rubs against him, that just—happens. He could hug a pine tree with the same result."

"You poor baby. My heart bleeds."

A tight, airless sensation banded his chest, and his blood hammered in his temples. "And it wouldn't mean my thoughts aren't focused on our boys."

She clucked her tongue. "It must be terrible, being so big and strong and *vulnerable.*" She wrinkled her nose and said in a singsong voice, " 'She rubbed against me, and I just couldn't *help* myself.' " Her eyes sliced the air between them. "Tell it to your mother. Maybe she'll buy it."

Tucker's patience snapped. If she wanted war, he'd oblige. "Are you really so worried about the kids, or are you just spitting fire because you're jealous?"

That got her goat. She slammed the trunk closed and stepped around to stand in front of him, her small chin jutting. That was another thing about her that he'd always found infuriating. In a temper, she never hesitated to belly up to him. He had over a hundred and twenty pounds on her, and to get nose-to-nose with him, she had to rise up on her tiptoes. Yet she never seemed to feel the least bit intimidated.

Not that he'd ever given her reason. No matter how pissed off he got, he would never smack a woman. That was an all-inclusive rule that applied even to a small blonde in serious need of an attitude adjustment.

She poked his chest with a pointy finger, finding just the right spot to hit a nerve. "Jealous?" Blue fire streaked from her eyes. Tucker almost expected steam to come rolling from her ears. "In your fantasies, Bucko!" She swung her arm toward Liz, who had moved several feet into the trees to find firewood. "Go for it! I couldn't care less if I'd had a lobotomy. The two of you deserve each other."

She whirled away. Tucker watched her storm from their would-be campsite, so blind with fury that she swept right past a bewildered Marvin without so much as a glance in his direction.

"Where's she going?" Marvin asked.

Tucker rubbed a hand over his face and blinked. "For a walk. She'll be back shortly."

Tucker meant to see that she was—if he had to throw her over his shoulder and carry her every step of the way.

Ellie ran short of breath partway up the hill. She wasn't sure if it was from exertion or sheer rage, but just in case Tucker was watching, she forced herself to keep going. *Jealous?* He was, hands down, the most arrogant, infuriating man she'd ever met. What did he think he was, God's gift to women? So his mind and feelings didn't have to be engaged, huh? A likely story. It sounded like a pat excuse for indiscriminate bed hopping to her.

Not that she cared. Tucker Grant could do whatever he pleased, whenever he pleased, and with whomever he pleased, but he could do it on his own damned time, not when her children were lost in a wilderness area. She refused to sit in camp when the light was still good, twiddling her thumbs, just so he could get it on with his big-breasted bimbo. As if she needed him as a guide? *Ha!* It was an easy enough thing to follow footprints. All she had to do was make a sweep along the ridge to pick up the boys' tracks. Then she would follow them until dark, making good use of the remaining daylight.

Staggering to a stop at the crest of the slope, Ellie

grabbed for oxygen, her lungs whining, her skin clammy with perspiration. While she stood there, struggling to catch her breath, she checked the compass to get her bearings and then cast about, looking for disturbed earth. Nothing.

When her heart rate finally slowed, she turned left to walk along the ridge. It stood to reason that the kids must have cut through here to get up the hill. She had only to keep walking. Sooner or later, she'd spot their trail.

Ellie no sooner thought that than she saw disturbed earth. Her pulse gave an excited kick and she hurried over to examine the tracks. With all the pine needles, it was hard to tell if the prints had been made by an animal or by humans. They were big enough and long enough to have been left by the boys, but the shapes were indistinct. She decided to follow them for a bit, hoping she might find a less blurred depression farther uphill. As she walked along, she counted the tracks, taking heart when she determined that at least four feet had consistently disturbed the earth through there.

Her mouth curved in a triumphant grin. Wouldn't it be something if *she* found the kids? *Put that in your pipe and smoke it, Tucker Grant.* There was nothing to this tracking business. He'd always made it look like a complicated science, crouching down to study the edges of the tracks and fingering the dirt. Now that she was on a trail herself, she knew all that nonsense had been for show.

Like she needed him to help find her kids? Ha. She could find them by herself, thank you very much.

*   *   *

Head bent, Tucker followed Ellie's tracks through a stand of Ponderosa pine. She'd picked up the boys' trail, he noted with an odd feeling of pride. Evidently all the things he'd tried to teach her hadn't gone in one ear and out the other, after all. Occasionally, he could see where she'd stopped to examine the prints. At other places, she'd turned about-face, probably to get her bearings. He could almost see her, palming her compass and frowning as she studied the dial.

Unfortunately, getting lost wasn't the only danger in these mountains. There were cougars and bears in these woods, and a lone hiker ran a greater risk of being attacked than people traveling in pairs. There were also broken limbs poking up from fallen trees practically everywhere he looked. What would she do if she slipped and fell? There'd be no one to stop the bleeding, no one to go for help. In addition to all that, there were the two-legged critters to worry about. Ellie wasn't much bigger than a minute. If she ran into a group of sleazy hikers, she could be in a peck of trouble. Most times, the men Tucker met along woodland trails were decent fellows, but there were always the exceptions.

At the thought, Tucker knotted his hands into hard fists. If anyone dared to lay a hand on her, he'd—well, no point in going there. At this time of year, there were few hikers in Baxter. Chances were good that she would encounter no one.

Even so, Tucker picked up his pace, hoping to find her soon. Damn fool woman, anyway. What had possessed her to come out here alone? In his opinion, it was a clear case of temper overruling common sense. He wan't even sure what had made her so furious.

What did she care if he and Liz had a thing going? Like she gave a hoot whom he slept with? He really would be dreaming if he started entertaining that notion.

It was all the stuff he'd heard Marvin saying to her, he guessed. Now, after all this time, he was suddenly asking himself, What if? What if he'd read it all wrong three years ago? What if Ellie really hadn't wanted him to leave? What if she actually had been jealous when she jumped him about Liz a while ago? A woman didn't almost dent the hood of a Land Cruiser with her bare hand unless she had deep feelings for a man. She either hated his guts—or she loved him to distraction. Which was it?

Damned if he knew. He'd grasped physics, impressed his professors in statistics, and pulled straight A's in every advanced math course offered at the university, but could he understand how Ellie's mind worked? Hell, no. She looked at everything differently than he did and came up with some of the most rattlebrained notions. With her, everything was about feelings. Well, he had news for her. There wasn't a man alive who had any control over his dick.

Tucker felt disgusted with himself for even thinking about her. After all he'd been through, only a fool would open himself up to more hurt, and that was exactly what he'd be doing if he let himself believe, even for a moment, that she still cared for him. After Sammy's accident, she had been the one who pointed the finger and couldn't forgive, and she'd been the one to turn her back on him, not the other way around. The marriage had been over before he ever walked out the door.

That was what he needed to remember, he told himself, and to hell with everything else. If Ellie hadn't had sex with Marvin yet, that was her problem. If, by some chance, she still had feelings for Tucker, that was her problem, too. At one time he'd loved her with every breath he took, needing her like he needed the air to breathe, and she'd tossed him away like so much trash. After the divorce, it had taken him two years to get over her. Now that he'd finally gotten his life back on track, she would whistle Dixie with her mouth full of peanut butter before he let her mess with his head again.

Surfacing from his thoughts, Tucker noted the position of the sinking sun. Directly over the mountains, the sky was streaked with gold and multiple hues of rose, but an ominous charcoal darkened the zenith. Within minutes, it would grow dark, making it impossible to follow her any longer.

Plunging into a lodgepole thicket, he cursed vilely. If he didn't find her soon, she'd end up spending the night out here. At least his boys were traveling together and knew how to take care of themselves. Ellie was a different story. If she lost that compass or read it wrong in the dark, God knew where she might end up.

"Ellie!"

No answer.

Tucker pushed through a dense network of limbs, spitting out bits of moss that slapped him across the mouth as he called her name every few feet. Still no answer. What the *hell* had he been thinking to let her storm off alone? The moment he found her, he was putting her on a leash.

*   *   *

Ellie slung her pack to the ground and looked across the small lake she'd stumbled upon as she emerged from the woods. *How beautiful.* There was still just enough daylight to see the adjacent shore where a doe and fawn had stepped from the trees to get a drink. An osprey circled and dived for a fish, sending up a spray of water. In the distance, a coyote howled to herald the night, its long, high-pitched call drifting on the breeze.

There was something so forlorn about the cry of a coyote, Ellie thought, rubbing her arms against the chill air blowing in off the water. She lifted her gaze to the deepening sky, feeling so small—and alone. Now that she'd stopped for the night, she was a little uneasy. Okay, a lot uneasy, she admitted to herself. But it was too late for second thoughts. It would be completely dark in twenty minutes, and she knew better than to think she could find her way back to the main camp without light to see by.

The first order of business was to gather some rocks and wood, she decided. A cheerful fire would not only soothe her nerves and provide warmth, but also keep creatures at bay. Once she had a healthy blaze going, she'd pitch her tent.

Taking advantage of the remaining daylight, she hurried back into the woods to collect fallen limbs. Five trips later, she had a large enough pile of fuel to last through the night. So far, so good. Maybe she didn't have much wilderness savvy, but she had gleaned enough from watching Tucker over the years to get by. Here in a few minutes, she'd put on a pot of coffee. The hot brew would go nicely with her trail mix and cheese, adding just the right touch to make her feel she'd had a full meal.

As she bent to arrange rocks around her prospective fire pit, a branch snapped in the trees off to her right. Jerking around to look, she half expected to see a bear lumbering toward her. But there was nothing. She shook her head and positioned another rock. Then another. As she worked, she heard a second limb break, and her nerves jangled with alarm.

Okay, so she was *extremely* uneasy about spending the night alone out here. No big surprise. She always had been a big chicken at night in the wilderness. The way she saw it, she basically had two choices. She could brave it out, telling herself there was nothing to be afraid of, which probably wouldn't work. Or she could devise some way to protect herself.

Better be prepared, she decided when another branch cracked behind her. Abandoning the rocks, she sorted through the firewood for a limb that would serve as a club. Her choice was a long, thick one with outcroppings of sharp, broken branches at the skinny end. After a couple of practice swings, she felt better. If any big creature came around, she'd bonk it on the snout and send it running.

Less nervous now that she had a weapon, Ellie finished building the rock ring and started a fire. She felt safer the instant the flames took hold. After throwing on more wood to provide light against the ever-deepening darkness, she stood for a while and warmed herself. Then, keeping her club near at hand, she pulled her tent from her backpack, quickly erected it, and crawled inside to unroll her sleeping bag. *Home sweet home.* She'd sleep like a baby, she promised herself.

She was about to crawl from the tent when she heard something sniffing just outside. Her body rigid, she stared at the tent wall, her heart pounding. *Oh, God!* She imagined a huge bear. According to Tucker, the creatures could pick up the scent of food from over a mile away, and they were extremely cantankerous if you got between them and their grub. Through the front opening of her shelter, she could see her backpack lying on the ground outside. For just an instant, she considered staying put. Maybe, if she remained absolutely still and quiet, the creature would find her trail rations and go away.

What was she thinking? The flimsy nylon of the tent offered no protection. With one sweep of a paw, a bear could rip it wide open, and her along with it. At least outside, she'd be able to see what was coming and defend herself.

On knees gone numb with fright, she crawled over to the tent flap. Club held high for battle, she leaned cautiously out, praying she didn't come nose-to-snout with a gigantic omnivore.

Chapter Seven

Tucker was so relieved to find Ellie that he felt weak at the knees. Not liking the feeling, he paused in the darkness beyond the firelight to gather his composure. He was just thinking of his boys, he assured himself. If something happened to their mother, they'd both be devastated, and Tucker would be left with the responsibility of raising them alone. Not a pleasant thought.

A grin tugged at his mouth when he saw Ellie peek out of her tent, a limb almost as big as she was held high over her head. She was clearly frightened half to death, a discovery that greatly improved his mood. Maybe next time she'd think twice before she stormed off alone and caused him no end of trouble.

Just deserts or not, he was glad Bucky had come along a few minutes ago to help him find her. Frightened as she was, she wouldn't have gotten much sleep tonight, and as a result, she would have tired more easily tomorrow. Unless he missed his guess, it would be a long, grueling day, chasing after those boys. She'd need all her stamina to keep up.

"Are you going to bean me with that thing if I come closer?" he called.

At the sound of his voice, she jumped nearly a foot and pressed a hand over her heart. "Tucker? *Oh!* You scared the sand out of me."

Tucker tried not to smile as he moved into the light. "I doubt it. You've got more sand than an ocean beach."

At the sound of Ellie's voice, Bucky abandoned the scent on the ground that had so intrigued him upon their arrival. With a glad bark, he raced around the tent and launched himself into her arms. With a startled "oof," she fell over backward and all but disappeared under a wriggling mass of black and gold fur.

"Bucky!" She made a sputtering sound, shoved at the dog, and rolled in the other direction to avoid getting licked on the face. "I just saw you a while ago. You act like it's been years! Off me, you silly mutt. Ugh."

Tucker walked to the fire. "I don't think he comprehends that this is a one-sided love affair."

"It isn't one-sided. I love him to death. I just don't care to swap slobber with him." Hair tousled, cheeks rosy from the struggle, she emerged from the tent on her knees, looking too cute by half for a woman who'd just seen her thirty-fifth birthday. Gracing him with an indignant glare, she asked, "What, may I ask, are you doing here?"

He held out his hands to the flames. "Oh, just out for an evening stroll. Thought I'd drop by and say hello."

"Very funny." Leaving her club inside the tent, she struggled to her feet and dusted off her jeans. Bucky danced at her feet, wagging so hard that his whole body undulated. Ellie took a moment to scratch his ears. Then, in that no-nonsense tone he'd heard her use with the kids a thousand times, she said, "Go lie down now. Go on." As Bucky ambled over to plop by the fire, she straightened. "I'm perfectly fine, as you can see. Regardless of what you may think, I can take care of myself."

"I never meant to imply you couldn't."

Her small chin came up, and her eyes turned a fiery blue. Tucker resigned himself to a quarrel. Since the divorce, nothing came easily with Ellie.

"I'm not going back to the main camp. If that's why you're here, forget it." She swung her arm toward the trees. "I found the boys' tracks."

"I know."

"And come first light, I intend to be back on their trail."

"No problem. That sleeping bag of yours is big enough for two."

Her eyes went wide. "Oh, no. Get that straight out of your head. You're not sharing my sleeping bag."

She looked so appalled at the thought, so *horrified* that he would even suggest such a thing, that Tucker could only wonder why. Granted, fitting two bodies into that bag would be a tight squeeze, but they'd managed a number of times when one of the kids had wet the bed.

Surely she wasn't worried that something might happen between them if they slept together? Tucker tried to push the thought from his mind, but it had the cling and stretch of melted mozzarella. That was exactly what worried her, he decided as he searched her expression. Given the fact that she knew him better than almost anyone, she couldn't possibly think he might force himself on her. Ruling that out, what did she have to fear?

Bewildered and more than a little intrigued, he treated her to a long study that made her fidget and avoid looking him directly in the eye. All his male instincts went on red alert.

"Would you *stop*?"

"Stop what?"

"Staring at me."

"Sorry." Tucker lowered his gaze to the fire. After a moment, he glanced back up. "Ellie, you aren't concerned about what may happen if we sleep together, are you? I mean—well, you know."

If possible, she looked even more appalled by that suggestion than she had before. "Don't be ridiculous. You and me?" She splayed a hand at the base of her throat and gave a shaky little laugh. "The thought never even occurred to me."

The lady seemed to be protesting just a little too much. He searched her face, every angle of which was engraved on his memory. In her eyes, he read myriad emotions, not the least of which were anger and bitterness, but underneath that, he glimpsed something more—an elusive something, there one moment and gone the next.

Had it been a trick of the light, or had he seen pain in those blue depths? He tried to delve deeper, but she bent her head. Before Sammy's accident, he would have stepped around the fire, caught her by the chin, and pressed the issue. Now all he could do was wait, wishing she'd look at him again. When she finally did, the shadows he'd seen in her eyes had vanished.

A pragmatist with both feet firmly rooted in reality, Tucker had never considered himself to be the imaginative type. He'd glimpsed something, he knew. He just wasn't sure what.

"I'm not going back down to the main camp with you," she said.

"Suit yourself."

"And you're not staying."

"Here's the way of it," he said softly. "You insist on staying here. I'm equally determined that you aren't staying alone. Where does that leave us?"

"With one tent, and me sleeping in it."

He shook his head. "Think again. It gets damned cold up here at night. I'm not freezing my ass off out here by the fire."

"Go back and sleep in your own tent, then."

"I'm not going without you."

She threw up her hands. "I'm perfectly capable of looking after myself. Even if I weren't, my welfare is no longer your concern."

"Technically, you may be right, but practically speaking, dead wrong. What'll I say to those boys if something happens to you?"

"That's dirty pool."

"That's reality. They love you. They'll hold me accountable if anything goes wrong. That being the case, you're either going back with me, or I'm staying here. Your choice."

She muttered under her breath and kicked at the dirt. "You can be so impossible sometimes. If you stay here, you'll have to go clear back down in the morning to get your gear. How does that make sense?"

"Didn't say it makes sense."

Her cheeks flushed with temper. "Which is the same as saying I don't make sense."

"Don't read between the lines. You're bad at it. All I'm saying is that I'm not leaving you here. It's a proven fact that lone campers and hikers run a greater risk of mishap."

"I think you pluck those facts out of your hat whenever you want to win an argument."

He chose to ignore that. "And that isn't to mention the risks a woman takes when she ventures off alone into a wilderness area. There's no telling what kind of characters are wandering around out here."

She hunched her shoulders inside her parka, pushing the blue nylon up around her ears. "It's a regular Grand Central. I can see your concern."

Tucker conceded the point with a shrug. "Yeah, well, call me too careful. You aren't making the newspaper headlines on my watch."

She rested her hands at her hips. After staring at the tent for a moment, she finally said, "Oh, all right, you win."

For a moment, Tucker thought she meant to let him share her sleeping bag. Then she kicked at the dirt again, this time sending a spray over the flames. "I'll pack my gear. You can put out the fire."

In less than ten minutes, they were ready to set out. Ellie immediately pulled a flashlight from her pack to light the way, which had the perverse effect of blinding Tucker more than it helped.

"We won't need that. I've got excellent night vision."

"I don't."

"I'll guide you. If you flash that light around, neither of us will be able to see past our noses."

With a disgruntled huff, she turned off the flashlight and returned it to her pack. "Are you happy now? I'm blind as a bat."

Even with his keen night vision, Tucker had to admit it was awfully dark under the trees. The boughs overhead blocked most of the moonlight. He curled a hand over her arm. "Your eyes will adjust. Go to your left."

Her footsteps faltered, and she pressed closer to his side. "I don't know how you can see anything."

"I couldn't read any fine print, that's for sure. But there's enough light coming down through the canopy for walking." Just as he spoke, he saw Bucky angling off through the trees. "Hey, Bucky, get back here!" he called.

The shepherd whipped around and barked excitedly, then darted deeper into the woods. For a moment, Tucker lost sight of him. Concerned that the canine might take off after an animal, he whistled shrilly. "Bucky! Come!" He felt Ellie jerk at every inflection of his voice and wondered at her nervousness. "Damn dog," he muttered.

She peered owlishly into the shadows. "Is he coming back?"

"You honestly can't see much of anything, can you?" Not really expecting an answer, Tucker drew her back into a walk. "Yeah, he's coming back." Keeping a hold on her arm, he bent to reward the returning dog with a friendly pat. "Good boy, Bucky." To Ellie, he said, "Stump, dead ahead." Firming his grip on her arm, he steered her around the obstacle. "Dead-fall. Step high."

"This is a nightmare." Like a blind woman groping her way, she moved cautiously forward. "I won't see a tree until I walk right into it."

"Trust me. I like that cute little nose too much to let you smash it."

The words were out before Tucker could stop them. He felt Ellie stiffen and draw away from him. What had possessed him to say that? Habit, he guessed. In happier times, he'd always loved her nose and teased her about it every chance he got.

Tucker couldn't say his taste had changed much; he still liked her nose. Compared to his high-bridged honker, it was impossibly dainty with small nostrils and a turned-up tip. When they had kissed—well, he probably shouldn't go there, he decided. If he started remembering how soft and pliable her nose had felt beneath his own, he might start remembering how soft and sweet she'd felt everywhere else. Not a good plan. He and Ellie were history, and things like that were best forgotten.

His traitorous mind didn't seem to recognize the danger. Despite his attempt to hold them at bay, memories assailed him. He saw himself at sixteen, rubbing noses with Ellie and cracking jokes to break the ice before he kissed her for the first time. What a smooth operator he'd been. Then later, after kissing became old hat, she allowed him to touch her breast—she'd been so shy, he so clumsy, their breathing ragged, their young bodies throbbing with needs neither of them completely understood.

After going a year with a perpetual erection, he'd

finally made love to her one night down by the river, an encounter that had cost him all three of the condoms he had on hand—not because he got lucky that many times, but because, in his eagerness, he managed to destroy two of the devices before he ever got them on. Later he wondered if the rubbers had rotted with age; after all, he'd been carrying the damned things in his wallet for nine months.

Remembering, Tucker smiled in the darkness, a gesture that soon became a grimace. Beneath his hand, Ellie's arm was rigid with tension. Was she recalling similar incidents herself? Memory lane, all because he'd made a stupid remark about her nose? *Damn*. They shared a history that had encompassed half their lives. What was he supposed to do, erase all those events from his mind?

It wasn't happening. In order to do that, he'd have to forget some very precious moments, like holding each of his sons for the first time. There were some memories he couldn't and didn't want to turn loose, memories that made him who he was, that would remain with him until he died.

"You know, Ellie, we aren't strangers."

She threw a startled look in his general direction. "Pardon?"

His gut clenched with irritation. "Is that the way you're going to play it?"

"Play what?"

Patience was a virtue, he reminded himself. "This conversation."

"I didn't realize we were having a conversation."

She moved even farther away from him, which hiked her captured arm to an awkward angle. Tucker would have loosened his grip, but he feared she might fall. "Rocks," he bit out, hauling her back toward him to guide her around the pile. "Would you stop trying to put distance between us? I don't bite, and I've had all my shots. It's an obstacle course out here. Tree."

She braked to a sudden halt and patted the darkness ahead of her. "Where?"

He chuckled in spite of himself. "Three feet, dead ahead." Bucky danced around them as Tucker tugged her back into a walk. "I like your nose too much to let you smash it, remember."

"Would you stop? You don't like anything about me anymore, and you very well know it."

She made that accusation with such conviction that it gave Tucker pause. It also made him feel incredibly sad. "I don't dislike you, Ellie."

"Right. You can't even talk to me without taking nasty shots."

"And you take none at me?"

She squeaked in alarm when her toe caught on a limb. "Do we have to have this conversation right now? I need all my concentration to navigate."

"I'll navigate. And, no, we don't have to have this conversation now if you'd rather not. Just understand that if we're going to be together all day tomorrow and possibly the next, I'm bound to say things now and again that maybe you'd rather I didn't. We were married for thirteen years. I can't watch every word I say so as not to remind you of that."

"I can handle occasional reminders, Tucker." Her hip bumped his thigh as they rounded another obstacle. "I'd just appreciate it if you would leave my nose out of it."

Tucker knew his comment about her nose had started this, but it didn't seem pivotal to the conversation now. "Your nose? Why?"

She dragged to a stop again and threw the tree directly behind him an exasperated look. "Because it has sexual connotations."

"Your *nose*?"

Even in the darkness, he saw her eyes spark with anger. Tucker was glad it was the tree taking the heat and not him. "You know very well what I mean. It was always a private joke between us, rubbing noses and making baby snots and all of that."

For a moment, he couldn't think what to say. Typical. She always had been able to wrap his tongue around a post and do a tap dance on the flapping end when they quarreled. "Noses aren't exactly erotic body parts."

"They were to us."

"We were just kids, for Pete's sake."

"Kids who grew up and—" She threw up her hands. "Oh, never mind. And you accuse me of playing dumb?"

"Okay," he conceded, "the nose thing once had sexual connotations. I admit it. But that isn't the point, is it?"

"That's *exactly* the point."

"No. The point is your reaction to an innocent remark. The nose thing was always a joke between us. It just popped out. Why get all bent out of shape about it?"

Tucker no sooner asked that question than he realized it was the crux of the entire issue—yet another piece of an emerging puzzle that baffled and intrigued him. Her tension electrified the air between them, and he had a hunch it wasn't only the topic of conversation that had her upset. Beneath his hand, her arm was still rigid, as if his slightest touch unsettled her. Even as he led her around obstacles, she tried to keep distance between them.

"I am not bent out of shape."

Her body language called her a liar. Keeping a firm grip on her arm, Tucker filed that observation away for later. For now, he had his job cut out for him just getting her back to camp. As though to drive that home, she stepped into a hole just then and emitted a breathless *harrumph*. He hauled her up onto level ground again. "You okay?"

She touched her fingertips to her lips. "I bit my tongue."

Tucker was beginning to wish he'd had the good sense to bite his own. If his suspicions were correct, he needed to be damned sure he wanted to deal with the outcome before he confronted her with any of them.

"Rock, northwest."

She panned the darkness. "Can you speak in terms of left, right, and straight ahead?"

"Straightish-leftish." He chuckled in spite of himself. "More leftish, actually."

"Thank you."

"Please tell me you didn't make sense of that."

"I made perfect sense of it."

"No wonder I never understood you."

She smiled slightly. "Yes, well, I never understood you, either—so there."

Even though he'd only meant it as a joke and she had responded in kind, Tucker wondered if lack of understanding hadn't been more of a problem between them than either of them had realized, possibly even the entire cause of their divorce. Right brain versus left brain, and all that. Only that afternoon, he'd been grumping to himself about how everything was about emotions with her while he tended to be analytical. It was such an elemental difference between them, one that caused problems sometimes, even when they'd loved each other.

Right after Sammy's death, he'd been so filled with pain that he'd gone on autopilot and concentrated on details to keep from breaking down—funeral arrangements, financial concerns, the day-to-day practicalities of caring for children and running a household while Ellie was incapacitated by shock and grief. At the time, it had seemed so important to him to hold it together and be strong for her. He'd been afraid to talk about his feelings for fear he'd fall apart. Men didn't cry. His father had drilled that into his head all his life, and he'd been determined to be the husband Ellie deserved during that time. In so doing, had he failed to be there for her the way she'd needed him to be?

Tucker didn't know. He honestly didn't know. That fact left him shaken in a way he hadn't experienced in three years.

Her breath coming in little puffs, she pulled to a stop and pushed at her hair. "I need to rest."

Tucker released her arm. "No problem. We can take five."

Bucky bumped against her legs. She bent to pet him. When she straightened, her eyes were wide and searching in the moonlight, unfocused even after she found his face. Tucker knew she couldn't see him clearly. That suited him just fine, for it gave him a chance to study her upturned features. He began with the nose he'd once loved so much, then journeyed to her soft, sweetly curved mouth, the point of her small chin, and the hollows of her fragile cheekbones. Even with her hair chopped off like a boy's and wearing clothing more suited to a man, she was completely and utterly feminine, the top of her fair head barely clearing his shoulder.

As if she sensed his perusal, she tugged at her jacket and straightened the collar of her shirt, her fingers traveling down to check all the buttons. For a woman who had so firmly closed the door on the past, she was awfully fidgety, he decided.

If that wasn't a result of sexual awareness, he'd eat his two-hundred-dollar hiking boots.

By the time Ellie and Tucker got back to the main camp, Marvin had prepared a fine meal of steak and baked potatoes, complete with a rich-bodied wine. They stood around the fire, eating the food from paper plates and drinking the wine from clear plastic cups. At any other time, Ellie might have enjoyed the novelty. It wasn't often that she was served a good steak and cabernet on a camping trip. Unfortunately, she was still so rattled from being alone with Tucker that she found it impossible to relax.

What was it about him, anyway? With one look from those intense hazel eyes, he could set her heart to pounding. With a mere brush of his fingertips, he could make her skin tingle with awareness. Just the deep timbre of his voice in the darkness had wreaked havoc with her nerve endings.

Pretending to be completely focused on her meal, Ellie studied him surreptitiously. He stood at the opposite side of the fire, his long, muscular legs braced apart. Balancing his plate on one broad palm, his wine cup clasped to his chest by his forearm, he looked at ease and completely in control. No struggling to cut his steak, no near spills of the wine. He was as comfortable out here as the creatures in the woods around them.

In the firelight, his hair gleamed like molten bronze, the waves that fell across his high forehead tipped with gold. Each time he chewed, his jaw muscle bunched. Everything about him was overpowering, from the way he stood, to the set of his broad shoulders, and even to the way he held his head.

He glanced up and caught her staring at him. The piece of steak she was chewing turned to rubber. His firm mouth twitched at one corner. His eyes warmed with teasing laughter. She tried to look away, but for the life of her, she couldn't. She swallowed the rubbery clump of meat and almost choked.

A feeling of wetness on her left breast jolted her back to her senses. She glanced down to see that she'd tipped her cup and sloshed wine down the front of herself. Fiery heat flooded her face. She hurried over to the trunk of the Honda.

Stupid, stupid, stupid. Now he really would have reason to laugh at her. Reluctant to set aside the wine for fear it might spill on the supplies and gear, she balanced her half-empty plate on Marvin's jar of peanut butter and kept hold of her glass. After managing to tear off a paper towel with only one hand, she scrubbed angrily at her shirt, hoping the cabernet hadn't soaked through to her bra, yet another lacy souvenir from her marriage. A stained bra might seem like a small thing to some people, but she couldn't afford another.

"Need some help?"

At the unexpected sound of Tucker's deep voice next to her ear, Ellie squeaked in surprise. Her left hand jerked, almost causing her to slosh more wine on herself. "Do you have to sneak up on me like that?"

"I didn't sneak."

His big, dark hand reached past her for the roll of towels. He jerked off a wad and leaned around to help dab at her shirt. One pass, two. Her nipple snapped to attention and was chanting *semper fidelis* before he made the third swipe.

She caught his wrist. "Do you mind?"

He stopped and flicked her a knowing look. "Not in the least. Just helping to clean up my mess. It was my fault you spilled it, after all."

"No, it wasn't."

"Sure it was." Swipe, swipe. On the sixth pass, his gaze dropped to the protuberance of her nipple that thrust against the damp flannel. He gave it a final rub, lifted his gaze to hers, and flashed a crooked grin. "It appears I still have one friend in the enemy camp."

Ellie almost doused him with the rest of her cabernet. As if he guessed what she was thinking, he slipped the cup from her rigid fingers and drained it in one gulp, his Adam's apple taking a sexy downward plunge as he finished swallowing. Still grinning, he returned the empty container.

"Better in me than on me."

She glared after him as he returned to the fire. Her face pulsated with heat. Just then, the cup snapped in her tightening grip, the sound going off in her ears like the report of a gun. She quickly tossed it in the trunk so no one would see.

Once back at the fire, she remembered her plate of food, still on the jar of peanut butter. Liz glared at her with green eyes that glittered with animosity. Marvin kept shooting her sideways glances, as if he'd just caught her and Tucker doing the dirty behind a bush. Ellie wished the evening were over. Her nerves were frayed. Her mood was grim. When she felt like this, the only thing to do was sleep it off.

To her dismay, she noticed that Tucker was studying her over the top of the licking flames. After searching her face for what seemed an endless moment, he dropped his gaze to the front of her shirt. When Ellie noticed his eyes shifting from left to right, she looked down to see what on earth was the matter.

The moment she dipped her chin, she wished she hadn't. Her right nipple barely showed, but the left one still stood at attention like a soldier at muster. She tried to tell herself it was a simple reaction to the chill air and dampness, but deep down, she knew better. Judging by the twinkle in Tucker's eyes, so did he.

Stepping over to the camp stove, he poured himself more wine. Or so she thought until he came to stand beside her and proffered the cup.

"No, thanks. I've had enough."

"Ah, come on. One side of you is still bone dry. For the sake of symmetry, if nothing else, you should have some more."

Ellie barely resisted the urge to smack the bottom of the cup. "It isn't what you think."

His eyes danced with devilment. In a voice pitched for her ears alone, he said, "Tell it to your mother. She may buy it."

After dinner was over and the mess had been cleared away, Tucker lighted a lantern, suspended it from a tree limb, and straddled a fallen log to study his topographical map.

Liz settled in close against his bent leg and began rubbing his back. Every pass of her fingernails raked his nerves the wrong way. He couldn't stay focused and kept losing his place. Finally, when he could bear the distraction no longer, he shifted away from her.

"Don't take this wrong, Liz, but I need to be alone right now."

She stiffened. "How can I not take that wrong?"

Tucker sighed. "I'm sorry. Try to understand, okay? It's been a really long day. I just need some space, that's all."

Her expression went soft with sympathy. Tucker had seen the sudden transformation before.

"Oh, of *course*," she crooned. "You poor baby."

"Thanks for understanding. You're a sport."

She beamed a smile, patted his cheek. "If you need me later, just holler. I'll be glad to help."

He glanced at his watch. "When I'm finished here, I plan to hit the sack. I'm totally beat."

She glanced around to locate Ellie, who was walking toward her tent. Apparently satisfied that her arch rival was about to retire, she yawned and nodded. "I'm pretty pooped myself." She leaned forward to give him a good night peck on the same cheek she'd just patted and stood up. "I guess I'll turn in."

"Good night, Liz. Have a good rest."

She gave him a warm, inviting look. "If counting sheep gets monotonous, you know where to find me."

"I'm too tired to do much sheep counting tonight."

Tucker watched her walk away. She swung her hips in such an exaggerated way, he was afraid she might throw her back out. He shook his head and returned his attention to the map. As he studied the trails that led to Tabletop, his thoughts drifted to his sons. This was their second night alone in the wilderness area. Tucker could only hope they were okay and that they would remain that way until he found them.

Kody's elbow was poking Zach in the ribs. When Zach tried to put some distance between their bodies, his little brother only squirmed closer. They'd been lying at the top of the ridge, watching their father's camp, for nearly an hour. Zach had a leg cramp from being still for so long, the icy chill of the ground had made his skin get goose bumps, and his belly itched from the pine needles that poked through his T-shirt. He didn't need any more aggravations.

"Move away, dumb butt," he whispered. "Your elbow hurts."

"It's dark out here." Kody wiggled closer yet. "Let's go back to our camp."

"It'll be just as dark there," Zach pointed out. "In so close, if we light a fire, Dad might see."

"I'm scared." Kody glanced fearfully over his shoulder. "What if a cougar gets us?"

"No cougar will get us," Zach said with far more certainty than he felt. In this small clearing, there was moonlight, but all around them, the woods were ominously dark. If anything sneaked up on them, they wouldn't know until it pounced. Zach's only consolation was that their dad was within shouting distance. "With all the large game in this area, the cougars have plenty to eat. They only jump humans when they're starving."

"I'm *scared*," Kody said again.

"You're never scared when Dad's with us."

"Dad's bigger than you, and he's strong. And he carries a gun for just in case. All you have is your pocketknife."

Though Zach would never admit it to Kody, he was scared, too. It was different, being out in the woods at night without their father. He always watched out for them and knew exactly what to do if something went wrong. Now that was Zach's responsibility.

Kody shivered. "I'm getting cold."

"Why didn't you bring your jacket?" Zach asked, even though he'd left his own back at their camp.

"It didn't feel that cold earlier."

Zach gave up on escaping his brother's elbow and moved closer. They might stay warmer if they shared each other's body heat.

"I'm hungry, too," Kody complained.

"Eat your chocolate bar."

"I already did."

Zach dug in his back pocket. "Here. You can have mine. Just remember I gave it to you. That's the last of the candy we got at the store yesterday. All the rest is that yucky stuff from Dad's house."

Kody made rustling sounds as he peeled away the wrapping. The smell of the warm chocolate drifted to Zach's nose, making his mouth water.

Kody stared downhill, watching their parents while he chewed. "Why do you think Mom and Dad brought Marvin and Liz?" he asked. "They'll ruin everything."

"Shh," Zach warned in a whisper. "Sound carries at night. You want them to hear you?"

Kody sighed. "Don't you get it? Dad can't make Mom fall in love with him again if Marvin and Liz are breathing down his neck. For this to work, they've got to be alone."

Right now, Liz and Marvin were the least of Zach's worries. "We can't let Bucky stay with Dad."

"Why not?"

"Because he'll lead Dad straight to us."

Kody considered that for a moment before whispering, "Uh-oh."

"Uh-oh is right. After they all go to sleep, we have to sneak down there and get him."

"But they might not go to bed for a long, long time, and it's spooky up here."

Zach ruffled his brother's hair the way he'd seen their father do. "Don't be afraid, Kody. Remember what Dad says; darkness is just the absence of light. Nothing's going to hurt us out here. If anything happens, we can holler for Dad. We're going to be fine."

Just then a twig snapped behind them. Zach tensed and scanned the darkness, staring so hard his eyes burned.

"What was that?" Kody asked.

Zach knew it could be any number of things: a deer possibly, or maybe even a bear. "Just the wind," he lied. "A limb broke."

His brother relaxed slightly. Zach wished there were someone to tell him comforting lies. He didn't like being out here all alone any better than Kody did. After a long moment, he gave voice to a thought that had been plaguing him.

"Maybe this was a bad move," he whispered. "Dad and Mom aren't going to get back together with Marvin and Liz along."

Kody flashed him a miserable look. "They *have* to get back together."

A tight feeling filled Zach's throat. He wanted their folks back together, too, but he was getting old enough to realize that the situation might be more complicated than either of them understood. Ever since Sammy died, their folks had gotten everything all twisted around inside their heads, blaming themselves and each other and saying awful stuff. Zach figured they needed counseling to iron things out between them, and even then, he wondered if they'd ever love each other the same way again. Some things hurt so badly, you just never got over them.

As if he guessed Zach's thoughts, Kody knotted his fists and tucked his elbows close to his body. "You big quitter. It's only the second night, and already you want to go home."

"I'm no quitter!" Zach winced at the loudness of his own voice. Hunching his shoulders around his ears, he lowered his pitch to add, "I'm just facing facts. Your plan can't work while Marvin and Liz are here."

"Then we gotta get rid of them."

"How?"

Kody frowned. In the moonlight, the creases that appeared on his forehead looked like lines from a black felt marker. "I don't know. We have to think of a way." He stared down at the camp below them, his mouth pursed in thought. "Maybe if we play a bunch of really mean tricks, Liz and Marvin will get mad and leave."

Zach figured it was a long shot, but he didn't have a better idea. "What kind of tricks?"

Chapter Eight

Tucker was intent on studying the forestry map again when the scuff of a footstep snapped his gaze to the left. Blinded by the lantern light, he squinted, half expecting to see Liz emerge from the shadows. He'd had about all he could take of her femme fatale routine. If she started in on him again, he was going to tell her, in no uncertain terms, that he wasn't interested, would never be interested, and wanted to be left alone.

"Tucker?"

At the sound of Ellie's voice, the tension knotting the muscles across his shoulders immediately eased. When she emerged from the fire-washed darkness, he said, "Hi. I thought you'd gone to bed."

"I started to." She gestured behind her. "Marvin's making so much noise putting up his tent that I figured I might as well wait."

She stepped closer, the wispy ends of her tousled hair shining like platinum in the lantern light. Judging by the thin set of her mouth, she was still a little miffed at him. Tucker didn't suppose he could blame her. He'd been pretty high-handed with her up at the lake, and his behavior during dinner hadn't been exemplary, either. He wasn't sure what had possessed him to flirt with her that way, but he'd greatly enjoyed her reaction.

"Ellie, about this evening."

She held up a staying hand. "I'm not here to discuss that, and I'd just as soon we didn't."

The blanket statement intrigued him. "Which part?"

A tiny frown pleated her brows. "Excuse me?"

"Which part of the evening are you not here to discuss?"

The creases between her brows deepened to furrows. "All parts."

Anchoring the map with his knees, he sat back to regard her expressive face. The mutinous set of her small chin had him biting back a smile. He wondered which of his offenses had pissed her off the most, the ultimatum he'd given her at the lake or his behavior by the fire. For reasons beyond him, he hoped it was the latter. "I'd like to apologize."

Her gaze chased from his, and she lifted her slender shoulders in a shrug. "That isn't necessary."

"Maybe not necessary, but I'll feel better."

She lifted her fair brows. "All the more reason not to let you."

Tucker chuckled in spite of himself. He'd felt the same way in reverse enough times to appreciate the humor. "From my standpoint, it's all the more reason to insist on it. I'm sorry, Ellie. I was pretty autocratic up at the lake."

Her irises darkened to so vivid a blue, they were almost violet. "Yes, you were."

"And I was out of line during dinner, as well."

Her cheeks pinkened, and her gaze went chasing off again. After a moment, she bent her head, hugged her waist, and made circles in the dirt with the toe of her boot. "Apology accepted."

Silence. He rubbed his hands over his thighs. It felt good to say he was sorry and receive absolution. So good, in fact, that he could only wonder why those two simple words had been so difficult for him to say over the last three years.

"I, um . . ." She scrubbed her palms over the hips of her jeans. "I said some things I shouldn't have, too. For all our difficulties, I know you love our boys and that you're as worried about them as I am."

"I'm worried, yes, but probably not quite as much as you are. I have the advantage of knowing first-hand how self-sufficient they are out there. If I were in a tight spot and given a choice between a grown man or one of those boys to get me out of it, I'd choose one of the boys."

"Really?" Her eyes clung to his. "You're not just saying that to ease my mind?"

"Nope. I trained them myself. They may not have a man's strength, but they're ace woodsmen." He smiled. "And they've both got their mother's brains."

She gave a startled laugh. "God help them. I'm lousy at wilderness stuff."

"Only because you've never cared enough to apply yourself. Tonight proved that. When push came to shove, you picked up their trail like a pro. I was impressed. In that kind of terrain with such a thick layer of pine needles to blur the trail, it takes skill not to lose it. There were several places where the prints disappeared completely, but you managed to find them again."

"I zigzagged back and forth the way you do. It wasn't that hard."

"Good job."

Looking pleased, she tipped her head to study the map. "I didn't mean to interrupt. I was just wondering what your strategy is for tomorrow."

Pointing to a large triangular shape, he said, "I'm studying the lay of the land leading up to Tabletop, trying to decide where they may have headed in. There are three trails they could have taken, all of which merge about halfway up."

She leaned closer to peruse the topography. After touching a fingertip to the spot he'd indicated, she asked, "Where are we right now, exactly?"

She was the only person Tucker knew who would ask where she was with a map of the area directly under her nose. During their marriage, he'd teased her about her lousy sense of direction and secretly loved her the more for it.

He indicated their location. "There's the highway we came in on this evening. Here's the dirt road we took to get where we are right now."

"How can you tell that's a dirt road?"

"If you aren't sure of the symbols, you can look them up over here." He showed her the legend and the type of line that designated unpaved byways. "I know it's confusing. Forestry maps are so busy, they look like chicken scratch."

"The writing's so small I can barely read it." She shifted her gaze back and forth from the legend to the map. "My goodness, are all those squiggly things between here and the mountain *hills*?"

Tucker struggled not to grin. That was another thing he'd always enjoyed about her, the ability she had to make him laugh when he least expected it. "Don't you remember going up there?"

"Of course. You have to hike through that awful canyon to reach the top, don't you?"

He took heart, thinking she remembered, after all. "That's right."

"And to reach the canyon, we have to walk up all those hills first?"

Tucker could only wonder where she had been all the times she'd hiked up there with him. Daydreaming, he guessed. She was a fine one for thinking deep thoughts while she did other things. Once, while musing over the contrast between deep red and pink, the colors some lady wanted in her bathroom, she'd nearly stepped on a rattlesnake.

"Yes, extremely *steep* hills. I'll warn you right now, Ellie, it's going to be an endurance test getting up there. If you don't think you and Marvin can make it, I'd advise you not to come."

"My sons are out there. I don't know if they're warm. I don't know if they have food. I'll keep up. Nothing—and I do mean *nothing*—is going to stop me from helping to find them."

He understood how worried she was. Nevertheless, he had legitimate concerns they needed to address. He inclined his head toward Marvin's half-erected tent at the opposite side of the clearing. "How about lover boy?"

For reasons he didn't care to analyze, he wished she would correct him and admit the man wasn't her lover. Instead, she merely said, "What about him?"

"He's not in the best physical shape."

"Looks can be deceiving."

"He's no nature enthusiast, Ellie. What if he falls behind and loses his way? The success of this search is going to depend on teamwork, with everyone carrying his or her own weight. If there's a possibility he might get lost, I'd just as soon leave him here."

Her eyes sparkled like prisms in the firelight. "Liz isn't exactly what I'd call a team player." She let that hang there for a moment. "Should we leave her behind, as well?"

Just that quickly, and they were at loggerheads again. It frustrated Tucker because they'd once gotten along so well. Thinking back, he could count the serious fights they'd had during their marriage on the fingers of one hand. Now they couldn't seem to discuss much of anything without one or both of them growing angry.

Why was that? They were the same two people. They undoubtedly still held many of the same opinions. Yet, for no apparent reason he could see, they disagreed about almost everything now.

"At least Liz knows how to find her own way. That's more than I can say for Marvin. Be fair about this, Ellie. I doubt the guy's gone camping in years."

Ellie was about to argue when she heard aluminum clanking. She glanced over her shoulder. A muttered curse drifted through the darkness.

"See what I mean?" Tucker said with a sarcastic edge to his voice.

"Some of those old-fashioned tents are very tricky to put together," she reminded him. "Just because—" Another curse rang out, cutting her short. Growing concerned, she turned toward the sound. "I better go see if I can help."

"You want me to come lend a hand?"

If not for the I-told-you-so smirk on his face, Ellie might have accepted the offer. "I think we can manage. We're both college graduates, after all."

Amusement warmed his expression. "I didn't realize they taught tent assembly in college."

Ellie didn't dignify that with a response. When she reached the sagging tent a few seconds later, she found Marvin inside, arms stretched above his head to support the aluminum framework. Ducking inside with him, she asked, "What seems to be the problem?"

Straining under the weight of the canvas, Marvin said, "I think a piece is missing or something."

Ellie craned her neck to see through the shadows. "It looks to me as if some of the poles are just in the wrong place." She reached up to check. "That's it, I think. This one goes there, and that one, here."

"You're right. I've got them hooked together wrong."

Before Ellie could think what he meant to do, he disconnected one joint. Left with insufficient support, the canvas came crashing down. Ellie felt as if a massive boulder hit her. The next instant, without knowing quite how she'd gotten there, she lay flattened under an oppressive weight with darkness all around her. Somewhere nearby, Marvin thrashed and grunted, and with his every movement, the pressure on her increased. For a moment, she thought he had fallen partially on top of her. Then she realized he only had a section of the side panel under him, the effect of which was to pull the canvas more tightly over her body each time he moved.

"Marvin, be still! You're squashing me." She struggled onto her side, hoping to find an escape route. She found only a rectangle of window mesh, which smashed against her face. "Don't roll any farther my way," she managed to say. "You're pulling the canvas tighter. I can barely breathe."

"Like I know which way is which?"

The tarp cinched tighter. Ellie was starting to feel as if she were in a straightjacket.

Tucker heard the tent collapse. There followed a collection of grunts and curses. It sounded to him as if the college graduates were experiencing a spot of trouble.

"Tucker!" called a muffled feminine voice. "Can you come here?"

After anchoring the map with a rock, Tucker swung off the log and started across the clearing. Once he circled the fire and could see more clearly, he had to swallow back laughter. Marvin's tent had collapsed, all right, with both of them inside it.

Tucker determined that the larger, undulating mass had to be Marvin. Judging by the clanking sounds, he was doing the horizontal tango with several tent poles. The smaller lump wasn't wiggling nearly as much, undoubtedly because Marvin's weight had her pinned full-length under the canvas.

"Well, this is a heck of a fix for two college grads to find themselves in," he couldn't resist saying.

"No wisecracks," was Ellie's muffled response.

When Tucker reached the tent, he bent forward at the waist, braced his hands on his knees, and said, "Hey, Ellie, you in there?"

"Of course I'm in here." She twitched and then went still. Now that he was closer, Tucker could make out the unmistakable outline of a shapely hip and leg under the dusty green canvas. "Don't just stand there, Tucker. Help us out."

"Point me in the right direction, and maybe I will. I can't see the door."

"If I knew where it was, don't you think I'd crawl that way?"

Tucker skirted the tarpaulin. He chuckled when he saw her face behind a window insert. Her nose and mouth were flattened and pulled into contorted shapes by the netting. Grimacing as she struggled under the weight, she curled her lips back to say, "This is *not* funny."

"I guess that depends which side of the canvas you're on. From out here, it's pretty funny."

Her eyes narrowed to slits. "Are you going to help us or not?"

Tucker waded out onto the collapsed tenting. "Stop thrashing, Marvin. I don't want to step on you." He pulled up a section of tarpaulin and ran it through his hands in search of the doorway. When he found it, he tossed the flap back and thrust his arm through the opening. "Grab hold, partner, and I'll give you a hand."

Marvin grunted and cursed. The next instant, they locked grips, and Tucker pulled him out. Ellie heaved a shrill sigh of relief. "I can breathe again. Thank you, God."

Grasping each corner of the sagging doorway, Tucker lifted it up to peer inside. Firelight coming through the canvas faintly illuminated the interior.

On hands and knees, Ellie emerged from under a section of tarp, her blond hair in a stir, her pixie face smudged with dirt. She crawled straight toward him and exited the tent between his spread legs. When Tucker glanced down, all he saw was her denim-clad fanny. He decided it was her best feature. Well—one of them, anyway.

"Thank you for your help," she said as she struggled to her feet. "Though I have to say, you took your own sweet time about giving it."

"Some moments are meant to be savored," he told her with a wink.

Long after lights out, Tucker lay awake, watching the flickering light of the campfire play over the walls of his tent. He could hear Liz snoring softly in the shelter next to his, but that wasn't what kept him from sleep. No matter how he tried to block them out, images of Ellie kept circling through his mind.

He'd been so afraid for her this evening when he'd been tracking her through the woods and it had started to grow dark. His only thought had been to find her before she got lost or hurt. He could tell himself it was because he didn't want to get stuck raising two boys alone, or because she was still, in some perverse way, a driving force in his life. But deep down, he knew that wasn't the whole truth. Up there on that mountain, when all his defenses had been stripped away by fear, he'd come face-to-face with the unvarnished and unwelcome truth, that he had never stopped loving her.

That was why he'd given her a hard time by the fire tonight and followed her to the trunk of her car to further bedevil her—because he still loved her. The realization had frightened him and made him furiously angry with himself. Instead of dealing with that in a rational, adult way, he'd resorted to tormenting her like an ornery ten-year-old boy.

He angled his arm over his forehead and clenched his teeth, cursing himself for a fool. It was over between them. Over. What the hell was he thinking, that this crisis with the boys might somehow get them back together? It wasn't going to happen. Why couldn't he just accept that? If he allowed himself to start thinking otherwise, he'd only be inviting more heartbreak.

Over the last three years, Tucker had endured enough pain to last him a lifetime. He wasn't about to set himself up for more.

That decided, he squeezed his eyes closed and paced his breathing, determined to go to sleep. All he saw was her face as it had looked earlier that evening—her beautiful eyes, her sweet mouth, and those impossibly fragile cheekbones. He tried to tell himself she wasn't all that pretty, that compared to Liz she rated about a three on a scale of one to ten. But facts were facts. Liz didn't appeal to him the way Ellie did. He loved her compact body. He loved her face. God help him, he even loved the way she stuck that sexy little nose in the air when she looked at him.

He rolled onto his side and hugged his sleeping bag to his chest, which only served to remind him of how he'd once held her in his arms as he drifted off to sleep. He could recall everything about her in vivid detail—how her soft little butt had felt, pressed against him—how her small breasts had been perfectly shaped to fit in his hand—how her breath had always hitched when he touched her nipple.

The memories made him want to jump up and make a beeline for her tent. Only then what? She wasn't his wife anymore. He had no rights, period. What did he plan to do, kiss her senseless and make love to her before she realized what hit her?

As the thought slipped into his mind, Tucker recalled how her nipple had hardened tonight when he grazed it with the paper towel. It had probably been nothing but an involuntary reaction. But what if it had been something more? He remembered how her cheeks had flushed and her body had stiffened, both sure signs that she'd been embarrassed. If it had meant nothing, why had it embarrassed her so?

He rolled back over to stare at the ceiling, once again tormenting himself with questions that all began with, "What if?" What if she still had feelings for him, just as he did for her? What if there was a chance, however minuscule, that they might patch things up and try again?

The very thought made Tucker nervous. If he allowed these feelings a foothold and she told him to take a flying leap, he wasn't sure he could handle it. On the other hand, though, what did he really have to lose? He'd already lost everything that had ever mattered a damn to him—his wife, his kids, and the life he'd worked so hard to build. Was he really such a coward that he was afraid to take a chance when he had so much to gain?

Tucker was his own worst critic, and he knew he had a lot of faults, but being a coward wasn't one of them. His boys were out there somewhere, all alone in the dark, gambling with their safety to get their parents back together. In light of that, how could he not, in good conscience, at least try to make that happen? If Ellie laughed in his face, it would hurt, no question about it. But at least he'd know he hadn't given up without a fight.

Leading the way, Zach crawled on his stomach the last few feet to their parents' camp. Kody slithered along behind him, the only sound he made an occasional soft grunt as he pulled himself over the ground. Holding his breath, Zach stopped to listen. *So far, so good.* It was sort of cool, actually, hearing so many snores all at once. He recognized his dad's, a rhythmic rumble and *whoo* that was unmistakable. From the opposite side of the waning fire, Marvin was really getting into it, too, making a whistling sound, then exhaling with a strangled sputter. Liz and his mom snored more softly, soft little huffs instead of snorts.

Kody crawled up beside him and flashed a pleased grin. "Listen," he whispered. "Mom and Dad still keep time with each other."

Zach cocked an ear toward their mom's tent. It was true, he realized. She was breathing in time with their dad, inhaling and releasing at exactly the same time.

"That's gotta be a sign," Kody murmured. "They're meant for each other."

Zach hoped Kody was right; otherwise, his parents were going to murder him. But that was a worry for later. Right now, he and Kody had work to do.

Bucky trotted from their dad's tent to greet them. Sitting up, Zach curled a hand over the dog's muzzle, a command to be quiet that their father had taught him. The shepherd shivered with delight but didn't make a sound.

"Good dog," Kody whispered. "You're the best, Bucky, the very best."

Using hand signals, Zach told Kody it was time for them to get started. They'd discussed their strategy up on the ridge, and they each had jobs to do. First on Zach's list was to slip inside his mom's tent and put some stuff in her backpack. Kody's was to quietly get in her car, pop the trunk, and search through the grocery items for something they could use to play pranks.

Zach's mission was riskier by far. His mom was a light sleeper. If he accidentally woke her up, it'd be all over. Being as quiet as possible, he crawled over to her tent and carefully lifted the flap. To his horror, Bucky followed him inside. Zach huddled in the corner, cringing when the Australian shepherd advanced on his mother's sleeping bag.

"Mmm," she murmured. "Go 'way, Bucky."

Zach expected her to suddenly sit up, point a finger, and say, "Ah-ha! Caught you!" He imagined his dad, grabbing him by the collar and demanding an explanation. Bucky was going to ruin everything. Zach felt sure of it.

Only his mom just petted the dog, rolled over, and jerked the sleeping bag over her head. "Good dog. Go 'way, now. Pester Tucker. Leave me alone."

Still crouched in the shadows, Zach grinned with relief. *Way to go, Bucky.* Even if his mom heard a strange noise, she probably wouldn't uncover her head now. She'd just think it was Bucky and ignore it.

He went straight to work. Seconds later when he slithered back outside, he saw Kody standing at the opposite side of the fire. In his uplifted hands, he held a gallon-size bottle of pancake syrup and a roll of toilet paper. Zach had to cup a hand over his mouth to keep from giggling. He gave his brother a thumbs-up and nodded.

This was going to be fun.

At first light the next morning, Ellie jerked awake to the sound of Tucker's deep voice.

"Wake up, everybody!" he yelled. "We overslept. Time to hit the deck!"

Ellie groaned. Eyes too bleary with sleep to read her watch, she squinted at the faint sunlight coming through the wall of her tent. Though she knew they should have been up before dawn, she wanted to pull the bag over her head and go back to sleep. *The boys*, she reminded herself. To find them before sundown, they needed to start up the mountain as early as possible.

Even though she'd slept in her clothes again, she still shuddered with cold as she rolled from her sleeping bag and pulled on her boots. The floor of her tent was damp with dew. Her jacket felt like a wet lump of ice when she reached for it, and she tossed it aside with a groan. During their marriage, Tucker had at least tried to make her camping experiences bearable. Now she was on her own.

When she pushed back the flap of her tent, she

saw that the ground was white with frost. Had the boys grown cold during the night? Had they taken enough food? Were they warming themselves by a fire even now, wishing they'd never pulled this crazy stunt?

"Bucky!" she heard Tucker call. "Here, boy!" After a moment of silence, he muttered, "That damn dog. Where the hell has he gotten off to?" He followed the question with a shrill whistle. "Here, boy! Come on! Here, Bucky!"

Ellie rubbed her arms as she stepped outside. Even though the icy bite in the air was forbidding, she took a moment to absorb the scenery around her. Its beauty made her forget the hardships of camping. The massive trunks of the old-growth Ponderosa rose like giant cinnamon sticks around the clearing, the boughs at their tops forming a flocked canopy over the forest floor. Unlike in the valley, the undergrowth here was far less dense, revealing a carpet of golden-brown pine needles that formed a perfect backdrop for the muted sage and the shiny green leaves of manzanita and slick leaf. Countless species of birds and squirrels heralded the new day with cheerful voices, the chorus creating a symphonic melody that fell easy on the ears.

She hauled in a deep breath, savoring the scents that drifted on the air, a blend of pine, sage, and a faint trace of vanilla. Taking stock of the pines, she thought she'd never seen anything so lovely. Sunlight shone down through the branches, the silvery shafts igniting the morning mist to form iridescent streamers. It was like waking up in a magical wonderland.

At the edge of camp, Tucker stood in one of the

shafts of sunlight. Legs spread, hands resting at his hips, he looked deliciously masculine, his denim-clad frame emanating strength. A nimbus of gold formed a halo around his tawny hair. The chill breeze sifted through the strands, making her fingers itch to smooth them.

"Bucky!" he yelled again. Glancing over his shoulder at Ellie, he said, "I'm worried."

The flick of his gaze made her skin tingle and her heart jump. The tips of his hair looked damp, his jaw shiny. By that she knew he'd already washed up and shaved. Remembering the incident yesterday morning, she brushed a hand over the seat of her jeans and looked quickly away. "Do you think he's taken off?"

"It isn't like him not to come. That'll be the crowning disaster, if those kids lose that dog."

The crowning disaster. Ellie knew he was thinking of all else the kids had endured over the last three years, most recently being uprooted and moved to a strange town.

She peered through the trees, trying to spot a furry black splotch in the shadows. "Maybe he's just making his morning rounds."

"I don't think so. He never wanders very far."

When her visual search turned up nothing, Ellie hugged herself, frowned thoughtfully, and then reached a difficult decision. "Maybe we should put off leaving to go look for him, Tucker. You're right about the kids. If something happens to Bucky, it'll be the straw that broke the camel's back."

He nodded. "God knows we can't go without him. They'll never forgive me if I leave that dog behind."

Deciding that the first order of business was to get her fleece sweatshirt, Ellie made a beeline for her car. Halfway there, she heard Marvin cursing. Boots in hand, he stumbled from his tent in his stocking feet. There were large, damp-looking brown splotches all over his clothes, and with every step he took, his white socks collected clumps of dirt, debris, and pine needles.

"Son of a *bitch!*" He ran a hand over his hair, making the thinning strands stand up in stiff spikes. Staring incredulously at his splayed fingers, he touched his tongue to his palm. "*Syrup!* The little bastards doused me with pancake syrup!"

Ellie couldn't fathom what he meant. Tucker strode up to stand beside her, staring at Marvin with the same startled amazement she felt. "What do you mean? Who doused you with syrup?" he asked.

"Your *sons!*"

For a moment, Tucker looked baffled. Then understanding dawned in his eyes. "The boys have been here?" He flashed Ellie a relieved grin, the lines of tension on his dark face easing away. "Ellie, the boys have been here! That's where Bucky went. They must have taken him!"

Her heart lifting with gladness, Ellie spun to search the woods again. Even though she caught no sign of movement, she smiled, barely resisting the urge to clap her hands and dance around the fire. If the boys had visited their camp during the night, that meant they were still safe. "Oh, thank you, God!" she cried happily. "That's the best news I've had in two days!"

Tucker gave a joyful whoop and grabbed her up in his arms to swirl her in circles. "They can't be far away!" he said with a laugh. "They were right here in camp a few hours ago, Ellie! Isn't that fantastic?"

Ellie was so happy her eyes filled with tears. "They aren't hurt—or lost. They know *exactly* where they are! And even better, they know exactly where *we* are!"

"I've done good!" Tucker said proudly. "That Zach is a hell of a kid, isn't he? He'd run circles around most men out there!"

"You've done better than good, *much* better than good. They've been out there two whole nights. How many kids could do that without something awful happening?"

Tucker suddenly stopped swirling. His gaze locked warmly on hers, and the expression on his features softened. "You haven't done so bad yourself, Ellie girl," he whispered.

"Excuse me?" Marvin cried. "I hate to break up this touching scene, but this is not cause for a goddamn *celebration*!"

Like a dash of ice water, the realization crashed over Ellie that she was locked in Tucker's arms. She felt him stiffen at exactly the same instant. They both jerked their heads around to stare at Marvin, who was holding his sticky boots aloft like tagged evidence for the prosecution.

"Who gives a shit if those kids are okay?" he cried. "Look at me! Just *look* what they've done!"

Ellie was trying to think of an appropriate response when a bloodcurdling scream ripped at her senses, startling her half out of her wits. Jerking from Tucker's hold, she spun around to see Liz burst from her tent, flailing her arms and swatting at her head.

Long streamers of what looked suspiciously like toilet paper billowed around her, some stuck to her hair, others to her person.

"Oh, God! Oh, *God*!" She ran in small circles, sputtering, swiping, and plucking helplessly at her clothes, which seemed to be stuck to her skin in places. "I'll *kill* them. That's a three-hundred-dollar sleeping bag! The little *monsters*."

Ellie heard Tucker make a choking sound she thought was a smothered laugh. She threw him an appalled look. He turned a suspicious shade of burgundy.

As relieved as Ellie was to know her boys were all right, she couldn't see the humor. Poor Marvin was soaked with syrup, which probably meant Liz's sleeping bag wasn't the only bedding that had been ruined. The deliberate destruction of property was something she could not condone.

Marvin stomped across the clearing, his socks collecting more debris with every step. As he stood in a patch of warm sunlight, the scent of syrup poured off him in waves. He thrust out his boots for Ellie's inspection. "Just *look* at this."

Ellie went up on her toes to peer into a boot. The insole was covered with sticky-looking goop. She wrinkled her nose and drew back. The smells of Marvin's feet and maple flavoring didn't marry well.

"Oh, dear," she said faintly.

"Oh, *dear*?" He was so furious his eyes were bugging. Holding his boots in one hand, he leveled a finger at her chest and began jabbing her breastbone to emphasize each word as he roared, "Now do you believe that kid's out of control?"

"I think they're both very confused and upset right now, yes," Ellie offered.

"Up*set*?" Marvin gave her chest several more pokes, this time so forcefully that Ellie lost her balance and fell back a step. "That oldest boy needs his ass kicked, and I'll be *glad* to do the honors!"

Tucker clamped a hand over Marvin's forearm. "Don't get physical, buddy. Nobody lays hands on a woman on my watch."

At that, Marvin's eyes really bugged. They reminded Ellie of oversize brown marbles. He jerked his arm free of Tucker's grasp. "Mind your own damn business. She's not your wife anymore." As though to drive home the point, he gave Ellie's chest another hard poke. "I'll put my hands on her any damn time I please!"

Marvin went down so fast that all Ellie saw was a blur. For a moment, she couldn't guess what had happened. Then she realized that Tucker stood over him with his fists clenched. To her horror, she saw blood trickling from Marvin's nose.

"Oh, *God*!" Ellie started forward, only to feel Tucker's hand clamp over her shoulder. She whirled on him. "You hit him!"

"Yeah, and I'll hit him again if he doesn't keep his hands to himself."

Ellie couldn't believe this was happening. She stared stupidly down at Marvin as he rolled around on the ground, trying to get up. When he finally gained his feet, his syrup-doused clothes and hair had collected so much dirt and so many pine needles that he resembled a vertically challenged Sasquatch.

"That's just great, Tucker," Liz said as she advanced on the scene, still tugging streamers of toilet paper from her clothes. "You can't blame us for being royally pissed."

"I don't blame you a bit," Tucker agreed, "but that doesn't give Marvin license to take it out on Ellie." Scowling ominously, he drew apart the front of Ellie's shirt. Startled by his unexpected touch, she tried to shove his hands away. He would have none of that. "Be still, damn it." His hazel eyes darkened with anger as he examined her upper chest. Turning back to Marvin, he said, "Pack your shit, you little punk. If you're not out of here in ten minutes, you'll think you're a mud hole I'm stomping dry."

Plucking bits of tissue from her face, Liz said, "Oh, for Pete's sake. He didn't seriously hurt her. It's only a few red marks."

"Red marks that'll be bruises by tomorrow," Tucker said, his voice so gravelly it bordered on a growl. He leveled a burning gaze on Marvin. "I mean it. Clear out."

"This is *absurd*," Liz cried. "Take your temper out on your kids, not him. That's half of what's wrong with the little brats. You let them get away with murder." She swung her arm toward her tent. "They poured syrup inside my sleeping bag and all over the floor of my tent. There's absolutely no excuse for such behavior!"

"I'm sorry about the sleeping bag and tent, Liz," Tucker replied. "I'll pay to have them cleaned or replace them if you prefer."

"That isn't the issue, and you know it. Those kids have gone too far! We have to get a handle on them."

"We?" Tucker repeated softly.

Liz flicked a glance at Ellie. "Yes, *we*. As your significant other, I deserve some semblance of respect from your sons. They can't be allowed to treat me like this."

Tucker's eyes heated and his jaw muscle bunched. Ellie had seen that look before and knew Liz was in for it.

"Let's get something straight," he said. "You are not and have never been my significant other, and you never will be."

Liz flinched as though he'd struck her.

"I've tried to spare your feelings and be nice about this," Tucker went on, "but apparently you don't register anything unless it's stated in point-blank terms. Our relationship, such as it is, gives you no right to expect any special consideration from my sons. I don't argue the fact that they're out of line or that they need to be reprimanded for what they've done." He glanced at Marvin, who was still brushing dirt from his clothes. "I apologize to both of you. But how the situation is handled from this point forward is none of your damn business. Is that perfectly clear?"

"*Someone* needs to mind your business," Liz cried. "You certainly aren't. Your out-of-control children are proof of that."

"We're doing the best we can."

"Yeah? Well, maybe you'd better buy a book," Liz suggested acidly. Several bees chose that moment to start buzzing around her head. She swatted them away. "Or take parenting classes. Your best isn't good enough."

Tucker's brows drew together in an ominous scowl,

his hazel eyes glittering with anger. "I think it might be a really good idea if you get a lift back to Bend with Marvin, Liz."

"I'm not *leaving*." She swatted at the bees again.

"Suit yourself," Tucker said, "but you aren't going anywhere with me. Both your sleeping bag and tent are covered with syrup. We have no way to clean them up." He gestured at the bees that were entering the clearing. "If you take that gear into the wilderness, you'll have a whole lot more to worry about than a swarm of yellow jackets. You'll attract every bear for fifty miles."

Liz's paper-dotted face flushed crimson as the truth of that sank home. She cursed under her breath and spun toward her tent, swatting away bees as she went. "Fine!" she cried. "This was what the little bitch wanted in the first place, to be alone with you. Far be it for me to spoil her plans. I regret the day I ever met you." At the entrance of her shelter, she spun back around. A purely evil gleam came into her eyes. "You're no great loss in bed, that's for sure. Twinkle Toes can have you."

Twenty minutes later, Ellie and Tucker were alone in camp. As she folded her tent and straightened her pack, she noticed that her chest was aching where Marvin had poked her. Tucker was probably right; tomorrow, the sore spots would be bruises.

Engaged in similar activities at the opposite side of the fire, he glanced up. "Are you okay?"

Ellie dropped her hand from the front of her shirt. "Yes, fine. Just a little tender."

Still hunkered over his pack, he studied her, his

expression solemn. Ellie struggled not to squirm. There was something different about the way he was looking at her this morning, she decided—a certain intensity she found unsettling.

He pushed to his feet and went to his Land Cruiser. After removing a five-gallon can of water from a rack on the front bumper, he walked over and doused the bed of hot coals from last night's fire. A cloud of thick gray smoke, ash, and steam rose from the ring of rocks.

After returning the can to the rig, he resumed his position at the opposite side of the pit. "I'm sorry I didn't stop him sooner, Ellie. Until he knocked you off balance, I didn't realize how hard he was poking you."

"I'm fine, Tucker, really."

He watched her through the smoky haze. "I hope you're not getting serious about him."

She bent her head, busied her hands again. "Not really, no. At this point in my life, serious isn't on my agenda."

"Good. A guy who flies into a temper and resorts to poking is only one step away from using his fists."

Ellie hadn't considered it from that angle. Instead she'd been thinking how uncharacteristic of Marvin the outburst had been, and concern for him had been gnawing at the edges of her mind. She knew how painful it was to love someone and not be loved in return. She suspected that was at least part of the reason Marvin had blown his cool, because she'd hurt him so deeply yesterday.

"Marvin isn't really a bad person," she said. "He's just—"

"A jerk?" he inserted. "We all get mad sometimes and do things we shouldn't. That's understandable, even if we're ashamed of ourselves afterward. But there are lines we don't step over, Ellie, things we just don't do. That's especially true for men. With the advantage of greater strength comes a certain responsibility."

Tucker would see it that way, Ellie thought. His father, Joe Grant, was a rough-and-rugged logger who'd never backed down from a fight in his life, but he was also one of the kindest, most fair-minded men she had ever known. He'd raised his sons to be just like him. In all the years of their marriage, Tucker had never lifted a hand to her in anger, and he rarely resorted to corporal punishment with his children.

Unfortunately not all men had had his upbringing, and they didn't look at things the same way.

"Marvin was very angry. Maybe he just lost it for a second. That happens. Perfectly nice people lose it sometimes."

"Make excuses for him if you like," he said. "Just understand one thing. If Marvin or any other man lays a finger on my sons, he'll answer to me."

"Marvin would never hit one of our boys."

"He threatened to kick Zach's ass," he reminded her. "If he follows through on that threat, it'll be the sorriest day of his life."

It burned Ellie that he believed she would allow anyone to mistreat one of the boys. Rather than cross swords with him over something that would never take place, she turned her attention to closing her pack.

"Do you have everything you need in there?" he asked.

"I think so."

"I'll have a look, if you don't mind."

She shoved her pack toward him. "Sure."

He hooked a hand over the straps. "What happened here?" he asked, palming what had once been one of the shoulder pads.

"The kids left my pack on the garage floor, and Bucky got hold of it."

He assessed the damage. "Pads protect your shoulders. Without them, the straps may dig in. You should have gotten new gear."

Ellie thought of the many unexpected outlays of cash that came with raising two sons. Tucker contributed a generous amount of support, and she made good money herself, but somehow, even though she stayed on a strict budget, she always ran a little short toward the end of the month. "I don't go hiking enough anymore to justify the expense."

He ran his thumb over a mangled pad, then turned his attention to the contents of her pack. Fairly certain that she'd done a fine job of arranging everything, Ellie clenched her teeth when he began taking stuff out. He paused to cast her a few questioning looks when he came across food items that weren't absolutely necessary, but to his credit, he said nothing. Just as well. She hadn't brought the canned goods for herself, but for Zach and Kody when they were found. They were peace offerings, she supposed, little treats to say she loved them. Though she knew they added extra weight, she wasn't about to leave them behind.

"Except for your tent, always carry the heavy stuff at the bottom," he said. "The weight's easier to manage that way and reduces the danger of you being caught by the wind on a cliff path." He angled her another sharp look. "I'd hate to fish you from the bottom of a canyon."

"Not as much as I would hate it, I assure you."

"You should have put everything in polythene bags. If we get rain or snow, your gear and clothing may get damp."

Ellie had been praying the good weather would hold. She glanced at the sky. "Do you think a bad weather front is moving this way?"

"Rule number one out here is to expect the unexpected. You'd freeze to death in damp clothing."

"I wasn't thinking, I guess. I completely forgot bags."

He strode across camp, opened his pack, and withdrew a handful of plastic. "I always bring a few extra in case mine get torn." As he retraced his steps, he muttered, "You can't forget things, Ellie, not out here. Once we're on that mountain, there'll be no turning back."

"I just forgot *bags*, Tucker." She grabbed some polythene and began putting her things inside. "Give me a break. Why are you being so grouchy?"

His jaw muscle started to tic. "I guess it gets my day off to a bad start when I stand there like a dumb ass while some bully takes his temper out on my wife." His high cheekbones went ruddy with color. "Excuse me, ex-wife." He tossed down a can of beef ravioli. "The point remains I just stood there and did nothing."

The anger in his expression touched her in a way she couldn't and didn't wish to define. "I'm all right, Tucker. It's only a couple of tender spots."

He glanced at her open collar. "Spots that are already turning black and blue."

Unsettled to think he'd been looking so closely at her, she pressed a hand over her chest.

"I can tell you this," he said in a low voice. "If we were still married, he'd have a lot more than a nosebleed to worry about right now."

Ellie didn't even want to think about it. "All's well that ends well."

"Yeah, I guess."

He thrust a hand into a side pocket of her pack. A bewildered look came over his face when he withdrew a white lace teddy and a rectangular white box with gold lettering that read, *White Diamonds*. Both the undergarment and scent still bore price tags.

All Ellie could do was gape. She hadn't put either item in her pack, had never even seen them before. The teddy sported smudges of dirt. She shifted her attention to the perfume box, which was crunched at the corners.

The last few years of their marriage, Tucker had always slipped a bottle of White Diamonds into her stocking each Christmas Eve with an accompanying note that read, "For later when you find time for Santa." It had seemed terribly romantic at the time, their little secret during the gift-giving hullabaloo. Until now, she hadn't realized the boys had known of the ritual, let alone that it had left such an impression on them.

"Oh, Tucker," she whispered. "Oh, *God*." Her eyes smarted with tears. "Bless their hearts."

"I take it this isn't your doing."

Ellie pictured their boys walking into a lingerie section with money from their piggy banks wadded in their pockets. She couldn't believe—just couldn't *believe* that they had put so much thought into this scheme or gone to such lengths to carry it off. They detested the ladies' underwear section and refused even to stand nearby while she browsed because they found it so embarrassing. She couldn't imagine them finding the courage to actually rifle through the racks to find a teddy in her size.

"No, of course it isn't my doing."

Tucker tossed down the box. Then he held up the teddy, huffed with laughter, and shook his head. "Those darned kids. Are they trying to set us up, or what?" He caught the garment in both hands and stretched the cloth. Peering at her through the lace, he whistled softly. "Wow. Put this on, and I'll follow you anywhere."

Ellie snatched the undergarment from his hands. "Don't make jokes. It isn't the least bit funny."

Tucker hadn't been joking, and he failed to see why she was so upset. It was only a teddy and some perfume, after all. He found it amazing that the kids had even thought of such things. They were definitely his sons, he thought proudly. Chips off the old block, and watch out, ladies. In another ten years, they'd be hell on wheels.

"Look on the bright side." He gestured at the undergarment. "At least it's not red or black."

She bunched the lace in her fists. "Would you be serious? Our sons went into a lingerie section and bought their mother a—" She broke off and stared at him with her heart in her eyes. "How can you *laugh*?"

Tucker had a bad feeling that the right brain, left brain thing was rearing its ugly head again. She was about to cry, and Ellie wasn't the type who opened the floodgates over nothing.

Assuming what he hoped was a suitably sober expression, he lowered his gaze to the teddy again, trying to think why she found it so disturbing. He decided maybe it was the sexual implications. Mothers looked at stuff like that differently, wanting to believe their boys were precious little angels.

"Where do you suppose they're getting such ideas?" he tried.

"Where do you *think*?" She rolled her eyes heavenward. "You are so obtuse sometimes."

Okay, fine, he'd bombed with that guess.

"Oh, this breaks my heart." She patted the center of her chest with the wadded lace, reminding him of a kneeling penitent saying, "Mea culpa, mea culpa."

Tucker sat back on his heels, regarding her in complete bewilderment and with no small amount of concern. Sometimes—not often, but sometimes—he wondered if they came from different planets.

"It is sad," he offered, thinking even as he uttered the lie that it was actually funnier than hell. What else did those boys have up their sleeves, champagne to set the mood? Nah. That was pretty high-tech for kids Zach and Kody's age. Too bad. When Ellie got tipsy, she lost all her inhibitions.

"Ellie, let's keep this in its proper perspective, all right?"

"And what, exactly, is the proper perspective, Tucker?"

"Look at the positive aspects," he advised.

"Such as?"

He considered for a moment. Opting for a note of humor, he said, "Well—they didn't supply us with a case of prophylactics. That's positive, right?"

Just as he spoke, Tucker returned his hand to the side pocket and felt several foil packets at his fingertips. *Uh-oh.* He froze and schooled his expression. If a teddy and perfume brought tears to her eyes, half a dozen rubbers would send her into hysterics.

What the *hell* were those kids thinking? More alarming, who was filling their heads with these ideas? Tucker no sooner asked himself that than he knew it was a dumb question. Kids nowadays were bombarded with "safe sex" messages. They probably knew as much about such things as Tucker did. There was an alarming thought. He'd already done his fatherly duty and talked to Zach, but he'd been putting it off with Kody, thinking he was still too young.

"They're just trying to set the stage for a reconciliation, Ellie," he found the presence of mind to say, not adding that he thought they were doing a damn fine job of it—better than she knew. *Rubbers?* He was going to brain the little buggers when he got his hands on them. "What we need to bear in mind is that we can't be led where we don't want to go."

The corners of her mouth quivered and she shook her head. Her eyes filled with accusation. "You honestly don't remember, do you?"

Tucker was feeling around in her pack, doing a condom roundup. With his thoughts thus occupied, her question caught him off guard. "Remember what?"

She snatched up the perfume box and shoved it in front of his nose. "*Read* that, Tucker! How can you not remember?"

He crossed his eyes, trying to focus. He'd found five foil packets. Human nature being what it was, he had a sneaking hunch the kids had thrown in six to make it an even number. Trying not to lose his grasp on any in the process, he dug his fingers deeper, searching for the last one. *Gotcha.* He closed his hand over it, then leaned back so he could see the perfume label.

"White Diamonds," he read, his voice going suddenly thick on the second word.

"Does that or does that not ring a bell?"

Tucker swallowed, hard. "Yes, it rings a bell."

"Now do you see why I'm so upset?"

He was beginning to, yes. Pulling his hand from her pack, he quickly transferred the contents into his jacket pocket and then rested his palms on his thighs.

"It's *our* perfume," she said shakily. "The kind you always bought for me, and they remembered."

Tucker slipped the box from her rigid fingers. Some mighty fond memories slipped through his mind as he gazed at the lettering. He looked back at Ellie, beginning to understand now why she had tears in her eyes. This wasn't just any perfume, but a very special reminder of precious moments they had shared. Had the boys meant it as such? Tucker believed they had.

"This is much more serious than I thought," she said. "What in the world are we going to do?"

Tucker had no idea. Curiosity piqued, he set aside the box to see what else the boys had slipped in her pack. Ellie's expression grew more stricken when he drew out a bottle of shampoo, one tube each of mascara and lipstick, a round case of blusher, and a plastic sack of disposable shavers.

"Oh, Tucker, they're hoping we'll make up and have a romantic interlude." Hands trembling, she began to stuff her clothing into bags. "I had no idea they were so desperately unhappy. They have to be to do something like this."

Tucker had tried to tell her that the very first night when he talked to her on the phone, but for reasons beyond him, it had taken this discovery to drive the point home.

"This isn't some crazy scheme they hatched up on the spur of the moment!" she cried. "They've been planning it for a while, and with an attention to detail that breaks my heart. They're honestly hoping we'll get back together, that we'll fall in love with each other again." She went back to doing the "mea culpa" thing, this time with a polythene bag clutched in her hand. "Oh, *God*. I didn't comprehend, I just didn't *comprehend*."

Tucker gazed off through the trees. She had a point. It was one thing when kids went off half-cocked and did something crazy. Parents could tell themselves they'd acted without thinking, that they hadn't considered the consequences. But Zach and Kody hadn't acted on impulse. They'd given their plan a great deal of thought.

Returning his gaze to Ellie, he couldn't help but think that there was a simple solution to the problem, namely giving in to the kids' demands. But he didn't think she was ready to consider that yet. "We'll talk

to them, Ellie, work things out, make a few conces-
sions. It'll be okay."

She swiped at her pale cheeks and shook her head.
"No," she said, "it won't be okay. They want the
one thing we can't possibly give them, Tucker: to be
a family again."

The one thing they couldn't possibly give them?
Tucker wanted to refute that, but caution held him
back. Better, he decided, to take a page out of his
sons' book and plan every move carefully. He
wanted her back in his life, but to get her there, they
had a lot of burned bridges to rebuild and some issues to resolve, none of them easy to discuss.

"Do you think it worked?" Kody asked as he
trudged up the trail beside his brother.

"I know it did. No way will Dad let Liz and Mar-
vin bring syrupy gear out here. It would attract—"
Zach broke off, half-afraid to mention bears for fear
he'd frighten Kody. "Wasps," he substituted quickly.
"These woods are full of wasps and yellow jackets.
You know how bad they sting."

"And bears, too," Kody inserted. He glanced over
his shoulder, ever watchful.

"It's getting a little late in the year for bears," Zach
lied. "There may be a few that aren't hibernating yet,
but most of them are probably sleeping by now."

Following Kody's example, Zach sneaked a look
behind them. Instead of a bear, he saw Bucky trotting
at their heels.

"Besides, what have we got to feel nervous about?
We've got Bucky now. If he smells anything dangerous, he'll bark to warn us."

Kody grinned and swung around to ruffle the dog's fur. "Right. I forgot about Bucky. You're our best camping bud, aren't you? I'm sure glad Dad brought you." He looked at Zach. "He was so cool last night. He never barked once."

"He knew who we were. He probably smelled us before we ever got down to their camp." Looking at the ground, Zach suddenly stopped. "We're there," he told his brother, pointing ahead. "Those are our tracks from yesterday." He grabbed Kody's arm. "Stand still. The next few steps we take have to lead into our old footprints exactly right, or Dad will smell a rat."

Kody stared at the unmarked expanse of trail that stretched between them and the footprints they had laid the previous day. "You sure this will work? Dad's an ominous tracker. What if he figures it out?"

"Just do like I say," Zach insisted. "When you start walking again, measure your strides so it won't look like you took baby steps before you reached the old footprints."

"And when I get there, step right where I stepped before, right?"

"Right." Zach took the lead, taking carefully measured strides. When he reached the footprints, he took great pains to place his feet in the old marks without blurring the edges. "Just like Dad showed us," he informed his brother with a grin.

Kody followed his example and soon stood beside him. "This is fun. He's sure gonna be mad when he figures out we tricked him, though. We might get grounded for a long, *long* time."

"He'll get over being mad by the time he catches

us." Zach turned his head to regard the pile of rocks beside the path, gauging the distance he would have to jump. "I'll go first," he said. "I can clear more ground than you. Then I'll catch your hand and help you make it."

Bucky cocked his head and barked, clearly puzzled by the boys' strange antics.

"Quiet!" Zach cried in a low voice. "A dog bark carries a long way. Dad'll hear you!"

Bucky lay down and put his head on his paws, whining mournfully. Zach coiled to jump on the rocks. He cleared the distance without a problem, caught his balance, and then turned to catch his brother's hand. Kody swung his arms to gain momentum.

"It's not *that* far," Zach admonished.

"Is, too."

"Is not! Just do it."

Kody sprang forward with all his might but fell short of the mark. Zach almost lost his footing as he grabbed his brother to pull him up onto the rocks.

"See? Piece of cake. You did it, no sweat."

The boys turned to regard their handiwork. Gazing down at their carefully laid trail, Zach felt fairly sure their father would notice nothing strange. By the time he realized he was no longer following fresh tracks, he would be several miles up the mountain.

Chapter Nine

Ellie stood on the knoll that overlooked last night's camp spot, watching as Tucker walked a slow circle around a section of disturbed dirt and pine needles. Huffing from the climb, she struggled to catch her breath, shifted her pack to ease the strain on her shoulders, and then stared at the ground, wondering what he found so fascinating there.

"The little buggers." He hunkered, touched a fingertip to an indentation in the needles, and glanced up at her. "They were up here, spying on us."

Ellie bent to look. "How can you be sure the boys did this?"

He indicated another indentation. Then, pointing farther over, he directed her attention to two more. "The toes of their boots made those marks." He motioned with his head. "Up that way, you can see where Kody had his elbows pressed into the dirt."

Ellie circled the disturbed area. After studying the marks, she could see where Zach, the taller boy, had lain beside his brother. "Why on earth would they lie here, watching us?"

Tucker straightened, shaking his head. "You've got me. Waiting for us to sack out, maybe?"

Ellie turned to search the surrounding woods. "I wonder where they are now."

"The only way to find out is to follow their footprints," he said.

As Ellie fell in behind him, she saw occasional depressions in the thick carpet of pine needles that had been made by her children's shoes. She also saw what she guessed were Bucky's prints, zigzagging back and forth in no apparent direction. In her mind's eye, she envisioned the shepherd, romping along, deliriously happy to be outdoors with the kids again.

Such fun, she thought glumly as she trudged ever upward. She wasn't sure what the elevation was, but she felt the thinness of the air every time she breathed. In the valley where she lived now, it ranged from one to two thousand feet above sea level, and her system had become accustomed to that. Over here, the elevation started at around four thousand feet and went up from there, sometimes to altitudes of well over six or seven thousand in the mountains. It took time to adjust to the change. Ellie could only hope her body did so quickly.

The boys' tracks led them to a formation of rock some distance away that cut into the side of a hill. Tucker once again hunkered to study the disturbances on the ground, touching some of the marks with a fingertip, and then moving to another spot. Ellie guessed the boys had camped there the previous night. *Okay, fine.* What more did they need to know? The kids were long gone now.

"What are you looking for?" she asked, trying to keep the edge from her voice.

Crouched some five feet away, he rubbed dirt between his fingertips and stared thoughtfully at the ground. His tawny hair caught the morning light, the sun-bleached ends glinting like polished brass. The fact that he looked deliciously handsome only made her more impatient to get going. The sooner they found the kids, the sooner she could get away from him.

"Are you about ready?" she pressed.

"In a minute." He rubbed more dirt.

Watching him, Ellie wondered what the Sam Hill was so important about the soil texture. "Have you found something important?"

"Sign always tells a story," he said distractedly.

"Would you mind sharing the tale?"

He glanced up. She didn't like the way he'd been looking at her all morning. It was something in his expression, she decided. While she hesitated to define it as a proprietary gleam, that was what immediately came to mind.

It was probably only her imagination. Tucker, feeling possessive? *Right*. She'd slept poorly the last two nights. As a result, she was exhausted, edgy, and her mind was playing tricks on her.

"It doesn't appear that they even bothered to pitch their tents," he informed her. "They laid out their sleeping bags, but I don't think they slept here."

"How do you know that?"

He pushed up. "Dirt's not packed where their bags were rolled out. I think they spent the lion's share of the night on that knoll above our camp."

Ellie gritted her teeth. As much as she appreciated the skill it took to determine such things, she couldn't see why he bothered. "Can we go now? Every second we waste puts us farther behind. I'm anxious to find them."

"Sure, let's go."

Instead of leading the way as she expected, he fell in beside her, his gaze fixed on the ground as he followed the boys' tracks up the hill. She tried to walk as fast as he did, but his legs were so much longer that she had difficulty sustaining the pace. Lungs burning, she picked up her momentum, taking two steps to his one. She could do this, she told herself. She *would* do this. Hell would freeze over before she complained that he was going too fast.

To her dismay, he seemed to sense that her energy was flagging and slowed his stride. Fearful that he might deem her physically unfit for the rigors that lay ahead, Ellie said, "Don't hold back on my account, Tucker. I'm fine."

"I do this so much with my work that I tend to walk at an unusually fast clip," was his only reply.

Ellie jerked with a start when he suddenly grasped her elbow to help her over a patch of rough ground. The heat of his hand radiated through the sleeve of her shirt and made her skin burn. When he shifted his grip, the movement of his fingers sent her heart into her throat.

"I can manage by myself, Tucker."

If he heard, he gave no indication. Even after they gained flatter ground, he maintained his hold on her arm. Farther up the hill, he finally released her only to curl a big hand over her shoulder, his long fingers extending well past her collarbone to ride above her breast. Every time his fingertips moved, Ellie felt as if she might part company with her skin.

"You okay?"

"Oh, yes, fine." Her heart was pounding so hard that her tonsils were pulsating. "Why do you ask?"

"You just seem tense, that's all. Careful here. It's pretty steep, and the earth's giving way." He fell back a step to grasp her at the waist and give her a boost from behind. "Steady?"

"I, um—yes, thank you." She caught her balance and turned to watch him scramble up after her. Struggling to hide her discomfiture, she said, "This is a different way than I came last night, isn't it?"

"Yeah, it is." He ran a thumb under the strap of his backpack and flexed his shoulders to redistribute the weight. Glancing up the hill, he squinted against the sunlight. "My guess is they're heading for the east trail up to Tabletop."

"Ah, yes. You said there are three that intersect farther up?"

"That's right."

As he fell in beside her again, he flashed one of those lopsided, charmingly boyish grins that had once made her feel weak at the knees. Then he cupped a hand under her elbow to assist her over a log.

By the time the sun was high overhead, Ellie was ready to be measured for her coffin. Ever since leaving the boys' campsite that morning, they had kept up a grueling pace. Being in superb physical condition and blessed with long legs, Tucker didn't seem to feel the strain, but she was about to die.

To his credit, he had offered to stop several times so she might rest. Pride and a well-founded fear that he might send her back to the Land Cruiser had prevented Ellie from taking him up on it.

It seemed to her that they'd walked up at least a hundred hills, all of them steep, and now they were scaling yet another one. On a bright note, the path they were following was narrow, forcing them to walk single file, which at least kept Tucker and his hands at a safe distance. But that was the only positive aspect.

Oh, she was tired. Her legs trembled with exhaustion, her back felt as if it might break under the weight of her pack, the straps were digging what felt like permanent trenches in her shoulders, and on top of that, she was getting a blister on one heel.

Even so, she refused to ask him to stop. They weren't going to find the boys before nightfall if she took too many breathers. After she hugged them and wept with relief, she was going to throttle them for putting her through this, she promised herself.

At the crest of the hill, Tucker stopped to look over his shoulder at her. As always, his sharp eyes seemed to see too much. He stood with one boot braced on a rock, his big body relaxed, his honey-colored hair ruffling in the breeze. He didn't even look winded, blast him.

Ellie straightened her aching back and tried not to drag her feet as she climbed the remaining stretch of trail. Kody's can of beef ravioli tapped her tailbone with every bounce of her pack. After six hours of constant thumping, she felt as if a spike were being driven through her spine.

"How you doing?" Tucker asked when she reached him.

Ellie suspected he knew very well how she was doing. How could he not? Even in her younger days, she'd never been much of an outdoors enthusiast.

"I'm just great," she managed to say, trying to smile even as she pushed her sweat-soaked hair back from her face. She couldn't admit how tired she was. They hadn't come far enough from last night's campsite yet, and she didn't want to give him a reason to send her back. "Isn't it gorgeous up here?"

For a long moment, he studied her thoughtfully. "Are you sure you want to do this, Ellie? I can draw you a map back to the Cruiser, give you the keys to my place. When I find the kids, I'll call you on the cell. It's only a short drive from Bend."

Ellie had been anticipating this, so she was ready with a reply. "I want to help find our sons, Tucker. I know I'm slowing you down, but overall, I haven't asked you to stop very often."

"It isn't that. I just hate for you to put yourself through this when it's not absolutely necessary."

"It's necessary to me. If the shoe were on the other foot, wouldn't you feel the same?"

"Yeah, I probably would. Strike that. I know I would." He trailed his gaze slowly over her face. "It's just hard to watch you do this to yourself, is all. You're so exhausted, you're trembling."

"I'll get my climbing legs under me. The first few hours are always the roughest."

She was relieved when he turned to take in the panoramic view below them. They stood on a ridge overlooking a forested gorge. Stands of Ponderosa and thickets of lodgepole pine lined the banks of a small stream, which wound like a silver-blue ribbon through the woodland.

Earlier that morning, Ellie had thought the Ponderosas were breathtakingly beautiful. Now she was starting to detest the very sight of them. She did her best not to look at Tabletop Mountain, rising against the horizon in the distance. If she allowed herself to think of all the miles that stretched between here and there, she might lose her determination to keep going.

"That's Flannigan Creek," he said. "If you can make it another mile, we'll have lunch by the water."

A *mile*? Ellie nearly moaned. "All right. Great."

"If you need to rest for a while before we head down, we won't lose that much time."

Ellie wanted to collapse right where she stood. "No, no. I'm anxious to catch up with them." It took all her effort to swing her arm toward the stream. Each of her limbs suddenly felt as if it weighed a hundred pounds. "Let's do it." At least it was downhill to the water, she thought. That was something. "I'll be right behind you."

He nodded and started down the hill. It was a steep decline with precious few stops, made all the more treacherous by patches of lava rock and loose stones.

"Watch your step through here."

He turned to give her a hand. Ellie almost accepted. Then she remembered how her pulse raced when he touched her and thought better of it. "I'm fine, Tucker. Really."

"You sure? I don't want you to slip and fall."

"I won't."

He swung away. Following his lead, she picked her way carefully, watching her feet and trying her best not to look toward the bottom. Heights had always given her a touch of vertigo, and it was a very long way down. Seemingly unconcerned about the sheer drop, Tucker descended the slope with impressive ease, his long legs marking off strides twice the length of hers.

Ellie wondered if he was part mountain goat. His boots never lost traction on the loose rocks. His shoulders, a good deal broader than his bulging pack, moved fluidly with each well-oiled shift of his hips, lending his gait an oddly graceful rhythm for so large a man. Normally she would have found his agility and strength attractive, but right now, all she could muster was resentment. She would have given anything to possess even half his stamina.

Taking her eyes off the ground was a mistake. She stepped on a small rock. The stone rolled under her boot, her foot shot out from under her, and the next instant, she was going down the sharp decline the fast way—on her butt.

Tucker heard her fall. He spun around but not in time. She skidded into him, catching him at the knees and knocking him off balance. The next thing she knew, they were both sliding down the embankment, willy-nilly.

All that stopped them from freefalling the entire way was a huge boulder. Tucker hit it, his breath *whooshing* from his lungs like a blowing whale. Before he could right himself, Ellie, sliding on her back, plowed into his outstretched legs, bounced over them, and came to an abrupt halt in a cluster of lava rock at the edge of the path. Her backpack was all that protected her from being badly bruised or cut by the sharp jags of stone. Stunned, she worked her mouth, grabbing for the breath that had been punched out of her by the fall.

"You hurt?" He pushed up on one elbow. "Ellie, are you hurt?"

Answering him was impossible. She lay face up, her spine arched over the pack, which had shifted from her shoulders to the small of her back. Arms flung wide, her fingertips barely touching the dirt, all she could do was lie there, doing a backbend over her gear while she whined for air.

Tucker sat up. "Are you hurt?" he asked again, his tone sharp with concern.

Finally managing to drag in a breath, she croaked, "I want my mother."

He chuckled weakly, then rolled onto his knees and crawled toward her. "Can I take that to mean you aren't hurt anywhere?"

She considered telling him her leg was broken so he would carry her the rest of the way. "Just a little bruised, I think. Nothing feels broken. How about you?"

"I'm fine." Twisting to sit, he crossed his arms over an upraised knee and rested his forehead on his wrists. "*Damn*. Talk about not knowing what hit you."

"I'm what hit you." She rubbed her right thigh, which still smarted from where it had connected with his legs. "Your shinbones nearly broke my femur."

She tried without success to roll onto her knees. She didn't know if it was the weight of the pack that anchored her in place, or if the nylon was snagged on the rocks, but she couldn't budge. She attempted to roll the other way. That didn't work, either. As a last resort, she decided to simply shed the pack, only to discover that the straps were pulled too tight over her shoulders.

Tucker slung off his pack. She sputtered at the dust that flew in her face.

"Sorry." He rubbed his hair to rid it of dirt, sending even more particulate matter her way. "Now I remember why I never let you go down a hill by yourself."

"Very funny."

He sent her a look of wry amusement. "Why don't you sit up? That can't be very comfortable."

Ellie would have loved to sit up. Her spine was about to snap. "I can't."

He sharpened his gaze on her face, which she felt pretty sure looked like a mud wallow. "What do you mean, you can't?"

"I think my pack is snagged on the rocks."

He cocked a molten eyebrow, and his eyes took on a mischievous twinkle. He glanced at the straps that dug in at her shoulders. "You mean you're stuck?"

"Don't you dare laugh."

His mouth twitched. "I wouldn't dream of it."

She squinted one eye to glare at him. "Well, don't just sit there. Are you going to give me a hand or not?"

"I don't know. It strikes me as a situation fraught with possibilities."

"Such as?"

A grin tugged at his mouth. "Mirror, mirror, on the wall, who's the best lover of them all?"

His expression turned teasing. She felt a giggle welling in her chest. It had always been this way. Since the first day she met him, he'd always been able to make her laugh.

"I'd rather endure Chinese water torture than tell you what you want to hear."

His grin broadened. "Have a heart. Do you know how demoralizing it is to be replaced by a short little toad with a bald spot and a rotten personality?"

"If your ego needs boosting, I'm sure Liz will happily pay you compliments, ad nauseam."

He sighed and shifted onto one knee. Grabbing the edge of her pack, he gave it a hard jerk to free the nylon from the rocks. Then he took her hand and pulled her to a sitting position. Ellie blinked, looked into his eyes, and then glanced quickly away.

For several seconds, the only sound around them was the wind whispering over the hillside. She hugged her ankles so her pack wouldn't pull her over backward.

"This is a hell of a way to go about getting a break," he observed. "You might've just asked."

She gave a startled laugh and tossed a pebble at him. "Get out of here. Like I fell on purpose?"

He chuckled and pushed to his feet. After swinging his pack onto his shoulders, he thrust out a hand to her. "Come on. We have two kids to go find."

Ellie laid her fingers across his palm. The heat and strength of his grip was wonderful in a way she couldn't define, his palm completely engulfing hers. With one pull, he lifted her to her feet. She drew her hand from his as quickly as she could without being obvious, then bounced on her toes to distribute the weight of her gear. When she was ready to go, she gestured downhill. "Lead the way."

When he didn't move, she glanced up to find him studying her. The look in his eyes made her heart catch. Smiling slightly, he reached out to rub his thumb over her cheek. The press of his fingertips in front of her ear and along the underside of her jaw set her skin to tingling.

"Dirt," he said as he lowered his hand.

"Oh." Ellie had forgotten how awful she must look. Suddenly self-conscious, she pushed at her hair and swiped at her jaw. "Better?"

He chuckled and caught her chin in his hand. "You made it worse. Hold still."

Once again using his thumb, he dabbed at her cheek and under her eye. When he finished, he leaned back to study her, his expression turning solemn. "How do you manage it?"

The look in his eyes made her stomach clench. She wanted to turn away, to pretend she hadn't heard. Instead, she swallowed and said, "Manage what?"

"To look so damned beautiful."

Ellie stared up at him, her mind momentarily blank. Then feelings flooded through her in a dizzying rush, pressure pushing up from her belly into her chest until she found it difficult to breathe. *Don't do this*, she wanted to cry. *Please, please, don't do this.* She'd worked so hard to get where she was. She had a fabulous job, a new circle of acquaintances, and a home she was buying all on her own. It was a life she'd built with painstaking effort, and she prided herself on the happiness and stability she had achieved without him.

Now, with only the graze of his thumb over her cheek and a husky compliment, he was shaking her world clear off its foundation, making her realize that she wasn't so content without him as she wanted to believe.

Swinging away from him, she tried to tamp down

the panic that welled in her throat. He had walked out on her, she reminded herself. He'd blamed her for Sammy's death, and he had abandoned her when she needed him the most, leaving her to get through the worst time of her life alone. And she'd done it, damn him. All alone and without his help, she'd clawed her way back to sanity and happiness. She wouldn't let him start playing with her feelings now—wouldn't allow him to worm his way back into her heart so he'd have the power to destroy her again.

No way, absolutely no way. Tucker Grant had used up all his chances with her.

Tucker had a lot to consider as he led the way down the slope, the thought hovering foremost in his mind that Ellie had looked scared half to death a moment ago when he'd touched her. On the one hand, he knew it was a gloomy portent, yet another indication of just how difficult it might be to bring her around. On the other hand, he took it as a very promising sign. When a female got that nervous around a man, it meant he was getting to her, that as much as she might want to feel nothing when he touched her, she couldn't quite pull it off.

A smile tugged at his mouth. Afraid of him, was she? Well, she had a right to be. This was war, and he was fighting for his life, no holds barred. He'd fight dirty, he'd fight mean. One way or another, this madness had to end. He was miserable. His kids were miserable. And whether Ellie wanted to admit it or not, he suspected she was miserable, too. That being the case, how did it make sense to go on as they were?

The long and short of it was that it made no sense at all. The kids had it right. No matter what it took, he and Ellie had to get back together. If it meant all of them going for counseling, so be it. If it meant screaming at each other until the anger and hurt lost its hold on them, that was okay, too. They had a host of problems, and it wouldn't be easy to iron them out. Tucker wasn't kidding himself on that score. But it could be done. It *would* be done. He wasn't easing up on her until he saw this through.

Looking back on it, he couldn't say why he'd ever allowed the divorce to happen in the first place. Granted, he and Ellie had lost a child, and, yes, he'd been instrumental in causing that child's death. The sorrow he felt ran so deep, he ached with it. Wasn't that punishment enough?

For almost three years, he hadn't thought so. As a result, he'd accepted anything that fate tossed his way—had almost welcomed it, in fact, believing, in some sick, masochistic way, that he deserved whatever he got. He'd killed his boy, so therefore he deserved to lose the rest of his family. He'd killed his boy, so therefore he had it coming when Ellie moved his other two kids to Springfield. He'd killed his boy, so therefore he had no right to any kind of happiness.

Now, suddenly, he felt as if he were waking up from a long, nightmare-filled sleep. Yes, he'd made a mistake, and his boy had died as a result of it, but that was all it had been, a terrible mistake. That didn't mean he deserved to be punished until the day he died. It didn't mean he deserved to lose everyone else that he loved. And, damn it, it didn't mean he had no right to be happy.

He wanted his life back, and he meant to take it back, no matter what.

Ever since last night when he'd reached that decision, Tucker had been feeling a resurgence of self-confidence, a commodity he'd had in short supply over the last three years. Ellie might resist him at every turn, but he felt assured of winning in the end. They'd been so very much in love before Sammy's accident. Surely there was something of that love left within her, even if she'd buried it under layers of bitterness and was doing her best to pretend it no longer existed.

Pretense was such a fragile veneer and could be so easily shattered. He knew Ellie, understood her in a way no one else did. Unless she'd changed drastically, which he was quickly coming to doubt, she would never give her body to a man unless her heart was part of the package. It was that trait he needed to concentrate on. If he had his way, that tendency would become her Achilles' heel. If he could seduce her, get her to make love with him, she wouldn't be able to look him in the eye afterward and deny her feelings any longer.

The thought made him smile again. Flirting with Ellie had always been one of his favorite pastimes. The greatest challenge, as he saw it, was to figure out the best approach. With any other woman, I might have employed sneaky tactics, working on her in a way that wasn't too obvious. He wasn't above being sly when the occasion called for it. But he instinctively knew that wasn't the right tack to take with Ellie.

They had avoided confrontation for too long as

it was. Oh, they'd quarreled—bitterly, heatedly, and almost continually—until it had reached a point that they were hard-put to speak a civil word to each other. They'd quarreled about all the wrong things— small things, big things, but all of them superficial, blowing so much smoke that they never got to the fire, never addressed any of the issues that really mattered.

Game playing, a psychologist would probably call it. Tucker thought it more apt to say they'd each climbed into a foxhole and lobbed bottle rockets instead of real grenades.

Well, damn it, a real explosion loomed on the horizon. He was tired of skirting the issues, tired of backing off and never pulling the pin. To solve the problem, they had to define it. To define it, they had to talk—honestly, no holds barred, down and dirty. No more guesswork, no more crawling away to nurse their wounds, no more confusing the issue with stupid arguments. He needed to take it head-on, be brutally truthful, and go for broke.

Jerked from his musings by the sound of a rock rolling down the hill behind him, Tucker whirled around, half expecting to see Ellie sliding down the steep decline on her butt again. When he saw that she was still on her feet, he relaxed, but only slightly. Her narrow shoulders were slumped under the weight of her pack, her sweaty face flushed with exertion. She looked absolutely exhausted. Before the divorce, he'd always tried to set a pace she could handle, and he felt ashamed of himself for not having done so today. She could have been injured in that fall.

From here on out, he would go slower, he vowed. The boys had left a clear trail for him to follow, and he felt confident he would catch up with them soon. That being the case, there was no great urgency.

She looked startled when he thrust out a hand to help her over a section of loose stone. "I'm fine," she assured him.

"I've heard that before."

Though she obviously preferred to have no physical contact with him if she could possibly avoid it, he kept his hand extended, determined not to take no for an answer this time. She stared at his outstretched palm for a second. Then she finally relented and reached toward him. Locking his hand over her forearm, he helped to steady her until she was safely abreast of him. Then he repeated the process all over again.

"You don't need to help me, Tucker. Last time, I wasn't watching my feet and stepped on a rock. I can manage. Really."

Struggling not to smile, he said, "It's no big thing. Right? I'm just giving you a hand. You'd do the same for me."

"I just hate to slow you down."

"I don't think we're that far behind them. We can afford to slow the pace a little."

"What makes you think we're not that far behind them?"

"In the past when I've taken Kody hiking, he's had trouble keeping up. I've been pouring on the coals all morning."

"I know," she said ruefully.

Tucker laughed. "Sorry about that." He helped her

over another section of rocks. "I'll try to be a little more considerate for the remainder of this ordeal. How's that sound?"

She smiled, nervously smoothing her shirttails as she drew away from him. "Just as long as we don't fall too far behind. Finding the kids is the most important thing, and I did insist on coming."

That smile. Her face had an enchanting mobility, her mouth curving sweetly at the corners and flashing a dimple in one cheek. Most of all, he loved the way her expressive eyes warmed with the gesture.

Over the last three years, she'd aged a little, of course. The emotional turmoil of a divorce tended to take its toll, and she'd had the added stress of mourning to contend with, as well. But the tiny lines etched at the corners of her eyes were barely visible. In a nutshell, she was still the most beautiful woman he'd ever known, and he was coming to accept that, in his opinion, she always would be. He'd lost his heart to her at sixteen, and now, all these years later, he still loved her, but more deeply. He'd tried to kill that love and had almost convinced himself that he'd been successful. But he'd been kidding himself. Ellie was his one and only. She always had been; she always would be.

When they reached the valley floor where the going was a little easier, Tucker let her take the lead for a while so she could set the pace. Bad move. Her face wasn't her only gorgeous feature. She had the nicest little ass he'd ever clapped eyes on—compact, but perfectly shaped. Displayed to best advantage by tight jeans, the hip action was enough to make him go cross-eyed.

He tried not to look. Fat chance. With her walking

only a few feet ahead, he could focus on little else. His trousers suddenly felt too short at the inseam. *Not good.* He was on a mission here. In order to accomplish it, he needed to keep a clear head, plan every move, and execute it with military precision.

He was giving himself a hard mental shake when he noticed she had meandered off in the wrong direction. "Whoa, Ellie, where are you going?"

"To the creek."

"Angle right."

She reeled to a stop and took in their surroundings. The thick stand of trees blocked their view of the stream, and they weren't close enough yet to hear the sound of the water. "Are you sure?"

Tucker bit back a grin as he stepped up behind her. "I'm positive. Head right."

She huffed with disgust and turned, pushing aside some bushes that blocked her way. As she passed through, a limb snapped back and nailed him right in the groin.

"*Hi-yuh.*"

Pain washed his vision with red. His lungs emptied of breath. Crossing his arms over himself, he bent forward at the waist. Now he knew why Indian braves had always insisted on their wives walking three paces behind them.

"What's wrong?" She pushed back through the bushes to reach him. "Tucker? What is it? Oh, God, talk to me." She bent down to peer up at his face and started rubbing his arm. "What's wrong?"

All he could force out was, "*Shee—ut!*"

"Oh, *dear.* Is it your stomach?" She swung off her pack and started digging through the side pocket. Mascara and blusher went flying. He had no idea what she was looking for. "Damn it. Where *are* they?"

He squeezed his eyes closed on a wave of nausea. "Here, here," she said softly. "Try these."

He narrowly opened one eye. What looked like two antacid tablets lay on her outstretched palm. "Won't—help," he managed to squeeze out.

"You don't have cramps?"

He shook his head.

She went back to rubbing his arm. "What is it, then? Did a snake bite you?"

Just the *thought* made him cringe. "No snake," he said. "A limb snapped back." He wondered if it hurt worse to get busted in the balls when you had a hard-on. Definitely a possibility, he decided. "Hit me in the nuts."

"Oh, *no*." Her eyes widened in dismay. "Are you going to be all right?"

He nodded. He could breathe again. "Just—give me—a minute."

She remained crouched beside him and continued to rub his arm. As the pain began to ease, he decided that it had almost been worth it just to have her touch him this way again. Sternly reminding himself that all good things had to end, he pushed slowly to his feet and carefully shook one leg. Gingerly rearranged his jeans. Things were still achy, but they felt functional once more.

"Whew."

She drew her hand from his arm. "Would you like to sit and rest for a minute?"

"Nah, I'll be fine now."

"Are you sure?"

"Positive." He gestured toward the creek. "I'll rest when we reach the water."

She forged back through the brush. Tucker was ready this time and caught the limb before it swung back and smacked him. Just as he relaxed and fell into step behind her again, she let go of a lodgepole branch and nearly nailed him on the chin.

They'd almost reached the creek when another branch swung back and almost caught him at the groin. Reeling to a stop, Tucker narrowed an eye on the back of her blond head as she continued toward the creek. He had a good mind to let her have it once and see how she liked it. Big problem: she didn't have the right equipment.

His gaze dropped to her backside, and his mouth twitched into a grin. All things considered, he was mighty glad she didn't.

Chapter Ten

Once at the stream, Tucker searched out a shady spot where they could rest while they ate their lunch. Determined to keep her distance, Ellie perched on a rock several feet away to eat her cheese and dried fruit. He reclined on the grass to chew on wild turkey strips that he'd smoked last spring.

Pretending to be intent on his food, Tucker watched her from the corner of his eye. Her movements jerky with nervousness, she kept sending looks his way, her eyes bright and watchful. Yep, he thought. He definitely had her worried. She was as jumpy as a frog on hot concrete.

When she finished eating, she abandoned her seat on the rock, waggled her fingers at him, and headed into the trees. No explanation was necessary. Out in the woods, the only ladies' room available was behind a tall bush.

"Don't wander off very far," he called.

"I won't. Just don't come looking for me. There are times when I don't appreciate company."

As Tucker watched her go, he noticed that she was limping slightly. "What's wrong with your foot?"

She stopped and glanced down. He didn't miss the guilty look that crossed her face as she said, "Oh, nothing. A bit of a catch in my ankle, is all. I must have twisted it a little when I fell."

Tucker had extensive training in first aid. "Want me to have a look?"

She waved the offer away. "No. It's nothing. Really."

She resumed her trek into the woods, the limp noticeably less pronounced now that he'd mentioned it. Tucker wondered if she was trying to hide how badly her ankle was hurt for fear he might send her back to the Land Cruiser.

Not a chance, he thought with a smug grin. He'd given her one opportunity to go back, hoping even as he made the offer that she'd turn it down. Now that she had, he wasn't about to give her the option again. He'd slow the pace, make sure she took no more tumbles, but he wasn't sending her back. Hell, no. He had the lady right where he wanted her— alone with him.

Given her ineptness in woodland settings, the situation was full of possibilities. She'd be dependent upon him for warmth, food, and protection. After seeing her with that club last night, he figured things could get really interesting after dark. If she got spooked, she'd have no one to cozy up to but him.

Tucker's grin broadened. These mountains were full of all manner of frightening creatures—snakes, bears, and cougars, to name a few. Recently they'd even spotted timber wolves in Oregon. The animals had been planted in Idaho and had migrated into the northeast section of the state. Tucker doubted there was much of a population yet, but Ellie had no way of knowing that. Not that he'd dream of lying to her. Only a low-down, mangy skunk would do that.

His sons had had their thinking caps on when they came up with this plan. When Tucker found them, he'd be obligated as a father to give them a lecture they'd not soon forget, but secretly, he'd be wanting to pat them on the back and say thank you.

Finished with his jerky, he pillowed his head on his arms and stared at the sky, wondering about Ellie's ankle again. He hoped it was nothing serious. If she had trouble walking, he didn't know what he'd do. He couldn't leave her behind, that was for sure.

She had never really shared his enthusiasm for outdoor activities, he guessed, just as he'd never completely understood her passion for interior design. Acutely aware of their differences and fearful of drifting apart, they'd made a pact early on in their marriage to be actively involved in each other's hobbies. It was a pact that they had kept until they parted company three years ago. On alternating weekends, he had gone with her to home shows and interior decorating events, and in turn, she'd gone with him to do the things he enjoyed. The arrangement had worked well, giving each of them equal time to pursue their interests. As a result, their life together had been rich with variety, and their sons had been exposed to a host of different activities, enabling them at a young age to distinguish a red-based blue from a brown-based blue almost as quickly as they could tell a red band trout from a native trout.

Tucker missed those days. Though he'd never developed a keen interest in decorating, he had enjoyed being with Ellie, no matter what the activity. After doing something she liked, she had always insisted on stopping at a motorcycle shop or an outdoor supply store on the way home, content to wander with him up and down the aisles while he drooled over stuff he wanted but couldn't afford to buy. Fishing supplies, camping gear, knives and guns. You name it; he had loved to look at it. She'd undoubtedly been bored to tears a number of times, but she'd never let on, pretending to be just as interested as he was.

Ellie. It suddenly occurred to him that she'd been gone an awfully long time. He bolted to a sitting position and called her name. No answer. He frowned and listened, hoping to catch the sound of approaching footsteps. Nothing.

"Ellie?" he called more loudly.

When she didn't answer the second time, he lumbered to his feet and angled off into the trees to find her. He'd walked about a hundred yards, which he personally felt was a hell of a long way to go just for privacy, when he saw the top of her blond head poking up above a manzanita bush. He tried to quietly retreat, but she glanced up and caught him.

"Oh!" she cried. Her head disappeared, then popped back up. "What are you doing out here?"

Tucker turned away to stare fixedly at a tree. "Sorry. I got to remembering how often you used to get lost, and I decided I better come check on you."

He heard twigs snapping and knew she was emerging from cover. "I appreciate your concern, but it wasn't necessary. I marked my trail."

"You did?"

She came abreast of him. He noticed she was still limping slightly, which gave him some cause for concern. "Yes." With a flourish of her hand, she indicated a broken slick-leaf branch to his left. "See? I did that every few feet. When you get turned around as easily as I do, you learn to compensate."

"I'm impressed." Tucker fell into a walk beside her. "How's the ankle?"

"The what?" Confusion clouded her eyes. "Oh." She laughed shrilly. "My ankle. It's fine. I'd forgotten all about it."

Acting on impulse, he reached to smooth a blond tendril back from her cheek. She jumped as if he'd stuck her with a pin, then started finger-combing her hair. "I know I must look a fright." She rubbed the end of her nose. "I don't have dirt all over my face, do I?"

"Nope." Watching her fidget, he struggled not to grin. She hadn't been this edgy even as a teenager. "And you don't look a fright, Ellie. Beautiful, more like. You're the only woman I know who can knock a guy's eyes out without half trying."

Embarrassment flooded her cheeks with rosy color. Fingertips dancing over the collar of her shirt, she grimaced and said, "Oh, well, I don't know about that." She stopped suddenly and frowned as she scanned the brush around them. "Hmm."

Following at her heels, Tucker couldn't think what the problem was.

She turned in a full circle. "I know it's here somewhere."

She wandered over to a bush, bent to look at it, and shook her head. Tucker trailed along behind her.

"What are you looking for?"

"My mark."

For an instant, he didn't know what she meant. Then it dawned on him that she couldn't find the branch she'd broken to mark her trail. Secretly pleased that he'd so completely distracted her, he chuckled and pointed out the way to their picnic spot.

Sighing, she headed in that direction. "Marking my way is a really good plan. I just have to fine-tune it a little."

Tucker figured a spray can of bright orange surveyor's paint might cure her problem. Short of that, she was in trouble.

By late afternoon, the blister on Ellie's heel was killing her, her legs had gone from exhausted to almost useless, her whole body hurt, and she was so hungry she could have eaten grub worms without batting an eye.

Where are those boys? The question streaked through her mind again and again, making her angrier each time. *How dare they pull a stunt like this? What on earth were they thinking?* Her and Tucker's problems weren't their concern, and they sure as heck couldn't be solved while they scrambled up steep inclines and fell down embankments.

Tucker suddenly came to a halt. Head hanging, Ellie almost ran face first into his backpack before she realized he'd stopped walking. With one look at him, she knew something was wrong. His body was rigid, and she could almost feel the waves of anger rolling off him.

"What is it?"

"I'm going to beat them within an inch of their *lives*," he gritted out.

Ellie saw he was glaring at the ground with pure murder glinting in his eyes. "What's wrong?"

"You don't want to know."

"Yes, I do."

He groaned and let his head fall back. "Those little *brats*. We've been following old tracks."

Ellie leaned over to stare at her sons' footprints. To her way of thinking, no tracks could be called fresh unless the boys were standing in them. "What do you mean, *old*?"

"I mean they tricked me. They laid a false trail."

"False, how? They walked through here, right?"

He swung around. The skin of his face was pulled tight with anger, making the ridge of each cheekbone stand out in sharp relief. "Just look at the damned prints, Ellie. What's missing?"

She turned her gaze back to the trail. She saw the footprints of both kids and couldn't think what he meant.

"Bucky," he ground out. "They have the dog with them today." He swung his hand to indicate the trail in both directions. "Do you see any dog tracks?"

Ellie frowned. "I'm sure I saw his tracks when we first started out. He could have just left the trail as they passed through here. You know how he loves to chase things. Maybe he saw a rabbit."

"Nope. I haven't seen his tracks for a while. I'm not sure when they disappeared, but at some point, they did, and I didn't register it."

Cursing vilely under his breath, he strode over to a tree, slinging off his pack as he went.

"What're you doing?"

"Sitting," he said unnecessarily as he plopped down with his back to the tree trunk. "They're playing with me. Just wait until I get my hands on them. I'm going to shake them until their teeth rattle."

When Ellie just stared blankly at him, he said, "Don't you get it? They reached the wilderness area sometime day before yesterday, long before I found their note and got up here myself. While we wasted all day yesterday trying to figure out where the hell they were, they were getting creative. They came out here and deliberately laid a false trail for me to follow. This morning they walked to it, and then they left the path to head God knows where, leaving me to waste half a day on a wild goose chase."

Ellie rubbed her aching temple. Then she held up a hand. "Wait a minute. Are you saying—?" She broke off and counted to ten. "Are you saying we've done all this walking for *nothing*?"

He nodded.

"You mean to say our sons may not even be *on* this stupid mountain?"

He nodded again.

She had an unholy urge to scream at the top of her lungs, pull her hair, and kick dirt. "How could that happen? You're an expert tracker, a modern-day Daniel Boone."

He narrowed his eyes.

"Well, it's true. If someone gets lost in this country, nine times out of ten, who do they call? How could two kids outsmart you like this?"

"It's quite simple. I've taught the little shits everything I know."

On any other occasion, Ellie might have taken exception to his calling their children "little shits." At the moment, however, her mood had deteriorated to a point that she could only agree with him.

"How could they do this?" she asked shrilly. "Do you know how many hills I've walked up today?" She thumped her forehead with her hand. "I can't *believe* it." She started limping in circles. The muscles along each side of her throat drew taut as she searched for a way to vent her frustration. "I know it's not your fault, Tucker. Please don't think I'm upset with you. It's just inconceivable to me that they'd do such a thing. What on earth has gotten into them?"

"A bit of the devil, I'd say." He passed a hand over his eyes and heaved a weary sigh. "I should have been paying closer attention. It's the oldest tracking trick in the book."

She scooped a hand through her hair, made a fist. "I know they don't want to be caught, and I can understand why they might lead us on a wild goose chase. But did they have to do it straight *uphill*? Why not on level ground, for heaven's sake?"

Her heel was hurting so badly that she had to stop pacing. She gimped over to join him under the tree, almost losing her balance as she swung off her pack. "Oh, God," she said as she dropped down beside him, hip to hip and arm to arm. "I'm so tired. When I think that I did all that walking for nothing, I could scream."

He snorted under his breath. "Don't waste your energy. If this is any indication, I have a feeling you're going to need it."

She groaned. "What're we going to do?"

"Before or after we murder them?"

Ellie heard the smile that had crept into his voice. She let her eyes fall closed, reminding herself that just this morning, she'd been extremely glad that he'd trained the boys so well.

"Don't you dare make light of this, Tucker Grant. It isn't the least bit funny. If they're not up on this mountain, we probably won't find them before dark. That means they'll have to spend another night out here alone."

"Almost guaranteed. They pulled this off, slicker than snot."

Ellie couldn't miss the husky note of fatherly satisfaction in his voice. She threw him an incredulous look. "You're *proud* of them."

"They're only kids. As pissed off as I am, I'm flat impressed. It takes a lot of planning and skill to lay a false trail. If it weren't for the dog's tracks petering out, I might still be following it."

Just the thought made her groan again.

"On a bright note, at least we know they've retained everything I've taught them."

"I suppose that's true."

"They know what they're doing out here, Ellie. They'll be all right."

She stared at the sky, wondering where the kids had gone. "Will it be difficult to pick up their trail again?"

He shifted beside her. Exhaustion had sapped all the starch from her spine, and she slumped against his arm. "Hopefully not. We'll double back until we find Bucky's prints again. That'll be near where they left the trail. I'll circle out from there to look for sign."

Ellie rubbed the top of her head, thinking her scalp felt sunburned. "You said 'hopefully not.' Does that mean it *could* be difficult?"

"Depends."

"On what?"

"How clever they were. If they left the trail on rocky ground or where they could drop off into a stream, I might have a devil of a time finding their tracks."

They sat there, staring off at nothing, defeated by their kids.

Finally she asked, "When you were teaching them how to lay a false trail, did you teach them how to use rocks and water to cover their tracks?"

He released a weary breath. "Yeah."

"Marvelous." She turned a questioning gaze to his. "Just out of curiosity, why did you teach them to lay a false trail in the first place?"

"To hold their interest." He shrugged. "To teach kids anything, you have to make it fun. It's also something every good tracker should know, just in case it's ever necessary to elude someone you don't want to find you."

"Like now?"

"Yeah," he agreed, "like now."

"What if you can't pick up their tracks again?"

"I'll find them. The only question is how long it might take me."

"Well," she said, "I guess the sooner we get going, the sooner that'll happen."

Every muscle in Ellie's body protested as she pushed to her feet, but she was determined to keep going. Tucker helped with her pack, sending zings down her arms and making her breath hitch with every brush of his fingertips. Ellie threw him a suspicious look. Was it only her imagination, or was he deliberately letting his hands linger?

He met her gaze, his expression a little too innocent for her peace of mind. Then he grinned and ruffled her hair. "What?"

"Nothing."

He gave her pack a jiggle to center it on her back, then shouldered his own. As they set out, she clenched her teeth. Her blistered heel had grown excruciatingly tender during the short rest period. Now every step was an agony, making her wonder how much farther she would be able to walk before she had to ask him to stop.

Dusk came swiftly in mountainous terrain. For about thirty minutes, the sun would hover above a ridge, spreading a red-gold and pink brilliance across the horizon, and then it took a fast dive, leaving the forest cloaked in a gray-blue gloaming. Ellie could tell by looking at the sky that daylight would soon start to wane.

She trudged determinedly behind Tucker, her thoughts centered on their kids. Tucker still hadn't found any fresh tracks. Their boys could be anywhere. In order to find them, she would walk until she dropped, and she absolutely wouldn't whine.

Tucker slowed the pace as they came around a bend in the path. Feeling numb, Ellie watched as he plucked something white from an overhanging tree bough.

"What is it?" she asked.

Paper rustled. "A note," he replied, smoothing the

crumpled page. "There's a message from both of them this time."

Ellie pressed close to his elbow, straining to make out the words. Sweat was in her eyes, making her vision blur. "What's it say?"

" '*Hi, Mom and Dad,*' " Tucker read aloud. Glancing at her, he inserted, "This part's from Zach." He resumed reading, " '*We didn't want Mom to be worried, so we doubled back to let you know we're both okay. We've got plenty of food, and our sleeping bags are warm, Mom. We're in absolutely no danger. Bucky keeps a lookout for trouble. Dad can tell you how alert he is, and he's not afraid of anything. Sorry for doing this, but it's the only way we know to make you guys see reason, and we aren't going to let you find us until you agree to our demands. We're sick and tired of being the ones to pay for Sammy's death.*' "

Ellie flashed Tucker a bewildered look. His only response was a shrug. He went on to read the short note from Kody. " '*Dear Mom and Dad, I hope you guys make up real fast. I'm having fun in the daytime, but it's really spooky out here at night without Dad, and I get scared sometimes. Please, try real hard to fall back in love fast, okay? Zach and me are anxious to go home.*' "

Tucker crumpled the paper in his fist. A lump came to Ellie's throat. "Is that how they see it?" she whispered. "That they've been made to pay for what happened to their brother?"

Even in the fading light, she could see Tucker's jaw muscle bunch. "Of course that's how they see it. It's true, isn't it? Nothing is the same for them now. The moment Sammy died, their whole world fell apart."

When she said nothing, he added, "Well, it's true. Think about it. Their brother died, we got a divorce, they all but lost their father, and their home life went to hell. Then they were moved to Springfield away from me, both sets of grandparents, all their cousins, and all their friends. Why shouldn't they feel that they've been made to pay, Ellie?"

"Why do I get the feeling you're placing all the blame for our separation on *me*?" Ellie asked.

"Why wouldn't I?"

Oh, how that infuriated her. She would accept the blame for Sammy, but the rest had been his fault, not hers. "That isn't fair. You were the one who walked out, not me."

An odd expression came over his face. For a long moment, he stared down at her. Then, without a word, he turned away, his movements jerky and angry. He took off his pack and slung it to the dirt.

"We'll stop here for the night," he said in a clipped voice.

"But it's not dark yet."

He jabbed a thumb at the sky. "Not quite, but almost." He inclined his head at the trees. "Once I get in the woods, I won't be able to see jack shit."

"Can't we just stay on the trail and keep going for a while?"

He gave her a sharp look. For several seconds, he held her gaze, and then the rigidity suddenly left his body. "You're something, you know it? What do you think about out here, Ellie, wall textures and color schemes? You sure as hell aren't concentrating on tracking."

"I've been thinking about our kids," she said thinly.

He let his eyes fall closed for a moment. When he looked at her again, he was smiling slightly. Shaking out the note, he flicked it with his fingers. "How do you think this got on that tree?"

"The boys left it there." She immediately saw where he was heading and felt a flush creep up her neck. Glancing toward the woods, she added, "Which means that, unless they developed wings, we can follow their tracks from here."

"Exactly."

Ellie felt stupid. The only thing she could think to say in her own defense was that she'd been worrying about the kids, but she'd already told him that.

He pinched the bridge of his nose. "I'm sorry," he said. "I'm biting your head off for no good reason. I'm sorry."

"Feel free. Apparently there's not much in it but air, anyway."

His mouth twitched. "Right. You danced circles around me in college, pulling a four-point-oh without half trying."

"I didn't have to know the scientific name of every fish and mammal in the Pacific Northwest and how to spell it correctly. Of course I danced circles around you. Basket weaving was such a breeze."

His smile took hold, curving slowly across his mouth. "Basket weaving? Did that come before or after trig and calculus?"

Ellie frowned as though she were trying to remember.

"Don't put yourself down."

"But it's so easy with your help."

He winced. "I'm sorry. It's just—" He broke off and shook his head. "Never mind. I apologize for getting testy. It takes all types to make the world go round. You're creative and imaginative; I'm analytical and pragmatic."

"It's called right brain, left brain."

"Yes, I know," he said with a grin. "I've been ruminating on that very thing a lot lately."

"Ruminating? There's a word I haven't heard in a good long while. Why have you been ruminating on right brain, left brain stuff?"

"It's one of the great mysteries of the universe, isn't it? Women think one way, men another. It's amazing we can even communicate."

"You mean we can?" Ellie feigned surprise. "Wow, what a breakthrough. When did that start happening?"

He laughed, pointed a finger at her as though it were a pistol, and pulled the imaginary trigger. "Don't knock what works. It's our differences that give the world balance."

There had been a time in the not-so-distant past when their combined differences had made for a very harmonious and interesting marriage. Ellie couldn't say they had created balance, but they had made a beautiful life together.

Resting his hands at his hips, he turned to survey the woods around them. "I'll have my work cut out for me in the morning. My guess is they went to great pains to cover their tracks."

"This is as good a place as any to make camp, I suppose."

He nodded. "Not bad. We're near the creek, and the ground's fairly level for our tents. I wonder if the little snots planned it this way. Hell of a note, isn't it, to think they're choosing our campsite for us?"

She cast a final, longing glance toward the woods.

"They'll be okay, Ellie. If they can double back to leave us a note, they aren't that far ahead, and they know exactly where we are. If anything goes wrong, one of them can come to us for help."

Ellie hadn't thought of that and felt somewhat reassured. Boneless with exhaustion, she followed Tucker's example and shed her pack. She briefly considered erecting her tent, but her throbbing foot changed her mind. The rushing sound of the creek beckoned to her. She could almost feel the soothing coldness of the water on her blistered heel.

She gimped her way down to the stream. After setting her things on the grassy bank, she struggled to unlace her boots and gingerly remove them. Pain thinned her lips as she peeled off her sock. She felt pretty sure some of her flesh went with it.

Clenching her teeth, she rolled up her pant leg and thrust her foot in the water. The icy shock sent a shaft of fire up her leg, and she gave an involuntary whimper.

"How's it doing?"

Ellie jumped at the sound of Tucker's voice directly behind her. She threw him a look over her shoulder. Judging by his stormy expression, he'd just spotted the blister, which was the size of a quarter and bloody raw.

"Damn it, Ellie, why didn't you tell me your boot was rubbing your heel?"

"I didn't want you to send me back. I know how you freak over foot sores."

"For good reason. Do you have any idea how easily that could get infected? And if it does, the complications you could have? I knew a guy who got blood poisoning from a blister once, and he damned near lost his leg."

He crouched beside her. None too gently, he slid a hand under her knee to lift her leg from the water. After a closer inspection of her heel, he said, "I can't *believe* you didn't tell me about this. I could have put some Second Skin on it and kept it from getting so bad."

"I was afraid you'd send me back, I told you. Besides, I won't get an infection. I've got some antibiotic ointment in my first aid kit. I'll rub some on after I've soaked it."

"You still should have told me. Now just look. You'll never be able to keep up with—"

"No matter what, I'm not going back," she cried. "I'll keep up. It just hurts a little."

"A little?"

He pushed to his feet and spun back toward camp. He returned moments later carrying a first aid pouch. Going down on one knee beside her, he looked at her heel again, then swore under his breath.

"I can't believe those boots did this," she said. "They're the same ones I used to wear. They fit me perfectly back then."

"You may have gotten them wet the last time you wore them." He opened the pouch and dug through it. "If you don't wear boots until they dry, the leather tends to shrink. In this instance, it also hardened with disuse. I'll rub them down with some saddle soap. It'll loosen up the leather and make it supple again."

Ellie jumped when he bent over her foot and touched the tender spot. "Sorry," he whispered. "I know it must hurt like hell."

After rolling up her pant leg a bit more, he carefully lifted her leg onto his thigh. Curling a hand over her ankle, he turned her foot so he could see the blister. Ellie made fists on the grass, acutely conscious of his hard, rough palm resting just below her knee. As he worked on her heel, cleaning the sore with an antiseptic swab, he traced circles on her shinbone with the thumb of his other hand. Light, tantalizing circles.

She clenched her teeth, willing herself not to notice how lovely it felt. It was just his *thumb*, for pity's sake. No big deal. Unfortunately, not noticing was beyond her. With every press of his fingertips and shift of his grip, her nerve endings hummed with delight.

She cast him a wondering glance. With his head bent over her foot, she couldn't read his expression. Was he touching her this way on purpose? He made another pass over her shin with his thumb, reminding her that she hadn't shaved her legs in over two weeks. She cringed, knowing he had to feel the stubble. Ah, well. Like she had time to worry about things like that? These days, she was doing good just to floss her teeth.

Still, it was embarrassing to have him feel the stubble, especially when she thought of all the smooth skin he'd probably caressed over the last year. Ellie told herself she'd be just as embarrassed if a total stranger were touching her leg, but deep down, she knew better.

"Do you mind?" she blurted.

He gave her a bewildered look. She wasn't fooled. He was doing his best to unsettle her, and they both knew it.

"Excuse me?" he said.

"Don't give me that innocent look. Stop caressing my skin that way. I don't appreciate it."

His lips twitched. "What do you mean? I'm not touching you in any particular way. It must be your imagination."

Ellie didn't think so. But she held her tongue all the same. He was pushing for a reaction from her. She wasn't sure what his game was, only that she didn't care to play.

When the blister was cleaned to his satisfaction, he applied a clear bandage with a cool, jellylike substance on the underside. It felt marvelous on her raw flesh. He glanced up. His eyes, she noticed, glinted with irritation even as he smiled slightly.

"Don't ever lie to me again," he said softly. "Not when we're out like this."

"I didn't exactly lie, Tucker. I just said I must have twisted my ankle a bit. It's possible I could have." She shrugged and pushed at her hair. "Sometimes injuries like that don't start bothering you until the following day."

"Don't split hairs with me, Ellie. If anything else goes wrong, I want to know about it immediately. A sore throat, a stomachache, or whatever else, you tell me, damn it. I don't want you having an appendicitis attack or something else equally serious, and letting it go until the condition gets critical."

"I'll tell you. I'm sorry about the fib. I was just afraid you might—"

He caught her chin in his hand. The press of his fingertips was firm yet gentle, barely hinting at the strength he held in check. "I won't send you back down the mountain, Ellie. We made those kids together, and we'll find them together." His voice went husky, and it seemed to her that his face drew closer. "Sometimes I wonder if you've lost sight of that fact."

"What fact?"

"That we made them together."

"I haven't forgotten that you're their father."

"Haven't you? Seems to me your memory could use a little refreshing." His mouth slanted into a dangerous smile. "I think you're trying very hard to forget that aspect of our relationship. Given the fact that it was, hands down, the very best part, I can only wonder why."

His features blurred. She blinked to bring them back into focus. Four twinkling hazel eyes continued to swim in her vision. "It was so good between us, Ellie," he said softly. "How can either of us possibly forget that?"

She leaned her head back to look up at him, and her heart sped to a gallop the instant she glimpsed his expression. She recognized trouble when she saw it. Planting a hand dead center on his chest, she said, "Tucker, I don't think—"

"What's the matter?" he challenged. "You afraid how you'll feel if I kiss you? That maybe you'll lose control and forget what the hell you're so pissed off at me about, why you hate me so much?"

"Don't be absurd. My days of losing control with you are history."

"Really?" His dark face drew closer. "Well, then? Where's the harm?"

She was still trying to think how to answer that question when his hard mouth settled over hers. At the first contact, Ellie's breath snagged behind her larynx, and her pulse leaped wildly. Silken heat. He caught her lower lip between his teeth and gave it a light tug that made her toes curl.

"Tucker," she managed to mumur, "I don't want—"

"Liar," he whispered against her mouth. "Don't tell me you don't want this, Ellie. I know damned well you do."

Oh, God, she'd forgotten how clever he was with his mouth. Sexy nibbles, teasing little drags of his tongue over her bottom lip. Before she could form a coherent thought, the blood rushed to her head and then drained out, leaving her dizzy and weak.

At the back of her mind, she knew she should push him away, but when she planted her hands on his shoulders, her fingers clutched at his shirt instead. It had been so long—so very, very long. He tasted of mint and crisp mountain air. The smell of his aftershave worked on her senses like a drug.

Tipping his head, he deepened the kiss, slipping his tongue past her teeth to taste the recesses of her mouth. One of them moaned—Ellie wasn't sure who—and the gentle pressure turned suddenly urgent. As though he feared she might jerk away, he slipped an arm around her waist, hauled her hard against him, and cupped a big hand over the back of her head.

Ellie couldn't have pulled away if her life depended on it. Oh, how she had missed this, missed *him*—being pressed against his hard body and feeling his strong arm around her, the force of his embrace nearly crushing the breath from her. His heart pounded against her breastbone, its steady cadence forming a sharp contrast to the erratic flutter of hers.

He made a fist in her hair, tipped her head back, and bent to catch the soft skin along her throat in his teeth. A feral rumble came up from his chest, lending the gentle bite a ferocity that ignited her senses and made her acutely conscious of the sheer power that surged through his long body. Male to female, a sharp yearning built between them that made her want with mindless urgency. Oh, God, how he made her want.

His breathing was uneven, quick and shallow, the exhalations warming her skin—setting it afire. He nipped his way up her neck, the prick of his teeth sharp and hungry, as if he were starving and wanted to feed on her very flesh. In that moment, she would have let him. He trailed kisses along the sensitive underside of her jaw to her ear, and then caught her lobe between his teeth. Her bones felt as if they were melting.

"Remember this, Ellie?"

She needed to say something, only she couldn't think what. Not with him breathing softly into her ear, not with his tongue circling over the sensitive hollow just beneath and making her nerves sing with delight.

His fingertips lightly caressed her scalp. Trailing kisses over her cheek, he found her mouth again and settled his lips over hers in a cajoling, tantalizing way that bombarded her already reeling senses. He knew her too well, she realized dimly. Just how to touch her, and where. Just how to excite her, then soothe her. She felt like a delicate stringed instrument being played by a master. Tucker Grant, at his best, was a force to be reckoned with.

A little frantically, she thought, *Pull away. Now, before it's too late.* Only it was already too late. It had been too late for twenty years. She'd loved him then, and God help her, she loved him now. It was madness. She knew it was madness, even as she sighed into his mouth, made tighter fists on his shirt, and pressed herself more firmly against him. She wanted what he offered, *needed* it on some level that ran deeper than reason. *Tucker.* Hunger lanced into her, creating an ache low in her belly that only he could ease. Oh, yes. She quivered under his hands, vulnerable in a way that both alarmed and aroused her. The same hunger radiated from him, electrifying her skin, making her pulse race.

Drawing hungrily on her mouth, he whispered, "How's your memory now, Ellie girl?"

The question worked on Ellie's swimming senses like a dash of cold water. She lifted her lashes, stared at the blur of his dark features. Memories plowed into her like fists. What on *earth* was she doing? This man had broken her heart into a million pieces and walked away without ever looking back. How many nights had she lain awake, dreaming of exactly this, praying he might come back to her and weeping until her pillow was soaked with tears—needing him, yearning for him, whispering his name?

Where had he been then?

Ellie knew exactly where he'd been—with another woman. Images spun through her mind with brutal clarity of Tucker running his dark hands over the flawless skin of a faceless lover. Nausea rose in her throat. She lowered her hands back to his shoulders and shoved against him with all her might.

Taken off guard, he nearly toppled over backward. Catching his balance just in time, he fixed her with a quizzical look.

"My memory," she managed to push out, "is picture clear."

Typically of Tucker, he regained his composure quickly. Never taking his gaze from hers, he blotted his mouth with the back of his hand. "And?"

"And nothing," she pushed out, her voice shaking.

She swallowed, hard. Her pulse was still pounding. Her bones felt as if they'd turned to warm jelly. She could easily envision herself flat on her back on the grass, begging him to make love to her while she tore at his clothes. Because she could see herself doing that, she reached deep for some shred of sanity. "Don't make the mistake of trying that again, Tucker. I'm not interested. Period."

His mouth tipped in a cocky grin, his eyes mocking her. "It didn't feel like a mistake to me, babe. In fact, I think it's the smartest thing I've done in three years. As for you not being interested, you may fool a stranger, you may even fool yourself, but you can't fool me. I know you too well."

He grabbed her boots and pushed to his feet. "I'll

get to work on these with the saddle soap. Wear your sock to keep that heel clean when you come back to camp."

He turned and walked away.

Ellie was still trembling when she walked back up from the creek. And, oh, she was angry. So angry that she wanted to jump on Tucker's back, claw at his face, and gouge out his eyes. *Damn him, damn him, damn him.* He was a bastard. She hated his guts. He was probably just bored and looking for a diversion. Well, he could count her out.

Hands shaking with fury, she dug in her pack for a fresh pair of socks. When Tucker finished rubbing saddle soap into her boots and brought them to her, she snatched them from his hands without a word.

"No 'Thank you, Tucker'?" he asked congenially.

Ellie considered bonking him on the kneecap. "Thanks," she bit out.

He clicked his tongue. "My, my, you really are pissed. Care to tell me why a simple kiss got your dander all in a stir?"

She jerked on a boot.

"Wrong foot."

She hissed air through her teeth when she saw he was right. She jerked the boot back off. "Leave me alone! Is that too much to ask?"

"All I did was kiss you. From the way you're acting, you'd think I forced the issue."

Oh, how it rankled that he hadn't found that necessary. When she remembered how she'd clung to him, she wanted to die. "I don't care to discuss it."

"You never want to discuss it. How many times

have I heard you say that? Has it ever occurred to you that the problems between us can't be resolved if you refuse to talk to me about them?"

"There are no problems between us. There's *nothing* between us, period." She shoved her foot into the correct boot and fumbled with the laces. "Just leave me alone, Tucker. I mean it."

"Or what?"

She paused to send him a bewildered look.

"There was an 'or else' hanging on the end of that. I'm just wondering what you plan to do if I don't." Devilment danced in his eyes. "Hang me out to dry? Throttle me, maybe?"

"Don't be ridiculous."

"You're right. It's absolutely ridiculous. I outweigh you by well over a hundred pounds." He crouched and brushed her hands aside to take over the boot-laces. "Whatever it is you have in mind for me, I guess I'll find out." He grinned and winked at her. "I sure as hell don't plan to leave you alone."

She tried to brush his hands aside to tie the laces herself. He braced his arms against her.

"Come on, Ellie. It was only a kiss."

Only a kiss? To him, maybe, but not to her. With that kiss, he'd made her heart hurt, and she'd never, ever forgive him for that.

He waited for her to slip on the second boot, then tied the laces as well. "How's the blister feel?" he asked.

The restored pliancy of the leather and the protective bandage had worked wonders. She pushed to her feet and discovered she could actually walk without her heel killing her. "It feels great. Thank you."

He straightened beside her. "Keep me posted. When it starts hurting again, it'll be time for more Second Skin."

He left her then to make fast work of pitching both their tents while she gathered rocks and wood to build a fire. She was scooping coffee into the basket of her small pot when he joined her by the flames. Feeling his gaze on her, Ellie missed her mark and slopped grounds onto her wet hand. Grimacing, she wiped them off on her jeans, then jammed the lid on the pot.

"You okay?"

Oh, she was just grand, she thought as she set the coffeepot on to boil. Aware of him in every pore of her skin, but otherwise, just grand. In all fairness, though, she didn't suppose she could place all the blame on him. He'd kissed her, yes, but the rest had been her fault. Clinging to him, wanting him. She needed her head examined. He'd left her, she reminded herself, and he'd been with countless women since, having the time of his life while she struggled to forget him and piece her life back together.

Where was her pride? She needed to find it, and fast, she thought acidly. Except for her boys, that was about all she had left.

He bent to shift the wood around, then straightened and brushed his hands clean on his pants. "I know you're probably hungry, but before I go down to catch our supper, I think I'll take a little walk."

Still crouched by the rocks, Ellie peered up at him through the gloom. "A *walk*? Are you nuts?"

He chuckled. "Not for pleasure. I thought I'd cut a wide circle to see what I can find out there."

Ellie's skin prickled. She started to glance around. "Don't look," he said softly. "I'm going to act as if I'm heading down to the creek to fish. Then I'll sneak out and around. After finding that note, it occurred to me that the little buggers may be staying in close at night because they're scared."

Ellie's neck felt suddenly stiff from the effort it took to keep her eyes on him. "Good thinking."

He winked at her. "Who knows? I may come back with a couple of good-size fish on my stringer."

"Oh, I hope so," she said. "Good luck."

Watching their folks was totally boring, Zach thought sleepily. Their dad was off fishing, and after purifying some water and filling the canteens, their mom had crouched by the fire again. Kody was already snoozing, and Zach, tired after such a long day, was tempted to follow his example. Bucky, curled up between them, snored softly. There was something about the sound of snoring that made a guy sleepy.

Zach twisted to get more comfortable and rubbed his face. His stomach was sore from lying on his belly so much. He was tempted to sit up, but it wasn't totally dark yet, and his dad had eyes like a hawk.

Just then a limb snapped. Limbs were always snapping in the woods, and Zach might have ignored it. But Bucky came instantly awake, sniffed the air, and started wagging his tail. *Red alert.*

Zach grabbed Kody's shoulder and shook him awake. *"I think Dad's coming!"* he whispered urgently.

Kody sprang erect, rubbed the sleep from his eyes, and then looked warily around. They held their breath to listen. Bucky whined softly. Then they heard the muted sound of footsteps.

Springing to their feet, they took off at a dead run. Bucky started after them, then wheeled to run toward their father. "Bucky!" Zach cried as sternly as he could in a voice that wouldn't travel. "No! Come!"

The dog danced in place for a moment. Then he obeyed Zach and came racing up the hill.

"*Zachariah*!" their father's voice boomed through the woods. "I hear you! Get back down here this instant!"

Zach picked up speed, grabbing Kody's arm to haul him along behind him. No way was he going to answer when his dad used that tone.

For a while, Zach thought he could hear their dad behind them, so he kept running until he thought his lungs might burst. When he and Kody could go no farther, they collapsed together under a tree, wheezing for breath and holding their sides. In the chill night air, their sweat smelled sweet and sticky.

"Do you—do you think he's still coming?" Kody huffed.

It was fully dark deep in the woods. Zach gulped and tried to listen. All he heard was a roaring sound in his ears. "Don't know," he gasped out.

Bucky lay down beside them. The dog no longer wagged his tail or acted excited. Zach took that as a good sign.

"I think he gave up. It's too dark to follow our

tracks, and we got a good enough jump on him that he couldn't follow our noise."

Kody slumped against the tree and drew up his knees. Still breathing hard, he angled an arm across his belly. In the darkness, the lettering on his sweatshirt glowed eerie white above his sleeve, the first two words of, I'M GONE FISHING, moving in a wavelike motion with every rise and fall of his chest.

"He almost had us. We're going to have to be more careful from now on."

Zach blotted beads of perspiration from his face. "Yeah," he agreed. "He's figured out that we're watching them. He may try sneaking up on us again."

"We can't let him catch us," Kody said fiercely. "Then they'll just take us home, and nothing will change."

Zach had his own reasons for not wanting it to happen that way, and at the start of this mission, he'd believed his brother's reasons were the same. Now he was starting to think that Kody might have even more at stake than he did. How that could be, he wasn't sure. It was just a feeling he had.

"If it doesn't get fixed, it doesn't get fixed," he said. "We'll just have to live with it."

Kody stared straight ahead, saying nothing. It seemed like forever before he finally spoke again. "It has to get fixed," he said. "It just has to, is all."

Ellie didn't like being in camp alone after dark. She couldn't see very well beyond the light of the fire, and she felt as if creatures were staring at her.

She just hoped none of them were large, long-toothed, and drooling.

She nearly jumped out of her skin when Tucker stepped suddenly into the light. Her heart did a nervous jiggle at the base of her throat as she tried to hide her discomfiture. "Well?"

"They were up there," he said, his voice hollow with weariness. "It's so dry, they heard me coming. They ran before I could reach them."

"You actually saw them?"

Stepping over to a cluster of large bushes, he broke off a stout, fairly straight branch. "No, but I heard them. And I know they heard me. I yelled for them to come back, but they kept going. I followed them for a bit; then I lost them."

Rocking forward onto her toes, Ellie stared thoughtfully into the fire. "At least we know they're hanging in close. It makes me a little less worried."

"Yeah, that's something, at least." He scanned the woods.

In the distance, a coyote yipped. At least Ellie thought it was a coyote until she saw Tucker stiffen and turn in that direction. The hair at her nape prickled. She very seldom saw him react to night sounds in the wilderness.

"What was that?" she whispered.

He cocked an ear and waited. When the sound came again, he narrowed his eyes thoughtfully.

"What is it?" she asked again.

He shrugged and smiled. "Probably just coyotes."

Ellie knew better. Tucker Grant didn't act this way over a mere coyote.

"It just sounded . . ." His voice trailed away. Then

he shrugged again. "I don't know. Different, some-how." He looked across the fire at her. "Probably just my imagination. Did it sound strange to you?"

Now that Ellie thought about it, she decided it had sounded strange. "A little," she confessed. Goose bumps rose on her skin. "What do you think it is?"

"Probably only coyotes."

"Probably?"

He nodded. "There is the very remote possibility that it could be a timber wolf."

"I didn't think there were any wolves in this country."

He ran the branch through his hands, testing it for straightness. "Haven't been any for years. Recently, though, there've been some sightings. They planted them in Yellowstone and Idaho a few years ago. Now they have them in the Washington Cascades and they're migrating into Oregon, as well. They found an Idaho radio-collared wolf at the north fork of the John Day River a couple of years back. They removed it back to Idaho, but later another one was struck by a car and killed just south of Baker City."

"That's not that far from here, not if they've man-aged to migrate clear from Yellowstone and Idaho."

"Nope. They've definitely moved into the state, the only question being how many are here."

Ellie rubbed her sleeves. "Oh, God. Do they bother humans?"

"I suppose they might if they're hungry. Wolves are very cunning, and they hunt in packs, so they're not afraid of much."

"What about the boys?"

"Nah, they're safe. They're together, for one thing,

and they've got Bucky to raise a ruckus. Wolves are pretty much like any other wild creature. If and when they get bold enough to take on a human, they prefer it to be someone who's all alone and can be taken by surprise."

That was reassuring. Sort of, anyway. Ellie was still worried, though. When the cry came again, she threw Tucker a frightened look.

He chuckled. "It's probably just coyotes, honey. In all the years I've hiked in these mountains, I've never once seen a wolf. I shouldn't have mentioned it. Now you're all upset."

"I can't help but think of the kids out there all alone."

"They're fine. Trust me. No wolves or anything else will get within a half mile of them with Bucky to raise an alarm."

Ellie sighed with relief. Then another thought occurred to her. "What about us? We don't have a dog to give us a warning."

"True." He peered off into the darkness. "No worries. We're together, and we've got the fire. Just stay alert."

Alert? Ellie glanced uneasily over her shoulder.

Pulling his pocketknife from his jeans, he hunkered down by the light of the flames to make a spear from the limb he'd selected. At its tip, he carved a sharp backward barb. When he finished, he fetched a flashlight from his pack and started toward the creek.

Ellie jumped to her feet. "Where are you going?"

He stopped, swung back. "Fishing. You're hungry, aren't you?"

She was too nervous to feel hungry. She heard the

coyote again. To her frightened ears, the call seemed to have moved closer. She hurried around the fire. "I'll just come along, if you don't mind."

His expression mirrored his surprise. "I thought you were pissed at me."

She sent another worried look at the trees that encroached on the clearing. Beyond the firelight, the night was dark as soot, and it was easy to imagine she saw things moving out there. "I'm all over that."

"Really? That's a record." His strong teeth gleamed in the firelight as a slow, knowing grin tipped up one corner of his mouth. "You're not worried about wolves, are you?"

"Sort of."

"Even if they're in this area, which they probably aren't, they won't come near the fire."

Ellie made fast tracks to reach him anyway. "That's good to know. All the same, I'd rather stay with you. There's safety in numbers, right?"

"I suppose that's true enough."

He fell into a walk. Ellie hurried to keep pace with him as the darkness closed in around them. The wind picked up and whipped through the trees. A loud noise made her leap with fright. "What was that?"

"What was what?"

"That cracking sound."

He chuckled and looped an arm around her shoulders. Hauling her firmly against him, he gave her arm a comforting pat. "We're perfectly safe, sweetheart. There's probably not a timber wolf within a hundred miles of us."

Sweetheart? It was on the tip of her tongue to protest the endearment, but under the circumstances, she decided that was an issue they could discuss later.

Chapter Eleven

Just before daybreak the next morning, Ellie was already awake when Tucker hollered at her to get up. Thanks to the wolves, or coyotes, or whatever the heck they were, she'd been awake most of the night. At one point, she'd grown so frightened that she actually considered joining Tucker in his tent, but good sense came to her rescue before she acted on the urge.

As a result, she was exhausted. Every muscle in her body screamed as she rolled from her sleeping bag and struggled to put on her boots. Oh, how she *hated* camping. During her marriage, it hadn't seemed so bad. Tucker's big body had kept her warm even on the coldest nights, and he'd always carried two wool blankets in his pack for use as padding under their zip-together sleeping bags. No such luxuries now, she thought testily.

After slipping on her jacket, she stumbled from her tent. Naked from the waist up, Tucker was crouched by the fire, shaving. His washbasin was perched on the edge of the rocks to keep the water warm. Ellie wasn't sure which she found most appealing, the pot of coffee simmering near the flames or the sight of him only half dressed. He'd slung a towel around his thick neck, and the white of the terry set his dark skin off to stunning advantage.

Shoulders, she thought. He had absolutely gorgeous shoulders, all bronzed from exposure to the sun and sculpted with muscle. In the past, Ellie had often studied them, marveling at all those dips and bulges. Sometimes, when the opportunity had presented itself, she had skimmed her hands over them, enjoying the silken texture of his skin, the incredible hardness beneath, and the warmth that radiated from him. More often than not, those touches had prompted him to touch back, and they'd sneaked away to make love, the location for the activity depending upon the hour and whether or not their kids were awake. Ellie couldn't count the times that her fascination with his physique had landed her in the coat closet—or in the utility room with the door locked.

The memories made her smile. Then she gave herself a hard mental shake. *No more.* With maturity had come indifference, she assured herself. Given a choice between shoulders or fresh coffee, she would now choose the coffee every time. She stumbled over to pour herself a cup. As she took a sip, her gaze landed on his well-padded chest, and she burned her tongue. He was driving her crazy on purpose, she decided. Any idiot knew it was inappropriate to run around half dressed in mixed company.

Not that he was running around. Then, at least, she might have found it more difficult to admire the view. As it was, he just crouched there, displaying his superbly fit body. Bent at the waist, most men's bellies rolled over the top of their jeans a little. Tucker's was so hard and ridged with muscle that not a hint of a spare tire showed. As he shifted to swish his razor in the water, the muscles in his thighs bulged beneath his jeans.

"How are you this morning?" he asked cheerfully.

"How long do you have?"

"That bad?" He grinned and angled her a questioning look. "How's the heel?"

"Amazingly, it's the only part of my body that doesn't hurt, so I guess it's better."

"That's good. What's the matter with the rest of you?"

"Ground sore. I feel like I went twenty rounds with the heavyweight champion of the world, and the creep didn't wear gloves."

He chuckled. Dropping the razor into the basin, he drew the towel from around his neck and dried his face. Then he ran his fingers through his hair, leaving wavy furrows that only made him seem sexier. After cleaning his razor and tossing away the water, he returned his shaving gear to his pack and tugged on his shirt.

"What you need," he said as he pushed to his feet, "is a nice, hot soak and an all-over massage. I can't conjure up a bath, but I'm good for the rubdown."

Ellie jerked up a staying hand. "No, thanks."

"Ah, come on." Buttoning his shirt, he circled the fire. "Why suffer all day when I can have you feeling great inside of ten minutes?"

That was what worried her, his ability to make her feel great. She felt a little like a rabbit being stalked by a large predator as he closed the remaining distance between them. He moved to stand behind her and curled his hands over her shoulders.

"I really don't want—" The rest died in her throat as his long fingers went to work, pressing in and releasing. She groaned like a woman in the throes of orgasm. *"Oh."*

"Feel nice?" He pressed his thumbs along her vertebrae and made fabulous little rotations over all the spots that ached. "That's the way. Just relax." He bent closer so his voice was a low rumble beside her ear. "Let me have my way with you."

Ellie gave a startled laugh. "Don't get any ideas. You'll be dead in less than a minute if you touch me anywhere you shoul—*O-hh*, that feels so *fabulous*." It took all her willpower not to lean her weight against the heels of his hands. "Oh, Tucker."

His clever fingers moved downward, seeking out the sore spots between her shoulder blades. "Lean back. I've got you." He put his hands at her waist and moved slowly up her ribs until his fingertips circled dangerously close to the swell of each breast. "Don't tense up on me. Stay limp so I can get the kinks out."

Her kinks had become the least of her worries. "I'm going to spill my coffee."

"Toss it out." His hot mouth skimmed up the side of her neck, his breaths whispery in her hair and tickling her nape. "God, Ellie, you feel so fantastic."

Her eyes, which had drooped almost shut, snapped wide open as it hit her what she was doing. She jerked erect, barely managing not to slop any coffee. "That's enough, thanks. I'm better now. Really."

His hands slid down to ride on her hips, his fingertips curling over her hipbones to get a firm grip. "What are you so afraid of, Ellie? Only say the word, and I always stop. You know that."

"Stop!" she squeaked.

He laughed and nipped her neck. "You're a cold woman. It'd be such a fabulous way to start the morning. It doesn't have to be complicated, you know. Think of it as a little stroll down memory lane, for old times' sake, if nothing else. We were so good together once."

Ellie stepped away from him. Clinging to her coffee mug as though it might lend her strength, she turned to face him. "I've sworn off."

"Off sex?" He sounded mildly horrified.

"Not across the board. Just sex with you."

"Why only with me?"

"I don't have indiscriminate sex. For safety's sake and a host of other reasons, I avoid intimacy with those who do."

His brows arched nearly to his hairline. "Are you accusing me of having indiscriminate sex?"

The innocent look on his face made her so angry she wanted to smack him. "I didn't stammer." She slung her hand to empty the cup. The liquid hit the fire with a loud hiss and sent up a cloud of steam. "And, *please*, don't bother to deny it. I heard all about the Jennifer Lopez look-alike with the tongue studs, Tucker, and I've seen Liz for myself. Heaven knows how many women there were in between."

"What the hell are you talking about? Jennifer *Lopez*?"

"Kody told me all about her."

"Kody?" Looking befuddled, he rubbed under his ear and frowned. "What, exactly, did he say?"

"Just that she was young, gorgeous, and you were totally gone over her."

His frown deepened. "Really? Isn't it interesting that I don't remember the woman."

"Girl," she corrected. "In my circles, it's called robbing the cradle."

He lifted one hand, palm up, and motioned her on with his fingertips. "Keep it coming. Specifics."

She could not believe his gall. How dare he pretend that he didn't know what she was talking about? Fury rolled hot into her throat. "Early twenties? Gorgeous tan? Pretty brown eyes? Built like a brick *outhouse*! Does that refresh your memory?"

He folded his arms. Narrowing one eye, he smiled. "No, actually, it doesn't. I never dated anyone who fit that description." He hesitated for a moment. "The fact of the matter is that I never dated anyone who fit *any* description. Except for Liz, of course, and only then in the most casual of ways, which is why I told her where to get off when she referred to herself as my significant other."

He could stand there denying it all day, but Ellie knew her boys wouldn't lie.

"That's why she made the crack about my lousy performance in bed," he added. "My performance sucked because I never performed, not with her or anyone else."

"Right. If you're selling the Golden Gate, I'll buy that, too."

He thrust out his chin. The green glints in his hazel

eyes told Ellie he was growing angry. That suited her just fine.

"While we're on the subject of Liz, let's get another thing straight," he went on. "Whatever you thought you saw yesterday when you jumped me next to the Land Cruiser, it sure as hell wasn't a hard-on."

"Really?" She stuck her finger through the handle of the tin cup and gave it a twirl. "What did you do? Stop by Photo Magic and get an enlargement?"

A vein in his temple popped up and started to throb. *Bull's-eye,* she thought happily. That one got him where it hurt.

"I don't recall you ever having any complaints in that area."

Ellie shrugged. "Of course not. I didn't want to bruise your fragile male ego. Besides, I had no standard for comparison at the time."

"And you do now?"

She only smiled sweetly again. Both his temples were pulsating now. It gave her no end of satisfaction. What had begun as a totally *awful* morning was suddenly looking up. "Are we finished with this boring conversation yet?"

"No," he growled. "I'm not finished."

She gave him a saccharine-sweet smile. "I am. Thanks for the update on your sex life, but I'm not interested, not for old times' sake and *definitely* not to take a stroll down memory lane. My memories of us aren't the kind I want to revisit." She swung away. "I suggest that you get dressed. We need to break camp and get cracking."

She heard his boot connect with the ground. The spray of dirt he kicked up almost hit her on the butt. She danced out of reach and turned to stare at him. Tucker had always been the calm one when they quarreled, the one who kept a lid on his temper.

He kicked dirt again and swore. "You always, *always* do this. Go ahead. Walk away, damn it. The conversation's over, *again*. You know what your problem is, Ellie? You're too big a coward to go toe to toe with me and have it out."

"I am not a coward!"

"Prove it."

She walked back toward him, stomping her feet with every step. When she reached him, she knocked the toes of her boots against his. "Fine! Here I am, toe to toe. You wanna talk? Start talking! Explain to me why your sons have given me blow-by-blow accounts of all your sexy girlfriends if there haven't been any girlfriends!"

He leaned down to put the end of his nose a scant inch from hers. "Maybe for the same reason they gave me blow-by-blow accounts of all your sexy boyfriends."

"My *what*?" Ellie winced the moment she spoke. No way did she want him to know she hadn't had any boyfriends, sexy or otherwise. Well—there'd been Marvin, she mentally revised. But he barely counted. All his kisses had ever done was make her think about her grocery list.

"You heard me," he growled back. "They gave me detailed accounts of all your boyfriends. I even saw one of them. Randall, I think his name was. Good-looking, dark hair, a suit type. One night when I dropped off the boys, he was coming out your front door. Zach said he was your new boyfriend. Talk about robbing the cradle. He didn't look a day over twenty."

"*Randall?*" Ellie inched her face back and blinked in confusion. As reluctant as she was to have Tucker know that she'd been celibate since the divorce, she didn't want him to think she'd been sleeping with a teenage boy. Unlike him, she had standards. "He's a Jehovah's Witness."

"I don't give a shit if he's Jewish, Catholic, or Muslim. He's a man, and according to the boys, you had a thing going with him."

"With *Randall*? He's just—" Ellie laughed and rolled her eyes. "Give me a break. He's only nineteen. He drops off religious pamphlets once a month. One night it was raining, and he was soaking wet. I invited him in to dry off, and we became friends. Now when he comes by, I always have him in for milk and cookies."

"Milk and cookies? How dumb do you think I am?" He sighed and rubbed a broad hand over his face. After gazing off into the woods for a moment, he puffed air into his cheeks and then released it through his teeth. "Strike that. I believe you, actually. I don't think you had a thing for Randall—or anyone else, for that matter. If the kids told you a bunch of whoppers, it only stands to reason that they told me a bunch, too."

"My sons do not lie."

"A week ago, I would have sworn they'd never run away. Now look what's happened." He gazed deeply into her eyes. "They're good kids, Ellie. But the way they see it right now, all bets are off and the rules don't apply. They've lied. They've run away. Where is it going to stop?"

She hugged her waist so hard that her knuckles hurt her ribs. Her boys had lied? She couldn't believe that. If there was a cardinal rule that she'd drilled into their heads, it was never to lie to her, not for any reason. "My boys don't lie," she said again, her voice ringing with more certainty than she actually felt.

"Have you been screwing Randall's brains out?"

The question snapped her chin up. "Of course not! I wouldn't go to bed with a kid that age."

"They implied that you were. When I got upset, Zach was quick to inform me that Randall only spent the night at your place when the boys were with me in Bend."

Ellie couldn't believe her ears. She'd never let a man spend the night, period.

"They lied," he assured her. "To both of us, evidently. I can only assume they were trying to make us jealous."

"Why would they do that?"

"Maybe they were hoping it would make us realize that we still love each other."

She let her eyes fall closed. "Oh, Tucker. That's so *sad*."

"Only if it doesn't happen." He grasped her by the chin, lifted her face. "Look at me, Ellie."

She kept her eyes closed, afraid of what she might see if she did as he requested.

"Please," he whispered.

His imploring tone made her slowly lift her lashes. When their gazes met and held, he smiled slightly and dragged a thumb over her mouth. "I haven't been with any other women, not with the Lopez look-alike or Liz or anyone else. Do you know why?" When she only stood there, staring up at him, he went on in a husky whisper. "Because I never stopped loving you, that's why. Never once, not for a single instant, did I ever stop loving you."

Tears rushed to her eyes.

"I wanted to," he rushed on. "I tried my best to hate you, in fact. But here I am, three years later, still in love with you. Hopelessly, completely, forever in love with you." When she started to speak, he touched his thumb to her lips again. "I know we have problems, problems that were bigger than we were right after Sammy died. I understand that we both have negative feelings to work through, that it may not happen overnight, and that even after all is said and done, we may still have unresolved issues. I don't know if we'll make it. I can't make any promises. All I know is that I love you so much I have to try."

"Oh, Tucker."

"The question is . . ." His voice trailed away, and he just stood there for a moment, his gaze clinging to hers. Then, his voice gruff with emotion, he began again. "The question is, Ellie, do you love me enough to try?"

Ellie could barely see him now through her tears. Oh, how she wanted to throw herself into his arms and sob out her answer, which was yes, a million times yes. It was one of the biggest heartbreaks of her life that the words wouldn't come, that they would have made no difference even if they had.

Because she'd lacked the courage to tell him the whole truth three years ago, he'd never fully comprehended her responsibility for Sammy's death, yet he'd blamed her for it anyway. How much more would he blame her now if she were to tell him the whole story?

He spoke of negative feelings and working their way through them? He spoke of love as if it were some magical panacea? Pretty words, and they sounded good. But how could he ever work through the fact that she had killed their son?

She'd loved this man with every fiber of her being three years ago, and that hadn't been enough to hold him. If he learned what had really happened that fateful afternoon, her love wouldn't be enough to hold him now.

He'd walk away—*again*.

If she let him back into her heart, he'd destroy her—*again*.

She didn't have the strength to endure that a second time and come out on the other side with her sanity.

Theirs had been the love of a lifetime—a sweet, innocent, incredibly beautiful love—but it was over. It had been over for a very long time, ending in that fateful moment when their son's motorcycle had careened into the path of a hay truck. They couldn't go back. They couldn't rebuild. A successful marriage couldn't be built on a lie, even if it was only a lie of omission, and she wasn't brave enough to tell him the truth. To what end? So he would have even more ammunition to wound her?

"I'm sorry," she whispered. "I'm so sorry, Tucker.

I wish I could say the words you want to hear, but I—just—can't."

For what seemed an endless moment, he didn't move, didn't seem even to breathe. Then he released her chin and stepped away to stand with his head bent, his hands resting at his hips.

When he finally looked back up at her, he said the last thing she expected to hear. "Round one, your win."

"Pardon?"

"You heard me." He straightened his shoulders, and a determined gleam slipped into his eyes. "I'm not giving up on you, Ellie. One way or another, we're going to give it another go. I'll drag you by your hair to counseling if I have to, get on my knees and beg if I have to, but I'll be damned if I'll throw in the towel this time without a fight."

Each word he spoke punched into her like a fist. He meant what he was saying; she could see it in his eyes. The knowledge scared her half to death.

A few minutes later, they were deep in the forest. Morning sunlight spilled through the canopy of Ponderosa boughs overhead, the shafts shimmering with dust motes. Red-winged blackbirds darted back and forth in the brush along the creek, their trilling voices filling the air with music. Ground squirrels scurried from their holes, already intent on foraging for food. With a shrill caw that drifted eerily along the stream, an osprey left its lofty nest atop an old snag and swooped skyward to catch a draft with its gracefully outstretched wings.

At any other time, Ellie would have been awestruck by such beauty, but this morning, she was too tense to appreciate it. Tucker was circling the area in search of the boys' tracks. She was hard put to keep up with him.

"Hello," he murmured when he finally found something. Crouching to examine the footprints, he touched a fingertip to the earth, then lifted his head to gaze uphill. "You ready for a climb?" he asked.

"As ready as I'll ever be," she replied.

He smiled and touched her cheek with the back of a knuckle as he walked by her. The casual caress sent her falling back a step, her nerves electrified, not only by the contact itself, but also by what it portended. He had no intention of observing a hands-off policy for the remainder of this trip. That much was clear.

Leaving her to make what she might of that, he strode away, his head slightly bent to scan the ground ahead. Ellie fell in behind him as he started through the trees. Her sore muscles screamed with every step. The 2nd Skin over her blister helped immensely, but the pack felt twice as heavy as it had yesterday. The straps cut into her bruised shoulders, and the weight bumped against her aching tailbone.

At the creek, Tucker stopped and slung off his pack. From a side pocket, he drew a pair of waterproof Gators, slipped them on over his boots, and tugged the elasticized tops up to just below his knees. Glancing back at her, he said, "Shed your pack, and I'll carry you across."

"Oh, you don't need to do that," she protested nervously. "I can make it."

"No arguments. I don't want you getting water inside your boots, not with a blister like that on your heel."

Ellie couldn't argue with his reasoning. Reluctantly, she tugged the straps of the backpack down her arms. Her gear no sooner plopped on the ground than he bent to pick her up.

She squeaked and clutched his shoulders. "Don't drop me!"

He straightened and gave her a jostle to get a better hold. "You never used to worry that I'd drop you."

"You had fewer reasons to lose your grip on me back then."

He chuckled. "Wishing you'd never heard of Photo Magic?"

Ellie cringed, which only made him laugh. "Don't worry. My fragile male ego isn't quite that fragile, and I'm choosy about how I get my revenge. Hold tight."

Ellie did as he suggested, acutely aware of how wonderful it felt to have his arms around her. She felt nothing but strength radiating from his big, rangy body.

Their noses were only a few inches apart. The faint scent of coffee laced his breath. Up close, she could see the tiny lines that fanned out from the corners of his eyes. Yet, oddly, she felt like a teenager again— an innocent fifteen-year-old girl who'd never been kissed. Tucker had stolen her heart all those years ago, and she had a feeling he would never give it back.

Judging by the expression that entered his eyes, he was remembering, too. His mouth tightened, deepening the slashes in his cheeks. The air around them seemed to thicken. Deliciously sensual memories filtered through her mind. She recalled exactly how it felt to have his big hands graze her skin, how it felt to slide into a slow, passionate kiss that heated her blood and made her pulse pound.

He plunged off the bank into the water. Ellie sucked in a breath when she felt his feet slip on the rocks. The stream was shallow, reaching only to his knees, but the current was swift, making it difficult for him to keep his footing.

She needn't have worried, she realized seconds later. He carried her across without a problem. At the other bank, he swung her up onto dry ground, steadied her until she caught her balance, and then waded back to retrieve their packs.

"Thanks," she said as he joined her on the bank and removed his Gators. "That water must be freezing."

Stomping his boots to rid them of excess moisture, he said, "Luckily, with the Gators, it wasn't bad." He guided her arms through the straps of her pack, helped settle the weight, and then tied the waist cinch. Once again, he seemed to purposely allow his hands to linger on her body.

As he donned his own pack, he turned his gaze up the hill. "You ready?"

"Ready," she said faintly, falling in behind as he began the ascent.

At a particularly steep place, he braced his feet and turned to help her. Not wishing to set a precedent by touching him any more than she absolutely had to, Ellie almost declined the offer. But then she recalled her painful tumble yesterday and decided she'd rather be safe than sorry.

Safe? As his hand closed over hers, awareness shot up her arm and her breathing quickened. Not so safe, she decided. His touch made her think about things she shouldn't—like how it might feel to make love with him again.

By midafternoon, Ellie was on her last legs. "Tucker?" she called. "I hate to ask, but can we take a short break?"

He turned to look back. "Sure. I told you, any time."

"I know. I just hate to make you stop."

Wincing, Ellie dragged the straps of her pack off her smarting shoulders and let the burden fall to the ground behind her. She didn't care if she broke her expensive water purifier—or anything else, for that matter. At this point, she was so exhausted that her one concern was to rest.

Frowning, Tucker retraced his path down the hill to her. When he reached her, he startled her by tugging the collar of her shirt open. A thunderous expression crossed his face.

"Holy hell, you're all black and blue."

Thinking he referred to the poke marks that Marvin had left on her chest, Ellie tucked in her chin to look.

"No, *no*, not there. Without pads, the damn straps are cutting into your shoulders."

He swore as he circled her. Ellie sank onto a rock and watched dully as he hefted her pack.

"That's it. I'm getting rid of some of this shit." He

started removing stuff and throwing it to the ground. "Can you explain this to me? I mean—I saw it the first morning, and I wondered about it at the time. Why didn't you ditch it when the straps started to hurt?"

Ellie stared stupidly at the can of beef ravioli, which she'd brought along for Kody. "I thought when we found them—you know—that some hot food would be nice."

He held up two cans of Vienna sausage. "Son of a *bitch*. No wonder your shoulders are bruised. You're carting a grocery store." He pulled out a can of spaghetti. "I don't know what I was thinking to let you carry all this stuff."

"That's Zach's favorite. Just in case they didn't take enough food. They might be hungry when we find them."

"So you loaded all this extra weight into your pack?" He continued throwing things aside. "I need my head examined for allowing it."

"What're you *doing*?"

"Lightening the load," he ground out. "Those kids don't need a damned feast when we find them. A kick in the pants, more like. And you don't need half this other stuff, either. I'll share mine."

When her tent joined the pile of discarded items, Ellie stiffened and threw him a heated glance. "Tucker, I need that for shelter."

He sent her a fiery look. "You can sleep with me."

"No way."

"Not in the same bag. We can share the same roof, can't we?"

Ellie wished to avoid that sort of closeness at all costs. "I'd rather not."

"Well, I'm afraid you're not going to get your druthers."

"That tent weighs hardly anything!" she cried. "You're just using that as an excuse. I am not, repeat *not* sharing a shelter with you."

"Your choice. I guess you can sleep under the stars."

"Very funny."

"We're leaving the tent, Ellie. Like it, don't like it. I really don't care." He sent her another searing look. "You're not going to make it, carrying a pack, and I can't keep up this pace if I carry two that are full."

Chapter Twelve

Ellie doubled her hands into throbbing fists as she watched Tucker trim her gear down to the bare essentials, leaving only her clothing, her sleeping bag, and the necessary food she'd brought along. It didn't escape her notice that the white teddy and perfume remained in her pack. Yet he left her tent lying in the dirt. How that made sense, she didn't know.

He shouldered both packs. "Are you rested enough to go on now?"

She struggled up from the rock. "What about all my stuff that you threw out?"

"We'll pick it up on the way back down. The gear isn't important, Ellie. You can always get more."

She reached out a hand. "I'll carry my own pack. I don't want you to do it."

"You'll do no such thing. Your shoulders are a mess."

Ellie clamped a hand over one of the throbbing places. Just the slight pressure of her fingers sent pain shooting down her arm. "I hate for you to tote double the weight because of me."

"I did it for years. You never objected then."

Ellie preferred not to think about those times. She settled for saying, "We were hiking for the fun of it then, not pushing ourselves to the limit like this."

He stepped over to catch her chin on the edge of his hand. "I'm nowhere close to reaching my limit. Just let me do this, okay? You're so exhausted you can barely walk. Carrying a pack, even a light one like this, might make you stumble and fall. I want to get you back down off this mountain in one piece."

Less than twenty minutes later, Ellie chanced a look over the edge of a cliff and nearly lost what remained of her lunch. She'd always hated heights and experienced vertigo. Today, in such an exhausted state, the nausea and dizziness were amplified.

She moved quickly back from the edge, closed her eyes, and gulped for breath. "I thought you said we wouldn't reach the bad part until tomorrow."

Tucker gripped her arm to steady her. Her weakness was such that she could muster no protest. "We won't," he affirmed. "This is a cakewalk compared to what lies ahead. Don't you remember the gorge?"

Ellie nodded, visions of deep cracks in the earth flashing through her mind. "Maybe we'll find them before they go that far," she said.

"We'll try, anyway."

To that end, they resumed walking, Tucker circling her to take the lead again. Numb with exhaustion, she admired the sure and easy agility with which he moved, his long legs pushing his weight up the incline with seemingly little effort. She didn't know how he did it. He'd been carrying both his pack and hers these last few minutes, most of it straight uphill, and he didn't even look winded.

She rolled her eyes and puffed at her bangs. Even without the pack to weigh her down, her legs were aching, and she tended to stumble easily. She thought of her sons and prayed that they'd make it safely. Had they already reached the gorge? Was Kody as tired as she was? Zach was very good with his little brother and usually watched out for him, but being so young himself, he might not notice if Kody's strength began to flag.

Ellie had hoped to find them before dark, but now, with it growing so late in the afternoon, the odds of that were dwindling. The Ponderosa and lodgepole pines cast long shadows, creating a premature twilight deep in the trees. When the sound of her heavy breathing wasn't too loud in her ears, she could hear the birds twittering as they darted from tree limb to tree limb. The squirrels were busily searching out their last tidbits of food for the day.

Darkness would come soon, blanketing the mountain in pitch black.

The footpath curved away from the cliff, winding upward through a bed of lava rock to a forested plateau. As Ellie followed Tucker over the flatter terrain, she sent up a prayer of thanks for the reprieve. With less exertion, her breaths came easier, her legs got a rest, and the sweat on her face dried in the breeze, cooling her flushed cheeks.

After only a few feet, the trail broke away from the trees to circle a lush green meadow bordered by a crag of lava rock at the far end. Startled by the unexpected intrusion of humans, a doe and fawn bounded away into the forest. A stream meandered through the clearing, a wide ribbon of mountain-clear water that babbled musically as it spilled over clusters of rock. The moist coolness of the air might have been heavenly if not for the swarm of mosquitoes that buzzed around Ellie's head. Never breaking stride, she slapped wearily at them.

"You didn't toss out my bug repellent, did you? If this is an indication, I'll get eaten alive tonight."

"I only got rid of unimportant stuff."

"Thank goodness. The last thing I need is a bunch of bug bites to make my day complete."

At the edge of the clearing where the path reentered the woods, Tucker skidded to a stop, forcing her to put on her brakes to keep from colliding with the packs riding his shoulders. "Another note."

Ellie knew by his strained tone that he was growing weary of this game their sons were playing. She suspected it was because he was concerned about her ability to keep going. That made two of them. At the outset of this journey, she'd never expected to be out here this long—or to be walking so far.

"You read it this time," he bit out.

She moved around him to pluck the paper from a tree limb that arched over the path. Sinking onto a fallen log, she swatted at a determined mosquito and then carefully unfolded the note, which the boys had affixed to the tree by puncturing one corner with a small branch.

The missive was in Zach's handwriting. A late grasshopper whirred in the dry grass near her feet as she began to read aloud. " 'Dear Mom and Dad: We hope you like this camp spot that we picked out for you tonight. It's a special place. Maybe it'll set the right mood.' " Ellie's fingers convulsed. "The right *mood*?" She looked up at Tucker. "Where is he getting all these *notions*? He's only fourteen, for Pete's sake."

"It's a different world these days, Ellie. Kids get educated fast."

"Until he leaves for college, he's never watching television again."

Tucker chuckled and turned his head to look up the trail. When he glanced back at Ellie, he was grinning broadly. "I'll be damned."

"What?"

He laughed and inclined his head at the paper. "First things first. What else does he say?"

Ellie searched to find her place. "'We tried to get you here early so you guys can really enjoy yourselves tonight. Don't be worried about us, Mom. We're not far away. No trying to sneak up on us again, Dad. It almost worked last night, but it won't again. We'll be ready for any tricks. Got to go. Kody's hungry, and I need to feed him. Have a great evening. *Please?*' "

Ellie sighed and crumpled the note in her fist. Swallowing to dislodge the lump in her throat, she said, "He underlined *please*. There isn't anything from Kody this time."

Tucker raked a hand through his hair. "You recognize where we are?"

She scanned the area. "In the woods?"

He grinned and shook his head. "Try again."

She looked more closely at the terrain. Then she shrugged. "I'm too tired for games. Where are we?"

"The hot springs."

Her nape went prickly. "You're kidding."

"Nope. Those ornery little whippersnappers brought us to our honeymoon spot. Can you believe it?"

Ellie didn't miss the satisfied gleam in his eyes. She dug her nails into the wad of paper. "You don't have to look so pleased."

He shrugged and winked at her. "Why not? One of my favorite places on earth, and my kids arranged it so I can spend the night here with the woman I love. Of course, I'm pleased."

"This isn't a pleasure outing." She flung her arm at the forest around them. "Our sons are out there. We're up here to find them. In order to do that, we have to stick together. Instead, I get the distinct impression you've joined forces with them against me."

"They aren't the enemy, Ellie."

"Don't be obtuse."

"Do you realize that's one of your favorite words?"

"You're avoiding the issue."

"No, you are. This isn't a war between us and the kids, or the guys against the gals, with you outnumbered. It's an issue between you and me. Fair odds, one against one, let the best man—or woman—win."

Ellie was so frustrated she wanted to scream. "You threw out my tent. If you think I'm going to—" Words failed her. She glanced toward the promontory of lava. "I am not sharing a tent with you here, end of discussion!"

"So that's what's worrying you." He gave her a crooked grin, looking entirely too rakish and sexy for her peace of mind. "Surely you don't think I knew about this in advance and ditched the tent on purpose?"

"I wouldn't put it past you."

He chuckled. "I wouldn't put it past me, either, but the fact is, there's no conspiracy going on between me and the kids. I just got lucky."

"Not yet, you haven't."

That really made him laugh. He spun and continued up the trail. "We'll see. Like I said, let the best man win."

"I'm not spending the night here!" she called after him.

"We don't have a choice. Their trail will take off from here, and it's getting too late to pick it up now. It'll be dark before we know it, and God knows which direction they went." When he reached the far end of the clearing below the stratum of lava rock that housed the hot springs, he started removing the packs. "Look on the bright side. For a wilderness area, these are five-star accommodations. You can have that hot bath we talked about this morning."

Huffing with anger, Ellie followed him. Everywhere she looked, she was bombarded with memories of their lovemaking. Two crazy college students who couldn't spare the money for a real honeymoon, they'd come home to Bend for a long weekend and hiked up here to celebrate their nuptials. It had been the most glorious three days of her life—but that was beside the point.

"I'm not staying here," she informed him again in a voice that vibrated with outrage. "If you have a shred of decency, you won't ask that of me."

He chuckled again. "I guess I don't have a shred."

"I am *not* spending a night here."

"Suit yourself." He dropped his pack and turned a slow circle, grinning from ear to ear. "Remember that tree—or more specifically, the grassy spot underneath it?"

Ellie was squeezing her fists so hard that the tablet paper had been compressed to the size of a marble. "*That* is exactly the problem. I mean it, Tucker. No way."

He cocked a tawny eyebrow. "Fine. Where do you plan to go? Let me know before you leave and I'll come get you in the morning."

Anger turned to helpless fury. He knew very well she wouldn't strike off on her own, not with wolves possibly in these woods. "Damn it, be reasonable. I don't even have a shelter."

He winked at her. "I'll be happy to share mine."

"You know very well why they brought us here."

"Yep. It was a stroke of sheer genius, if you ask me."

"It isn't going to happen," she said shrilly.

"Fine." He lifted his hands. "It isn't going to happen. So relax. Laugh it off. Congratulate yourself on raising two kids who can come up with a scheme like this and pull it off without a hitch. They didn't plan this in an hour, that's for damned sure. They must have spent days cooking it up."

She had already considered that, and thinking about it made her heart hurt. Her sons wanted more from her than she was able to give. Tucker wanted more from her than she was able to give. And, God help her, he *had* joined forces with them against her. She saw it in his eyes. He was hoping all the romantic memories would get to her, that she'd succumb to sentiment and make love with him under that tree again.

Well, she had news for him. Having sex wouldn't solve their problems. It wouldn't even start.

She was so upset she could scarcely believe her ears when she heard him start to laugh. Not just a halfhearted chuckle. Oh, no. This was more a guffaw—raucous and straight from the gut. She turned to see him striding across the clearing toward the rocks.

"Would you *look*?" He swung around, one hand clamped over his belly as if the laughter pained him. "If I wasn't seeing it myself, I would *not* believe this."

Bewildered, Ellie glanced past him. At the base of the lava on a broad, flat-surfaced rock, was what appeared to be an arrangement of flowers in a dog food can, flanked by two bottles of wine. She blinked, convinced she had to be seeing things, but when her vision cleared, the items were still there.

"They even left a corkscrew." He flashed her a broad smile over his shoulder. "The roses are artificial, but, hey, pretty classy, if you ask me." He picked up one of the bottles and let loose with another guffaw. "The little *hooligans*. They raided my wine rack and stole my merlot. Nothing so fine as Marvin's stuff, unfortunately. I buy on the cheap, but it's not bad stuff for the price."

Ellie didn't give a rip how good the wine was. She had no intention of drinking any. "Tucker," she said, using a cajoling tone this time, "I really don't want to stay here. Can't we move down from here a bit? We can pitch the tent along the creek somewhere and come back in the morning to pick up their trail. This place is rife with so many memories."

"It sure is." His voice dipped to a husky timbre. Setting the wine back on the rock, he turned to take in the clearing. Pointing to her left, he said, "Over there, for instance. Remember that night, Ellie? We stood in the moonlight on that exact spot and renewed our wedding vows. You'd just found out you were pregnant with Sammy. You'd been green with morning sickness twenty-four hours a day, but that night you felt okay."

His expression sobered. Ellie wasn't sure what had made him melancholy, whether it was his recollections of that night or the mention of Sammy's name, but his eyes went dark with pain.

"Do you remember what you said to me that night?" he asked.

Ellie didn't want to go there.

"You promised to love me forever. You said nothing, absolutely nothing, would ever change how you felt about me."

Her feelings hadn't changed, she thought sadly, but everything else in her life had.

"What happened, Ellie?"

She forced herself to meet his gaze. "The very fact that you need to ask should answer that question." She pushed at her hair. The strands were as stiff as piano wire. "If we're staying here, I'm going to make use of those springs and take a bath."

"Want some company?"

She threw him a stony look. "No, I do not. If you come anywhere near those springs while I'm bathing, I'll drown you."

*   *   *

When Ellie returned to their campsite forty minutes later, Tucker had set up the tent, built a roaring fire, already caught fish in the nearby creek for their supper, and was in the process of pouring wine into their tin coffee mugs.

"None for me, thanks," Ellie said as she moved to stand at the fire.

Though she'd just had a hot bath, the night air was chilly, and it had a bite when it seeped through her clothing to touch her still-damp skin. She held her hands out to the flames and shivered. Her hair was still wet, which didn't help to ward off the cold.

Ignoring her refusal of any wine, Tucker sloshed a measure into her cup anyway. "Come on. Have a little. It'll warm you right up."

Ellie thought she would be better served to put on her jacket. Spirits of any kind tended to dull her wits. Around Tucker, that could prove dangerous. "No, really. I don't care for any."

"Why? Afraid you'll lose your inhibitions and end up in bed with me?"

Ellie wouldn't dignify that charge with a response.

"Ah-ha. You know what that means, don't you?" He slipped the cup into her hand and then stood beside her to sip from his own. "Deep down, you want to go to bed with me. If the desire isn't there when you're sober, it won't suddenly come upon you when you're drunk."

Ellie shook her head. "Can we talk about something else?"

"I'd rather you answer my question."

"I didn't realize you asked one."

"Are you afraid to have any wine because you'd like to go to bed with me?"

She considered lying and then discarded the thought. "Yes."

For a moment, he regarded her with a mix of stunned bewilderment and incredulity. Then he recovered and smiled. "A few sips won't hurt. I promise to be a perfect gentleman."

Ellie laughed in spite of herself. "Right. You've never been a perfect gentleman in your life."

"I have so. I have never once forced you to do anything you didn't want to do."

"Force, no. But pushing and prodding aren't beyond you."

He clicked his cup against hers. "I'll drink to that."

She automatically took a sip of the wine before she thought. As it slid down her throat, she shot him a frown. He chuckled and tapped his cup to hers again. "To our sons, the most wonderful boys who ever walked. You have to drink to that."

"Unfair."

"I know. Hear, hear." He started to drink, then lowered his cup slightly to gaze at her over the speckled rim. "You know what happens when you don't drink to a toast?"

"No, what?"

"You get a hairy wart on the end of your nose and your toenails turn yellow."

"Oh, dear. Really?"

"Have I ever lied to you?"

She didn't know why she found it so impossible to resist him, but she did. "Cheers." She took a small sip, assuring herself that a tiny bit of wine wouldn't hurt.

"Here's another one you can't ignore. To our success in finding our kids, safe and sound."

Ellie definitely had to drink to that one. And so it

went. Before she knew it, her hair was almost dry, it had grown fully dark, and Tucker was refilling her cup. "I really shouldn't have any more."

He poured anyway. "Ah, come on. Live a little, live a lot. You only get one go around. Why not go around with me?"

"I already tried. Remember? Somehow we got onto the roundabout together but turned off on different roads."

"We turned off together, Ellie. I distinctly remember that much—staring at each other but not really connecting anymore."

"I guess our communication lines shorted out."

He refilled his own cup and set the bottle on the ground beside him. "I guess so. Why did that happen, do you think?"

She took another tiny sip of merlot. "It wasn't because I said, 'I don't want to discuss it.' I know that much."

Tucker dug at the dirt with his heel. "Then why?"

A heavy feeling filled her chest. In a thin voice, she said, "You walked out. Just up and walked out." She clanked her cup against his. "To remembering. Isn't it grand?"

It was Tucker who didn't drink this time. For a long moment, he simply stared into his wine. Then he finally slanted her a hard look. In the flickering firelight, his eyes cut like glass. "Why do you do that?"

"Do what?"

"Let on like I abandoned you."

"Because you did." His stony expression prompted her to add, "I'm sorry. Maybe I remember it wrong. I could have sworn it was *me* who was left standing alone in the living room, with the sound of the slamming door reverberating in *my* ears. Correct me if I have it reversed."

"Goddamn it."

"Hear, hear, I'll drink to that." She tipped back her head to drain her cup. Then she held it out to him for a refill. "I'll need some more. There are so many things to drink to, after all, like the fact that *you* left me, and now, here you are, trying to convince me we should give it another try. As if I'm the one who walked out on you, as if I'm the one who gave up on the marriage in the first place?" When he didn't refill her cup, she clanked it against his anyway. "I really think we should drink to that, Tucker. It's so classic, isn't it? Pure Tucker Grant. You've changed your mind, so now I should revise my thinking, rearrange my life, and fall back into your arms."

"You're doing this on purpose. You want to pick a fight. If you can piss me off, you'll feel safe."

She touched her cup to his again. "To whatever works."

He tossed out the rest of his wine, his eyes glittering with anger. "You want to fight, fine by me. Only this time, it'll be by different rules."

She didn't like the sound of that. "What rules are those?"

"Rules of fair play. No blowing smoke. No lying. No skirting the real issues. You still game? Or are you afraid to take me on?"

"I'm not afraid of you, and I've never blown any smoke."

"Bullshit. You do it constantly. Like our marriage,

for instance, and me abandoning you. How is it that you twist everything around to make it my fault?"

"Why does everything have to be about *blame* with you?" she volleyed back.

"There, you see?" He laughed bitterly. "Instead of addressing the question, you launch a counterattack. That's rich, coming from the queen of accusation herself."

That was so unfair, she couldn't quite believe he'd said it.

Before she could respond, he rushed on to say, "No matter how much at fault you may be, you somehow convince yourself that you're in no way to blame. Take this mess with the kids. When I called to tell you, your first thought was that I must have done something to make them run away. Screwing Liz in the living room while they were watching television was the first thing that popped into your mind."

"I never believed you'd be *that* crass."

"And that excuses you? No. It never crossed your mind that maybe you had laid the groundwork for this whole mess yourself."

Ellie couldn't believe he'd worked it around in his head to make it all her fault. Now it was her turn to start growing angry. "I beg your pardon?" she asked icily.

"The move to Springfield, for starters. Do you think I *wanted* you to take the kids over to the valley? Do you think I *wanted* my time with them cut back to almost nothing? Do you honestly believe, deep down, that I thought being separated from me would be good for them?"

"We have joint custody. If you thought it would be so bad for them, you could have stopped me from going."

"And have you hate me for refusing to let you leave Bend? There were already enough counts against me. I didn't want to add another to your list. You said it was killing you to stay in that house, remember? That it was having a bad effect on the kids, as well. You told me every nook and cranny reminded you of Sammy, and you thought it might be easier if the three of you could make a fresh start somewhere else. New surroundings, new friends, new experiences. Remember that phone conversation, Ellie? What was I supposed to do, be a bastard and say no?"

"I see," she said. "So this whole mess with the kids has nothing to do with Sammy's death, nothing to do with our divorce. The whole problem, in a nutshell, stems from the move to Springfield, for which you take no responsibility. If anything happens, you'll hold me entirely responsible."

"Yeah. How does it feel?"

Ellie felt as if he'd slapped her. She splayed a hand over her heart and just stared at him. "Yes, I put out feelers for another job," she admitted tremulously, "and yes, I relocated. I had lost my child, if you'll recall, and shortly thereafter, I lost my husband, as well."

"Excuse me, but Sammy was my child, too. You seem to forget that. I'll also remind you that it wasn't only your marriage that fell apart."

"I have never forgotten, even for an instant, that Sammy was your son. I just think we should have faced the grief of losing him together, the way parents are supposed to, side by side, supporting each other, helping each other through it. Instead, you walked out and left me to go through it alone."

"And you think I wasn't alone?" he retorted.

"Not in the same way I was."

"At least you still had the kids."

"Oh, yes. What a comfort that was. Two kids whose whole world had fallen apart. Two kids who'd lost not only their brother but their father, as well. I could barely hold myself together during that time. Everywhere I looked, there were a thousand memories to haunt me. I couldn't run from them like you did."

Even in the firelight, she saw the blood drain from his face. He flung aside his cup. The tin clanked loudly when it hit the rocks. He stood with his hands balled into fists, every muscle in his body quivering, his eyes flashing with rage. For the first time since she'd known him, Ellie was afraid he might strike her.

"*Run* from them? You little *bitch*." He leveled a finger at her face. "I'm sick to death tired of you insinuating that I ran out on you. *Enough.* Blame me for everything else, damn you, but not our divorce! You didn't lose your husband, Ellie. You threw him away."

That was so completely outrageous she could think of no response.

"I was the one who walked out," he continued. "Guilty as charged! But you were the one who drove me to it."

"Drove you to it?"

"Yes, damn it. Night after night, lying beside you in bed, feeling you cringe every time you thought I might touch you. What did you expect me to do, Ellie, stay there and live with your constant condemnation?"

"I never condemned you." Hurt and outrage pushed into her throat. He'd been the one who condemned her, not the other way around. "How can you say that?"

"Oh, come off it. You hated me so much you could barely stand to look at me. I'd killed our boy, for God's sake! Don't you think knowing that and having to live with it every waking second was punishment enough without you crucifying me every chance you got?"

Her mouth worked, but no words came out.

Saving her the need to speak, he rushed on to say, "I've had it." He made a slashing motion near his forehead. "Right up to the damned eyebrows. I'll accept the blame for Sammy. I went against your wishes and bought him the stupid motorcycle. I also forgot to lock the shed to make sure he couldn't get in there. Because of my stupidity and negligence, he ended up dead. On that count, I haven't got a leg to stand on. My fault, all the way, much to my sorrow for the rest of my life! But I refuse to accept the blame for our divorce. No *way*, lady. You're the one who ended the marriage, the one who turned your back on me. It didn't count for shit that I'd loved our son as much as you did. All the sacrifices I'd made up to that point to be a good husband and father didn't count for shit, either!

"You were hurting. I understood that. You

couldn't forgive me for Sammy's death, and I understood that, as well. But I'll be damned if I'll stand here and have you add abandonment to my list of sins! I left because you made it impossible for me to stay! Excuse me, but where the hell do you get off?"

He stalked away into the darkness, leaving her to stare stupidly after him. Tucker blamed *himself* for Sammy's death? She could scarcely believe her ears. As he'd reminded her countless times, *she'd* been the one at home. She'd been the one who hadn't been watching him closely enough. If not for her negligence, their son never would have been able to sneak out to the shed and climb on the motorcycle unsupervised in the first place.

Ellie clamped a hand over her mouth and squeezed her eyes closed. She was shaking so hard that her legs would barely hold her up. *Oh, God. Oh, dear God.* All this time, she'd believed that Tucker blamed her. Because she had believed that so completely, she'd never found the courage to tell him the truth about what had really happened that afternoon. She'd been afraid it would only make him hate her all the more.

Now she realized he'd never blamed her at all.

"Can you believe they're fighting?" Kody said crossly. "They're supposed to be making up. What is *so* difficult about that for them to understand?"

Lying on his belly again and staring at their parents through the brush, Zach could only shake his head. Citing a favorite adage of his father's, he said, "Maybe things have to get worse before they get better."

Kody huffed. "How much worse can things get?"

That was a question Zach didn't want to answer. He had a bad feeling things could get a whole lot worse. He'd never seen their dad get so mad at their mom that he trembled and doubled his fists. "I don't know," he settled for saying. "Who understands adults?"

Their mother hunkered back down by the fire. Looping her arms around her bent knees and rocking rhythmically onto her toes, she looked so sad that Zach wished he could go hug her. This crazy idea of Kody's had seemed like an okay plan back in town, but now Zach seriously questioned the wisdom of it. Their parents had been through enough. It seemed to Zach that all he and Kody had accomplished so far was to make them more miserable.

"That clinches it," Zach whispered when he saw his mother's shoulders start to jerk. "Mom's crying. I'm calling this off."

Kody lashed out a hand and grabbed Zach's arm. "No, wait! She's getting up. See? She's gonna go after him."

Zach wasn't sure that was good. To his recollection, their dad and mom had never gotten physical during a fight, but there could always be a first time. Dad was pretty pissed. Tucker Grant didn't believe in smacking women, but what if he got so furious, he forgot his own rule?

"Come on," he said to his brother.

Kody sent him a bewildered look. "Where are we going?"

Zach hadn't thought that far ahead yet. He only knew he needed to get his brother away from there. Even if their mom and dad only yelled and screamed at each other, they'd probably say a lot of ugly stuff that Kody shouldn't hear.

"Come on, I said. You'll find out where we're going when we get there."

Chapter Thirteen

Head in his hands, Tucker sat on a log near the creek. The rushing sound of the water didn't soothe him as he'd hoped it might. The comparative silence of the small clearing worked no magic, either. He was furious, and he doubted the emotion would leave him any time soon.

He wasn't sure if he was angrier with Ellie or with himself. She had maneuvered him like a chess piece, and he'd let her. He should have kept his cool and laughed at her attempts to piss him off. But, oh, no, he'd allowed her to push his buttons and make him lose his temper, which had been her aim from the start.

He could almost see her, dusting her hands and smiling over a job well done. No romantic evening, no walks down memory lane, no more worries that she might be tempted to make love with him. Just that easily, and he'd been dispatched. She was probably cuddled up in her sleeping bag right now, munching trail mix for supper and smirking at her cleverness.

"Tucker?"

At the sound of her voice, he nearly jumped out of his skin. Pushing erect, he spun to face her. She stood some ten feet away, arms locked around her ribs, shoulders hunched. She reminded him of an actress in one of those vampire flicks, her eyes glittering pools of darkness in her bloodless face, the skin so tight over her cheekbones that she looked almost skeletal. He decided it must be a trick of the moonlight.

"I, um—n-need to t-talk to you." Her voice was eerily high-pitched, each intonation faint and shaky. "Can you give me a c-couple of minutes?"

"I'm finished talking for tonight. Anything else you need to say, save it for tomorrow."

She bent her head. "I c-can't. I have to s-say it now. I'll lose my courage if I wait." Her shoulders gave a violent jerk. "I'm s-sorry, so sorry. I don't expect you to forgive me, but, oh, God, I'm so *sorry!*"

Tucker clenched his fists, battling the urge to go to her. He'd always been a sucker for tears, probably because she so seldom played that card. On the few occasions that she had, he'd never been able to stay mad at her.

Well, not this time. He was pissed, royally pissed, and he intended to stay that way. She could cry until her eyes swelled shut. How dare she upbraid him for abandoning her? Even worse, she'd accused him of running from the grief and memories. As if a person could? The world wasn't a big enough place to escape that kind of pain, and he hadn't tried.

"Tell me how sorry you are tomorrow," he bit out. "Right now, I'm just that close"—he measured off a half inch between thumb and forefinger—"to losing my temper in a way that will make Hiroshima look like a cap gun going off. If you're smart, you'll back off and leave me alone."

"I c-can't do that. I need to get this said."

He wasn't surprised. She had backed away from very few things in her life, and he'd never been one of them. He folded his arms, assuring himself that it was only a precaution to make sure he didn't strangle her, not to keep himself from closing the distance between them and gathering her into his arms. She was shaking, he realized, shaking horribly, and her pallor wasn't a trick of the moonlight, after all.

"I, um—" Her breath caught wetly in her throat, and she gulped to steady her voice. "I always thought you blamed *me* for what happened."

She lifted her head to look at him again. He'd never seen such pain in anyone's eyes.

"I thought you b-blamed me because I wasn't watching Sammy closely enough that afternoon," she went on shakily. "You did say that to me." She gestured limply with her hand. "You said it never would've happened if I'd only b-been watching him closer. Remember?"

He remembered, and he wished to God he didn't. Nausea curled through his stomach. *Why?* The question circled in his mind. Why, a thousand times, why? It wasn't like him to be deliberately cruel to anyone, yet he had purposefully wounded Ellie, the person he loved most. At the time, it had seemed necessary somehow—vital to his own sanity in some convoluted way. He'd been responsible for their child's death, he'd seen the accusation in her eyes, and that had hurt so much he'd felt compelled to shift some of the blame, to hurt her as deeply as she was hurting him.

"That's why I never t-told you," she went on in that awful, quivering voice that cut him to the quick with every inflection. "I need you to understand that up front. I, um, didn't intend to hurt you. I just didn't think it would make a d-difference. If I told you, I mean. I reasoned that it would only make you hate me more, and you already hated me enough as it was. So I just never t-told you."

Tucker had no idea what she was about to say. He only knew he wished she wouldn't. She looked so small, standing there—small and horribly fragile. He couldn't shake the feeling that she might shatter like glass if she said another word, and he'd never be able to piece her back together again.

He barely felt his feet move as he took a step toward her. "Ellie, let's not do this."

She threw up a quivering hand. "I have to. You n-need to know. I would've told you. Honestly I would have. If I'd known you blamed yourself, I never would have kept it a secret, I s-swear. As it was, with you thinking it was all my fault anyway, I couldn't see how telling you mattered." She gulped and made a mewling sound, then cupped a hand over her eyes, her fingers jerking as though electric jolts were shooting through her body. "Now I realize I caused you a lot of unnecessary heartache. When you walked out on me anyway, I should have told you. I know that now. But I just didn't have the courage."

There it was again, the charge that he had walked out on her. Back at the fire, the accusation had made him see red. Now, all he felt was sick. That really was how she'd seen it. In her mind, he'd just up and left her without just cause. That was so far from the truth, he wanted to argue the point, but defending himself no longer seemed important. The reasons for their divorce had never been based on facts but on feelings. That was what he needed to focus on right now, how she must have felt back then, rightly or wrongly, and how that had prompted her to think and behave.

She held her breath, her tear-filled eyes clinging to his as she struggled to hold back sobs. Her body began to quake—huge, violent tremors that nearly rocked her off her feet. Finally, on an expulsion of breath, she cried, "I killed him." Her voice was so muted he almost couldn't hear her. "Not the bike, not you." The tendons along her throat convulsed. She swayed and caught her balance. "It was me who did it. That was why I couldn't bear to look at you. Not because I detested you, Tucker, but because I detested myself."

Tucker wasn't sure what he'd expected her to say, but it hadn't been this. How could she possibly blame herself? He'd been the one to buy Sammy the motorcycle, and he had been responsible for leaving the shed unlocked, as well.

"Oh, Ellie," he whispered. "Don't even go there, honey. You loved him so much. Let's just—"

"Would you *listen*?" she cried. "J-just for a *minute*, please. I'll never find the courage again. You have to listen."

Because he could see she was hell-bent on finishing, he nodded. "I'm sorry. I'll listen. Of course, I'll listen."

She laced her fingers together, bent her knuckles

backward. "You said I wasn't watching him closely enough, but I was. Through the window while I fixed his birthday dinner, I was w-watching while he rode the bike."

Tucker stared at her in bewilderment. "How could you have been watching him?" He shook his head. "That can't be, Ellie. He was—"

"He didn't sneak out to the shed and get on the motorcycle without asking." Her voice went oddly flat, her eyes blank and glassy, as if she were seeing things he couldn't. "That's what everyone thought, what I allowed everyone to believe, but the truth is, he came in, begging to ride the bike, and I gave him my permission." She fixed him with a tortured look. "You didn't forget to lock the shed, Tucker. I gave him the key. After he opened the padlock, he brought it back in the house to me."

The words hit Tucker like fists in the solar plexus, shoving the breath from his lungs and making his legs feel watery. He just stood there, staring at her, his heart pounding in his ears like a fist on sheet metal. "*What*?" he pushed out. "I expressly said he wasn't to ride the bike when I wasn't there. You *knew* that. Why in God's name would you have given him permission?"

Her face twisted, the muscles around her mouth quivering spasmodically. "Because," she said thinly, "I was trying to get ready for his party, and he kept standing in my way, begging to ride the bike. Just in the fenced field, he said. There were no trees or anything for him to hit. It was his birthday, and he wasn't a baby anymore." She touched her fingertips to her lips, a dry, tearing sob coming up from her chest. She swallowed, dragged in air through her nose with such force that it flattened her nostrils. "I wanted to get him out of my hair for a little while." Her voice went shrill on that last word, and she squeezed her eyes closed, tears coursing down her cheeks. She paused, gulping for breath. Then in a ragged whisper, she said, "Be c-careful what you wish for, Tucker. You just might get it. He's out of my hair now. *Forever*."

"Sweet Christ." The meaning of all she'd just told him started to sink in, and anger flared within him. "How could you have kept this from me, Ellie? Not just for days or weeks, but for three frigging *years*? How could you? Do you have any idea how many nights I lay awake, cursing myself for leaving that stupid shed unlocked?"

She shook her head. "I didn't know, Tucker. I would have told you, I swear. I never even thought of you blaming yourself for that. If I had known—"

"You never even thought." Tucker's whole body tensed. "Our son killed himself on a bike that should have been inaccessible to him, and you never once stopped to think that maybe I blamed myself for leaving the damned door unlocked?"

As though his words were knife blades, she winced and whirled away into the darkness. She took only three steps before her toe caught on a fallen limb that sent her sprawling. Seeing her fall, hearing her body hit the ground with such force jerked Tucker back to his senses, and the anger drained out of him like water from a sieve.

"Ellie, wait. I—"

"I'm sorry!" she cried. "I'm *sorry*!"

Tucker bolted after her, but she scrambled back up like a wild thing, running again before she fully gained her feet.

"Ellie!" he shouted.

Before he could reach her, she was gone. Swallowed by the blackness. *Gone.* Tucker's first reaction was panic. He could hear her footsteps as she raced through the forest. Recalling her poor night vision, he cringed. The woods were full of obstacles she couldn't see.

"Ellie, I didn't mean it!" His words bounced back at him as if they were hitting a wall. "Ellie? Not in the *dark*! You'll get hurt out there!"

No answer. Judging by the crashing noises, she didn't even slow down. Trying to follow the sounds, he set off, his boots striking the littered earth with such impact he felt the jolts clear through his body. A tree branch smacked him across the forehead, nearly knocking him off his feet. He staggered, caught his balance, and kept going.

"Ellie?"

He was making so much noise himself that he could no longer hear her. He reeled to a stop, held his breath to listen. Off to the left, he caught the sound of limbs snapping, only now they seemed more distant.

"Ellie!" he screamed. "Damn it, don't do this! I didn't mean it! Do you hear me? I didn't mean it!"

Calm, he had to stay calm. She was running blind, veering first one way, then another. God knew where she might head next. He needed to not only follow her but also keep track of the turns she took. That way, even if he lost her in the darkness, he'd have a fix on her general location.

"Ellie!" he yelled, knowing even as he called her name that she wouldn't heed his voice, might be so upset she didn't even hear it. "Ellie, please!"

He broke into a run again, his mind screaming one question. Where the hell did she think she was going? *Away* was the only answer that came to mind, away from the pain—away from him. And why shouldn't she? For three years, she'd kept that awful secret, afraid to tell him for fear of his reaction. And what had he done when she finally found the courage? The first words out of his mouth had been angry and accusing.

Tucker had longer legs, had the advantage of speed, but he was foiled by her zigzagging path. As he ran after her, a dozen thoughts spilled into his head and out of it, the most frightening of all that it would be his fault if she got hurt. She had preceded her confession with an explanation for her silence. *I thought you blamed me, that it would only make you hate me more.* On the surface, that seemed like such a weak excuse. Only hadn't he done essentially the same thing? Yes, and for similar reasons. How could he reproach her?

Wave after wave of regret crashed through him as he veered through the trees. God forgive him. If Ellie fell and impaled herself on a sharp branch, he would have to live with it for the rest of his life.

The sounds ahead of him suddenly stopped. He staggered to a halt, cocked his head. His lungs wheezed each time he inhaled, the rushing sounds echoing against his eardrums and making it difficult to hear. *Gone,* he thought. She'd simply vanished.

Madness. She was flesh and blood. He was letting fear do his thinking. A woman didn't simply disappear. Only a second ago, he'd been able to hear her footsteps. That meant she had either fallen or stopped running, not that she'd vanished. It also meant that she could probably hear him—if she was still conscious.

"Ellie?" Tucker turned a slow circle, his heart still pounding so loudly that he could hear very little else. He envisioned her draped over a log, seriously injured or dead. The pictures made him so frantic he shoved them angrily away. "Sweetheart, won't you answer me?" He bunched his fists, wishing she'd say something. "Let's go back to the fire, have some wine, and talk about this." He paused, listened. He clung to his self-control by a thread. "Ellie, damn it, you're scaring me to death. At least tell me you're all right!"

"I'm f-fine."

Her voice seemed to ricochet off the trees around him, a whispery quaver that might have been no more than a sigh of the wind. Frustrated and more than a little afraid for her, he spun, trying to pinpoint where she was. He imagined her crouched behind a tree, trying to block out the sound of his voice.

"Go away, Tucker, *please*? I—need to be—alone right now."

He whipped to his left, stared into the blackness until his eyes ached. Nothing. She sounded close—twenty, maybe thirty feet away. Only he wasn't sure which way to go. "That's what landed us in this mess in the first place, backing away and leaving each other alone." Frustrated, he pinched the bridge of his nose. "We need to hash this out, Ellie. Sit down and talk about it."

"I *can't*. You're already furious, and I don't blame you! If I told you the rest, you'd *despise* me."

"I'm not furious, Ellie." He moved due east. "You just caught me off guard, is all."

"Right! Just go away. Leave me *alone*."

Her voice came at him from the right. He whirled to peer through the shadows. "Nothing you can say will make me despise you, Ellie."

"You don't know. You just don't *know*."

Tucker figured it was high time that he did. She'd been carrying that horrible secret around for three endless years, lacerating herself with guilt. And apparently there was even more she had yet to tell him. He wasn't walking away, not again. No matter what she'd done—or failed to do—Sammy's death hadn't been her fault. She'd loved that child with her whole heart and soul, just as he had. He knew she never would have done anything to harm him. Not deliberately, anyway.

"I know it isn't easy to talk about it," he said hoarsely. "That it hurts."

"Yes. Down deep, where no one else can see, it hurts so bad you want to die."

He homed in on her voice. His skin prickled, and his senses became keenly alert. Taking care to make no noise, he moved toward her.

"We can't die, Ellie. That'd be too easy, and it isn't how life works. I wished for death a hundred times. I wanted to just go to sleep and never wake up. But morning always came, and the feelings were still there. After a while, I learned to live with them."

"Yes."

"We both have our demons to live with," he went on. "You don't honestly believe you're the only one with awful secrets, do you?" Tucker swallowed, knotted his hands. With the darkness all around him, it wasn't as hard to face the memories and dredge up the words. He'd thought them a thousand times, after all. "You know what haunts me? I put our son's life at risk to save a few bucks. You tried to tell me the bike was too large for him, but all I could think about was how fast he was growing, that I'd end up having to get him the larger motorcycle in only a few months and lose several hundred dollars on the trade-in. I thought if I laid down safety rules, if I monitored him closely, he'd be perfectly safe on the larger bike, so I ignored your concerns." He grabbed for breath, closed his eyes. "I killed my son to save a few measly bucks."

"Oh, Tucker." He heard her breath catch, caught the soft huff of a sob. "Oh, *God*."

"It's true." He was shaking so hard that his vocal cords quivered. "I could never tell you that. I wanted to, I tried to, but the words just wouldn't come. I was afraid, I think. That you'd detest me, never forgive me." He passed a trembling hand over his eyes. "I should have bought him the smaller bike. Instead I assured you that the larger one was perfectly safe, all because I didn't want to lose a bunch of money on the deal." An awful, tearing pain lanced through his chest. "Do you know how I felt, Ellie, knowing that? At the funeral, and later at the cemetery—*Jesus.* I kept thinking of dollar bills—how they felt in my hand—just pieces of paper that meant nothing. How can I ever forgive myself for that?"

Silence. It pulsated in his ears, throbbed in his temples. He held his breath, waiting for her to say something, anything, even if it was to scream at him.

Instead, she only said his name, her voice ringing with an awful weariness that mirrored his own. He felt sucked dry, emptied out, and as weak as if he'd just suffered a bout of dry heaves.

"I'm sorry," he said raggedly. "I'm so sorry, Ellie. If I could undo it, I would. I thought I was being practical. He was growing so fast, we couldn't keep him in pants. It seemed so foolish, buying him a bike that would be too small for him by spring. I'm sorry."

"If I had followed your rules," she said hollowly, "he wouldn't be dead. It wasn't your fault. It was mine, all mine."

Her voice trailed through the darkness, as thin and shrill as a reed whistle. Tucker continued toward it. "Maybe we should just be done with it and draw straws."

"What?" Bewilderment laced her voice.

"To decide who's more to blame. I'm convinced I am, you're convinced you are. There must be a fair way to decide, once and for all, which of us was the most terrible parent."

"We don't need straws to determine that. I win, hands down. You can say what you want about the money thing, but the truth is, you would've sold everything we owned for him—gone broke and lived in a shack for him."

"Same back at you." Tucker sighed, let his head fall back. "Out of your hair, Ellie? I can't believe you said such a thing. You would have died for that boy, done anything on earth for him. How can you even think that way?"

"Because it's true."

"Ellie, listen to me," he implored. "I listened to you. It's only fair for you to give me a chance now." Tucker waited a beat, wishing she would say something. When she didn't, he tried to sort his thoughts and plunged on. "It's not as if you gave Sammy permission to actually go riding somewhere off our property. You said he could putt around in a fenced field right beside the house. In addition to that, you were watching him out the window. By all rights, he should have been perfectly safe."

"He wasn't supposed to ride when you weren't there! I bent the rule, and he ended up *dead*!"

"He hit a chuckhole. Inexperienced riders tend to pull back on the handlebars when they panic. When Sammy did that, he accelerated and lost control. It could have hap—"

"I knew better than to say yes," she inserted with a sob, cutting him short. "Say whatever you want, but I knew better, and I gave him permission anyway."

Her voice sounded closer with every careful step he took. "You made a bad call. We all make bad calls sometimes, honey. When you have kids, it goes with the territory."

"A bad call that *killed* him, and all for what? So I could impress people?"

"Impress people?" he repeated.

"Yes! You know how I was back then. Appearances were *everything*. It was his birthday, and all our relatives were coming for the party. I wanted it to be perfect."

Tucker's heart twisted. Picking where he stepped, he continued toward her. "You know what I remember, Ellie? How hard you worked to make it a special party. For days in advance, you were planning the dinner, trying to decide how to decorate his cake. You made it all so special for him. His big day. Remember how excited he was?"

"Details!" she cried. "Stupid *details*."

A branch snapped under his boot. Wincing, he stopped and listened to see if she would run. When he heard no sounds to indicate that she had, he pressed forward again. "They weren't stupid details to Sammy. He was going to be twelve. It was a big day for him, and you were planning a huge party to celebrate that."

As if he hadn't spoken, she rushed on to say, "I'd had a beastly morning at the shop, and it put me way behind schedule. I got home over an hour late, we had a houseful of company coming, and I was racing against the clock to get dinner fixed. You called to tell me you were running late, too. I was afraid you wouldn't get to the bakery in time to pick up the cake."

Her voice went quivery and was squeezed to silence. He heard her breath catch in her throat as she struggled to continue.

"I remember like it happened yesterday. Those last

moments. They're burned into my brain, I think. Even how his hair smelled—that wonderful mix of sweat, grass, and shampoo, with just a trace of doggy odor mixed in."

A burning sensation washed over Tucker's eyes. He knew the smell she meant, and remembering made him ache. *Ah, God. Sammy.* Would the pain of losing him never ease?

"None of his presents were wrapped yet," she went on in a taut, quivery voice. "I had all of that to do, plus fix dinner and tidy the house. Practically the whole family was coming to the party—your parents and mine, plus all your brothers and their families. You know how I was about the house back then, especially when company was coming. I wanted everything to be exactly right." Regret thickened her voice. "It sounds so stupid now. Fixing the perfect meal, having the table just so, and making sure the bathrooms sparkled. None of those things mattered. Not really. But they seemed to at the time. My nerves were completely frazzled, and I was running around the kitchen like a chicken with its head cut off. I'd just gotten the meat into the skillet for the stroganoff."

"Stroganoff," he murmured. "His favorite."

"Yes, his favorite," she rushed on. "He would have been just as happy with pizza—or even hot dogs. But, oh, no, I had to make a big production."

"Of course you did." Tucker came around a tree and finally saw her some ten feet away, huddled on the ground with her back to a log, her knees clasped to her chest. She stared off at nothing, her face a caricature of the one he knew, each feature stark with sadness. "It was his birthday," he reminded her, "a time to make a big production."

"It wasn't about *him*. It was all about *me*. Back then, it always was. The fact that it was *Sammy's* day faded in importance, and all I could think about was the stupid party." She leaned her head back, her throat working convulsively. "Do you really want to hear all this? You'll *hate* me afterward."

Tucker couldn't have spoken in that moment if he tried. Watching her, seeing the agonized expressions that crossed her face, he loved her as he'd never loved anyone, and he hurt for her even more than he hurt for himself. Hate her? Never. All he wanted was to grab hold of her and never let go—to somehow ease her pain even though he'd never yet figured out how to ease his own.

"Back then, I was Superwoman without a cape, juggling marriage, motherhood, and a demanding career, all without ever dropping the ball."

He remembered those days—and how very proud he'd been to have her as his wife. Ellie Frost, the prettiest girl at Newton High, a physician's daughter with all the advantages of wealth, and she'd married a poor logger's son. He'd never quite been able to believe his luck, never quite gotten over the miracle of it. She'd been *his*, the only truly fine thing he'd ever had in his life.

"I wanted everyone to look at me and say, 'Wow, how does she do it?'" she confessed. "I wanted your brothers to tell you how lucky you were. And, oh, God, this is purely evil, Tucker, but I wanted to outshine all their wives because none of them worked."

"You did outshine them," he said. "Without half trying, Ellie, you outshined them all."

She realized his nearness then and jerked her head around to try and find him in the shadows. Moonlight gilded the tears on her cheeks, turning them to silver. Her eyes were swimming spheres of luminescent pain. He wanted so badly to close the distance and catch her up in his arms. It was what he should have done three years ago. He knew that now. Unfortunately, back then, all he'd seen in her eyes was accusation, and that had held him back. Almost afraid to breathe for fear she might bolt, he leaned a shoulder against the pine and crossed his ankles.

"He kept standing in my way," she whispered raggedly. " 'Please, Mom, please, Mom,' he said. Remember how he used to do that?"

Tucker nodded. Like Ellie, he sometimes felt that the memories had been burned into his brain.

She lifted her hands, shrugged helplessly. "I reasoned that he was right about not being a baby anymore, and I thought it would be safe to bend the rules just a little and let him ride in the field if I kept an eye on him through the windows."

Tucker sighed and gazed at the patch of starlit sky above them. He didn't know what to say to her. He wished he did, but the sad fact was that there were no words to ease their troubled hearts or make sense of the loss. Somehow they simply had to live with it. They'd done a piss-poor job of that so far.

He felt so tired. God, he felt so awfully, horribly tired. He wondered fleetingly if she felt the same way, almost let the thought slip away, and then backed up to analyze his reason for doing so. Habit, he guessed. When something hurt this much, it was so much easier never to voice his feelings, to concentrate instead on simply surviving, moment by moment, because thinking too deeply about anything only made it worse.

Now, when it was far too late, he wondered if Ellie had needed him to talk to her about Sammy's death, to share his feelings with her. *Probably.* And instead he'd closed her out. Back at the fire, she had accused him of trying to run from the grief and memories, and he'd responded with a furious denial. But maybe there was more truth to the charge than he wanted to believe. In a sense, he had run from his feelings by refusing to talk about them.

"Ellie," he said in a raspy voice, "how long are we going to do this to ourselves?"

Catching her lower lip between her teeth, she only stared at him, her eyes mirroring myriad emotions, the one that touched him most a hopeless remorse he'd felt himself a thousand times.

"We can't go back, sweetheart," he pointed out gently. "We can't change any of it, no matter how much we might wish we could."

"No," she agreed forlornly. "I'd give anything if I could, *anything.*"

Tucker pushed away from the tree and moved cautiously toward her. "If you could go back, what would you do differently?"

"Everything! I'd say to heck with stroganoff and fix hot dogs. And I'd let the house go. I wouldn't worry about details, period, and I'd just"—her shoulders jerked—"hug him. I'd just *hug* him."

Tucker lowered himself to the ground beside her.

Emotion clogged his throat, and this time when his eyes seared over with tears, he couldn't blink them away, wasn't even sure he wanted to. He'd hidden behind his macho image for too damned long as it was, rigidly adhering to the tenets taught to him by his big, brawny father—namely that tears were for women and men had to be strong.

Such bullshit. Ellie had needed him to cry with her, and instead, he'd held his feelings in check, dealing with the funeral arrangements and the police and all the practicalities, priding himself on being able to keep it together.

"Come here, Ellie mine." He touched a hand to her back. "You can't go back and hug Sammy. But I could really use a hug right now."

With a low cry, she launched herself against his chest, her slender arms circling his neck. "I'm sorry, so sorry," she cried. "All this time, you blamed yourself. I should have told you. I'm sorry."

Tucker enfolded her in his embrace and pressed his face against the curve of her neck. It had always been his favorite place to nuzzle, so soft and sweet smelling. He drew her slight body across his lap and more firmly against him, loving the feel of her in his arms. It was exactly where she belonged, where she had always belonged. He'd lost sight of that for a while, but he vowed he never would again.

"I would have blamed myself anyway, Ellie," he assured her. "I still do. I think I always will."

"Me, too," she squeaked. "Me, too."

"You know what I'd change if I could go back and do just one thing differently?"

She shook her head.

He ran a shaky hand over her hair. "I'd cry with you. I'd let everything else go, and I'd just hold you like this and cry with you."

"Oh, Tucker," she whispered.

"I suppose you think I should wish I hadn't bought that bike."

"No. I didn't say that."

"You don't have to. I've wished it myself plenty of times. I really screwed up, buying it for him. But you know what, Ellie? I've thought long and hard on this, and I think we might have lost him, anyway. On that bike or a smaller one—or on a regular bicycle— maybe it would have happened, no matter what. I'll never understand why or reconcile myself to the fact, but I believe Sammy might have left us anyway, that maybe he was meant to go."

He pressed a kiss to her hair, breathed deeply of the smell. "That being the case, I wouldn't waste my wish on things I couldn't change. I'd want to make different choices afterward and be there for you like I should've been. I'm sorry I wasn't."

Cupping a hand over the back of her head, Tucker began rocking her, whether to soothe her or himself, he wasn't sure. It didn't really matter. He was holding her again. That was all that counted.

So many things that had baffled him up until now suddenly made perfect sense—her reluctance to talk to him about Sammy, her defensiveness, the drastic change in her appearance. With all her heart, she believed that she had sacrificed her son on the altar of perfection, and she'd been striving to correct the mistake ever since. That was why her hair was chopped off like a boy's, why she wore no makeup, why she didn't take time to shave her legs, and no longer wore attractive clothes. In a way only another parent who'd lost a child could understand, she was trying to atone for her sin.

"I love you, Ellie. I'll always, *always* love you. There's nothing you can do to make me stop." He smiled against her hair. "Forever, Ellie girl. Until the rivers stop flowing and the ocean goes dry, I'll always, *always* love you."

She squeezed his neck more tightly, her shoulders jerking with soft sobs. "Oh, Tucker, I love you, too," she squeezed out. "I love you, too."

That was all he needed to hear. The rest would come with time.

Three years ago, Ellie hadn't been able to cry, and now she couldn't seem to stop. Plastering her body to Tucker's, she wrapped clinging arms around him, pushed her face hard against his shoulder, and let it come in great, wrenching sobs that rushed from her yawning mouth and shook her whole body. Swearing softly, Tucker clamped a big hand over the back of her head, buried his face in the lee of her neck, and started to cry with her.

At the farthest edges of her mind, Ellie realized he was rocking her—slowly, rhythmically—back and forth, back and forth—the swaying motion a comfort in and of itself. This was how it should have happened before, she thought dimly. They should have clung to each other in just this way, soothing each other, holding each other fast. Perhaps then they might have helped each other heal.

It felt so right to be in his arms again. So wonderfully *right*. Ellie hugged him harder, wishing the embrace might never end.

Afterward she couldn't say how long they cried. It could have been for only a minute or for as long as an hour. Time ceased to matter. Reality didn't intrude. They simply sat there, locked in a rigid embrace, ridding themselves of old hurts that cut so deep they couldn't be expressed with words. It was a pain that only the two of them could understand and share—the irretrievable loss of a child they had both loved better than they loved themselves.

When the storm finally passed and they drew apart, they sat on the ground in the moonlit shadows with their backs against the log. "You know what it amounts to?" he asked softly.

"No, what?"

"We both need help." His mouth twisted in a ghost of a smile. "You in your way, me in mine. Don't you think it's about time we finally got some?"

"Are you talking about counseling?"

He nodded.

The muscles in her belly clenched like fists. "I'll think about it, Tucker. I'm not sure that's the right avenue for me."

"What is the right avenue?"

"I don't really know."

He reached over to smooth her hair back, and then grazed his thumb over her mouth. "Until you decide, let me leave you with one thought. You were a *wonderful* mother to that boy, the very best. If you don't believe me, ask the individuals who know better than anyone else, your other two sons."

Ellie curled her fingers over his wrist. "Thank you

for that, Tucker, but the sad fact is, I know better, and I don't think some psychologist will change my mind." She paused for a moment. Then she whispered, "I heard the truck brakes scream. Did you know that?"

He went perfectly still. "No, I didn't know that."

She released his arm and rubbed her hands over the knees of her jeans. "I was wiping off the stove. I heard them scream, and then there was this awful thud. I've heard that sound a million times in my nightmares. Do you know what it was, Tucker, that awful thud?"

He averted his gaze, swallowed, closed his eyes for a brief instant. "Oh, God."

"I was polishing my range top." It took all her strength to finish. "Shining my *stove* when he died. I wasn't a wonderful mother. I loved him, yes. But I wasn't the mother he deserved. I cared too much about a hundred other things that didn't matter."

He released a shaky breath. "Ah, Ellie."

"My stove is a mess these days," she confessed. "The whole house is a disaster, in fact. I don't care. I learned my lesson. I'm just sorry I learned it too late."

"You know what I think?" He leaned around to make her look at him. "I think we were the best parents we knew how to be. I believe that's what a counselor will say to both of us as well, that we did the very best we could. All parents make bad choices. At some point, they all make mistakes. It was just our misfortune that our mistakes cost us and our son so dearly."

Ellie knew he was probably right. They could flog

themselves with guilt until hell froze over, but the bottom line was, what had happened to Sammy had been a terrible accident. Neither of them could have foreseen it; neither of them had been able to prevent it. It had simply happened, and nothing would ever change it or bring him back. Maybe there was some truth to Tucker's theory that Sammy had been destined to leave them. He was certainly in heaven now, one of God's special angels, and nothing could ever harm him again.

A sense of peace filled her—fragile at first, but gaining strength as she gazed into Tucker's eyes. Maybe it had been fate; maybe it had been God's will. She didn't know. She guessed she never would. She only knew it was time for both of them to bury their ghosts and move forward.

As though he read her mind, he pressed a kiss to her forehead and set her off his lap to get up. "It's getting cold out here. I don't want you to take a chill."

Ellie allowed him to pull her to her feet. Once standing, she leaned against him when he curled a strong arm around her waist. Warmth wrapped around her. He ran a hand over her back and sighed as if he were utterly spent. She shared the feeling. Her legs felt boneless, her body limp. Oddly, it didn't matter. The darkness couldn't touch them. The cold couldn't penetrate. As long as they had each other, they had everything.

Ellie couldn't say how long they stood there, clinging to each other. When he finally stirred, he kept one arm firmly locked around her waist as they set off. It felt so right, walking with him through the dark woods. Their bodies shifted together in an easy rhythm that came from familiarity.

Once back at camp, he sat on the ground by the fire and pulled her down between his bent knees. As she settled in, he rested his chin atop her head and snugly clasped an arm around her waist.

"I've missed this," he whispered. "I've missed you. I can't tell you how much."

Ellie sighed and relaxed against his sturdy chest. His big hand splayed over her ribs on one side, his hunched shoulders shielding her from the cold. She felt as if she'd been lost for a very long time and had finally found her way home. At the thought, tears filled her eyes, making the firelight blur and shimmer like a huge pool of liquid amber.

She gazed dreamily into the swirl, thinking how much she loved having his arms around her. His heart thrummed a steady cadence, the muted thumps vibrating against her shoulder blades. *Tucker*. He smelled of the wind, pine trees, grass, and wood smoke, with a faint musky maleness underscoring the blend. Strength emanated from his body, even in repose, making her feel safe and cherished.

She loved him so—a feeling that claimed not only her heart, but her mind and body as well, permeating her so completely that even her bones seemed to ache with it. She yearned to press closer, to simply be absorbed by him. The thought of being apart from him again made her feel frantic.

He ran his free hand lightly over her hair, his long fingers incredibly gentle. She loved his hard, work-roughened palm, the thickness of his wrist, the leashed power she felt in each graze of his fingertips over her temple. She couldn't help but imagine how it might feel if he were to touch her this way everywhere. *Bad timing.* This wasn't a moment for the physical. They needed simply to be for a while, absorbing the fact that they were together again.

The night breeze lifted, stirring and intertwining the strands of their hair. Ellie gazed at the stars, wondering for a moment if Sammy was up there, watching them and smiling. In her heart of hearts, she knew he never would have wanted them to be apart, and that if he was watching, he was surely glad to see them together again.

But enough of that. Sammy was gone, and tonight was for the living.

"I love you, Tucker."

He bent his head to press his face to the side of her neck. She felt his firm mouth curve in a smile. "I know," he whispered. "That was my only hope these last two days—knowing the love still had to be in you somewhere, that it couldn't have just died."

She tipped her head to nuzzle her cheek against his hair. Her eyes drifted slowly closed. "It was always in there. It just sort of got buried." She swallowed, waited a beat. "Did you mean it when you said you haven't been with anyone since the divorce?"

She felt his grin broaden. "You still jealous of Jennifer and her tongue studs?"

Ellie stiffened, which prompted him to chuckle. He tightened his hold on her. "You're not going anywhere, lady. And, yes, of course, I meant it. There's been only one woman for me." Mimicking her diatribe from early that morning, he said, "Gorgeous?

Blond? Huge blue eyes to drown in? Does that refresh your memory?"

"What about my gorgeous body?"

He sighed. "That, too, but I'm trying not to think about it right now."

"Why?"

"Because I'll carry you to the tent and ravish you, and I don't think the timing's right."

Ellie had thought the same thing herself, only somehow that didn't make her need him any less. None of this would seem real to her until they made love, and she wanted very much to believe it was real.

He nibbled at her ear. Sighed again. "Don't you feel drained?"

"Yes. Only—" She broke off, afraid her thoughts, spoken aloud, might sound silly.

"Only what?" he pressed.

"I need you to hold me. To know in my heart that this is all really happening, I need you to hold me. I know it sounds dumb, but—"

"It doesn't sound dumb at all." His arm tightened around her. "I know exactly what you mean."

She turned to search his gaze. The love she saw burning in those hazel depths lightened her heart, and suddenly it didn't seem like such bad timing for the physical, after all. "Make love to me, Tucker. Please? Have you any clue how *long* it's been for me?"

He searched her eyes. "No, how long?"

"Three years, twenty days, sixteen hours, forty-one minutes, and three"—she glanced at her watch—"correction, four seconds." She rubbed the end of her nose against his. "And counting."

He groaned. "Don't do that. I'll rip your clothes off and have you right here in the dirt."

She rubbed noses with him again.

"I'm warning you. I can't resist that nose." He leaned back. "Are you telling me you haven't been with anyone else either, Ellie?"

She saw the incredulous hope in his expression, and seeing it brought tears to her eyes. "Do I look like a bed hopper to you, Mr. Grant? Of course I haven't been with anyone else."

He rested his temple against hers and simply held her to his heart for what seemed an endless time. Finally he whispered, "You can hop into my bed whenever you like. Just name the time."

"I'd like. And the time is now."

"God help me, I'm stranded with a seriously horny woman."

"Yes. What do you intend to do about it?"

He slipped a hand up to cup her breast. Her nipple sprang taut the instant he touched it. The hazel of his irises went dark with arousal. Ellie's breath snagged at the back of her throat. She let her head fall back against his shoulder. He unbuttoned the top of her shirt and slipped his hand inside to tease her aching flesh, making her body jerk with every pass of his fingers.

"Now *that* is a serious problem," he murmured huskily. "I can see I've got my work cut out for me tonight."

"Yes," she said with a delighted sigh. "And if you hope to get any sleep at all, you'd better get to it."

"Have plans for me, do you?"

"I do."

He drew his hand from her shirt. "Problem."

"What?"

"Our kids. What if they're up there, spying on us?"

Ellie tensed. "You think?"

"I think."

"Well, hell."

He laughed at her disgruntled tone. "We can go in the tent."

She relaxed slightly. "That'll work."

"Or . . ." He let that hang there for a moment. "We can go up to the springs. They can't get close enough to spy on us there without me seeing them."

Ellie considered her choices. "The springs," she said, remembering their honeymoon. It seemed right to her that they should begin again in that place where they had so many beautiful memories. "Definitely the springs."

Tucker loosened his arms from around her. After she twisted away, he pushed easily to his feet and hauled her up beside him. Before Ellie could guess what he meant to do, he bent, caught her behind the knees, and tossed her bottom-up over his shoulder.

She shrieked and laughed. "What in heaven's name are you doing?"

"Taking you to the springs."

He set off toward the lava promontory. At its base, he detoured to the rock to collect the unopened bottle of wine and the corkscrew. Ellie made fists over his belt to lever herself up so the blood wouldn't rush to her head.

"Surely you don't intend to carry me all the way up."

"I carried you up sixteen years ago."

"Not like this."

"I didn't have wine to carry then." He gave her a bounce to get a better grip on her before he started up the rocks. "Hold tight, Lady Godiva with the shorn locks."

Ellie giggled. "I'm not naked."

"You will be shortly."

Chapter Fourteen

As Tucker climbed the last few feet to the springs, Ellie craned her neck to see ahead of them. In the darkness and upside down, she soon abandoned the endeavor. Not only was she unable to see much, but trying made her dizzy, as well. She clung more tightly to Tucker's belt when he lengthened his strides and jumped from one rock to another to make the steep ascent.

"How on earth can you see where you're going?"

"Just because you're half blind at night, it doesn't mean everyone is. I can see fine."

She felt the change in the air before she could see the springs or hear the gurgle of the water. Suddenly, a steamy warmth enveloped them. The misty vapor was odorous, but not unpleasantly so. With unerring accuracy, Tucker traversed a treacherously uneven surface of rock and came to stand at the edge of the pool. With a quick bend of his knees, he set her down.

As he placed the wine at the edge of the pool, he asked, "How much weight have you gained in the last three years?"

"Oh, *you!*" She punched his arm. "Not an ounce."

"Take off those clothes. Let me judge for myself."

A cloud had moved over the moon, making the light faint. All Ellie could see of him was a huge, hulking silhouette. Tucker, however, had eyes like a cat. She pressed a hand to the front of her shirt. Glancing toward the water, she strained to see where the rocks dropped away to form the pool. All that met her gaze was cavernous blackness. The faintly acrid smell of the mineral spring curled up to her nostrils.

"Should we be doing this?" she asked. "Our sons are out there somewhere. It seems sort of irresponsible to be thinking about—"

She jumped when he suddenly clasped her face between his hands. "Our sons are out there expressly to make this happen. I can't track them in the dark, Ellie. There's nothing more we can do until daylight."

"I know. It's just that—I feel sort of guilty, I guess."

"Don't. This is what they want." He lowered his hands to unbutton her shirt. "You're not feeling nervous, are you?"

She felt the chill air wash over her chest. The next instant, the flannel began sliding down her arms. She shivered when it fell away, leaving her with only the protection of her bra and jeans. "Oh, no." Then, with a tremor in her voice, "Just a little, I guess." She sought his gaze in the darkness. "It's been so long since we—"

"I love you, Ellie." He bent to kiss the side of her neck and then her shoulder as he reached around her to unfasten her bra and remove it. As he straightened away, he dropped the strip of lacy cotton and elastic to the rocks. "Dear God, you are so beautiful. I had almost forgotten."

Self-conscious, she crossed her arms over her chest. Her hair must look a fright, she thought. That wasn't to mention that it had been three years since he'd seen her body. Three very difficult years of sleepless nights and relentless depression that had taken a toll on her face and skin.

"How can anyone be so perfect?" He curled his hands over her upper arms to set her back a step, and then he slowly circled her, looking his fill.

"Oh, Tucker, don't." She pushed at her hair. "I'm such a mess." She realized where he was looking and dropped her arm to shield both breasts again. "Don't look too closely. At thirty-five, gravity starts to win the war."

He pressed a fingertip to her lips. His voice throbbed with sincerity when he whispered, "Ellie, would you stop?" When she flashed him a questioning look, he caught her chin, lifted her face, and stepped close to trail tantalizing kisses over her cheek. "You're beautiful. The most beautiful woman I've ever seen. And when you're ninety, I'll still think so. Don't you know that?"

"Oh, Tucker." She let her eyes fall closed.

He tugged her arms down to her sides. Then his big, warm hands cupped her softness. Her breath caught in her throat. She let her head fall back, powerless to resist the way he made her feel. It had always been this way. With only a touch, he could make her forget everything but him.

He grazed the tips of her breasts with his thumbs then rolled them between his fingers. The thrill of it went through her like an electric jolt, making her feel weak at the knees and dizzy.

While she tried to right her senses, he unsnapped her jeans and drew the denim down her legs. "I've been fantasizing about doing this again ever since that first morning."

"What?"

"When you spilled coffee on yourself," he explained. "When I jerked your jeans down. The sight of you—*damn*—it was all I could do not to gawk. You were wearing French-cut pant—" He broke off, staring at the triangular swatch of lace that shielded that most feminine part of her from view. "You still are."

"These are a different pair."

"They're enough to make a man swallow his tongue."

Ellie giggled nervously. "You bought them for me."

"I did?"

"Christmas, our last year. Remember? I hid them away after the divorce, but then my sensible ones wore out, and I couldn't afford new, so I brought them back into service a few weeks ago."

Still crouched before her, he gave the lace a burning look. "I'm glad. They're almost as good as the white teddy." He grinned and winked at her. "You're not off the hook, by the way. It wasn't in the cards tonight, but I fully intend to see you wear that soon."

"Maybe when we're back in civilization," she compromised, shivering and rubbing her arms. "It's too cold up here for lace teddies."

"True," he agreed. Then he grinned wickedly. "That's okay. It gives me something to look forward to." He ran his hands lightly down her legs to her ankles. "You shaved when you came up earlier."

"I had the razors handy. I decided I might as well."

"Glad again. Your skin feels like satin." As he lifted her feet from the puddle of denim, he whispered, "I'm shaking."

"Why?"

"Why?" he echoed incredulously. He pushed erect and kissed her lightly. "You're not the only one who's nervous. I've dreamed of you—yearned for you—and now that we're together again, I can't believe you're real. What if I'm only dreaming? What if I wake up, and I'm still all alone?"

She understood exactly how he felt. "Oh, Tucker, you aren't dreaming. This is real. I'm real."

"Promise me. Tell me you'll never leave me again."

Her chest had grown so tight that the words came hard. "I never left you, but I'll promise, all the same. Just please don't ever leave me again."

"Never," he assured her. "That's one thing you can count on, lady. From now on, you're stuck with me."

That was precisely what she needed to hear.

"This reminds me of our first time together," he said. "Remember that?"

How could she forget? Two kids, fumbling with buttons and zippers, so nervous they could barely make their fingers work. The shy unveiling of body parts, while cheeks flamed with embarrassment and gazes went chasing off. The hesitant sweetness that followed when they touched each other for the first time.

They'd been only teenagers then, but so very deeply in love. Ellie still remembered how he'd stopped and pulled away when she cried out in pain, and how she'd had to coax him to try again. She'd wanted him every bit as much as he wanted her.

It was a need that had never left her, as strong tonight as it had been nearly twenty years ago.

Clouds still covered the moon. Straining to see his features in the darkness, she heard the whisper of cloth as he stripped off his shirt, the faint popping of metal buttons as he unfastened the fly of his Levi's. She shivered and hugged herself against the cold while he balanced first on one foot and then the other to tug off his boots and jeans.

"As beautiful as you look in those panties, would you mind removing them now?" he asked with a laugh.

"Oh." Ellie tucked her thumbs under the elastic and wiggled her hips as she tugged it down. "Sorry."

"Sweet Lord."

She could feel his gaze on her, and once again, she felt exposed, vulnerable, less than what she wished she were. Finally, he came to her. The heat of his bare skin against hers was a shock after the chill of the air. She gasped as he slipped an arm around her and led her to the water. She gasped again when she sat on the cool rocks.

The instant she slipped into the hot water, she felt

neck deep in liquid heaven. "Oh, *Tucker*, this is fabulous!"

The clouds broke apart just then, and moonlight washed over the rocks above her. She saw Tucker bent over his jeans, fishing in the pocket for something. Muscles rippled in his back and shoulders, a fascinating shadow play on muted bronze. His hair glinted like molten brass. With every movement of his arms, tendons bunched and flexed. She especially loved his legs. They were long and lean, yet as sturdy as tree trunks.

When he finally turned toward her, he laid a bar of soap beside the wine.

"You brought *soap*?"

"I put it in my pocket earlier, thinking I'd come up later and have a bath." Bracing a hand on a rock, he vaulted agilely into the water. The resultant splash nearly swamped her, and she sputtered not to choke. Before she completely caught her breath, he was settling his hands at her waist. "I just never dreamed I'd have such a beautiful bathing companion."

The silence, broken only by the sounds of their breathing and the lapping of the water, curled around them, heavy with all the feelings neither of them could think how to express: love—so very much love—and a sense of wonder that they were with each other again. It was a miracle, this reunion, something they'd both yearned for but despaired of ever happening.

Very gently, he pressed her back against the rock wall of the pool and then retreated to put some distance between them. He trailed his hands up her arms, the graze of his palms moving over her skin like the underside of silk.

Her heart pounded so loudly she felt sure he could hear it. She hauled in a burning breath as his fingertips slipped over her shoulders and traced the V of her collarbone. With agonizing slowness, he trailed his touch down from there to the cleavage of her breasts.

"I stand corrected," he said in a gravelly voice laced with amusement. "This is far better than the first time. Then you were only a promise, Ellie girl. Now that promise has been fulfilled. Do you have any idea how very much I love you?"

A tight feeling banded her chest. "I only know how much I love you."

A wealth of emotion was reflected in his eyes. He smoothed a hand over her hair, cupped a palm to her cheek. In a voice gone husky with tenderness, he said, "Being with you again—it's a precious gift. Not just now, as fabulous as that is, but knowing I'll be with you always. I haven't felt whole for three long years, and now suddenly I do." He searched her gaze. "Why is that, do you think?"

The airless sensation in her chest made it difficult for her to speak. "Because we belong together?"

He nodded, moved his hand down to her shoulder, and rested his forehead against hers. "Yeah, we belong together," he whispered. "All my life, I've heard people talk about matches made in heaven. Until this moment, I don't think I fully understood what they meant. We were made for each other, Ellie mine. Without you, I'm only one half of what I should be."

Tears burned in her eyes. "Ah, but together, we're dynamite."

His hand tightened on her shoulder. She felt his body grow tense. He drew her against him and simply held her for a moment. Ellie felt him trembling and grew concerned.

"Tucker, are you okay?"

"Perfect. I just—give me a second. I have a very important thank-you to say before we take this any further."

Ellie rested her chin on his chest and let her eyes fall closed, sending up a prayer of thanks herself. By the world's standards, maybe their reunion wouldn't qualify as much of a miracle, but to her—and to Tucker—it was the real McCoy. She had his arms around her again.

"I love you," he whispered shakily.

Ellie circled his neck and clung to him. He tightened his embrace to hold her fast. Time and the world around them ceased to exist for a while, and they just stood there, absorbing the essence of one another and trying to assimilate the fact that the impossible had occurred.

She wasn't sure how long they held each other. She only knew a lifetime of feeling his arms locked around her wouldn't have been long enough. Finally Tucker leaned back. When Ellie looked up, she saw that he was smiling.

"We are so lucky."

"Blessed," she corrected.

He kissed the tip of her nose. Then he moved his hand down from her shoulder to lightly caress her arm. Searching his eyes, Ellie forgot all her concerns about appearance and gave herself up to the sheer joy of being with him again. His touch felt so right— so wonderfully, beautifully perfect—as he explored the curve of her hip and the indentation of her waist.

"When we were apart," he whispered, "I tortured myself, thinking of all the things I never did to please you. Little things, big things. It made me so sad because I didn't think I'd ever get another chance. Now, here we are, together again, and damned if I know where to start."

"Just start at the beginning, Tucker. If we don't get it exactly right the first time, we'll have the rest of our lives to work on it."

He smiled and caught her at the waist to lift her high. She grasped his shoulders and braced her arms, gazing down at his moon-silvered features through the droplets of water that clung to her lashes. Shimmering and dark, his eyes held hers for a long moment. Then he lowered her back into the water, letting her body slide down his until her feet found purchase on the rocky edge of the pool.

"I ache for you," he whispered huskily, "but there's no way I'm going to rush this."

"Do I have a vote?"

"No," he said with a low laugh.

He toyed with her fingertips, then drew a tantalizing circle on the palms of her hands before moving up from there to her wrists, then her forearms, and finally to the sensitive bend of her elbows. The smile fled his dark face, to be replaced by an almost worshipful intensity that was entirely centered on her.

The storm of feelings he stirred within her was so devastating that Ellie could scarcely think. He caressed her as though he meant to commit every line and curve of her body to memory.

"Ah, Ellie, my love."

A pent-up breath rushed from her lungs. She

longed to move closer to him, to feel his strength and heat. As though he sensed that, he returned his hands to her waist and held her fast against the rocks.

"I want to enjoy you," he whispered. "I need to make you mine again. Do you understand?"

She wanted to tell him that she'd always been his. *Always.* But the words wouldn't come.

His big, hard hands slid slowly over her hips, his palms just rough enough to feel slightly abrasive but silken, as well. His long fingers kneaded her flesh, pressing deep, then releasing, the burn of them remaining long after he moved to another spot. The surface of the water struck her at midchest, the bone-melting warmth of it lapping up onto her nipples and then falling away to leave her defenseless against the cold. The contrast between heat and coolness aroused her, torturing her nerve endings and making her flesh pucker even before Tucker teased her there with kisses.

Her spine arched when he ran a broad palm up the inside of her thigh. As his fingertips came close to the tops of her legs, desire coiled low in her belly, and her secret, inner places convulsed with expectation. Much to her disappointment, he stopped short of his target, choosing instead to run his hand down the inside of her other leg.

Ellie clung to his shoulders. Her breath began to come in shallow little rushes. She parted her lips, feeling disoriented. He smiled and dipped his head to kiss her, gently at first, and then more deeply, his tongue thrusting to find every sensitive recess of her mouth.

She moaned and pressed closer to him, feeling as if he were the only solid thing in a suddenly spiraling void. He caught her to his chest and stepped off into deeper water where only he could touch bottom. Dimly she realized that he wanted to have complete control. She didn't care. This was Tucker, her one true love. She trusted him as she'd never trusted anyone.

Lifting her slightly, he abandoned her mouth to suckle her breasts. Ellie gasped at the shock of it. Her flesh went instantly hard, the crests of her nipples swelling and thrusting in blatant invitation. He captured one throbbing peak between his teeth, the gentle pressure making her whole body jerk. With merciless drags of his tongue over the tip, he continued the sweet torture, making her cry out.

"Tucker?" Blinded now with need, she made fists in his hair and gave herself to him, arching her spine to better accommodate his mouth. "Oh, Tucker."

She couldn't formulate a request. She only knew she wanted him, *wanted* him so much. And still, he teased her. Until her breath rasped in her throat. Until her body churned with unsatisfied yearnings. Until she nearly wept with it. Feverishly she sought his mouth with her own and ran her hands over his skin, her memories of him and the reality of him colliding sweetly in her brain. *Tucker*. She could scarcely believe he was there with her again.

Every time with Tucker had always been a journey of discovery, and it was no different now. It was only the two of them, just as it used to be, a wonderfully sweet joining of hearts and bodies.

Dimly she was aware of him lifting her to sit on

a smooth rock at the water's edge. Bewildered, she couldn't think what he was about until he nudged her knees apart and used his hand to pleasure her. With the first shock of sensation, Ellie cried out. She made a fist over his hair, drawing him closer, unable to do anything but surrender and ride the waves of sensation.

When she thought she could bear it no more, he sent her over the edge. Release rolled through her in explosive surges.

Afterward, before her muddled mind could clear, he pulled her back into the water, his arms closing around her like padded steel. Ellie was too spent to hug him back. Instead, she floated against him, content to go with the flow of the water and him. *Anywhere.* Deep within her was a sense of belonging.

She knew he felt the same by the way he held her, his arms locked tight, his body tensed. He kissed her hair and skimmed a big hand over her shoulder, his fingers kneading, then gliding, his touch eliciting tingles just beneath her skin.

He held her like that for an interminable space of time, until her breathing evened out and the slight spasms racking her body subsided. Then, catching her behind the knees, he lifted her to ride his hips and plunged his manhood into her with one smooth thrust.

The shock of entry made her cry out with sheer pleasure. It had been so long—so very, *very* long. Her mind slipped into the dark, dizzying place that only Tucker could create. She locked her hands over his shoulders, glorying in the rush. *This* was why she'd been born a woman—to be with this man in exactly this way—one with him, their hearts pumping in an exhaustive beat, the unsynchronized rhythms creating a perfect harmony.

She lifted herself and then sank down, meeting his thrusts, loving the sensation of fullness and streaking fire. When he suddenly stiffened, all her senses sharpened in a breathless hush. Beneath her palms, the flesh and muscles over his shoulders suddenly bunched and went rock hard. Then, with pulsating intensity, bursts of heat rushed into her, carrying her up and over the crest with him into a swirling vortex of sheer rapture.

When it was over, they drifted in each other's arms, the water forming steam curtains around their heads to create a cocoon of privacy. Resting her cheek against his neck, Ellie felt boneless, her body clasped against his, her feet dangling. Off to the right, she could hear water dripping—a slow and faint *plip-plop-plip* that made her eyes feel heavy. She had no idea how many minutes passed, only that eventually their breathing evened out and their hearts stopped pounding.

"Guess what?" he finally whispered.

"What?" she murmured.

She felt his lips curve in a smile against her wet hair. "We forgot to drink any wine or use the damn soap."

She laughed and nuzzled her cheek sleepily against his neck. "Is that all? For an awful moment, I thought you were going to say we forgot a contraceptive."

He stiffened. "I never even thought about it."

"Me, neither," she said, struggling to hide her smile.

"Are you protected?"

After the divorce, emotional stress had wreaked havoc with her cycle, and the doctor had put her on the Pill to keep her regular. But it was so much fun teasing him that she couldn't resist. "Why would I be protected? I haven't been at risk."

"Holy hell," he muttered. "Without protection, I can't hang my pants on your doorknob without getting you pregnant."

Ellie couldn't suppress her laughter another second. When he realized she was giggling, he growled low in his throat and dunked her.

By the time they got back to camp, Ellie was deliciously sleepy and wanted only to go to bed. Evidently Tucker was thinking the same thing. After building up the fire and joining her in the tent, he enlisted her aid in zipping their sleeping bags together, talking to her as they worked.

"If they're headed for Tabletop Mountain like I think, they've nearly reached a point of no return. There's only one way in and one way out through the gorge. They won't be able to double back and slip past us."

Ellie prayed the boys made it safely through. Recalling the rocky terrain and sheer drop-offs, she shuddered with dread at the thought of them going through there without their father.

Finished with his side of the zipper, Tucker sat back on his heels and rested his hands on his knees. "We'll find them tomorrow," he assured her. "I'll be able to pick up their trail, no problem. Once they enter that gorge, they'll be boxed in. There'll be no more side trips, no more circling back around to spy on us."

He opened the sleeping bag, turned to sit down, and removed his boots. After slipping into bed fully clothed, he held out his hand to her. "Come here."

She peeled off her shirt and moved to lie beside him. Gently, he drew her into his arms and kissed her forehead. She rolled into him and pressed her face against his shoulder. "Hold me, Tucker. Please, just hold me."

He did as she asked, his arms creating a warm haven around her. Pressing his lips to her hair, he said, "I'll find them tomorrow. I promise. Tomorrow night, they'll be at home, safe and sound." He tucked in his chin to look down at her. "Your only concern is deciding which home we're going to take them to."

For a moment, Ellie couldn't think what he meant. Then it dawned on her that they were divorced and living in different towns. She had a separate life from his now, a job and responsibilities. "Oh, dear, I hadn't thought that far ahead."

"Well, start," he whispered. "When we find the kids, we need to have some idea of how we plan to iron out all the wrinkles." He hugged her closer. Silence fell between them. After a long while, he swallowed and said, "I want you to quit your job and come home to Bend, Ellie."

It was what she wanted, too. More than anything. Only how could she possibly? Tucker made fairly good money, but his salary wouldn't cover the expenses of two households. Even empty, the Springfield home would be costly, with monthly charges for electricity, water, fire insurance, and the mortgage payment continuing uninterrupted until someone else bought it.

That could take months.

The thought of being away from Tucker that long made her ache. Not *now*, when they'd just gotten back together.

"We'll get married again as soon as we can," he whispered. "My place is large enough for all of us. With the boys coming to visit twice a month and inviting friends over like they do, I got a place with four bedrooms. It's a cracker-box special—thin walls, cheap rugs. You'll hate it. But it'll do us until we can find a fixer-upper that you'll be happier with."

"How do you keep up with a four-bedroom house?"

"I clean one room a day, deep clean twice a month."

"You deep clean? I didn't know you knew how."

He pinched her bottom through her jeans. "I learned watching you." He sighed. "I think maybe I need to unlearn a few things. It occurred to me tonight, listening to you talk, that I've become the perfectionist who worries about stupid stuff now. I haven't made life very easy on our boys, trying to be a perfect father." He told her about his health-food kick and the list of house rules he'd taped inside a cupboard. "I don't think I'm very much fun anymore."

"I've been learning to play football."

"*What?* The last time I took you to a game, you cheered when a kid ran the wrong way with the ball."

Ellie giggled. "You *would* remember that. I've learned a lot since then. I bought *Football for Dummies*, and I've read it, cover to cover. I work with Zach on his spirals, and I attend most of his practices. I'm usually the only mom who shows up."

"Dear God, no wonder our kids are so unhappy. Their parents have flipped out. Football, Ellie?"

"And basketball. I'm a champion dribbler."

"That I've got to see."

She smiled. As always, Tucker had worked his magic. A moment ago, she'd been worried sick about the boys. "I'd love to go back home with you," she admitted. "But I'll have to give notice at the shop and sell the house first."

He startled her by pushing up on one elbow and rolling her onto her back. With his chest anchoring her down, he brought his face close to hers. "No way in hell. I'm not spending a single night away from you from this moment forward. You can quit the damned job without giving notice, and we'll tend to the business of selling the house from Bend."

"That's not a responsible way for me to handle the situation."

"I don't want you to be responsible," he retorted. "Don't you want to come home?"

"Oh, yes," she said softly.

"Then it's settled. You can call your boss from my place and tell him the bad news. We'll enroll the kids in their old school as soon as we get back. They'll be happy as clams about it."

Ellie smiled dreamily, her gaze fixed on the play of firelight on the ceiling of the tent. "It'll be expensive, moving all my stuff to Bend. And if the house doesn't sell right away, we'll have double payments. I really should keep my job, Tucker. What'll we do without my income?"

"We'll eat macaroni and cheese made with eggnog."

Ellie burst out laughing. "College. I remember. We ran out of milk and I used eggnog someone had given us."

"Simplicity. Don't think of all the pitfalls. Just jump in with both feet." He bent his head to kiss her, deeply, thoroughly. "You trusted me to take care of you when I was only nineteen. Trust me to manage now."

Looking up at him, Ellie knew she would trust him with her life. And whether it was practical or not, she didn't want to be three hours away from him. "All right." A wonderful, light feeling filled her chest. "To heck with being a responsible career woman. I'll quit and find a job as fast as I can in Bend."

"Nope," he said, nibbling seductively at her mouth. "For at least a month, I'm going to chain you to the bed so I can have my way with you a dozen times a day."

She giggled. "Well, put like that, I may wait a month to find another job."

"I don't want you to go back to work," he said. "Not for someone else, anyway. I put my half of what we got for our old house into the one I have now. I can borrow against the equity to supplement our income until we sell the Springfield place."

"But, Tucker, I enjoy my job."

"You've always wanted to start your own consulting business. When we sell your place, we'll have the extra cash for you to do that."

"It takes time for an interior designer to build up

a clientele," she pointed out. "As much as I'd love to try it, we'd be without a second income for months, maybe even a year."

"I'll make it work. We're a family, Ellie. Being together again right away is important, not just to us, but to the boys. And it was never your dream to work for someone else. This is a new beginning. Why not do it with pizzazz?"

"With both the boys in school, I won't have that much to keep me busy. Until I build up a customer base, what will I do with myself all day?"

"You can take care of the baby."

Ellie blinked, convinced she hadn't heard him right. "What baby?"

"Our baby, the one we're going to make together." He flicked his tongue over her bottom lip. "I want another child."

She stared blankly up at his dark face. "When did you decide this?"

"Tonight—when you let me think I'd made love to you without protection." His voice dipped to a hoarse tenor. "My first thought was, 'Oh, God, I'll get her pregnant.' And right on the tail of it, I realized I'd be glad."

"Oh, Tucker." She framed his face between her hands, loving him as she'd never loved anyone. "I'm thirty-five years old now. My biological clock is running out."

He winked at her and grinned. "If there's one thing I can absolutely bank on, it's my ability to get you pregnant without half trying. It'll still be safe enough for you to have a baby if we get right to work on it."

"You'll still have a child in college when you're about to retire."

"Which means I'll have tons of time to devote to on-campus activities. Father-child weekends, fundraisers, ball games. Being retired won't necessarily be a drawback."

"It will if you're living on a fixed income and trying to pay tuition."

"I'll start another college fund, and by then, your consulting business will be worth a mint. When we sell out, we'll invest the proceeds. Tuition won't be a big deal. Just think of it, Ellie. A new baby. We can fill up that empty bedroom. We're young. Why not? Maybe we'll have a baby girl who looks just like you."

Until this moment, Ellie hadn't even considered having another child. Why, then, did it suddenly seem like a dream she'd been holding close to her heart and simply hadn't acknowledged? *A baby.* A little person to love, not a replacement for the child they'd lost, but an entirely new life to round out their family. After all she and Tucker had been through, it seemed right, beautifully and perfectly right, to make a brand-new start, and what better way than to create a brand-new life?

Ellie could almost see a chubby little girl with tawny curls and hazel eyes, sitting in a high chair. She could imagine how wonderful it would feel to hold her—how sweet she would be after her bath, all warm and damp and wrapped in a soft towel.

"She may end up looking like you," she said. "The boys do."

"God forbid. A girl with my nose?"

Ellie laughed and hugged his neck. "I don't think we can special order. Now that I come to think about it, your nose wouldn't do at all for a girl. Maybe I should just stay on the Pill."

"It's only ninety-nine point nine percent safe."

"Meaning?"

"Meaning that's all the opportunity my swimmers need." He trailed his lips down her throat. "And on that thought, I'm ready to put a few more to work."

"Right *now*?"

His only reply was to slip a hand under her bra and claim her mouth in a searing kiss.

It was all the answer she needed.

Zach sat slumped by their tiny fire, his head cradled in his hands. Because he didn't dare add much wood for fear his father might see the light, the flames sputtered and put out little warmth, but it was better than nothing. The night wind cut through their clothing like razor-sharp ice blades.

Kody hunkered beside Zach, feeding his face with dry Cheerios. "Everything's ruined," he said for at least the fiftieth time. With his mouth full of cereal, the words mushed together, but Zach got the drift. "They're so mad at each other they might never make up."

Miserable and completely disheartened, Zach straightened to glare at his brother. "Just don't blame me. It is not my fault this time. It's Sammy's. He's the one who died. He's the one who ruined everything for the rest of us. I *hate* him."

Kody paled. "How can you say that? It's not Sammy's fault he got killed."

"Whose fault was it then? *Yours?* It sure as heck wasn't mine. He's the one who got on the stupid bike. He's the one who crashed through the fence and got hit by a hay truck because he didn't mind Dad's rules. And now *he's* the only one they care about. If it's not his fault, whose is it?"

Kody glanced quickly away. Zach was too upset to care what his brother's problem was anymore. It was starting to look as if they had done all this for nothing. Their folks might never get back together now, no matter what they did.

Pushing the zipper-seal bag of Cheerios aside, Kody tossed what remained in his fist to Bucky and flopped down on his rump. After dusting his hands on his jeans, he said, "What're we gonna do now?"

"I don't know." Zach gathered saliva and spat into the fire. The glob of spittle made a hissing sound when it hit the coals. "Keep going, I guess. Maybe in a couple of days, they'll get over being pissed."

"Maybe." Kody heaved a long sigh. "I'm getting tired of this, though. Why can't they just make up so we can go home?"

"I don't know."

"They love each other."

"How do you know? People's feelings change."

"Not theirs!" Kody said fiercely. "They're just unhappy because Sammy died, and both of them blame themselves. They still love each other, deep down. Nobody gets that mad at someone else unless they're in love."

If that was the case, Zach hoped he never experienced the feeling. It made people act totally crazy.

"We can't give up," Kody said. "Not now, when

we're so close. If we don't follow through, we'll graduate high school in Springfield."

"Gag me with a spoon," Zach said. Not that Springfield was really a bad place. It just wasn't home.

He balled his hands into fists. Maybe he'd messed up by telling his folks all those lies to make them jealous, and maybe it had been a stupid move to run away, but at least he'd tried to fix things. That was more than he could say for either one of them.

He was tired of having his whole life ruined because of Sammy. His mom and dad had had three children, not just one, and it was about time they started to realize it.

Chapter Fifteen

Icy air nipped at Ellie's cheeks. Still half asleep, she burrowed under the covers and snuggled close to the big, warm body beside her. It was only when her hand grazed a hairy, well-muscled chest that she snapped completely awake. What was a man doing in her bed?

Her eyes flew wide open. She peered out over the edge of the covers, expecting to see the familiar, cream-colored walls of her bedroom. Instead she was surrounded by swimming-pool blue. The first faint glow of daylight filtered through the azure nylon, barely illuminating the small enclosure.

For a moment, she couldn't recall where she was. Then it all came rushing back to her. The boys running away—she and Tucker traipsing through the wilderness to find them—their lovemaking last night.

The tension eased from her body, and she tightened her arm over Tucker's side, loving how he felt. She flattened her hand over his chest and pressed her cheek against his shoulder blade. It was nothing short of a miracle, being with him again. The only things missing to make her happiness complete were their sons.

"Good morning," he said, his voice thick with sleep.

Ellie touched her lips to his skin and breathed deeply of his scent, which was as familiar to her as her own. "Good morning."

He rolled over to face her. His arm felt heavy and wonderfully right where it came to rest just above her hip. The splay of his hand over the small of her back made her skin hum with awareness. He smiled sleepily, his hazel eyes only partially open, his tawny lashes fluttering. "God, Ellie, you feel good. I can't believe you're actually here."

Since she'd been thinking the same about him, she only sighed.

"I wish we didn't have to get up," he whispered, running his hand up her back. As his palm slid forward over her side, his fingertips grazed the underside of her bare breast. "You feel so good."

She wanted to arch her spine in invitation, but the sun was coming up, and there were other, far more pressing things to do. "If wishes were horses, poor men would ride. We've got to find our boys."

He groaned and nuzzled her hair. "Rain check?"

She hugged his neck. "Absolutely, and collectible any time."

He trailed his lips to her ear, then rose up on one elbow to kiss her lips. With hard-won restraint, Ellie kept it short because she knew anything more would end with another lovemaking session. As much as she wanted that, they couldn't spare the time.

"You're a cruel, heartless woman," he informed her, his voice already gruff with desire.

She laughed and pushed away to sit up. "It's as painful for me as it is for you." Shuddering with cold, she fished through the pile of clothes lying on the floor of the tent. When she found her bra, she thrust her arms under the straps and reached back to fasten the clasp. "It's so c-cold my goose bumps are freezing."

He chuckled and sat up. Reaching past her, he grabbed his shorts and jeans. "I'll get a fire started. Why don't you stay put until I holler?"

Ellie resisted the temptation. Somewhere on this mountain, her sons were enduring the cold, as well. The sooner she and Tucker found them, the better she would feel.

Zach stared at the swift, deep creek below them. A big log bridged the water, stretching from one bank to the other. He and Kody had walked across it plenty of times with Dad when they were much younger, and Zach had no misgivings about doing so again. Dad always said log bridges, firmly anchored to both banks, were as solid as any modern-day structure designed by an engineer.

"You and Bucky go first," Zach told Kody. "That way I can help if you start to lose your balance."

"Right. Fall in with me, probably."

Kody put a foot on the log. The water below the natural bridge was deep—and swift.

"Be careful!" Zach called. "I don't want you getting hurt. Mom and Dad will have my head."

"I won't fall." Just as Kody spoke, the log seemed to shift slightly, and he almost fell. He waved his arms to regain his balance. "Whoa! What happened?"

"I don't know. Maybe the old guy is getting rotten. Go on across. I'll wait until you're off."

Kody made it the remainder of the way without mishap. Zach was about to step out onto the log when a sudden concern came to him. He drew off his backpack, fished through the side pockets, and drew out a piece of paper.

From the other side, Kody yelled, "What now? They're only a few hours behind us! We gotta maintain our lead!"

"I'm writing Dad a note to warn him about the log!"

Kody nodded. "Good idea." He looked down into the churning water. "It'd be awful if it broke!"

After he finished, Zach affixed the folded paper to a sharp nub that stuck up from the exposed tree roots. Standing back to survey his handiwork, he worried for a moment about the brisk wind carrying the paper away.

"What now?" Kody called.

"What if it doesn't stay?" Zach yelled back.

"It'll stay. They've gotten all our other notes."

Zach hoped Kody was right. He pulled his pack back onto his shoulders, tightened his waist cinch, and turned to face the log. After seeing it shift under Kody's weight, he was sort of scared to get on it.

Gathering courage, he flexed his fingers, made tight fists, and relaxed his grip. Then he finally stepped out on the log. The opposite bank looked awfully far away.

The sun was straight up when Tucker stopped for lunch. After over five hours of nonstop walking, Ellie was more than ready for a rest and eagerly collapsed under a big pine.

"I'm beyond being tired," she said miserably. "I think I'm dead and this is hell."

"How's the heel?"

"That blister is the least of my miseries. My whole body aches."

He winked at her. "I'll bet you don't say no to a massage tonight."

Ellie winced as she crossed her ankles to sit Indian-style. "I'm ready to have one now."

"Don't tempt a man that way." Tucker grinned as he sat beside her on the patchy yellow grass. After bracing his shoulders against the tree's massive trunk, he opened his pack to dig out some food. "How's about we share rations? I've got some trail mix and dried fruit."

Ellie drew her apricots from a side pocket. "Any apples?" she asked.

He peered over her arm at the apricots, winked at her, and then tossed her a sandwich bag. "Dusted with cinnamon, just the way you like them."

It touched her that he remembered that. She handed over her apricots, then opened his bag. "Yum. Did you dry these yourself?"

"Yep." He gave her a sidelong grin. "After the divorce, I bought my own drying rack. I had to learn by trial and error, but I finally got it down. They still aren't as good as the ones you do, but close enough."

"Geez. Now that you're so accomplished in the kitchen, you may not want me around after the newness wears off."

He frowned, pretending to mull that over. Then he winked at her. "It's not your cooking that's the big attraction."

Ellie giggled and slugged his shoulder. Then she helped herself to a handful of his trail mix, as well. "Would you like some cheese?"

"Cheddar?"

"Extra sharp."

He snatched the package from her lap. "We should have shared food yesterday. Having some variety makes the meal a lot less boring."

Ellie settled back to munch on the granola and apples. It was funny how she'd forgotten so many little things about him, only to have the memories come rushing back now that she was with him again. Every time he took a bite, he dusted his fingers on his pants.

She had missed being with him so much. Oh, God, how she had missed him.

When the worst of their hunger was appeased, he cracked open his canteen and offered her a drink of filtered water. "I've got my own, thanks." She reached for her canteen and drank deeply. Her throat whistled as she came up for air. "Ah, that tastes good."

"Anything wet tastes good when you're out like this." He returned his canteen to his pack. "I could sure go for a hot cup of coffee right about now."

"Mm." She rubbed her arms, chilled by the breeze that had suddenly picked up. "Does it seem colder to you this afternoon?"

"A little, I guess." A pensive expression came over his face. Ellie knew without asking that his thoughts had turned to their sons. "I wish they were here with us."

"I've been trying to keep a positive attitude," she

told him, "and for the most part, I've been successful. But every once in a while, a huge wave of panic hits me, and I almost can't breathe."

She wished he would reassure her. Instead, his eyes went dark with sadness.

"When I was younger," he said in a rough voice, "I didn't think anything bad would ever happen to us. Our boys were healthy, we went to church every Sunday, we prayed together, and we tried our best to be good parents. Somehow, I had it in my head that God watched over us more closely than He did everyone else because we were doing all the right things. Sort of a pact, you know? As long as we did everything right, God would keep His end of the bargain." He swallowed and cleared his throat. "I know it sounds bad, but back then when I heard about some poor parents losing a kid, I secretly thought that maybe it was somehow their fault—that maybe they hadn't been watchful enough—or that they hadn't been strict enough about safety."

Ellie rubbed her arms again.

"I knew it was wrong to have those thoughts," he said softly, "and I'd chase them away as soon as they came, but they'd sneak into my mind, all the same. God, Ellie, I was so smug."

"I think maybe we all are until something terrible happens," she said. "It's easy to feel smug when life has never knocked you flat."

"Now I'm older and a little wiser," he went on. "I understand that bad things happen to perfectly nice people, despite all their efforts and precautions. Going to church, and praying, and being as decent as you can aren't an insurance policy."

"No," she said hollowly.

"In short, life is a crapshoot. Some people are lucky, others not so lucky, and there isn't a damned thing any of us can do to change it."

Ellie couldn't think what to say. "Have you lost your faith, Tucker?"

He took forever to reply. "I did for a while," he admitted. "Now I believe again, only in a different way. God gave us free will to make our own choices in life. If we make the wrong ones, it's our fault, not His."

There it was again—guilt that cut like a knife. Ellie couldn't finish the apple slice, so she tossed it away for the squirrels. She and Tucker had both made wrong choices, one compounding the other, and they'd lost a son because of it.

They'd also lost each other for a very long time.

She remembered suddenly how Tucker had worked all the overtime he could for a year to save for those motorcycles. It had been his dream to go for woodland rides as a family—to simply take off on back trails and camp beside a stream somewhere. That same afternoon after they bought the bikes, they'd gone for a family ride. Sammy had had no difficulty controlling the motorcycle Tucker had insisted on buying him, which had greatly allayed Ellie's misgivings about its speed and power.

They had had so much fun on that ride. Because it hurt, Ellie hadn't allowed herself to think of that afternoon very much—until now. Puttering along winding trails with the wind in their faces. Riding fast over humps to feel their stomachs come up in their throats. Laughing and yelling to each other and whooping in sheer delight. It had been an afternoon to remember always.

Tucker's dream come true—or a wrong choice? That was the question. He'd worked so hard to make it happen. And he'd had only the best of intentions, to give his sons yet another fun and wholesome family activity that would keep them busy and out of trouble. No gangs and drugs for the Grant boys. Tucker had devoted all of his energy to prevent that, taking his sons to church, teaching them right from wrong, and, most important, being their friend as well as their father.

Other people bought their kids high-speed bicycles, and no one died.

Other people let their kids ride skateboards, and no one died.

Other people rode snowmobiles and went water and snow skiing, and no one ever died.

Why, then, had buying motorcycles been such a wrong choice?

"I'm sorry," he said huskily. "Why is it we always get off on this?"

Ellie nearly pointed out that just the opposite was true; they hadn't talked about it nearly enough. It had hurt too deeply. Now that the pain had dulled a bit, they were beginning to open up. And bleed again.

"You didn't make a wrong choice, Tucker," she said. "You were and still are the best father I've ever known."

He had stopped eating now, too. Eyes closed, face drawn, he rested his head against the tree trunk. "Are you afraid, Ellie?"

She wasn't sure what he meant.

He cracked open one eye. "Not just now. Obviously we're both worried right now. I mean other times. I catch myself not letting the kids do lots of things because I'm afraid. Going roller skating, for instance. Just two weeks ago, they begged to go with their friends on Saturday. We used to let them do it all the time. Remember? Mrs. Robinson offered to take them and pick them up. I knew all the boys, and they're nice kids. But I said no. The thought of letting them go made me feel panicky. I'd read somewhere about a kid getting hurt doing the whip. You know, that thing they do, all holding hands and skating in a circle really fast? He lost his grip on another kid's hand and went flying into a wall. He hit the brick headfirst."

Ellie winced at the image his words formed in her mind. "I thought they'd stopped letting kids do that."

"Not everywhere, I guess. And it killed him," he said. "It wasn't in Bend. Somewhere else—I can't recall where. But just like that, he was dead. When I read the news story, I kept thinking of the parents and how they were feeling. For the rest of their lives, would they regret that they let him go skating?" He pressed his lips together and shrugged. "Skating's dangerous. Most parents let their kids go, but we all know it's dangerous. How do they feel about that?"

"I don't let them ride their bicycles very much anymore," she confessed. "Just around the neighborhood, and only then on the sidewalks. And it's absolutely against the rules in the evening when the neighborhood traffic increases. Zach *hates* it. He keeps telling me he's not a baby anymore." Her voice went thin. "That was exactly what Sammy said to me, right before. 'I'm not a baby anymore, Mom.' "

He sighed and let both eyes drift closed again. "We're a mess. No wonder our kids are miserable. Bicycles and roller skating are right up there with apple pie." His throat convulsed as he swallowed. "How can they learn to get along in the world as adults if we try to protect them from every damn thing?"

"I just want them to live through childhood so that adulthood becomes a worry."

He snorted, the laugh catching him by surprise and nearly choking him. Ellie, who'd been feeling so maudlin, was taken aback for a moment. It was all so awful—so *heartbreaking*—how could he see it as funny?

Only suddenly it was. Perhaps heartbreakingly so, but funny, all the same, and she chimed in with a choked giggle that soon burst forth into full-blown hilarity. Raising kids—how did anyone live through it and stay sane?

When her mirth subsided enough for her to speak, she squeezed out, "Kody runs around the house with his toothbrush in his mouth. I keep telling him it's dangerous, and he ignores me. One night I got so upset, I slapped him."

Tucker grinned. "Well, you proved your point. Running around with a toothbrush in his mouth is dangerous."

Suddenly they were laughing again—hysterically, until their sides hurt, with tears streaming down their cheeks. Ellie wasn't sure *why* they were laughing. Somehow, that didn't matter. It felt good. Weren't they allowed to feel good sometimes?

Finally, when they were slumped in exhaustion against the tree, Tucker said, "Maybe the boys have it right, and we really should get counseling. We aren't letting our kids be normal kids."

"I told you last night that I'll think about it, but to be perfectly honest, I'm hesitant."

"Why?" he asked.

"How is some counselor who's never lost a child going to help us?" she asked. "On what page of the book is there a cure for waking up in the middle of the night to check on your kids and finding one bed empty?"

His lips went colorless.

"People encouraged me to gut Sammy's room," she rushed on. "Did you know that? 'Throw everything of his away,' they said." She pushed angrily at her hair. "How do you throw your child away? Damn them all, with their solutions and platitudes. They don't know. They have no *idea*. I still have his things, stored in the attic. And deep in one of my dresser drawers, I have the last T-shirt he ever wore. I keep it sealed in plastic so his smell won't go away."

"Oh, honey," he whispered.

She blinked to clear her eyes. "Sometimes, when I'm sure no one will catch me, I hold it to my face and breathe in his smell. Then I cry myself sick. Not so often anymore. Not nearly so often. But I still do it sometimes."

There was blood on that T-shirt—*his* blood. He'd been her firstborn. Sammy, her little love. She'd never throw him away. Never.

"I wish the boys hadn't done this," she whispered. "Don't they know how much we love them?"

"Sure, they know." Glistening moisture came into his eyes. "Over the last three years, that's been my only comfort. However else we may have screwed up, Sammy always knew how much we loved him. I've never doubted that for a minute."

Ellie agreed. Sammy had known. She had tortured herself with feelings of guilt in a thousand different ways, but unlike many other grieving parents, at least she'd had no regrets on that score. Both she and Tucker had told Sammy they loved him every day, and they'd done their best to show him, as well.

Even the motorcycle that killed him had been a gift of love.

Tucker intruded upon her thoughts by saying, "I think they're still headed for Tabletop. At least they haven't changed direction on us."

Ellie thought of the place. There was a beautiful little lake in a nearby draw that teemed with trout.

"You think you can make it?" he asked.

"I'll make it," she said. "I may strangle them when we find them, but I'll make it."

He smiled. "It'll be rough going, I admit. But if it's any consolation, we won't get to the bad part until sometime later today."

"I thought the plan was to find them today," she reminded him.

He rubbed a hand over his face and blinked. "Yeah, that was the plan." He shrugged. "We're not covering quite as much ground as I hoped. The little hooligans are deliberately taking us over the roughest terrain they can find."

Ellie bent her head. She knew she'd been slowing him down. If not for her, Tucker probably would have already found them. "Maybe I should make temporary camp down here and let you go on without me."

"And stay out here alone tonight? No way."

"Better me than the boys."

He arched an eyebrow. "By whose estimation? Those boys are perfectly at home out here. You aren't. I'm not leaving you alone."

"I'd be fine, Tucker. Honestly. With me holding you back, you may not find them before sundown."

"Then I won't. It's as simple as that."

He returned all his food to his pack and pushed to his feet. "Stow your stuff. It's time to head out."

Ellie wanted to feel angry with him for being so dictatorial, but deep down, she knew they wouldn't be faced with this situation if not for her own stubbornness. She'd insisted on coming, foolishly disregarding all his warnings.

"I'm sorry," she said in a low voice as she cinched the pocket strings of her pack. "I should have stayed home."

"Would you stop? You're here. We'll find them. No worries. It's just going to take a little longer than I hoped, is all."

An hour later, Ellie had to ask Tucker to stop so she could dig her jacket from her pack. "It's *chilly* this afternoon," she complained. "Usually I'm so hot, I'm dying at this time of day. Now I'm freezing."

"We're climbing," he explained. "The higher we get, the cooler it'll be."

As Ellie rifled through her things for her parka,

Tucker stared at the mountains. When she pushed erect again, he glanced at her. "It is windy."

Ellie lifted her face to it. "You're right. I noticed it earlier at lunch. You don't think a weather front is coming this way, do you?"

He scanned the sky. "No clouds that I can see. When we stop to rest again, I'll tune in to the weather channel to see how it's looking."

He slung both packs over his shoulders. Then he started off. Ellie noticed that he had picked up the pace as she fell in to follow. She sensed without being told that he was a little worried about the wind picking up. "How much farther is it to that creek we have to cross?"

"Only a few more minutes. Once we reach the other side, there's only one trail up through the canyon. If they try to double back, they'll run into us on the way down."

As Tucker had predicted, they reached the creek less than ten minutes later. Because she was afraid of heights, Ellie had always hated walking across the natural bridge. As she and Tucker approached the water, her stomach did nervous flips. She tried to tell herself it was silly. Even if she fell, it wasn't all that far a drop down to the water. Nevertheless, it looked like a mile when she finally stood on the bank looking down.

"I'm not sure I'm ready for this."

He flashed her a knowing grin. "Putting it off won't make it easier."

He didn't hesitate to step out onto the log. He started across with an impressive display of grace and balance for such a large man. When he realized that Ellie hadn't started across after him, he shifted the packs and turned around. "Come on, sweetheart. You always do this, and it's silly."

It didn't feel silly to her. Heart slamming, knees knocking, she stepped out on the log. "I'm just nervous, is all. I know it's wide, and I probably won't fall, but I always think I might."

He leaned forward to catch her hand. His grip lent her confidence, and she closed the distance between them with three long steps. He bent to kiss her. Just as he did, Ellie could have sworn she heard wood crack.

Her nerves leaped. "What was that?" She glanced down, started to feel dizzy, and jerked her gaze back to Tucker's smiling face. "Oh, God. One of these times, this old log is going to break. I just know it."

"Not in your lifetime. This old fellow is as sturdy as a rock."

To prove the point, Tucker firmed his grip on her hand and bent his knees to bounce.

"No, don't!" Ellie cried. "Oh, God. Please, don't, Tucker."

"See?" he said with a confident laugh as he went up and down. "Sturdy as a ro—"

A sharp report, like that of a high-powered rifle, split the air, and the next instant, the log disappeared from under Ellie's feet. She screamed. Tucker made a wild grab for her. And then they were falling.

Down, down, they went. The shock of it froze Ellie's lungs. Tucker lost his grip on her hands. The water was dark—so horribly dark. She flailed wildly with her arms, wondering which way was up, feeling as though her chest might burst.

Suddenly she popped to the surface. The swift current caught her in a rough embrace and swept her downstream. Wildly she scanned the surface.

"Tucker!" she screamed. "Tucker?"

He surfaced about ten feet behind her, still struggling to rid himself of the packs. When he finally freed both arms from the straps, the large blobs of blue nylon were caught by the water and swept right past Ellie, who was swimming frantically against the current to stay with him.

"Toward shore!" he shouted.

His hair was plastered to his head. Water streamed down his face. He gulped frantically for air as he swam for the rocks. Ellie pumped her arms, doing her best to follow him, but the pull of the creek was stronger than she was. If not for Tucker reaching out to grab her shirt, she would have been carried away from him.

They scrambled onto the rocks together, gasping at the cold, heaving for breath. Rivulets of water poured from their drenched clothing. As they gained their feet on a craggy boulder, Tucker caught her close in a hug.

"Are you all right? Are you hurt? Did the log hit you?"

"I'm f-fine." Ellie's lungs grabbed for oxygen. For a moment, she just clung to Tucker, too weak to do anything else. "I'm okay. H—how about you?"

"I'm fine." He smoothed the water from her hair. "What the hell happened?"

Ellie laughed hysterically. "The log broke. Behind you, at the other bank, I think. You bounced, and it snapped clean in two."

Tucker gazed upstream at what had once been their natural bridge. His eyes turned dark as umber, the pupils shrinking to pinpricks. "I can't believe I did something so stupid."

"You've bounced on it for years," she reminded him.

"Exactly. Nothing lasts forever. I should have looked at it more closely before I started jumping on it."

He grabbed her hand and started up the bank. Ellie scrambled behind him to keep pace. "Where are we going? Don't we need to go find our packs?"

"First things first. We have to get these wet clothes off before our core body temps start to drop."

"But we have no other clothes."

"We'll wring these out, build a fire." When they reached high ground, he released her hand and began gathering fallen limbs. "Thank God I have my magnesium and flint on me."

Taking her cue from him, Ellie started collecting pieces of wood, as well. When they'd gathered enough for a fire, Tucker arranged the pieces and went to work with his fire starter to set flame to the kindling. After adding more wood to the feeble blaze, he stood and stripped off his coat and shirt. "You, too," he ordered.

Sensing his urgency, Ellie struggled to shed her jacket and blouse. To her surprise, the wind felt warmer against her wet skin than her soaked clothing had.

After hanging his dripping jacket over a tree limb, he wrung out his shirt and put it back on. Then he plucked Ellie's blouse and jacket from her trembling hands and began wringing the water from those, too. Returning them to her, he said, "They're still damp, but at least they're not soaking wet. Until I find our packs, we'll have to make do with wet jeans."

Ellie tugged her upper clothing back on. "I can't believe how cold it is," she said with a shiver.

"Once you start moving, you'll feel warmer." He helped pull her jacket up over her shoulders. "I want you to start gathering wood to build a windbreak here by the fire. Under no circumstances do I want you to stop moving, Ellie. When you've finished building the break, walk in circles around the fire if you have to, but don't stand still. You need to keep your blood flowing to stay warm. Otherwise hypothermia is liable to set in."

Ellie didn't need him to tell her how dangerous that could be. Nodding as she buttoned her blouse, she searched his gaze. "What will you be doing while I build the windbreak?"

He gestured downstream. "I'm going after our packs. Without them, we'll be in a hell of a fix."

"Shouldn't I come with you? There's no telling how far they may have drifted in that swift water."

He shook his head. "Chances are, they've caught on the rocks and won't be that far away. I probably won't be gone very long. Keep hauling up wood to throw on the fire and get something erected to shield us from the wind. When I get back, I'll need the heat and windbreak to get my temp back up to normal."

It occurred to Ellie in that moment how truly serious their predicament was. They had no dry clothing, no tent, and no provisions, and at this elevation, the ambient temperature was several degrees colder than it had been farther down the mountain. When the sun sank behind the ridge later, the temperature would drop even more.

"Be careful going downstream," she implored him. "If you get hurt, we'll be in trouble."

"I'll be careful." He stepped around the small fire to give her a quick hug. "I'll be on the move the entire time. That'll help keep me warm. You just be sure to do the same. Promise?"

Ellie wrapped both arms around his neck to return his hug. She was shivering powerfully. "Don't worry about me. I'll be so busy gathering wood, I won't have time to stand still."

He pressed his cold face against the curve of her neck. His breath wafted steamily against her chilled skin, making her wish she could burrow closer. "I love you," he said. "Keep moving. Get the windbreak erected so I can get warm in a hurry when I get back."

"I'll be worried the entire time you're gone." She leaned her head back to see his face. "What if you can't find the packs?"

"*Can't* isn't in my vocabulary."

One mile and a host of curses later, Tucker spotted a backpack floating in an eddy formed by a formation of rocks. Not much farther downstream, he found Ellie's pack, hooked on a tree limb that had fallen across the creek.

Miraculously, the packs had remained closed, and

none of their things had been lost. There the miracles ended. The polythene bags had helped protect their sleeping bags and clothing from getting completely soaked, but everything was wet in places and damp everywhere else.

Tucker wasted no time in returning to the make-shift campsite where he'd left Ellie. He was pleased to see that she had erected a waist-high pile of limbs near the fire to provide protection from the wind.

"You found them!" she cried when she saw him walking up from the creek with the packs slung over his shoulder.

"We got lucky," he called back. "They didn't come open, so we didn't lose anything."

Once at the fire, he dropped the packs to the ground. Ellie hurried over to help sort through their gear. With the sudden cessation of physical activity, her teeth began to chatter, prompting Tucker to give her a long, hard look. "Your lips are turning blue. We've got to get you warmer."

He gathered more tree limbs to throw on the fire, and then dug through her pack, hoping to find some dry clothing. Her jeans and tops had gotten damp, but he found a shirt of his own that was somewhat drier. Then he set himself to the task of stripping Ellie to the skin, removing her boots as well, and helping her into the fresh clothing.

"What about you?" she asked through chattering teeth.

He started shedding his own clothes and pulling on replacements. "We'll have to make do with wet boots." He tossed hers at her feet. "With halfway dry socks, maybe they won't be too bad."

"I feel better already," she replied as she shoved a foot into one of her boots. "Damp is better than drippy."

Tucker couldn't help but grin. Nobody could ever accuse Ellie of being a whiner. He knew she had to be freezing even in the drier clothing, but at least her lips no longer looked blue. "Can you start gathering more wood to build us some drying racks?" he asked as he tugged on his boots. "Our sleeping bags need to be hung up to dry. Yours is soaked in places, but mine's only damp. We'll hang it closest to the flames so we'll have at least one bag to sleep in tonight."

She tied her bootlaces and struck off into the woods. While she was gone, Tucker drew out his cell phone, which he'd wrapped tightly in plastic. After checking to make sure it had stayed dry, he dug around for his weather radio and sighed with relief when he saw that it was still sealed in polythene.

When Ellie returned, dragging several large limbs behind her, he helped her to fashion some racks to dry their things. "My phone and radio survived the dunking."

"Good." She brushed her hands clean and stood back to survey their work. "All and all, we haven't sustained too much damage then."

They spread his sleeping bag by the fire. Then they gathered more limbs so they could hang other wet items near the flames. The result was a cozy shelter all around them, which served to block the worst of the wind and retain the heat of the fire.

Tucker visibly relaxed once that was accomplished. "We'll be okay now," he informed her. "Hypothermia was my biggest worry. In wet clothing with a wind chill, a person can lose body heat and be in big trouble fast, even with a fire going."

Ellie spread her hands over the flames. "I believe it. Even now I feel like my jeans are freezing to my backside."

He chuckled. "That's a good sign. It's when you get so cold you don't feel anything that you're in big trouble."

Teeth clenched to prevent them from chattering, she turned to warm her rump. "So it's good that my butt's freezing?"

He glanced up from his pack. "I'll help warm it up here in a second."

She giggled. "Here in a second, I'll be a human icicle."

Grinning, he pushed to his feet and came to her. Standing at her back, he wrapped both arms around her. The heat of his body surrounded her, and she sighed, pressing closer against him.

"Better?"

"Much," she agreed. "I just hope our bedding dries out. What will we do tonight if it doesn't?"

"With this shelter around us, we'll manage to stay reasonably warm," he assured her. "We'll gather more wood. If the bags don't dry out, we'll cuddle here by the fire all night."

"Mm," she murmured, reveling in the warmth that radiated from his big body. "That sounds good."

"Cuddling with you always sounds good," he whispered near her ear.

They remained locked together until the worst of the chill had been chased away. Then he left her to rummage through his pack for additional layers of clothing. It seemed to Ellie it took forever before he returned with a slightly damp fleece sweatshirt. After tugging it over her head, he helped to stuff her arms down the sleeves.

"What about you?"

"There's another shirt," he assured her. "Stand here by the fire, all right? Keep warm while I go put it on."

Minutes later that seemed like hours, he returned to her. Drawing her into his arms again, he pressed full-length against her back. "The fire will dry our damp spots," he assured her. "My sleeping bag isn't that bad. It'll be usable in a few hours. Before dark, anyway. We'll be fine for the night. Won't be the first time we shared a sleeping bag. Right?"

"R-right," Ellie said on the tail end of a shiver. "Fine. We'll be fine."

For three miserable days, the stretch between dawn and sundown had seemed like an eternity to Ellie. Now, when daylight was their only salvation, it seemed to her that the sun was in a race to slide behind the mountain. Before full dark, Tucker caught some fish for their supper. While he cooked, Ellie held their nylon tent to the flames and heated one section at a time. Their shelter was as dry as it was going to get by the time Tucker finished preparing their meal.

"We're damn lucky our packs stayed closed and the polythene protected our food," he said as he forked up some rice and fish. "If the rice bag had burst, we wouldn't be enjoying haute cuisine, that's for sure."

Ellie sighed. She felt halfway warm for the first time in hours, and while the food wasn't quite on a par with haute cuisine, it was fabulous. "What I wouldn't give for a bottle of Marvin's cabernet right now."

Tucker arched an eyebrow. "I don't have any cabernet, and I left the merlot, but I do have a flask of whiskey."

"*Whiskey?*"

He winked at her. "For medicinal purposes, of course. You wanna play doctor with me?"

She giggled. "Nah."

His face fell. "Ah, come on. Why not? We're stuck out here. Our kids saw to that. We may as well enjoy it."

He finished cleaning his plate, walked down to the water to give it a quick rinse, and then returned to set up their tent. When their shelter was erected and the dry sleeping bag was laid out inside, he rifled through his pack and drew out a small black thermal flask. "Voilà," he said as he lifted the flap. "It's cheap stuff, but it'll warm our innards."

He came to sit beside her, took a slug from the protruding mouth of the whiskey bottle, and then passed the flask to Ellie. "Bottom's up, lady."

"Are you trying to ply me with liquor or keep me warm?"

"A little of both. It's colder than hell tonight." He turned his gaze to the nearly dark sky. His brows drew together in a frown. "I'm starting to worry that a storm is coming."

Ellie took a sip of the liquor and passed it back to him. "Don't even say it. Bad luck."

He took another swig of whiskey, then capped the bottle. "Maybe I'd better check the weather."

Ellie looked anxiously at the sky. A storm would be disastrous, not only for them but also for the kids. "Oh, Tucker, you're frightening me."

Digging in his pack for the radio, he said, "I should have listened to you earlier. It *is* colder, Ellie. I don't like the feeling in the air." He crouched at the opposite side of the fire and tuned the dial to pick up the weather station. "Maybe it's just that we got so chilled."

Ellie didn't think so. Now that she came to think about it, she'd noticed a change in the temperature last night, warming herself by the fire, though she hadn't registered it as a sign of bad weather then.

As Tucker fiddled with the radio, she peered at the slate sky. No stars had peeked out yet. The moon was nowhere to be seen. That might mean dense cloud cover had moved in overhead.

A tight, cold feeling seized her chest. "Oh, dear, Tucker, do you think it might snow?"

"I hope to hell not." He moistened his finger and held it up to the wind. "It feels nippy enough, though." He went back to adjusting the radio dial. Static belched. A moment later, the weather report came in, broken but audible. Tucker held the radio to his ear and listened to the forecast with a deepening frown.

"That's just great," he said as he flicked off the power to squelch the static. "A storm is heading our way. It'll hit sometime tonight or tomorrow."

Ellie didn't need him to tell her what that could mean. At these heights, most storms brought snow, sometimes even in the middle of summer. She sat erect on the blanket. "Does Zach carry a radio?"

Tucker nodded. "He's undoubtedly tuned in and knows bad weather is brewing. I've taught him to check if he feels a change in the air." His mouth thinned into a grim line. "The question is, will he heed the warning?"

Ellie greatly feared Zach wouldn't. He and Kody were on a mission, and nothing, including bad weather, was going to make them give it up. Her heart froze at the thought of her sons being caught in a high-mountain blizzard. The temperatures could drop to well below freezing, and the hiking paths would become icy and treacherous.

She closed her eyes, feeling sick. "Oh, Tucker, he won't call it quits. You know he won't."

"No," he agreed. "This is too important to them."

Cupping a hand over her brow, Ellie sat with one elbow braced on her upraised knee. "Oh, God, what are we going to do?"

His voice rang with hollowness. "I think it's time to throw in the towel."

Ellie jerked her hand down to stare at him. "What do you mean?"

"If our clothes aren't dry by morning, we can't go on. Our jackets are soaked, our boots are wet. At these temperatures, we'll get hypothermia if we leave the fire. I think it's time to call in the cavalry."

He reached for his pack, drew out the phone. As he peeled away the plastic and turned it on, he said, "It was one thing when the boys were playing hide and seek, and leaving us notes. I knew they were okay, that they were staying in close. This is a whole new kettle of fish."

He looked down at the digital display on the cellular. "Sweet Christ."

"*What?*"

"No signal."

"It's not working, you mean?"

"I'm sure it's working fine." He gazed out into the darkness. "We're near the canyon. We're in a hole here, and it can't pick up a signal."

Ellie's heart had started to thump with fear. When Tucker decided he needed to call in reinforcements, he was genuinely worried. "Maybe we can find higher ground to call out."

"No *we* to it." He pushed to his feet. "You're staying put by the fire. I'm going to hike back out where I can pick up a signal."

"You're *what?*"

"I have to do it, Ellie. I don't know how bad a storm is moving in. Probably just a skiff of snow that'll melt off. But with our boys out there, I can't take the chance. There may be a full-scale blizzard coming."

"But the only dry thing on you is your shirt, and that's not really—"

He held up a hand. "I've got the body density to handle it. You don't. I probably won't have to walk that far."

Ellie knew he was lying. She saw it in his eyes. To her knowledge, it was the first out-and-out lie that Tucker had ever told her. By that she knew how very concerned he actually was about their sons. He would risk getting hypothermia to hike back out.

He started gathering more wood for the fire before he left. Ellie scrambled around with him, loading her arms with limbs, twigs, bark, and anything else she found that might provide fuel for the flames. When they had piled enough wood by the fire to last until morning, he took her in his arms.

"I love you, Ellie girl."

She pressed her face against his shoulder, horribly aware as she did that his shirt felt much damper than hers. She hadn't noticed it earlier. Now she realized he'd given her the drier garment. She hugged his neck, loving him so much she couldn't express it with words.

"We're switching shirts," she insisted as she drew away. Not giving him time to argue, she stripped hers off and stood there half-naked, waiting for him to shed his. "No arguing, Tucker. I'll have the fire for warmth. You won't."

"I'm fine in this shirt."

She pushed hers closer. "Switch or watch me turn to an icicle. I'm not putting this one back on."

He sighed and stripped off the damper shirt. They both hurried to redress, their movements jerky in the freezing air. When they were both covered again, he locked his arms around her.

His hazel eyes delved deeply into hers. "Tabletop Mountain is due west. If something happens with your compass, walk toward it. You'll head straight up through the canyon."

Ellie was shaking. She knew Tucker wouldn't be telling her this if he felt sure he would make it back. "You're frightening me."

"Nothing to be scared about. Just a safety precaution. If I'm not back by daylight, someone's got to go after those kids, and that'll leave you." He caught her face between his hands. "No decorating anybody's john while you're walking. You hear? Pay attention to where you're at, what's around you."

Ellie nodded. An awful, aching sensation spread through her chest. "How long do you think you'll be gone?"

"I'm not sure. No longer than I have to be. I may not have to go that far to find a high place." He dipped his head to kiss the end of her nose. "I'll be all right, Ellie. Even if I'm not back by daylight, you can rest assured I'll be following you up the canyon."

"What if you get hypothermia?"

"Nah. I'll take some magnesium and flint. If anything goes wrong, I'll build a fire to keep warm." A twinkle slipped into his eyes. "Hey, I'm a modern-day Daniel Boone, remember?"

He kissed her deeply. Then he grabbed his wet coat and put it on. "Better than nothing," he told her. "My body'll heat the lining, and the denim will break the wind."

Ellie didn't want him to go. She wasn't worried for herself, but she was terrified for him. She nearly begged him to stay. But then she thought of the boys and kept silent. They'd lost one child. She understood Tucker's determination not to let it happen again.

He would rather die himself—and she felt the same way. This was something he had to do. She wouldn't make it difficult for him.

"I'll hold down the fort," she assured him. "Keep the home fire burning and the bed warm."

He flashed her a slow grin. "That'll be worth coming back for." At the edge of the clearing, he hesitated. "Remember the other night when we heard those coyotes howling, and I said it might be wolves?"

She glanced uneasily over her shoulder. "Yes."

"I was lying. A few have been spotted in Oregon, but as far as I know, none are in this area yet."

Ellie stared at him in bewilderment. "Why'd you lie?"

"To make you uneasy so you'd stick close to me." He shrugged. "It seemed like a great idea at the time."

Ellie gave a startled laugh, remembering how she'd practically climbed inside his jeans with him on the way down to the creek. "Tucker Grant, you ought to be ashamed of yourself!"

He flashed her a sexy grin. Then he vanished into the darkness.

The next four hours were among the longest of Ellie's life. She paced back and forth by the fire, her ears pricking at every slight sound in the woods around her. Tree limbs kept snapping in the darkness. The first few times, she felt sure something was out there. A hundred snaps later, she grew inured to the sound.

She imagined Tucker, walking along the trail they'd come in on, his breath fogging the night air, his clothes turning as cold as ice from the frigid temperature. How far would he have to go before the phone picked up a signal? At first, she prayed he wouldn't have to go far. After three and half hours, she just prayed God would keep him safe.

It was shortly after eleven when he suddenly stepped back into the firelight. He was moving slowly, almost woodenly. As he drew closer to the light, she saw that there was a gray cast to his skin and that his eyes were unnaturally bright.

"Tucker!" she cried gladly as she circled the fire to hug him. When her hands curled over his jacket sleeves, her fingers felt the crust of ice that had formed on the denim. "Oh, Tucker, you must be freezing. Did you manage to call out?"

He looked at her oddly. Ellie's heart caught. The confused expression in his eyes frightened her.

"What is it?" she asked. "Tucker?"

His lips parted, but he didn't immediately speak. He seemed to be groping for words. "Couldn't call. No signal."

Ellie's heart sank. "Oh, *no.*"

"Walked and walked. A long way. Kept trying. Couldn't get out." He swallowed and dipped his head to rest his brow against hers. "Ellie?" he said softly.

"Yes?"

"Listen close. Okay? I'm hypothermic. Not real bad yet. You have to—" He sighed as though he were too exhausted to finish. "Have to warm me up. Fluids, food. Build up the fire, get the sleeping bag. We need to strip down and huddle."

Fear clamored in her brain. "Oh, God, Tucker."

"Steady warmth," he said, sounding as if each word took great effort, "or I'll go into rewarming shock. Bad news. You understand? Keep me by the fire, share body heat. I'm prob'bly dehydrated. Need lots of water."

Ellie caught his face between her hands. His cheeks felt as cold as stone. "I can do that."

As though his legs would no longer hold him up, he sank down by the fire. He wasn't shivering. She'd read somewhere that that was a very bad sign. She raced for the tent to get the sleeping bag.

Tucker drifted in a gauzy world of images where nothing seemed quite real. He wanted to sleep, but Ellie wouldn't allow it. She asked him questions. She lightly tapped his jaw. Every time he tried to drift off, she called him back. Ellie, bathed in firelight. Ellie, holding the canteen to his lips and making him drink. Ellie, forcing warm food down him. She was golden, his Ellie.

When she slipped naked into the sleeping bag with him, Tucker felt as if sunshine was pressing against him. He held on to her for warmth—he held on to her for comfort. He wanted nothing more than to cuddle her close and sleep. She wouldn't let him close his eyes.

"You have to stay awake, Tucker. I read somewhere that it's dangerous to sleep when you're hypothermic."

Some time later, Tucker gained enough clarity of mind to check his watch. He saw that it was almost three. He had no idea how long Ellie had been taking care of him. He only knew she'd done a damned fine job of it. The fire still burned brightly, which told him that she'd been up and down, feeding wood to the flames. The canteen lying near his head was full, an indication that she'd gone down to the creek to purify more water. Given the fact that she lay naked beside him now, he could only imagine the kind of night she'd had so far, stripping off to share her body heat, then throwing her clothes back on to ward off the cold when she left their makeshift bed.

His head was clearer now. More important, her body next to his no longer felt as warm as sunshine, which told him his core temperature had risen even though his skin was still chilly.

"Hey," she whispered. "You're back with the living."

He smiled drowsily. "You gonna let me sleep now, you little witch?"

She ran a hand over his arm. "Nope. You're still cool. You can sleep when you're warmer."

In the leaping amber thrown over them by the fire, she looked so beautiful with her small features, big blue eyes, and the tousled cap of golden hair. Tucker knew he'd survive when he felt her hardened nipples stabbing his chest and a certain part of him went hard in response.

"If you won't let me sleep, then give me a good reason to stay awake." He nuzzled her ear. "I knew I'd get you to play doctor with me if I worked it right."

She giggled. Then she pushed at his head. "Be good. You have hypothermia."

He teased the silky hollow below her earlobe with his tongue. "Chronic. That's different from acute, and it was only the beginning stages. When it improves to this point, one of the best ways to raise the body temp the rest of the way is to exercise."

She giggled. "Hmm. Maybe you should jump up and take a few laps around the fire."

He kissed his way to her collarbone. "I was thinking about taking a few laps of a different kind."

She smiled dreamily. Her lips parted. She sighed as he rolled her onto her back. He moved down on her and caught the peak of one breast between his teeth. She jerked as though he'd touched her with an electric prod. Her slender hands slipped into his hair.

When she arched up, offering herself to him, he applied himself to the pleasurable task of taking her, immersing himself in the sweet, moist warmth of her and carrying them both over the edge into a swirling, pulsating haze of sheer delight.

Afterward, she hooked a limp arm around his neck, buried her face against his shoulder, and whispered, "Don't ever get hypothermia with anyone but me."

Tucker was still smiling when he finally fell asleep.

Chapter Sixteen

Dawn was just breaking. The fire had burned down to a few licking fingers of orange. The storm-laden sky was pewter above the mountains, darkening in graduating degrees from there to a still-dark charcoal directly overhead. Ellie stirred in Tucker's embrace, frowned, and then ducked her head under the sleeping bag to escape the ice particles that kept pelting her face.

The moment she dived for cover, her brain kicked into gear and clarity sharpened her muddled thoughts. *Snow!* She stiffened and grabbed Tucker's arm to shake him awake.

"It's snowing. We have to get up!"

No conversation was necessary. They leapt to their feet, both of them on the same wavelength as they scrabbled to dress in their still-damp clothes and break camp. No coffee this morning. No ablutions. No quick nourishment. They put everything into their backpacks, regardless of whether it was dry or wet, and within ten minutes they were heading downstream to go find their sons.

They walked for a mile before they found a natural

bridge across the creek, yet another log that gave
Ellie heart palpitations as she walked across it.

Once across the stream, Ellie breathed a sigh of
relief, only to have another bad moment when they
started up through the canyon. The path was steep,
and the freezing snow made the footing all the more
slick and treacherous. As she followed Tucker ever
upward, she said a silent prayer that her sons had
passed through here before the snow had started to
fall. If she remembered correctly, Tabletop Gorge was
rife with crevices in the lava rock, many of the drop-
offs plunging distances of fifty to sixty feet.

As they wound their way along the edge of a cre-
vasse, Ellie searched for splotches of dark blue on
the rocks below. Both boys wore dark blue parkas.

When they came to a place where the way grew
particularly steep, Ellie's boots slipped from under
her. She fell and slid some five feet downward on
her stomach. Tucker came racing back down after her,
his long legs spread, his boots grabbing and slipping
on the jags of rock at the edge of the path.

"Are you all right?"

The breath had been knocked from her, but other
than that, Ellie felt fairly sure she'd done herself no
injury. Even if she had, it wouldn't have mattered.
Her boys were up there ahead of them somewhere.
Inside her mind, the ticking clock was measuring off
the seconds. If her blister pained her, she no longer
felt it. If her lungs grabbed for breath, she ignored
the burn. The game of hide-and-seek had suddenly
turned deadly.

She felt nothing, saw nothing but the path that
angled upward in front of them. She vowed she

would make the climb if she had to claw her way up, crawling every inch of the way.

"We have to turn back." Zach scrambled to his feet after slipping on the ice. When he straightened, he saw just how close he had come to sliding over the edge of the path to the jagged teeth of lava below. Last night when they'd made camp at the lower end of the canyon trail, Zach had listened to the weather channel. He'd tried to tell Kody then that snow might be coming their way. But Kody had refused to listen. "This is crazy, Kody. What good is it to get Mom and Dad back together if we're both dead?"

Kody stood some five feet below him. Heaving for breath, he rested a hand on Bucky's head, his fingers embedded in the dog's thick fur. "Go ahead and turn back if you want. I'm gonna keep going."

Snow drifted down between them, the flakes meandering this way and that. In any other place, at any other time, Zach would have thought they were beautiful. He'd lived most of his life in central Oregon, and he'd loved the snow ever since he could remember. Living south of Bend, you either liked the white stuff or you were miserable all winter.

"What do you mean, you're gonna keep going?" Zach had sensed that Kody was more driven to do this than he was, that somehow the stakes were higher for him. But this was the first time that they'd gone to loggerheads. "We're in this together, and I'm the oldest. If I say we quit, we quit! It's snowing, Kody. This storm could get worse. You want to get stranded up here and maybe freeze to death?"

There was a funny, burning look in Kody's eyes.

Too late, Zach realized that it had been a mistake—all of it. He never should have agreed to this crazy scheme in the first place.

"I don't care if I freeze," Kody said. "I just don't care anymore. I know you don't understand. That's okay. I can go the rest of the way by myself."

To Zach's dismay, Kody scrambled up the path toward him. In places, he had to claw his fingers through the snow to find dirt so he wouldn't slip. Watching him, Zach knew that his brother really meant to keep going. The only way to prevent him would be to physically restrain him, and this narrow path was a dangerous place for a wrestling match.

Afraid suddenly because he felt himself losing control of this situation, Zach fell back on the only trump card an older brother had. "Fine. Go without me. I don't care. You'll be sorry when you get up there and start to feel scared because you're all alone."

As Kody came abreast of Zach, he stopped to catch his breath. Tears glistened in his eyes, lending the burning look a feverish brightness. His chin trembled as he met Zach's gaze. "I've been all alone for a long, long time," he said. "This is something I gotta do."

"*Why?*" Zach didn't mean to yell, but he couldn't help himself. He was starting to get really scared. Something was troubling Kody, something really, really bad that Zach didn't know how to fix. "Who cares at this point if Mom and Dad patch it up? Come on, Kody. Don't be dumb."

"I care," Kody replied in that same, oddly flat voice. "It's my fault they're apart. I can't fix the other, but I can fix this." He rubbed his eye with his fist. "I have to fix this one thing."

Zach searched his brother's face. He found no answers there. He only knew that a power play wasn't going to work this time. Kody honestly believed that he had to carry this out, and to do it, he would go on alone if he had to.

Zach watched his little brother continue up the trail. When Kody and Bucky reached the crest and started to drop down the other side, Zach called out. "Wait! If you're going, I'm going!"

Kody stopped and turned. From a distance, his eyes looked like burning embers in his pale face. "You don't have to. I don't want you to get hurt, too. Maybe it'd be better if you went back down."

Zach couldn't think what Kody meant. As far as he knew, no one else had been hurt. His brother wasn't making good sense.

It didn't matter. Whether Kody was making sense or not, he was Zach's little brother, and Zach felt responsible for him. He couldn't let him hike the rest of the way through the canyon by himself.

"We're Grants," he said fiercely. "For better or worse, we stick together!"

When Tucker and Ellie finally reached the top of the ridge, they hoped to see their sons. Instead they saw only their footprints heading east, clearly delineated in the snow. Huffing from the climb, Ellie had no choice but to pause for a rest. Well above the timberline, the trees at that elevation were smaller than those farther down the mountain, and the underbrush was far less dense, greatly increasing the visibility. Heartened by the unimpeded view, she scanned the distant reaches of the plateau for any sign of movement. When she spotted nothing, she couldn't help but sigh.

"At least we know they're up here," Tucker said, his breath fogging the air. He laid a hand on her shoulder and gave it a squeeze. "Now all we have to do is find the little buggers."

They set off again as soon as she caught her breath. "It seems to me that all I've done for an eternity is follow footprints. If this keeps up much longer, I'm going to be tracking them in my sleep."

Tucker chuckled. "I know, but it's almost over. They've boxed themselves in this time. The only safe way off this ridge is through the gorge, and we'll see them if they double back this way." He flashed her a smile over his shoulder. Snowflakes peppered his hair and jacket. "I wish now that I hadn't tossed away the hot chocolate packets. That and some beef ravioli would sure go good when we find them."

Ellie couldn't fault him for lightening the load. He'd been carrying her pack and his own for two days now. Or was it three? Incredulous, she realized that she'd lost track of how long they'd been out here. "We can do without it." She studied the sky. So far, the snow had been falling sporadically, but the darkness of the clouds gathering overhead didn't bode well. "If it snows much more, will we be able to make it back down the mountain?"

"If we can't, I can always call out for help. Up here, we'll be able to pick up a signal, no problem. More than likely, though, the worst that will happen is that we'll get stranded overnight. That won't be a problem. I can build some kind of shelter to keep the worst of the snow off our tents. Come morning when the sun starts to melt it off, we'll head back down."

Ellie thought of the many narrow, steep places that they would encounter on the descent, and her stomach knotted with worry. She shoved the concerns away. If the path grew dangerously slick, Tucker would see to it that no one fell by tying them all together with rope.

Soon they would find their sons. Once Tucker was in charge, everything would be fine.

A few minutes later, he stopped to let her rest again. Grateful for the reprieve, Ellie sank onto a snowy rock. The chill seeped through her still-damp jeans, and her fingers immediately started to ache when she braced her hands beside her. "I wonder what the temperature is."

"Probably about twenty degrees."

She shivered and chafed her arms through the sleeves of her jacket. "No wonder it feels so cold up here."

He frowned as he scanned the area ahead of them. "This is warm compared to what it'll be tonight."

"I take it you think it's going to snow a lot more."

"Possibly." When he met her gaze, his eyes filled with understanding. "I know it's your job as a mother to worry, but it's okay now to relax a little bit. They can't be more than a few minutes ahead of us. We'll find them before the storm gets worse."

Ellie laughed and rolled her eyes. "Am I that transparent?"

"Like glass."

"I'm sorry. I can't seem to help it. I keep thinking that we have a second chance and need to make the most of it, but I'm afraid something awful will happen to mess it up."

"No negative thoughts. That's an order."

Yes, sir." She gave him a mock salute. "No more fretting, I promise."

"Once we find them, I'll build a big fire," he assured her. "We won't freeze, and it may be a lot of fun. Like old times. I think they're heading for our old campsite."

Ellie followed the direction of their sons' tracks with her gaze. A tight feeling came into her throat as memories assailed her. Images of Sammy automatically took shape in her mind. It had been here, on this plateau, that they had last camped out with him—here that they'd last gone swimming with him, fishing with him, and roasted hot dogs with him. It hurt, being here.

"Oh, Tucker."

"Don't. New beginnings, remember?"

Ellie nodded, knowing he was right. "It's easier said than done sometimes."

He extended a hand to help her up. "I know. Believe me, I know. But that's okay, too. We're only human." He dipped his head to kiss her cheek, then drew her into a walk. "I think it's time to start forgiving ourselves for not being perfect, don't you?"

Their boots made scrunching sounds on the snow, the cadence picking up as they began walking faster. "I think it's past time." She managed to give him a smile. "We need to move forward now, as a family."

Thirty minutes later, Tucker stood in front of a flat-surfaced boulder, protected on three sides from the wind by a pile of larger rocks. He stared solemnly at the display his kids had left behind—three framed photographs, one an eight-by-ten of Sammy, the other two five-by-sevens of Kody and Zach. What struck Tucker most about the arrangement was that Sammy's picture was out in front and held center stage while the smaller pictures of Kody and Zach were tucked in behind and almost hidden from view.

Tucker felt as if he'd just been kicked in the stomach. He recognized the photographs as ones removed from his living room. Until this moment, he'd never thought about Sammy's picture being so much larger, nor had he stopped to think of the message he'd been sending his other two sons.

Sammy is most important.

I loved him the best.

No matter what you do—no matter how you excel— you'll never mean as much to me as he did.

Ellie came to stand beside him. When she saw the pictures, she made a strangled sound low in her throat. "Oh, my God," she whispered.

Snowflakes pelted Tucker's face. An awful pain welled up in his chest. He'd never meant to make Zach and Kody feel second rate. *Never.* He'd loved Sammy, yes, more than words could convey. But he loved the other two boys just as much.

His gaze came to rest on Sammy's picture. Hazel eyes, much like his own, stared back at him. A dozen sweet memories flashed through his mind. Sammy, taking his first step. Sammy, riding his first tricycle. Those were things a father never forgot, things that haunted him later, when that child was gone.

In his grief, he had placed the eight-by-ten of Sammy on his mantel, creating a shrine of sorts, and also punishing himself. Because of him, Sammy was dead, after all. What kind of father could allow himself to forget that?

It had never occurred to Tucker until now that the

other two boys had felt slighted. They'd still been with him, after all, and the photograph of Sammy was all that he had had left.

"Oh, Ellie. What in God's name have I done?"

He felt her hands curl over his arm, her fingers biting through the sleeve of his wet jacket. "Not just you. I've done it, too. God forgive me, I've done it, too."

They leaned into each other. The icy wind gusted across the flat, whipping their clothing and chilling them to the bone. Tucker curled an arm around Ellie, needing her close to him.

Funny, he thought, how guilt blinded a person to all else. For three years, he had wallowed in it, hating himself, feeling sorry for himself, and punishing himself, never once stopping to wonder what he might be doing to the people around him. He'd been so wrapped up in his pain—in how *he* felt—that he hadn't given a good goddamn about anyone else.

With shaking hands, Tucker reached for the letters the boys had left. He didn't want to read them. Seeing the pictures had been painful enough. But on some level, he knew reading these letters was something he needed to do.

Still clinging to his sleeve, Ellie stood beside him as he plucked the folded sheets of paper from the protective plastic. The first letter was from Zach.

His voice gravelly, Tucker forced himself to read it aloud.

> *Dear Dad and Mom: I guess both of you are royally pissed at me by now. I wanted to turn back when I tuned in to the weather channel and found*

*out a storm was coming. Honestly, I did. But
Kody had a cow and threatened to go ahead without
me. So here I am.*

*Something's up with him. I've been really worried
about him for a long time. Practically all he does
is watch TV anymore. That, and writing in his stupid notebook. I knew it wasn't normal, but what
was I supposed to do? You guys were never around
to notice.*

"Oh, Tucker." Ellie pressed her face against his
arm. Her fingers dug hard through the frigid lining
of his jacket. "I've been working six days a week. It's
true. I'm hardly ever around."

"You had to make a living," he said. "And since
the divorce, I'm not there to take up the slack. Naturally the kids are left alone more. Let's keep it in
perspective. All right? They aren't the only kids on
earth with divorced parents. Far from it."

"Somehow that doesn't make me feel better."

It didn't make Tucker feel better, either. Most kids
from broken homes weren't also dealing with the
death of a sibling. His stomach burned as if he'd
swallowed acid.

Clearing his throat to steady his voice, he continued to read.

*It was Kody's idea to do this wilderness thing. He
got it in his head that you guys might fall back
in love if we could get you off alone together. I didn't
think it would work, but I'd already messed up
so bad, trying to make you jealous, and it wasn't
like I had a better idea. He went along with my*

plan and didn't rat on me when I told you all those lies. It only seemed fair to give his plan a fair shot.

About the lies I told. I guess you've figured out by now that I made a lot of stuff up. I thought feeling jealous might make you see how much you still loved each other. It was so totally obvious to Kody and me. When people love each other like you guys do, it's dumb to be divorced. Only nothing we said or did could make you see that. So I tried making you jealous. I'd say I'm sorry, but I'm not. At least I tried to fix things.

Once again, Tucker was forced to stop reading for a moment. He gazed over the top of the letter at the pictures of his sons. He remembered with vivid clarity the moment when Ellie had told him she was pregnant with each of them and exactly how it had felt the first time he held each of them in his arms. He'd had such plans back then—big dreams and high hopes. How, then, had he come to be standing here now, feeling nothing but regret?

Tucker read on.

Both of you have been seeing other people pretty steady for a while now. Kody was scared we'd get Liz for a stepmom and Marvin for a stepdad, and so was I. No offense, but they both make us want to puke. We hate living in Springfield. We hate being bounced back and forth between the two of you. We decided we had to do something, and fast, before one of you did something totally stupid, like get

*married again. Once that happened, we knew we'd
be sunk.*

*Anyway, that's how this all came about. I know
I'm the oldest, and you're both going to blame
me. That's okay. I'm used to it. I get blamed for
everything else these days, so why not this?*

"Damn," Tucker whispered. "Is that true? Do we
blame him for everything?"

Ellie's face had gone bloodless. Her lashes fluttered. When she met Tucker's gaze, her eyes were
dark with regret. "I do place a lot of responsibility
on him while I'm at work."

Tucker wanted to say that wasn't the case at his
house. But when he really thought about it, he knew
it was a lie. He often had to work on Saturdays, even
on visitation weekends, and while he was gone, he
left Zach in charge. "I guess I do, too," he confessed.
"I try not to nitpick. I don't get to have them all that
much, but I've been a stickler about the house the
last year, wanting it kept tidy and the kitchen clean."

"And we've elected Zach to carry the load."

Tucker nodded, glad now that he'd chosen to read
these letters before haring after the kids. As difficult
as it might be to face, he and Ellie had made some
grave mistakes, and it was high time they corrected
them.

The remainder of Zach's letter was a heartrending
portrayal of a teenage boy's outlook on life that was,
in many ways, more insightful than his parents'.

*I know you guys still grieve for Sammy, and I
don't want to make you feel worse, but there are*

*things I just have to say. The first is that I loved
Sammy, too. Both of you seem to forget that. He
was my big brother. We always played together because we were practically the same age. Suddenly
he was gone. That was really, really hard for me.
And, to make it even worse, I lost my parents,
too.*

*I know. You're both thinking that isn't true. But
I did lose you, Mom and Dad, not just because
of the divorce, but in other ways, too. Everything
stopped when Sammy died. Dad got rid of the
motorcycles. You guys never took us anywhere as a
family after that. You live apart, and now you're
always sad.*

*I'm sick and tired of the sadness. I miss Sammy,
too. We all do. But that doesn't mean all our lives
should come to a big, screeching halt. You make me
feel like a non-person, someone who doesn't
count, and Kody feels the same way. Maybe you
don't mean to make us feel that way, but you do.
It's always about Sammy now, and never about us.
Remember when Sammy did this? Remember
when Sammy did that? You look at us, and think
of him. Christmas totally sucks. Even our birth-
days are screwed up now. It's like you guys relive
Sammy's last birthday every time, remembering
how he died, instead of being happy to celebrate mine
or Kody's. How do you think that makes us feel?*

*I'm also tired of never getting to do anything fun.
I know it's awful of me, but I hate Sammy now.
Him dying has ruined my whole life. You're so
afraid I'll get hurt, you both say no to practically
everything. I can't go skating. I can't ride my bike.*

I can't have a skateboard. I can't have a motorcycle. I can't do much of anything. Mom doesn't even like me to stay all night at a friend's anymore. It's like, if I'm out of her sight, she thinks something bad will happen to me.

Accidents happen. Sammy had an accident, and he died. That doesn't mean me and Kody are going to die, too. I'm fourteen now. Next year, I'll get my driver's permit. That should be a real kick. Maybe, if I'm lucky, you'll let me drive when I'm twenty-one. I should be able to ride my bike to town if I want, and go swimming at the river with my friends. You guys aren't letting me be a normal guy.

That's all I'm asking. I just want to be normal. I'd like our family back, too. But instead of trying to patch things up, like Kody and I asked, you're fighting and acting nuts. We saw you screaming at each other. If you think we're going to come home when you're still acting like that, think again. We're sticking to our guns until you agree to our terms.

I guess that's about all I've got to say. I don't know if I said it very good. Love, Zach.

Tucker started to scrunch the paper in his fist. Then he thought better of it and neatly folded the letter to put it back inside the bag. It was worth reading again, maybe more than once. Zach had poured his heart out, no question, and even though some of the charges seemed a little unfair, they were still indicative of how he'd been made to feel.

Both he and Ellie needed to think long and hard about that.

Kody's letter was a bit less stinging but even more heartbreaking, an eleven-year-old's plea for love. Ellie wept as Tucker read it aloud.

> *I can't be Sammy. I tried to be for a long, long time because I know how you miss him, and that makes me feel so bad. No matter how I try, though, I'll never be as good at soccer or basketball. And I'll never be as good at math, either. I'm sorry it was him and not me. I never told you this, but what happened to him was my fault. I was afraid to tell you. I knew it would make you hate me. I wish I could fix things, bring him back again so you'd be happy, but I can't. Getting you back together is all I can do. And maybe I can't even do that. I'm sorry.*

After reading both notes, Tucker slipped them into his pocket and started to walk off, his one thought to find a place where he could be alone. He took no more than two steps before he realized what he was doing and turned back to pull Ellie into his arms.

"I'm sorry," he told her. "Old habits die hard. No more. From now on, we face everything together. Right?"

Her body was shaking. He gathered her closer, relieved when she put her arms around his neck. *Together*. That was where they'd gone wrong before, he thought. They'd let the pain create a wall between them.

"Oh, Tucker," she said, "why does Kody blame

himself? I had no idea. Why on earth does he think he was responsible?"

"I have no idea. No idea in hell. It doesn't make sense. But, then, when I think about it, we haven't made a lot of sense ourselves. I blamed myself, you blamed yourself, Kody blames himself. It doesn't have to make sense, I guess. It hurts, all the same."

"It bothers me that he's tried to measure up to Sammy. What have we done to make him feel he needs to?"

It was a question Tucker wasn't sure how to answer. In his recollection, he'd never once compared Kody to Sammy or expressed disappointment in him, and he couldn't believe that Ellie had. But after seeing the arrangement of pictures, he was starting to realize that they'd sent their kids a host of signals they'd never meant to send.

"First things first," he settled for saying. "We need to find them and make sure they're safe. Then we'll worry about the rest."

She tightened her arms around him. "I don't know what to say to them."

Tucker ran a hand over her hair, acutely aware of the melting snowflakes that came away on his fingers. The storm was building. If they were going to pass a reasonably comfortable night on this plateau, he had to find the boys and get a shelter of some sort built before the snow got too deep.

"We'll tell them we're sorry and how much we love them," he said. "When you boil it all down, what else is there to say?"

She drew back and wiped her cheeks. Then she nodded and managed a wobbly smile. "That sounds like a good place to start."

Turning toward the rocks, she reached with trembling hands to rearrange the pictures, pushing Sammy's way to the back and putting Zach and Kody's out front. When she finished, the likeness of their dead son was almost hidden by the grinning faces of his brothers. That was as it should be.

Tucker's eyes burned with tears, yet, at the same time, he felt a sense of rightness move through him. They would never forget Sammy, they would never stop loving him—but it was time to say good-bye.

"We're going to be okay now," Ellie said as she turned to face him. "We're all going to be okay."

"You bet we are," Tucker agreed. "Together we stand, divided we fall. We just lost sight of that for a while."

Chapter Seventeen

Tucker took Ellie's hand. Drawing her along beside him, he began following his sons' tracks again. Her fingers felt icy in his grasp, reminding him yet again of the dropping temperature and their damp clothing.

"I'm surprised they left the old campsite," she said. "Where do you think they're headed now?"

Tucker fixed his gaze on the tracks ahead of them, which had now switched directions and were going due north. "I'm fresh out of answers," he replied, picking up the pace. "There's not much over that way, just rocky flatland and a few scraggly bushes."

"Are you sure going through the gorge is the only way down?"

"Positive. Unless, of course, you have wings. The north face of Tabletop is solid granite, practically straight up and down, and it's not much better to the south or west." He led her around a pile of pumice. "I've seen a few climbers rappel down, but otherwise, those routes are pretty much impassable."

As Tucker spoke, a sense of unease gnawed at his guts. He frowned slightly, recalling Zach's note. *If you think we're going to come home when you're still acting like that, think again.* It was almost as if Zach had felt confident of making good their escape. Given the fact that going through the gorge was the only way to get off Tabletop, that made no sense. Zach had to know they couldn't double back without being caught.

"Oh, God," Tucker said. His chest suddenly felt as tight as a drum, and his heart was starting to pound. "Oh, Jesus."

Ellie's fingers clutched at his. "What?"

"The boys and I did some rock climbing this summer."

Her blue eyes widened. "You what?"

"Not extensively," he elaborated. "I just taught them the basics, stuff every good woodsman needs to know in case of an emergency."

He reeled to a halt. He didn't want to believe his boys would do something so foolhardy, yet a part of him was very much afraid they might. *We're sticking to our guns until you agree to our terms,* Zach had written. How could he have felt so certain of success when there was only one way off the mountain?

He'd worked with his sons last summer, teaching them how to rappel. They'd both learned the technique well. Tucker had cautioned them never to try it alone unless there was an emergency. But wasn't that exactly what this was to them, an emergency? They were fighting to save their family, and in order to do it, they would risk a dangerous descent down the face of a cliff rather than chance being caught.

Just as Tucker had worked his way around to that conclusion, he heard Bucky barking. He glanced up to see the dog tearing toward them through the snow in a flat-out run. When the Australian shepherd reached them, he grabbed the leg of Tucker's jeans in his teeth, braced his hind legs, and began to pull frantically.

Tucker released Ellie's hand, shoved the dog loose, and broke into a run. "Take me to them, Bucky! Find Zach and Kody!"

The shepherd gave a glad bark and whirled to retrace his steps. Tucker fell into a run behind him, thanking God that the dog had found them. Bucky could take them directly to the boys, saving valuable time.

"Ellie, they're trying to rappel down the north face!" he yelled over his shoulder. "Follow my tracks. I have to get there before they start down!"

Ellie had never been a very fast runner, but fear lent her speed she hadn't realized she possessed. This snow would make the rocks on the north face slick, increasing the danger greatly. If memory served her right, in several places there were drops of nearly a hundred feet. If one of the boys fell—oh, dear God, if one of them fell, he could be killed.

Legs churning, heart slamming, she prayed mindlessly as she ran that God wouldn't take another child from them. *I'm sorry, so sorry.* She'd never meant to make Zach and Kody feel that they mattered less to her than Sammy. What a nightmare to think that she and Tucker could lose one or both of the children they still had because they'd grieved so deeply over the one they'd lost.

Why hadn't they taken stock of their countless

blessings and tried to be grateful for those? Yes, they'd lost one son. But they still had two to love. Why had it taken something like this to make them realize that life must go on?

Bucky led the way, his barks a claxon to guide them when he grew nearly invisible behind the veil of falling snow. Not even Tucker's much longer legs gave him that much of an advantage. Ellie raced along behind him, scarcely aware of the burning in her lungs as she panted for breath. *Slipping, sliding.* Reaching the boys became her one consuming thought. Fists clenched, arms pumping, she fairly flew over the snow-covered rocks.

When the north face came into view, she scanned the terrain, searching for their sons. Nothing. There were so many large rocks along the edge of the cliff, creating dark splotches in the snow. Two kids in dark jackets might not stand out.

"Can you see them, Tucker?" Though she screamed the question, she was so breathless from running that her voice barely carried. "Are they there?"

If he heard her, he gave no indication. Instead, he veered suddenly to the left and picked up speed. Falling well behind, Ellie changed directions, too, craning her neck to see past him as they raced over the plateau.

Finally she glimpsed a splotch of blue. Kody was crouched on his hands and knees at the edge of the cliff. As they drew closer, she could hear him sobbing. Bucky had already reached the child. After checking Kody for injuries, the dog raced back to Tucker and Ellie, his barks frantic and shrill, his feet in constant motion. The dog darted in and out around them, providing escort the remainder of the way.

As Tucker covered the last few feet to reach Kody, he yelled, "Where's Zach?" When the child failed to answer, he cried the question again. "Kody, where's Zach?"

"He f-fell!" Kody cried. "He lost his h-hold on the ropes, and he fell!"

"Oh, dear God." Tucker dropped to his belly beside his son to look over the cliff. When Ellie staggered up beside them, he swung out his arm. "Stay back from the edge. It's straight down."

Ellie sank to her knees and grabbed hold of Kody to pull him safely away. Wailing shrilly, the child threw his arms around her neck. "He's h-hurt really bad, Mom. I think he's dead. It's my f-fault! It's all my *fault*! First I killed Sammy and now Zach."

Ellie felt as if the earth shifted beneath her. She tightened her arms around her son, her mind spinning at the implications of what he'd just said. "No. Oh, Kody, no. Sammy's accident wasn't your fault, sweetie, and this isn't, either."

"Yes, it was! You don't know 'cause I never told. He didn't lose control of the motorcycle because he hit a chuckhole. He—" Kody broke off and gulped. "I dared him to do a wheelie. That's how come he crashed. He was afraid I'd call him a chicken if he didn't try!" After punctuating that with a keening wail, he added, "He said he didn't know how, but I egged him on, anyhow. Finally, he gunned the gas and jerked up on the front wheel. The bike almost came over on top of him. He lost control, and when the front tire touched down again, he didn't let off the gas. The bike crashed through the fence, right out in front of the hay truck!"

In that instant, the years fell away, and Ellie was once again standing on the road, staring at her dead son. For the life of her, she couldn't recall where Kody had been, and God forgive her, she had no recollection of his whereabouts later. All she'd been able to see was Sammy, all she'd been able to feel was pain. The other two boys had been home that afternoon, but right after the accident, they'd all but ceased to exist for her. Dimly she recalled Tucker's brother Jeff coming to take Zach and Kody to his place. Sometime after the funeral, he'd brought them home again. In the interim, she'd been so numb that all she'd felt was a sense of relief not to have them underfoot.

Never once had she stopped to think that Zach or Kody might harbor feelings of guilt over their brother's death. "Oh, Kody," she whispered brokenly. "Oh, my sweet boy. You were just a little fellow when it happened. No matter what you said or did, it wasn't your fault. It wasn't your *fault!*"

Kody's body jerked with a tearing sob. "You don't hate me? You aren't mad?"

Oh, God—oh, God. He had kept this ugly secret for three long years, afraid to come forward, terrified to confess his imagined sin. Cupping a hand over the back of his head, Ellie clasped him tightly to her body and met Tucker's tortured gaze. For a heartbeat of time, the world seemed to stop moving. They were frozen there, like statues on an icy tableau, their mistakes and failures suddenly picture clear.

"We could never hate you," Tucker said firmly,

"and we'd never, *never* be mad at you over something that was never your fault in the first place."

Ellie could feel Kody shaking—an awful, horrible shaking, the kind that resulted only from terror or shock. "It's all right. It's going to be all right," she assured him again.

"Don't let Zach die, Dad. Please, don't let him die. Please, make him be all right!"

"Shh, shh," Ellie soothed. "Of course he won't die. Don't even think it."

Tucker pushed to his feet. Over the top of Kody's head, he met Ellie's gaze once more. "His fall was broken by an outcropping of rock. It looks like his arm is broken."

This isn't happening, Ellie thought stupidly. *It can't be. I'm only dreaming.* But she wasn't. This was real. And somehow she had to deal with it.

"Is he conscious?" she forced herself to ask.

Tucker shook his head. Then, as if he knew how terrifying that news would be, he added, "Thank God for that. This way, at least, he isn't in any pain."

"He went d-down first because h-he's the oldest," Kody squeaked out. "Once he m-made it, I was s'posed to lower Bucky and our gear down to him. Then he was gonna h-help me make my descent."

Tucker started pulling up the rope, which was tied off to a huge boulder several feet behind them. After testing the anchor to make certain it would bear his weight, he passed the end between his legs from the front, brought it around to the left of his body, across his chest, then over his shoulder and down his back.

"Kody, I need you to spot for me, partner," he said.

Kody shook his head no. "I was sp-spotting for

Z-Zach, and just look what h-happened! Have Mom do it."

Ellie started to get up, but Tucker flashed her a look that stopped her cold. Shifting his gaze back to their son, he said, "Mom doesn't know how to spot. You do. To bring your brother up, I'm going to need your help."

Kody straightened away from Ellie. His face was pinched and deathly pale, with bluish circles under his tear-reddened eyes. Ellie wanted to intervene, to tell Tucker he shouldn't push the child right then. But once again he gave her a look that held her in check. She realized then that Tucker felt Kody needed to help, that playing a part in saving his brother might be cathartic.

"All right," Kody agreed tremulously.

Tucker nodded. "I knew I could count on you. What's the first rule in an emergency?"

Kody scrambled to his feet. Gulping down a sob, he said, "To keep your head."

"What's the second rule?"

"Figure out what needs to be done," Kody said in a wobbly voice, "then figure out a way to do it without putting yourself in danger."

Tucker nodded. "That's exactly right." He reached out to hook a hand over the back of Kody's head. Hauling him forward, he gave him a hard hug and ruffled his hair. "Why do you suppose someone made rules for emergencies?"

Kody buried his face against his father's jacket. " 'Cause accidents happen sometimes, and we have to kn-know what to d-do."

"That's right. Accidents happen. Today Zach has

had an accident. It wasn't his fault. It wasn't yours. It just happened. Do you understand what I'm saying?" When Kody nodded, Tucker caught him by the chin and tipped his head back. "No more blaming yourself. Okay? Zach needs you to be sharp right now, and so do I."

"Okay," Kody said. "I'll do my best."

"I know you will. I'll need you to be my eyes," Tucker said as he hunkered down to ease toward the edge again. "I won't be able to see behind me very well when I reach the ledge."

"I know." Kody dropped to his knees and crawled with his father to the precipice. "I know what to do, Dad."

As Tucker lowered himself over the side, he looked back at Ellie. "Kody'll need your help to pull Zach up. Scoot over on your belly. Before you stand up again, move well back from the edge. I don't want either of you getting dizzy and doing a swan dive."

"Be careful," she called.

He grabbed the rope with his left hand, hitched a loop around his left wrist to give himself extra support, and dropped over the edge. "I always try to be careful."

The next instant, he was gone. Digging in with her elbows and toes, Ellie scooted over to lie beside Kody. When she looked over, all she could see at first was Tucker, abseiling down the face of the cliff. Booted feet planted firmly apart, he leaned out from the rock at an alarming angle, letting the rope around his thigh and along his back support his weight. Stepping slowly downward, he controlled his rate of descent by playing out line through his right hand.

Just watching him scared Ellie half to death. She'd never seen him do any rock climbing. Not surprisingly, he executed the technique with the same athletic grace with which he did everything else, making it look absurdly easy. Ellie knew better. One mistake was all it would take, and he could fall forty feet.

"A little more to your right, Dad!" Kody called.

Following Kody's directions, Tucker propelled himself sideways. The shift of position allowed Ellie to finally see Zach. She was glad to be in a prone position because she almost fainted. Sprawled on his back, her son lay on a ledge of rock barely as broad as his shoulders. His hair was speckled with snowflakes. One leg already dangled over the edge, and the slightest movement might send him plummeting to his death on the jagged rocks below.

Nausea punched her in the stomach. She dug her fingers into the snow, barely feeling the cold. Twisted sharply at the elbow, Zach's right forearm was bent unnaturally outward from his body at a forty-five-degree angle. Even with a heavy jacket sleeve to camouflage the breaks, Ellie knew he had severe compound fractures. After thirteen years of marriage to Tucker, she was also familiar enough with first aid to know that the two broken bones in his forearm could, if moved, sever a main artery, resulting in almost certain death.

With a frightened gaze, she took in Zach's face—the awful stillness of his pale features, the faint purple hue of his white-rimmed lips. He looked—oh, dear God—he looked dead already.

Black spots blinked out her vision. For an awful second, her swimming head felt disconnected from her shoulders. She squeezed her eyes closed, clenched her teeth, and dragged in breaths through her nose.

"You okay, Mom?" Kody asked in a quivery little voice.

Her throat burned as if she'd just guzzled a full bottle of Drāno. She swallowed, her vocal cords stretching taut. "Yes." Deep breaths. Deep, deep breaths. "I'm fine."

"He's not dead," Kody assured her. "He isn't, Mom. See? Watch his chest."

Ellie tried to focus. Couldn't. "He's breathing, then?"

Kody made an affirmative sound. "I don't think he banged his head real bad, either. When he first fell, he was awake, and he could talk. It was only later, when he tried to sit up, that he passed out. I think it hurt real bad to move his arm."

She was going to vomit. Gulping frantically to hold it down, she closed her eyes again.

"Okay!" Tucker called up. "How am I doing, Kode?"

"He's right under you," Kody called back. "About ten more feet."

Tucker craned his neck, trying to see. Apparently failing in that, he looked back up. "All right, you guys, this is where it gets tricky. I need to set down on the ledge, but I don't want to step on him or move him. There's not a whole lot of room to spare, so you've got to direct my feet."

Kody inched closer to the edge. "This is where Zach fell," he whispered. Then to his father, he yelled, "Watch out there, Dad. I think the rock is icy."

Kody no sooner hollered the warning than Tucker's boots slipped on the granite. His body swung hard into the rock. For several seconds, he just dangled there, grabbing for the breath that had been knocked out of him.

"Don't turn loose, Dad!" Kody cried. "Don't lose your grip!"

Ellie's pulse pounded in her ears like a drumbeat. Every muscle in her body strained with Tucker as he fought to get a foothold. To her horror, his boots kept slipping off the rocks, making it impossible for him to rappel.

"Oh, God," she whispered. "Oh, my God."

"The rock juts out here and caught snow," he called up. "It's slick as snot. Must've melted and froze."

The wind caught his body, twisting him on the rope. Ellie heard the hemp whine under his weight. She could only pray that no sharp edge of stone on the boulder would cut through the braid.

Tucker glanced over the face of the cliff. "I'm gonna propel sideways, try to get away from the ice."

"He can't hang there for long. The wind is freezing cold," Kody said in a tight, urgent voice. "If his hands get numb, he'll lose his grip and fall, Mom, just like Zach."

Ellie couldn't drag her eyes off Tucker to comfort her son. Using the rope like a swing, he began pumping his feet, trying to gain a sideways momentum. She realized that the half-cradle of rope no longer supported his weight as it had before. Instead, it bit in around his thigh, which had to be painful. To lessen the pressure, he was holding on for dear life with his hands and bearing most of his weight with his arms.

Ellie knew that took incredible strength. A lesser man would have fallen—just as Zach had.

Not Tucker. At first he barely moved, but then, ever so slowly, his shifting weight created a pendulum effect. As he began swinging in wider arcs, he tested the rock with his boots. Finally he found a surface that wasn't icy, enabling him to plant his feet against the rock once more.

Leaning back against the line, he rested for a moment. Then he jiggled his right leg to stimulate the circulation. "Whoo!" he said. Glancing down over his left shoulder, he studied the lay of the cliff face between him and Zach. "To get around the ice, I have to go straight down from here, then work my way back over and up," he called. His hazel gaze singled out Ellie. "To do that, I'm going to need more rope."

Until that moment, Ellie hadn't noticed that he had very little line left to play out.

"Zach forgot one very important rule in rock climbing—to make sure he had enough line to reach the bottom."

Ellie's stomach felt as if it plunged the entire sixty feet to the rocks below. Her son had started down the face of a cliff without enough rope? "How can I get you more line?" she called.

"You'll have to tie on." He directed his gaze to Kody. "Do you have more rope, son?"

"Yeah." Kody pushed up on his hands and knees. "But I haven't learned all my knots!"

"Your mother can tie knots." Tucker flicked another glance at Ellie. "It's not that difficult, honey. The hardest part is that you'll have to loosen the rope from around the boulder while you tie on another section. That means you and Kody will have to hold my weight while you're making the knot. Kody knows how to belay, using the anchor as leverage. He can show you how. When you've added the extra rope, you just tie off to the anchor again."

"Tucker, I can't tie a knot to support your weight! Oh, God, don't ask that of me. Please. What if it doesn't hold?"

"It'll hold." He stared up at her, his expression completely calm. "A plain old square knot will probably work."

"*Probably?*"

"Bad choice of words. You can do it, Ellie. You've got to." He flashed her a weak grin. "Sorry, darlin'. I made the stupidest mistake in the book. Rule number one in rock climbing, always check your own gear. I assumed that Zach knew enough to measure out enough line."

"He measured it," Kody called down. "We just didn't know how far it was to the ground."

Tucker puffed air into his cheeks. "Yeah, well. There's a lot to learn before you try to rappel alone. Accurately guessing the distance of a drop takes some practice."

Ellie pushed up on her hands and knees.

"Don't stand up near the edge!" Tucker yelled.

"I won't."

She crawled a safe distance away before she rose to her feet. Her legs were watery with fear, and her hands shook so badly, she doubted she could hold a rope, let alone tie a trustworthy knot.

No choice. Both Tucker and Zach were in a hell of a fix, and she was the only person available to get them out of it.

Kody ran to get the extra coil of rope from Zach's pack and then went with Ellie to the boulder. Bucky danced around Ellie's legs, slowing her down. "Sit!" she cried sharply. For the first time since puppyhood, Bucky obeyed her instantly, dropping back onto his haunches. Ellie made a mental note to treat him to a T-bone steak when they got home. She wiped her hands on her jeans. "Okay, Kody, how do you belay?"

"It's not that hard, Mom. We can do it." He motioned her over to the rock. "When I untie the rope, we both grab hold, you out front, me back here. Brace hard with your feet and lean back, using all your weight. While I'm loosening the rope, we can use the boulder as an anchor to help hold Dad's weight. When I've got the end loose, I'll take over while you turn loose and get behind here .with me to tie the knot."

Tucker outweighed Kody by a hundred and fifty pounds. "What if you can't hold him?"

"I can hold him. With the rope partway around the rock, I'll have enough leverage." Evidently he caught her dubious look. "I've done it before, Mom. Lots of times. Dad taught me how last summer. It'll work. I promise. It's not a matter of strength and weight, but leverage."

Ellie could only hope.

She gripped the taut section of rope in her hands and braced her feet. "Okay. Loosen anchor."

From the corner of her eye, she saw Kody scrambling about at the opposite side of the boulder.

An instant later, the rope slipped in her hands, the rough hemp burning her palms and taking skin. She tightened her grip and leaned back with all her weight.

Suddenly the tension against the rope lessened.

"Okay!" Kody said triumphantly. "Gotcha covered."

Ellie threw him an incredulous look over her shoulder.

"I've got it, Mom. You can turn loose now and come around to tie the knot."

Prepared to grab hold again, just in case Kody had problems, Ellie slowly slackened her grip.

"See?" Kody said when she'd turned completely loose. "I've got him."

Ellie hurried around the boulder. With quivering hands and fingers that had turned to rubber, she fumbled with the two ends of rope, trying frantically to make a strong knot. When she was finished, she tugged to check her work, thinking as she did that the true test would be the full force of Tucker's weight.

"Done?"

Ellie tried to say yes. Her voice wouldn't work. She could only give a nod.

"Okay, then. Let's play out the length." He craned his neck to yell over his shoulder. "We're done, Dad. Start taking in rope!"

Ellie's heart bumped up in the back of her throat as they fed out the line. At any moment, she expected to hear Tucker scream as he free-fell toward the rocks. When nothing happened, her legs nearly buckled. The knot she'd tied was holding. *Thank God.*

After the new section of rope had been played out,

Ellie helped her son tie off to the boulder again. By the time they returned to the edge of the cliff, Tucker had rappelled around the section of ice and was already working his way back to Zach.

Ellie held her breath as her husband hooked a leg over the outcropping and then pulled himself up onto the ledge with their son. When he gave her a thumbs-up, tears filled her eyes. Relief, fear, joy—the mix of emotions churned within her, impossible to untangle or clearly define. On the one hand, she rejoiced because he'd finally reached Zach, but on the other, she despaired because there was still so much to accomplish before they'd both be safely off the ledge.

For the next thirty minutes, Ellie and Kody were kept busy searching for limbs, sticks, and green bark that Tucker could use to fashion a splint for Zach's arm and a sling to lift him up the side of the cliff. Given the fact that they were above the timberline and trees were in short supply, they had to go to the east rim of the plateau, just above the canyon, to find the needed items.

During that foray, Ellie thanked God at least a hundred times that Tucker was so well trained in first aid. Zach was badly hurt; she didn't kid herself into thinking otherwise. But with Tucker in charge, at least he had a chance.

Later, as she watched Tucker working over their son, Ellie knew her faith in him was well deserved. With only a first aid kit, rope, and strips of cloth he'd torn from their clothing, Tucker immobilized their son's fractured forearm with a splint and then fashioned a stretcher, using the limbs they'd found as side rails. It was a time-consuming process, and at times, Ellie feared that Tucker would never signal for her and Kody to pull Zach up.

Before that moment arrived, Zach regained consciousness, only to pass out again from pain when Tucker had to lift him onto the makeshift stretcher. Ellie's heart felt as if it might pound its way from her chest while she and Kody worked together to pull her elder son to safety. If the line snapped—if the wind picked up—if Zach regained consciousness and panicked—he could fall to his death.

Perhaps there were angels who lent the stretcher wings, or maybe it was the steadying Hand of God— or, perhaps, it was only Tucker's fine workmanship— but nothing went wrong. The ropes didn't break, the wind held its breath, and soon the stretcher was on safe ground.

"Thank you, God," Ellie cried as she crouched over her injured child. "Thank you, thank you, thank you."

She wanted to check Zach everywhere for other injuries. Leaving his side was one of the hardest things she'd ever done in her life. But until Tucker had scaled the cliff and was safely beside them, she had no choice.

Crawling on her belly, Ellie left her sons and returned to the edge of the embankment to watch her husband make the ascent. *Yes, my husband*, she thought when she mentally started to correct herself. Maybe she and Tucker were legally divorced, but she knew now that they had never been divorced in their hearts. They'd only gone their separate ways for a while.

When he finally reached the top and swung up a leg, Ellie grabbed handfuls of his jacket to help pull him the rest of the way. He rolled over the edge, coming to rest on his back. Sobbing with relief, she bent over him, raining kisses on his face even as tears streamed down her own.

"Oh, Tucker, I've never been so scared in all my life."

He hooked an arm around her neck and pulled her down on top of him. For a moment, they just lay there, chest to chest, heart to heart, glad—so very glad—just to be alive.

"He's going to make it," Tucker whispered near her ear. "It's just a broken arm, sweetheart. He's going to be fine."

Ellie could only nod.

Tucker sighed and loosened his arms from around her to sit up. After gaining his feet, he drew her up beside him, and together, they hurried over to their boys. Zach had regained consciousness again, and he managed a faint smile before letting his eyes drift closed. Tucker examined him for other injuries.

"He's okay, Ellie," he finally pronounced. "The arm may hurt like the devil, but he's going to be fine."

While Tucker called for help on the cell phone, Ellie sat beside the stretcher, holding Zach's uninjured hand, her other arm looped around Kody's shoulders.

"Dad says he's going to be all right," she told her eleven-year-old. "Did you hear that? Good news, huh?"

Tears welled in Kody's eyes. His chin wobbled as

he nodded. "Yeah, real good news. I thought he might die, and it would've been all my fault again. He wanted to turn back, and I wouldn't."

Ellie pressed her cheek to the top of Kody's head, wishing she were incredibly wise and knew exactly what to say to him.

"Sammy's accident wasn't your fault, sweetie. It wasn't anyone's fault." Not hers, not Tucker's, and most especially not Kody's. "I've always blamed myself for what happened," she whispered. "Did you know that?"

Kody nodded. "I kind of figured. Lots of times, I wanted to tell you it was me that caused it to happen, but I was afraid you'd hate me."

"Never," Ellie said fiercely, hugging him again to drive home the point. "I could never hate you, Kody. Never in a zillion years."

"But I called him a chicken," Kody cried. "He wouldn't've popped that wheelie and plowed through the fence if it wasn't for me."

"Ah, but he wouldn't have been on the bike at all if it hadn't been for me," Ellie countered. "I broke the rules and let him go riding when your dad wasn't home."

Tucker walked up just then. "I've got you both beat. There wouldn't have been a bike, period, if it hadn't been for me buying him one."

Ellie smiled and ruffled Kody's hair. "There, you see? We've all been blaming ourselves, each in our own way. Which of us is guiltiest, do you think? Maybe we should draw straws, the shortest straw loses."

"That'd be dumb," Kody said.

"No dumber than all of us dragging our bottom lips on the ground for the rest of our lives, blaming ourselves for something we never meant to happen." Tucker hunkered down to look his youngest son dead in the eye. "Sammy's gone, Kody. We'll always miss him. Deep in our hearts, we'll always wish things had happened differently. But we can't let that spoil the rest of our lives. Sammy wouldn't want that. This guilt thing is tearing all of us apart. It's time to let it go."

Kody nodded. "I'd like that. It makes me feel awful inside."

"Excuse me, I'm dying over here," Zach injected hoarsely. "Forget about Sammy for once and think about me, why don't you?"

Tucker winked at Ellie and reached past her to check Zach's pulse. "Wiser words were never spoken. How you feeling, sport?"

"Like, *awful*. My arm hurts."

Tucker nodded. "I know it does. A rescue copter is on the way. Before you know it, a pretty little nurse will be spoon-feeding you Jell-O."

"I don't want *Jell-O*." Zach wrinkled his nose. "I haven't had anything good to eat in three days. I'm starving."

"Hunger is a very good sign," Tucker assured him. "I'd say you're going to live."

"I better." Zach closed his eyes, clearly spent. "If I don't, all three of you will be on another guilt trip for three years."

The words hung there on the air, stark and brutally true. For a moment, Ellie was so taken aback, she couldn't think how to react, and then she burst out laughing. Tucker soon joined her. Kody took a little longer, but soon he was giggling, too.

Never opening his eyes, Zach smiled wanly. "That's a really good sound," he said faintly.

It was a beautiful sound, Ellie thought. The most beautiful sound on earth, in fact.

The Grants were a family again.

Epilogue

Patches of golden sunlight spilled down through the branches of the trees, dappling the winding dirt road with yellow. Puttering along on her trail bike behind Tucker and the boys, who rode their motorcycles slowly so as not to kick up dust, Ellie lifted her face to the breeze, loving all the wonderful smells that came from the surrounding woodlands. Pine and juniper, sage and manzanita, the scents of home. This was where she'd been born and raised, and where she and Tucker had chosen to raise their children. Little wonder. Central Oregon was, in her opinion, one of the most beautiful places on earth.

An osprey circled above them, its belly and the underside of its wings flashing white as it swooped low over the trees. Above the sound of the motorcycles, its two-syllable cry drifted on the air, a shrill *ka-whee, ka-whee* that was soon echoed by its chicks, confined to a treetop nest somewhere in the nearby forest.

Tucker signaled to turn right, leading his followers to a lovely grassy meadow bordered by dense woodlands. Eager to eat, the boys and Ellie parked their bikes behind his, cut the engines, and swung off their saddle seats. The blessed quietness of the woods suddenly surrounded them, which really wasn't quiet at all when you listened closely. A crystal-clear stream ribboned through the grass, its gurgling adding yet another beautiful element to an already gorgeous afternoon. The osprey still circled overhead, calling to her babies. The breeze whispered in the forest, the gusts and lulls creating a hushed sound.

"This is *perfect*," Ellie called to Tucker, who was loosening the straps that secured their picnic basket to the back of his trail bike. She threw her arms wide and turned in a circle. "I can't believe how wonderful it feels."

"Check out that ospey!" Zach cried. "Don't they usually nest near lakes?"

Tucker shook out the blanket and spread it on the grass. "That's right, lakes or streams." He gestured with a swing of his head. "About a quarter of a mile from here is Hazel Lake. It teems with trout, good hunting for an opsrey."

Ellie leaned her head back to watch the bird search tirelessly for sustenance. With a nest full of babies, the osprey had her work cut out for her. Spring was such a lovely time of year. Everywhere one looked was a sign of new life and the never-ending cycle of renewal. Even the light green new growth on the trees, tipping the boughs like candle tapers, seemed part of the celebration.

As Ellie went to help Tucker lay out the food, she touched a hand lightly to her waist and smiled to herself. Tucker glanced up and frowned in concern. "Are you feeling sick?"

"No, I feel wonderful!" Oddly, that was true. She'd had no morning sickness so far. Of course, it was still early on. She knelt on the blanket to empty the basket. Calling out to the boys, who'd wandered over to explore the stream, she said, "First come, first served! If you want your share, you'd better get dibs. I'm starving!"

Tucker grinned and helped himself to a chicken leg. After taking a bite, he said, "Your appetite has sure picked up. Watch it, lady. I like that figure of yours just the way it is."

Ellie might have informed him that her waistline would soon expand beyond his wildest expectations, but that was news she wanted to share in private. She'd only gotten the word herself yesterday. She wanted to hug the secret close for just a little longer.

The boys joined them on the blanket to partake of the picnic. Soon they were all too busy eating to talk. When Tucker dusted his fingers clean on his jeans, Kody mimicked the action, making her smile. It was so good, so very good to be out here as a family again, enjoying the forest and nature.

No more feelings of guilt. No more sadness. Kody was a normal, happy boy now who seldom had time to watch television and never wrote in his notebook. Zach was slowly working through his feelings of anger toward Sammy, which, perversely, had filled him with guilt until the counselor had assured him that such feelings were natural.

As for her and Tucker, they no longer blamed themselves for what had happened, either. Sammy's death had been a terrible accident—something neither of them could prevent. As parents, they had to turn loose now and let their children take some risks. Life, according to Zach, wasn't worth living if you never got to have any fun. Ellie supposed there was a great deal of truth in that.

It had been a long journey, one that had lasted most of the winter, but their weekly counseling sessions had worked a miracle. Under the direction of Harold Mooney, their psychologist, she, Tucker, and the kids had taken it step by slow step. Zach and Kody had been given more freedom in increments. Now they were allowed to ride their bicycles to town, they owned Rollerblades, and they went skating with their friends on a regular basis. Ellie still had her moments of irrational terror for their safety, but with each passing day, it was getting easier for her, and she thought it was getting easier for Tucker, as well.

Three months ago, she'd taken an important step forward by going to a beauty salon to have her hair styled. Tucker had celebrated the change in her appearance by taking them all out for junk food that evening, a major hurdle for him to leap over. When she'd started wearing makeup a week later, he'd marked the occasion by throwing away all the carob-coated nuts and raisins in the cupboard. As for their house, Ellie would never allow herself to fall back into the trap of being a perfectionist, but she and Tucker did muck out each room once a week, working together, side by side. What touched her the most about his willingness to help was each night when they cleaned up the kitchen. Tucker had never yet allowed her to wash off the stove.

One day soon, Ellie vowed, she would polish the range again, but she was in no hurry. If she'd learned anything from all the counseling, it was to be patient with herself and with her family. Overall, she felt that all of them had made amazing progress.

Now, after months of therapy, they had finally sold the Springfield house, allowing them to take the final and most difficult step of buying motorcycles again. This trip today was their first real outing. The short rides they'd taken together before this had been more for the sake of instruction than pleasure, with Tucker providing the lessons and laying down safety rules. Ellie hadn't expected to enjoy herself. She'd been so sure it would only bring back painful memories. But instead she felt joyously free.

"Penny for them," Tucker said as he selected a cookie for dessert.

"I'm just thinking how *fun* this is."

He winked at her when the boys chorused their agreement. After making quick work of the cookie, he stood and offered her a hand up. "Let's take a walk."

Ellie glanced at the kids. "Will you guys be okay?"

"Like, what are we gonna do, Mom, drown in knee-deep water?" Zach asked.

"Point taken." Ellie laughed and reached for Tucker's outstretched hand. He lifted her easily to her feet. She leaned happily into him when he slipped a strong arm around her shoulders. "Nevertheless, stay out of the water while we're gone!" she called back.

As they entered the tree line, a hush settled over the forest. Ellie imagined little squirrels diving for cover to peer nervously out at them. "Oh, Tucker, isn't this something?" she said. "It's so beautiful here, I can scarcely believe it."

"You're beautiful," he informed her huskily and,

without any warning, swung her around to press her back against a tree. "So beautiful. After three years of starvation, I can't seem to get my fill of you."

Ellie giggled and slapped at his wandering hand. "Behave. The boys might follow us. What'll they think?"

"That their dad is one lucky fellow."

He kissed her then—a slow, sweet joining of mouths that made her pulse start to race. Ellie melted into it. He was her everything, she thought dreamily, the other half of herself.

When he came up for breath, she gazed up at his dark face. The small forest residents had resumed their activities. A squirrel chattered nearby. She could hear tiny claws skittering over the rough bark somewhere above her head. The osprey call came again, a distant *ka-whee* that drifted musically on the breeze.

Ellie had meant to tell Tucker her news at a special moment, but now she knew there would never be a more perfect time than now. She looked deeply into his hazel eyes. Her heart gave a glad little bump. "I've got some really wonderful news to share with you," she whispered. "Remember that night at the hot spring, when you realized you wanted another baby?"

His face went still. His hand convulsed on her back. "Yeah," he said cautiously, "I remember it very well."

"Your wish came true. Dr. Pruitt called yesterday to tell me the news. I'm not irregular because I've gone off the Pill. I'm very, very pregnant."

A suspicious shine came to his eyes. He stared down at her, as if he couldn't quite believe his ears.

Then, with a loud whoop that startled her, he swung her up into his arms and turned in dizzying circles, laughing and yelling, "Yes!" at the top of his lungs.

When his initial joy subsided, he stopped spinning to kiss her again, his hands moving gently over her body as though she were suddenly made of fragile glass. Trailing his lips over her cheeks, he whispered, "And you're riding a motorcycle? I should paddle your fanny. You should have told me. I would have postponed the bike thing until later."

"We can't put this on hold for seven months." She caught his face between her hands. "Dr. Pruitt says it's perfectly safe as long as I go slow and stay off rough roads. I'm fine, Tucker. And so is our baby girl."

"You already know the sex?"

"Not for sure. I just have a feeling. I'm not sick this time. Not at all. This pregnancy is totally different from the other three. I think a girl agrees with my system."

He chuckled and bent his head to rest his forehead against hers. "A baby, Ellie. Just think of it. I'm so happy!"

Ellie was happy, too. Happier than she'd ever imagined she might be again. Life did go on. Time truly did heal all pain. When she thought of Sammy now, she had mostly good feelings, and her memories made her smile.

"Oh, gag!"

Both Ellie and Tucker jumped at the unexpected sound of Kody's voice. Still locked in each other's arms, they turned to see both their sons walking toward them through the trees.

"You guys aren't supposed to get all mushy in front of us," Zach chimed in. "Do you want us to get warped?"

"We love each other," Tucker said with a chuckle. "Live with it."

Zach elbowed his brother and did an about-face. "Come on, Kode. Let's leave the lovebirds alone."

Kody followed his brother, complaining with every step. "I always miss the good part. At this rate, I'm gonna be twenty before I know anything about anything. Why can't I watch to see what happens next?"

Tucker turned a laughing gaze back to Ellie. When the sound of their sons' footsteps drifted away, he rubbed noses with her, then gently kissed her forehead.

"Tell me, Mr. Grant, what part *does* come next?" she asked.

All the amusement left his expression. For a long moment, he looked deeply into her eyes. Then, in a voice gone husky with emotion, he replied, "The forever part comes next, Ellie girl. And that's going to be the very best part of all."

The collision nearly knocked Chloe down. She lost
her grip on her son and her purse. Lipsticks, pens,
car keys, and loose coins spilled over the floor as she
staggered to catch her balance.

Large, capable hands clamped over her shoulders
to keep her from falling. "Are you all right?" a deep
voice asked.

"I'm fine." Chloe was so jarred by the impact that
she couldn't focus for a moment. Her nose hurt. She
registered the pain only a fraction of an instant before
embarrassment washed over her. She couldn't believe
she'd barreled into someone this way. "I am so sorry."
She realized she was apologizing to a shirt button,
broke off, and lifted her startled gaze to find the face
that went with the chest and shoulders. "I should have
been paying attention to where I was going."

"That makes two of us. I didn't mean to mow you
down like that."

His voice was a rich, vibrant tenor with a raspy
edge. Even with the brim of a brown Stetson dipping
low to shadow his face, she could see that his fea-

tures were striking. High, sharp cheekbones underscored eyes so clear and intense a blue they were
startling in contrast to his dark skin and jet-black
brows. Deep creases slashed his lean cheeks, brack-
eting a perfectly shaped mouth that might have
looked hard if not for the sensual fullness of the
lower lip. He had a strong, angular jaw, defined by
corded muscle that bunched and rippled, giving him
the look of a man with turbulent emotions roiling
just beneath the surface.

"Are you sure you're not hurt?"

"No, no, I'm—fine. Really."

The collar of his blue shirt lay open at the throat,
revealing a circlet of cobalt beads from which was
suspended a crude stone medallion with a starburst
etched on the face. Chloe had never seen anything
quite like it. Slipping free of his grasp, she bent to
collect her things.

When he crouched down to help, she said, "Oh,
no, please. I can manage."

Ignoring her protest, he began picking stuff up, a
blur of blue and sun-bronzed skin as he shoved items
back in her bag. He had the hands of a man who
labored outdoors. The sleeves of his shirt were folded
back to reveal thick, sinewy forearms with only a
sparse dusting of dark hair.

Low in her abdomen, Chloe felt a quickening. It
had been so long since she had experienced the sensation that it took her a moment to realize it was
sexual attraction. Surprised at herself and more than
a little unsettled, she forced her attention back to the
task at hand.

As the mother of a small boy, she had developed

a bad habit of carrying a little of everything in her purse. The collection was a junky-looking mess. When the stranger picked up an unwrapped peppermint candy with more hair on it than stripes, Chloe wished the floor planks would swallow her. His hard mouth twitched as he dropped the candy back in her purse along with an emergency tampon that had been in a side pocket so long the wrapper had nearly disintegrated.

"Thank you," she said.

"No problem." Still hunkered at her eye level, he nudged up the brim of his hat to regard her with unsmiling intensity. "I just hope I didn't hurt you."

Chloe waved a hand as she pushed to her feet. "I'm fine. Next time maybe I'll watch where I'm going." Smiling at Jeremy, who'd backed away to stare, she added, "My little boy just got a new puppy, and we were searching for the dog food section."

"Ah." He glanced at the child. Then he tipped his hat to Chloe and said, "I'll leave you to it, then."

And he walked away. . . .